Half Past Dead

D0169929

Half Past Dead

ZOE ARCHER
BIANCA D'ARC

BRAVA

KENSINGTON PUBLISHING CORP.
www.kensingtonbooks.com

BRAVA BOOKS are published by

Kensington Publishing Corp.
119 West 40th Street
New York, NY 10018

Copyright © 2010 Kensington Publishing Corp.
"The Undying Heart" copyright © 2010 Ami Silber
"Simon Says" copyright © 2010 Cristine Martins

All rights reserved. No part of this book may be reproduced in any form or by any means without the prior written consent of the Publisher, excepting brief quotes used in reviews.

All Kensington titles, imprints, and distributed lines are available at special quantity discounts for bulk purchases for sales promotion, premiums, fund-raising, and educational or institutional use.

Special book excerpts or customized printings can also be created to fit specific needs. For details, write or phone the office of the Kensington Special Sales Manager: Kensington Publishing Corp., 119 West 40th Street, New York, NY 10018; Attn. Special Sales Department. Phone: 1-800-221-2647.

Brava and the B logo are Reg. U.S. Pat. & TM Off.

ISBN-13: 978-0-7582-4697-4
ISBN-10: 0-7582-4697-8

First Kensington Trade Paperback Printing: January 2010

10 9 8 7 6 5 4 3 2 1

Printed in the United States of America

CONTENTS

The Undying Heart

Zoe Archer

Chapter One

L adies never hunted humans.

Fortunately, Cassandra Fielding never truly concerned herself with how ladies should and shouldn't behave. As she crouched in the shadows of a stonemason's yard, pistol ready in the folds of her skirt, she kept her focus off such inconsequential things as decorous, ladylike behavior and on the front of the tavern opposite the yard. Her prey was inside the tavern. She needed to be ready to move, to follow. To hunt.

The windows of the tavern glowed yellow, and within the taproom, raucous male voices rang out—laughing, boasting, debating. Within was Cassandra's intended target. Colonel Kenneth Broadwell. Entirely unaware that his every moment was being monitored, Broadwell had been spotted several days ago in the vicinity after years abroad. As the Blade closest to where Broadwell had been seen, Cassandra was dispatched to follow him. Her orders were clear, however: track Broadwell, but do not engage. So Cassandra now waited in the stonemason's yard, her cloak wrapped around her against the night's chill, a pistol standing by should it be needed.

Her parents, tolerant though they were of her campaigning for factory conditions reform, would most definitely *not* approve of their daughter skulking about on her own in the middle of the night. But Cassandra never told them she was an operative for the Blades of the Rose, had been one for nigh on a year. It was for her parents' protection as much as her own.

Right now her protection nestled in the folds of her skirt, and her pocket held a goodly handful of bullets. Not that Cassandra had ever shot anyone before. As soon as she'd received her assignment, she'd gone out and bought her very own gun. Borrowing one of her father's would raise questions, questions she couldn't answer, so she purchased her own. The weapon was necessary, but it felt strange and alien in her hand. Yet she would use it if she had to.

She prayed she didn't have to. Her goal had always been to improve people's lives, not end them.

Moonlight spilled into the yard, and the hulking forms of uncut stone turned to creatures of silver and darkness. Cassandra hid herself behind one slab of granite, entirely alone except for the stone. Overhead, the night sky was a black, glittering void. All the decent citizens of this small town had been asleep, safe in their beds, for hours. No one walked the streets, and the wind cut down the narrow lanes with soft, keening sounds.

As a child, she'd been afraid of the dark, thanks to her brother Charlie. He'd once locked her in the cellar as a prank, luring her down there with promises of treacle tarts. She'd spent terrible hours crying in the darkness, until Mrs. Walsh, the housekeeper, heard her sobs and let Cassandra out. For months afterward, she couldn't sleep without a lamp burning.

But that was long ago. Cassandra now knew that things really *did* creep in the darkness, but they were often just as afraid of her as she was of them. She took some comfort in that as she hid herself in the stonemason's yard.

Her childhood imagination must now enjoy taunting her. How else to explain the sinister feeling lurking among the shadows with her, a presence that felt palpable, malevolent.

A slight shifting, the merest suggestion of displaced air. Cassandra whirled around, gun pointed. She knew better than to dismiss instinct. One of the first things she learned when she joined the Blades: never shrug off intuition. That's where the true danger lay, for magic dwelt in the margins of awareness.

In the gloomy darkness, she saw nothing. No person, no animal. Yet nothing could shake her sense that something was there. A presence that loomed just beyond the boundaries of sight and perception. Unnamed, unknown, drawing closer. Closer. Her heart stuttered as her every nerve became a plucked string, reverberating with tension.

She knew it now without a doubt.

She wasn't alone.

Fighting the sudden lump of fear in her throat, Cassandra pressed herself against the granite slab. Not for protection, but to better see whoever, *whatever,* prowled in the darkness. She held her breath, waited.

There, again. A justified chill of fear scraped down her neck. Someone was sliding from shadow to shadow, movements so swift, so silent, anyone who wasn't trained to spot such subtlety would have missed it. Who could it be? Another Heir of Albion, like Broadwell? It couldn't be a Blade, for Cassandra had been unable to send a telegram to let them know Broadwell's whereabouts. Someone else, then.

Something else. The shadows gathered, shaping themselves into the form of a man gliding from darkness to darkness—tall, long-limbed, powerfully built. Twenty feet away. At a slight sound, he turned to investigate. His eyes literally glowed. Hollow and white, unearthly.

Cassandra stifled a gasp. Oh, it was one thing to read about and study magic. Entirely different to sense it, *see* it.

Whatever this . . . man . . . was, he moved with unearthly speed and stealth. She could not see his face as he shifted back into the shadows, more subtle and elusive than any human or animal. *What was he?* Before she could study him further, he melted into darkness, disappearing.

For several moments, Cassandra peered into the night, straining for another sense of him. Yet he was gone, absorbed into the fabric of shadow like a half-remembered dream. Cassandra, trying to refocus, turned back to keep her vigil on the tavern.

The unknown man stood right in front of her. They both started, neither expecting the other. Her pistol came up immediately.

Ambient light from the tavern revealed his face, the glow of his eyes vanished, and her fingers around the trigger slackened in shock. The tall man also started again, as shocked as Cassandra.

It could not be. Yet it was. She took a step forward, lowering her weapon, hardly daring to believe what she saw.

"Sam?" Her voice was a stunned whisper. "Samuel Reed?"

"Cassie."

Oh, God, she knew that voice. Knew it as well as she knew the deepest recesses of her own heart. A low, masculine rumble, much deeper now than it had been ten years ago, but it was him. Sam.

"Cassandra now," she said automatically as she grappled with understanding. Nothing made sense. It could not be that Sam was the creature she had just witnessed prowling through the darkness. "What the blazes are you doing here?"

Sam emerged slightly from the darkness, wariness evident in the guarded movement of his long, lean body. He'd been only eighteen the last time Cassandra saw him, verging into adulthood. Now there was no debate. Sam had grown up. He was, positively, a man. She noted it in the breadth of his shoulders, his broad chest, and powerful limbs. Even in shadow, even dressed in clean but slightly threadbare clothing, she could see it. Sam had left boyhood long ago. This man radiated potent strength, barely restrained.

Cassandra stared up at his face and felt another jolt of shock. The softness of youth had vanished entirely. Sam's face . . . there was no other way for her to describe it . . . it was *hard,* a collection of sharply chiseled planes that made no allowance for leniency. Bold jaw, tight-pressed lips, sharp nose, and forbidding, dark brow. Too severe to be handsome, but undeniably striking. Such a change from the boy he'd been.

"I should ask you the same damned question," he growled. "You shouldn't be out. Alone." He moved, as if to reach for her, but his hand stopped, curling into itself and falling to his side instead.

Fear suddenly danced along her neck. His voice was rough, almost menacing. But that was ridiculous. This was *Sam*, her brother Charlie's best friend, the boy she'd known—and adored—almost her whole life. Ten years ago, he and Charlie both bought commissions, joining the army and serving in the same unit together, as they had done everything together. Including—

"For a lady," Sam growled, "you're pretty damned free with that gun."

She glanced down at the weapon in her hand, then tucked it into her skirts. Proper young women did not carry pistols. Certainly not during the day, and most assuredly not in the middle of the night while lurking in deserted stonemason yards.

"Pistols are all the rage this season," she said. She could not tell Sam anything about her mission, bound by a code of silence, as well as for his own protection.

Although, she amended, gazing at Sam, he seemed perfectly capable of protecting himself. If forced to use only one word to describe this man, the word she must choose would be lethal. She'd never met a man who held such dangerous intent in his body, including the most seasoned Blade field agents. He did not even offer a veneer of a smile at her attempt at humor.

"Nothing good brings a woman out at night," he rumbled. "Some kind of assignation, then. A husband? Lover?" He raised a brow.

Cassandra wondered what kind of lover necessitated having a gun. "I might not be the same girl who collected spiders in jars," she said, "but I'm not the sort of woman who arranges moonlight trysts." However, she wasn't a maiden any more. She'd seen to that a few years ago, though she wasn't about to tell Sam.

Truthfully, she did not know what to say to Sam. She'd so often dreamt of this moment, how she would greet him upon his return. She had even contemplated something as frivolous as the dress she would wear. It would show him she was no longer a girl with dirt under her fingernails, but a grown woman, with a grown woman's desires. And he would see her as if for the first time, a slow smile of wonder illuminating his face, and realize that what he had been searching for had been at home all along. Her nails, too, would be clean. She curbed the impulse to check them now—for often, after touring factories and inspecting conditions, her fingernails did get dirty. But that was a minor detail compared to seeing Sam again.

Her dream of their reunion had ended two years ago, but she remembered it vividly, an imprint of abandoned hope burned into an afterimage on her heart.

Yet this . . . fierce, dangerous man . . . was entirely unlike the Sam she'd longed for, resembling him only in the most superficial way. He burned with a deep, profound coldness that seeped into her own bones.

She realized that it *had* been Sam, stalking the darkness. Moving with an eerie fluidity. More at home within the realm of unnatural shadow than light and life. But how could that be possible?

"I've no idea who you are anymore." Sam's voice glinted like a knife in the darkness.

"That feeling," she said, "is mutual."

Truthfully, she had no idea who he was. Or, her mind whispered, *what* he was. She tried to push that thought away, but it would not be staved off.

Unfamiliar, this terror. Something clammy and frightened uncoiled in her stomach as she stared up at his impassive face. The changes wrought in Sam went beyond the shift from youth to maturity, from civilian to veteran soldier. Yet she did not know what, exactly, was different, was deeply, profoundly not right.

A burst of noise careened out of the tavern. Both Cassandra and Sam shot alert glances toward it, but no one exited the building. As Sam continued to rake the tavern with his gaze, Cassandra could feel the waves of anger and purpose emanating from him, palpable as frost. The gentling of his expression was gone. Nothing gentle in him now.

Sam had been a soldier, a major, the last she'd heard, and still held himself with a soldier's vigilant, capable presence. He wore civilian clothes, yet carried, she saw at that moment, an officer's sword and wore tall military boots. The war in the Crimea ended two years ago. What had become of him since then?

"This makes no sense," she said. "I was told . . ." Her words dried as he swung his gaze back to her. Even in the weak light from the tavern's windows, she saw his eyes were the same palest blue, edged in indigo, only now his eyes did not dance with humor or mischief. They were . . . *haunted*.

"I was told," she began again, "that you were dead."

He stared at her with those anguished, cold eyes. And said, "I am."

Cassie—Cassandra—jolted. Her eyes rounded as she took a step back. Sam hated putting distance between them, the girl he'd known for almost his whole childhood, but it was necessary. He didn't want her close to him. She was a relic, a reminder of the life he'd lost and everything he could never have.

He waited for her to dispute him, claim that he was, in fact, *not* dead, since he stood right in front of her, talking like any ordinary man. But Sam wasn't an ordinary man. Far from it.

And Cassandra just stared at him, her familiar whiskey-gold eyes gleaming with shock. Sam kept himself silent, watching, waiting.

Cassie Fielding, a grown woman. He remembered her, trailing after him and Charlie as they rambled over Sam's father's estate, or the much smaller park around the Fieldings' home. She'd been a scrawny thing, all eyes and bones, a mass of chestnut hair. But her delicate appearance belied a girl with strong opinions and a will of iron. Always abandoning her deportment lessons and embroidery hoops to join in the boys' mischief—building fortresses in the woods, playing pirates, digging in the dirt for odd and interesting rocks. Sam's own sisters were nothing like Cassandra and often snickered at private family dinners that the neighbor's daughter made a far better boy than a girl. Sam, to his shame now, never defended her. Just shrugged and kept on eating, adolescently indifferent.

When Sam left for the army, she'd been on the cusp of womanhood, almost ready to make her debut. A debut that Cassandra did not want. The closer she came to being out in society, the less she readied herself for it. There were fights, Charlie told him, yelling matches between Cassandra and her parents, slammed doors, threats, and pleas. Cassandra called the whole business of having a Season "hogwash for ninnies," which made her mother furious and her father retreat to his study. Sam wondered if she'd had her debut, after all that turmoil.

His mother had sighed, saying that Cassandra would never be beautiful. Now that Cassandra was a woman, his mother's prediction had been proven both true and untrue. Cassandra wasn't a society beauty, her looks were far too singular for that—she still had those large, canny eyes, a jawline that verged on handsome rather than pretty—but she had matured into herself with a self-awareness and strength that stirred him.

Damn it, he thought savagely, turning away, he had no right to be stirred. He had only vengeance, and, when that had been meted out, he had nothing. Just the hope of rest. Finally, rest.

And the man who'd cost Sam everything was in that tavern right now. Sam wanted to run across the street, slam into the tavern, and simply cut Broadwell down with Sam's old officer's sword. But he couldn't. Not with innocents around who could be hurt. He had no idea what he would do when he finally unleashed himself on Broadwell. Sam's control would be gone, and he'd lose himself to the beast of his retribution, and nothing and no one would be safe. Not even Cassandra.

Incredibly, despite what he'd just said to her, she actually took a step *closer* to him, not away. He recoiled. But she persisted, coming yet nearer, raising one slim, gloved hand and, when he tried to slip farther back, she managed to take his own hand, her fingers pressed to his wrist.

He stilled, wanting to shut his eyes against the flood of sensation. It had been so damned long since a woman—since *any-one*—touched him. But he forced himself to stare down at her as she felt for his heartbeat. He was certain that horror and re-pulsion would cross her face, as she realized what he truly was, and why she should run, run like hell.

"Satisfied?" he sneered as something he thought already broken shattered within him.

He saw it then in her expression. Full understanding. Steal-ing like an eclipse. Yet she didn't look anything but sad, deeply sad. She raised her eyes to his, and he found himself staring into them, finding in them a warmth he never anticipated, and did not want.

"You're very close to home," she whispered.

His sneer fell away. Home. His parents' estate was only a dozen miles from here. And Cassandra's family home adjoined the boundaries of that estate. Memories assailed him, swirling as thick and dangerous as ocean currents, threatening to drag him out to sea, drowning him. Childhood, the cheerful knowl-edge that he was a third son and hadn't his older brothers' re-sponsibilities, the reckless carousing of adolescence, he and Charlie drinking and wenching at the very same tavern where he now lurked. His mother's exasperated sighs. His father's stern admonishments that he must make a man of himself. At Sam's urging, his father bought him a commission, and so the adventure of life truly began. And ended.

His parents must never see him again.

"Not coming home," he growled. He pulled his hand from hers, and missed her touch at once.

Just then, the very man Sam wanted stepped from the door of the tavern. Sam's heightened hearing caught the sound even before the man emerged. Sam's eyes narrowed, his body tens-ing, as he watched his former commanding officer tug on a dark coat and look up at the glinting night sky. A smug smile tugged on the corner of Broadwell's mouth. Doubtless the bas-tard was planning his next defilement. But Sam would stop him before that.

Sam almost forgot Cassandra standing beside him, until he

heard her short, indrawn breath. He glanced over to see her also intently watching Broadwell with a look of recognition. What the devil? Was she here for that son of a bitch, too? If that bastard had hurt her, Sam would gut him and force him to watch the spectacle.

Broadwell strode away from the tavern, heading down the deserted street. He still had the same arrogant gait, as if he owned the world and the world should be grateful for the honor. Sam waited until the colonel was well away from the tavern—and civilians—before darting after him. He'd end this tonight.

"Sam, no, wait!" Cassandra's hissed warning behind him did not register. All he saw was Broadwell's retreating back, all he heard were the hated bastard's footsteps upon the cobbled street.

Broadwell rounded a corner, heading toward where his horse was stabled. Noiselessly, Sam drew his sword, then pressed himself against the wall, listening to the sounds around the corner. He heard the colonel enter his horse's stall and lead the animal out. The shuffling of hooves and feet in straw. The stable boy must be asleep somewhere. Broadwell was alone and had not yet mounted the horse. *Now*, when the swine wasn't paying attention.

Sam sprang around the corner, leaping over a low, spiked iron fence that enclosed the stable yard. He raised his sword, ready to strike. Only the alarmed horse alerted Broadwell to his attack. The beast whinnied in fear, dancing to one side, and Broadwell spun around just in time to dodge Sam's blow. His sword caught in the curve of the saddle, cutting into the leather. Sam pulled it free immediately, but Broadwell had been a soldier, too, and nimbly darted away before Sam could strike again.

"Still on my trail, Major Reed?" Broadwell smirked in the darkness of the stables. God, that face, so thin and cruel, the face of a so-called gentleman—it was burned into Sam's mind. All around them, animals shifted nervously in their stalls.

"Won't stop until you pay," Sam growled. He lunged for Broadwell again.

Broadwell dashed to the side, narrowly avoiding the slicing

blade. He grabbed a whip that leaned against a wall. "Your bloody tenacity." The whip snapped out, biting at Sam's sword hand, but Sam didn't let go of the blade. "Thought it was an asset once," Broadwell sneered. "Now it's just a damned nuisance."

Sam swung, and caught Broadwell across the shoulder, cutting through the fabric of his clothes to the flesh beneath. The colonel hissed, sounding more annoyed than in pain.

"I'll give you a hundred more of those before I kill you," gritted Sam.

Furious now that he'd been wounded, Broadwell tossed the whip aside just as he launched himself at Sam. The two men grappled, the air thick with the sounds of their boots scraping on the cobbles, their grunts of rage, fearful horses whinnying. And the faint sound of a woman's running steps coming closer. Hell—Cassandra.

At her approach, Sam's attention wavered for less than a moment. But it was enough. Broadwell shoved Sam back. The heel of Sam's boot caught between two stones, costing him his balance. He stumbled backward and then—

Cassandra gave a quick, horrified cry.

A dull white echo of what once had been pain speared through Sam's chest. He tried to spring forward for another attack, but couldn't move. Something held him immobile. He glanced down and saw a spike of the iron railing protruding from his chest.

He swore, struggling to pull himself up and off the spike. As he did this, Broadwell leapt upon the back of his horse. The horse wheeled around, snorting and anxious.

"Such a pleasure, Major Reed." Broadwell turned to Cassandra with a threatening glare. "Whoever you are, you'd best forget everything you've seen here tonight." He gave a mocking salute, and kicked his horse into a run. As he did, bolting from the stable, he sent Sam a glance of pure malicious glee. Sam snarled with fury as his intended prey evaded him yet again.

* * *

A litany of swears and prayers fell from Cassandra's mouth as she ran toward Sam. He partly lay, partly knelt upon the ground, thrashing angrily as—good God—a wicked iron spike jutted from the left side of his chest. Such a wound should kill, if not cause excruciating agony, but Sam just glared down at the spike, as though it were no more than a splinter, as he tried to extract himself from it.

"Easy, easy," Cassandra murmured. "Let me help." She'd read about field dressing. She reached for him.

He pulled back as much as he was able. "Don't touch me," he snapped, eyes cold blue fire in the darkness.

Cassandra stayed where she was, but pulled her hands back. She could only watch as Sam, with a grunt, struggled to stand. He lurched forward in slow increments, and the spike retreated by inches from the front of his chest. He ought to be screaming in pain, but he only clenched his teeth with the effort to pull the spike from his body. At last, he tugged himself free and then rose swiftly to standing. He glanced down at his torn coat and shirt, scowling. She drifted closer, looking at the patch of flesh revealed by the shredded fabric. With a wince, she saw his torn skin. It seemed the spike had pierced him between the ribs, spearing through his lung. Yet she heard no rasp of his breathing. And . . .

"No blood," she breathed.

His jaw hardened as his eyes moved back and forth between her face and the wound in his chest. "And there won't be. Never again."

As she stared, she saw his skin shift. The wound shrank, his flesh knitting together, sealing itself up, until the gaping puncture from the spike contracted and then disappeared completely. Within seconds, only a bit of raised skin indicated that he'd been hurt at all.

No.

Her eyes burned.

He gave a low, hollow laugh. "Good as new." Then his glance shot to her. A frown of confusion appeared between his dark brows. "You always had a tough constitution, but why the hell aren't you screaming or fainting?"

Cassandra continued to stare at the bit of Sam's chest revealed by his torn clothing. From what she could see, his pectoral muscle was well-sculpted, precisely delineated, and faintly dusted with dark hair. This, almost more than watching him heal from a mortal wound before her eyes, unsettled her. Sam. She'd dreamt of him for years. And now, the impossible had happened. He was back. But this was not the Sam she once knew, for so many reasons.

Had she not been a Blade, she wouldn't have believed such things were possible. But, within the past year, she had learned—mostly in theory—that the world was full of such impossibilities.

Realizing that she stared, Cassandra brought her gaze up to Sam's. She tilted her head back to look him in the eye. He'd grown taller, as well as filled out. He must have been a sight, striding across a battlefield, commanding men with his sword upraised. The battlefield where he had died. And, somehow, risen again.

Sam loomed over her, palpably dangerous. "You should be praying that this is just a dream—or a nightmare."

Chapter Two

Cassandra turned from him—the known world was shifting, tilting, and she needed balance. It seemed as though fate was daring anyone foolish enough to take it on, merciless and mercurial.

Seeing only the street before her, she walked, dazed. She took refuge in responsibility, in her mission for the Blades. Yes, the mission. It would guide her when all ballast was gone.

"Fleeing me," Sam rumbled. "Wise."

She spun around—but he was gone. Staring into the night, Cassandra found herself entirely alone. She took a few steps back, to try and find him, then shook herself and moved on. Determination pushed her forward. She refused the life of a society wife for a reason, because she needed more than pretty rooms and teas and dinner parties where she tried to be a charming ornament. She wanted purpose, a greater contribution. Now, when challenged, she must show her true mettle. With or without Sam.

She walked through the dark streets. When she reached her destination, she stood outside the building, her breath misting on the windows in the chill of early morning. Everything within was dark and quiet. Considering that dawn was only just creeping over the horizon, this wasn't a surprise. Yet her task was still urgent.

"Midnight assignations, pistols," Sam said behind her, "and now telegraph offices. Not the Cassie Fielding I knew."

She jolted. Then fought for steadiness, refusing to turn around. "Cassandra," she corrected. "You were damned quiet. I didn't hear you following me."

"You wouldn't," he answered, "unless I wanted you to."

She checked the posted hours in the office window. A painted sign boasted that the shop opened at six every morning in order to send telegraphs to such cosmopolitan locations as St. Petersburg and Berlin. Thank goodness for provincial pretensions, otherwise she would lose precious hours before sending her message.

She had to let the Blades know that not only was Broadwell in England, he was on the move. Once she sent the telegram to Blades headquarters in Southampton, other operatives would take the next train north and join her. No Blade undertook a mission alone—the dangers were too great. But frustration rose at the sight of the closed telegraph office. She burned with impatience to successfully accomplish her assignment.

"Steady, Fielding," she muttered to herself. "You've just got to wait a little."

"Not alone, you won't," came the growled response.

Her pulse leapt at the sound but with awareness, not fear. Cassandra glanced over her shoulder. Sam had moved silently so that he now leaned against the storefront opposite the telegraph office. His arms crossed over his chest as he watched her. There was nothing indolent or careless about his posture. A brutal, ready awareness radiated out from him. In addition to his sword, he carried a pistol, the form of the weapon hinted at beneath his jacket. But the most dangerous weapon was Sam, himself.

As the sky began to lighten, she could see him more plainly. He still had ink-black hair, though it was worn a little longer now, brushing his collar, as if he hadn't time or concern with things as frivolous as barbering. His rangy body was a coiled beast, primed to pounce. Only minutes earlier, she'd witnessed him fighting with Broadwell. Cassandra didn't have much experience watching men fight—she'd never been allowed to watch the boxing matches at local fairs. Yet she knew there was something fiercely beautiful about the way Sam fought, as though he was made for the one purpose and met that purpose with savage grace.

Cassandra crossed the street to stand with him. As she neared, he began to lean closer, but then seemed to force himself to edge slightly away, keeping distance between them.

"The gun I have isn't decorative," she said. "I can protect myself." She hoped she sounded more confident than she felt. At the gun shop, she'd been allowed to use a shooting range in the back to test the weapon. It had roared in her hands, but she'd at least hit the target. That had been the first and, so far, only time she'd used the pistol.

Sam's forbidding expression grew even more grim, yet somehow resigned. "Not from me you can't. You can't understand what I am. If you did, you'd be terrified." He began to turn away, but her hand on his arm stopped him. They both stilled at the contact, even with her gloves and his coat and shirt between them. Beneath her hand, his arm was unyielding, taut with muscle.

"Aside from that time Charlie locked me in the basement," she said, "have you known me to be afraid?"

He made a soft exhalation, very nearly an amused snort. "You scared the hell out of him with that snake you caught once."

She almost smiled at the memory, "I chased him around the yard with the snake, until my mother made me let the poor beast go."

He pressed his lips together, as if fighting a smile, then grew yet more serious, as if challenging his own desire to smile. "I'm worse than a grass snake, or even an adder."

"I'm still not afraid of you." Far from it.

He gave a stiff nod. But moved so that her hand fell away from him, like an autumn leaf. And he remained silent.

She would have to extract it from him, the diseased flesh of memory. So she gave him what she carried within her, "Charlie wrote me," she said. "The things he described . . . the disaster of Balaclava . . . the punishing winter." She still had those letters, despite the fact that some were gruesome records of suffering.

"You sent us socks." Sam's voice held the faintest trace of warmth, an echo of sunlight.

"Terrible socks," she added. "I can't knit worth a damn."

"We wore them anyway. Too cold to care if the socks were all different lengths. And thicknesses."

She smiled. "Must have been truly desperate."

"We were. Not bullets but disease took half the men."

Her smile died. "Charlie's letters didn't say much about that."

"No—he wouldn't. He wouldn't allow any of us to wallow in our misery, no matter how bad things got."

"What would he do?" She craved anything of her brother, any small memory.

"Told jokes, sang nonsense songs so that we laughed even as we starved. The men loved him. The men came to me when they wanted guidance, but it was Charlie they loved." Here, his voice warmed again slightly, and a spectral smile hovered around Sam's mouth. Cassandra's heart seized, seeing the tattered vestiges of the old Sam. Then it was gone.

"The last letter he sent," she said, "was a month before he died. Nobody ever knew what truly happened, only that he'd been killed in action at the Redan."

Sam stared, unseeing, at the windows of the telegraph office, as though they reflected the past and not the spectral forms of Sam and Cassandra standing opposite. "A damned mess," he growled. "The commanding officers wanted it captured, and threw men at it. The dead piled up. Broadwell commanded our unit, and one morning he gave the attack orders that I knew would slaughter us. Even though it was grounds for court martial, I tried to move the men, get them out of the way of enemy bombardment. Better to lose my life at the end of a rope than the hundred men of my company should be killed for nothing."

That *did* sound like Sam, who gladly put himself in harm's

way to protect others. More than once, he'd stepped between her and Charlie when her brother had been hell-bent on teasing her mercilessly. The two boys had even traded punches over it. Of course, Cassandra had been able to hold her own against her brother, biting and scratching like a rabid badger, but Sam's actions had earned him her fervent adoration. She wondered if he even remembered those fights between him and Charlie. Likely not, given that much greater events had transpired since then.

Events he continued to narrate, shaking his head. "No good. The enemy chopped us to pieces. Charlie . . ." He swallowed hard, and Cassandra felt her own throat burning. She wanted to cover her ears and run. She wanted to hear every word. Charlie's love of practical jokes had been the bane of her childhood, and she had loved him desperately, seeing later in those tormenting jokes his only way of expressing fraternal affection. Although she'd had enough of frogs down the back of her dresses. She got him back, though. He never drank another cup of tea without giving it a cautious sniff first.

"Charlie took it hard," Sam rasped. "But he died fast. Couldn't say the same about everyone else. I was . . . lucky. Took a bullet to the leg, and I went down. It wasn't fatal."

"But," Cassandra breathed, "the letter my parents received . . . it said *everyone* in the company died."

Sam smiled, brittle as winter morning. "I died. While I was lying there, bleeding, I saw someone making their way through the fallen. Methodically firing and reloading his revolver. Those who weren't dead got a bullet in the heart. I readied my sword, thinking it might have been a French soldier, but when he got closer, I saw I was wrong." His voice hardened. "It was Broadwell. Killing his own men."

"Oh, my God." Cassandra thought she might be sick, but fought the wave of nausea.

Sam continued on, relentless. "Broadwell got to me. I tried to fight him off, but I'd lost a lot of blood and was . . . weak. He laughed and said I'd be a good addition, and then shot me. Right through the heart. Fiery pain starting in my chest and exploding outward engulfing everything, my blood coursing out of my body, my heart slowing. And I was angry, so goddamned angry, that it was ending like *this*. Then I died." His hand drifted up and he absently touched the place on his chest where he'd received his death wound.

"It was . . . peaceful. But it didn't last." Sam stared down at his clenched fists. "Next thing I knew, I felt this slam of pain, like a battering ram straight to my chest. Broadwell was standing over me, holding something in his hands that glowed while he chanted something in a language I couldn't recognize. When he saw my eyes open, he jeered at me, said I wouldn't be defying his orders any more. He told me to stand up. I couldn't refuse. And when I looked around, I saw all the fallen men standing, like me, except the ones who'd been too . . . damaged. None of us understood what had happened, how we could be alive. But we soon learned. Charlie was one of the truly lucky ones. Me and the others . . ." He tightened his jaw. "We weren't alive. And our will . . . wasn't our own."

Sickened to her deepest self, Cassandra breathed, "What do you mean?"

Before he could answer, a whistling middle-aged man ambled up to the telegraph office. Keys jingled in his hand. In the growing light, he looked curiously at Sam and Cassandra, his gaze lingering on Sam with a puzzled frown. Sam glanced away, as if trying to deflect the man's curiosity. With a shake of his head, the man turned back to the office door and unlocked it.

"Old friend of yours?" Cassandra whispered.

"Never seen him before."

The door to the office opened and the man entered. Cassandra hurried after him, Sam close at her heels.

"Good morning, Miss," the telegraph operator called out cheerfully as he puttered about the office. "And, uh, Sir." The room now filled with sunlight, revealing the plain floors, the counter, the telegraph machine proudly displaying its modern convenience on a desk. The telegraph operator lit a fire in a squat stove and set a kettle on top. As he rubbed his hands to warm them, he turned to her. "So terribly sorry the lines were down yesterday. We'll send your telegram this morning, though! Never known the lines to go down for more than half a day. Brought a friend with you this time, I see." Again, he glanced at Sam standing beside Cassandra, unable to hide his disquiet.

"I need to draft a new telegram," Cassandra said. She tugged off her gloves to take the operator's proffered pen and slip of paper.

As she began to write, the telegraph operator cleared his throat uncomfortably and stared at Sam. Sam, catching the operator's scrutiny, moved from her side to study the advertisements pinned to a nearby wall, seemingly intrigued by what he saw there. His alert posture and rigid shoulders told her he was anything but interested in a few scraps of paper touting the latest in wheat-threshing devices or ladies' bonnets.

Cassandra peered up through her lashes to observe the operator. An expression of deep unease flitted across his jowly face, growing more and more apprehensive the longer he looked at Sam. But what was it about Sam that so disturbed this very ordinary man? Sam had been careful to hide the tear in his clothing, and he certainly did not look like a disreputable character. If anything, Sam radiated military bearing. His authoritative presence should be reassuring. Yet something, some . . . uncanny aura around Sam troubled the operator.

She hurriedly finished her telegram and handed it to the telegrapher. He started, as if surprised to find her there, then read it through.

"You sure you want to send this, Miss? It seems a lot of nonsense to me."

Precisely. All written communication between Blades had to be encoded. "Yes, please do send it exactly as it's written."

He shrugged as he sat himself down at the telegraph. With her message propped up at his elbow, he began to tap the key. He frowned down at the machine, then tapped the key again. Still frowning, he rose and checked the wires running from the telegraph.

"What's the matter?" But Cassandra already knew.

The telegrapher shook his head. "I just don't understand it,

Miss. The lines have never been down this long. There's no accounting for it."

Cassandra suspected that there was, in fact, a clear reason why the typically reliable telegraph lines weren't functioning. The Heirs of Albion were powerful enough to block them, particularly if they were trying to hide the movements of one of their men. She fought a shiver—aside from seeing Broadwell earlier, she'd had but one other encounter with some Heirs, and that had been mercifully brief. But now she was beginning to have a truer sense what they were capable of.

"Perhaps you can come back later today," the telegraph operator suggested. Then his gaze slid to Sam, grew uncomfortable again. She could almost hear the telegrapher's thoughts, *I hope she doesn't bring* him *with her.*

Sam had his back to the man, but he turned his head slightly, catching the operator's tangible sense of agitation.

Cassandra put several coins on the counter. "I'll pay now. Just send the telegram as soon as the lines are up." Then she stepped quickly to Sam and looped her arm through his.

He tensed at her touch, but allowed her to lead him toward the door. "Good morning," Cassandra called over her shoulder, and then she and Sam were out on the street, striding briskly away from the telegraph office.

As they walked, passing sleepy-eyed servants and delivery wagons, Cassandra held onto Sam's taut arm. His crystal gaze snapped down to where her bare fingers rested on his sleeve. Flickering in those pale blue depths came the barest suggestion of longing, but it vanished before she could be certain.

"You shouldn't," he growled.

"Shouldn't what?"

"Touch me. I repulse you. Just as I repulsed that bloody simp at the telegraph office."

"You couldn't disgust me, Sam."

His eyes flashed, glacial blue. "You don't know what the hell you're talking about."

Cassandra stopped walking abruptly. When he tried to pull away, she gripped his arm tightly and she glared up at him.

"And I don't think *you* know who the hell *you're* talking to. *Me*, Sam. Remember how you and Charlie used to hide when I'd try to tag along? I never let you hide then, and I won't now."

"This isn't children's games, Cassandra," he gritted. He shoved his wrist into her line of vision, and she stared at the corded muscle and tendons there. "See something missing?"

All she saw was the strength of him. "No—"

"Look closer."

She did, and then saw it. The stillness of his skin.

"No pulse," he growled. He pulled his wrist away.

Aware of a maid and a crossing sweeper openly watching them, Sam tugged her into a narrow alley. He glowered down at her, crowding her against a wall. On either side of her head, he planted his large hands, and leaned close. Despite his size, his effective caging of her and the biting fury in his gaze, she did not back down.

"Don't let your childhood fancies turn something rotten into a fairy story," he snarled.

A quick burst of anger flared within her. "I never said—"

"Remember how I said that after Broadwell turned me and the other men, that our will wasn't our own?"

She nodded slowly, anger dissipating, as a miasma of horror began to creep through her.

"The thing he used to transform us, it gave him power over us. We had to obey his *every* command. We were forced to do things." His voice dropped into a harsh rasp. "Can't . . . can't even tell you what those things were. Don't want those images infecting you. They were . . . repellent. Disgusting."

Fresh sickness pushed through her. "Murder?" she breathed.

"And worse." He fought against a tide of emotion, his mouth pressed tight. The column of his neck moved as he swallowed. "We were still at war, and we were still soldiers, but we went far beyond even the most depraved marauders. None of us could stop ourselves, no matter how hard we fought. Broadwell controlled us, and, for his own gratification, we could only watch as he forced us to violate all of humanity's morals."

Sam's eyes squeezed shut as if to block the images that now

seethed through his mind, his head hanging down. A lock of black hair fell across his forehead—just as it would when he was younger and bent over a particularly engaging book. Which she inevitably would try to snatch away.

But no book could ever contain what Sam must have seen, what he had done. Cassandra could not begin to comprehend what that must have been like for strong-willed Sam to have his will taken away, to be impelled to commit crimes not only against others, but against himself. An unbearable torment, but one that *had* to be borne, because there was no other choice. Dear God, no wonder he looked at the world with a cold, remote gaze. It had to be the only way to survive, or else be driven mad by memories.

Cassandra raised one shaking hand and placed it against his jaw. His eyes flew open and they both inhaled at the contact of flesh to flesh. Beneath her palm, his skin was marmoreal, hard and cool. Yet she also felt the tiny tremors that wracked him.

"It's not your fault," she said.

He sucked in a breath that he did not truly need. "Damned quick to forgive me," he growled. "When I can't forgive myself."

She wouldn't accept his self-reproach. "*Broadwell* did those things, not you. You said yourself that you had no control."

Sam pushed against the wall, swinging away from her. He stared down the length of the alley, where two cats nosed the rubbish. Empty bottles, bones from someone's supper, a newspaper. Such an ordinary scene from any little English town, so far from what Sam had witnessed—and done.

She knew then that she hated Broadwell, hated him in a way she thought she could never feel. As if she could level cities with her rage. This went far beyond what her mission entailed. What he'd done to the men of Sam's company infuriated her. And what he had done to Sam turned her blood to fire. Broadwell had to be stopped.

"I broke free," he said on a guttural rasp. "After about a year of that hell, I somehow broke the hold he had on me."

Incredible. "If anyone has the strength of will to sever a supernatural chokehold, it would be you. Such an obstinate bastard."

He snorted at her coarse language, but didn't deny that he was exactly what she called him.

"You were able to fight back," she said, stepping closer. She spoke to his broad back. "There's your proof. No blame falls on you. It's Broadwell's alone."

"Should have broken free of it sooner," he muttered.

Now she was getting frustrated. He was so determined to punish himself. "Did any of the other men break Broadwell's hold?"

"No."

Cassandra stepped in front of him. "That kind of magic—I know something about it, and the fact that you were able to free yourself *at all* from it is bloody miraculous."

He stared at her, and there was a tiny, nearly imperceptible gentling, even though his face lost none of its striking angularity. "I cannot understand you." His voice was low, smoky. She felt herself drawn closer. "Why are you not sickened by what I've said? How can you bear the sight of me, knowing what I am and what I've done? Aren't you horrified?"

"Make no mistake," she answered. "Everything you've told me, it's torn me open, down to the heart of me." She curled a fist over the center of her chest. "Yet, despite it all, I know you, Samuel Acton Reed. *I know you.* And I'll never turn away from you."

"Clinging to the past," he muttered, yet his gaze warmed.

Was she? Were her girlhood dreams manipulating her woman's judgment? Perhaps she so desperately wanted the fantasy she had created in her youth, she willingly overlooked evidence that could shatter such finely wrought constructs. This man before her was not Sam, not as she knew him, and, by his own admission, he'd done terrible, ghastly things. He had been killed and rose again as the living dead.

And yet, gazing into his diamond-blue eyes, that seemed to yearn without knowing they did, the instinct on which she so assiduously relied told her no. He'd undergone the most profound change possible, alive, then dead, and then this awful amalgam of both. The things he had been forced to do . . . no wonder he had to cauterize his emotions. Anyone would have been turned into a true monster from such suffering. But not him. Not Sam.

"I've cut free from the moorings of the past," she said, taking his cool hand between her two warm palms. "The current of the present has brought us together now."

He stared down at their joined hands—his large and roughened from soldiering, hers smaller and slender, but stronger, she hoped, than they appeared. She inwardly grimaced to see slight crescents of grease under her nails, but she'd only just returned from inspecting a cotton mill when the Blades' summons came. No time for washing up, she'd dashed back out the door.

If now he saw the grime on her hand, he didn't seem to care. For a moment, his hand lay motionless in hers, but then, very slightly, his thumb rubbed against her wrist. A shiver ran through her, sparking sensation. They both glanced up at each other, and their gazes held with a new awareness.

They broke apart at the sound of a woman stepping into the alley and beating a rug. The woman gave the worn rug several good thwacks with a wire carpet beater, then stared openly at Cassandra and Sam with commingled curiosity and distrust.

Without speaking, Sam offered Cassandra his arm, and they both strode quickly from the alley and down one of the larger streets. The town was too small for their movements in the early morning hours to go unnoticed, yet she didn't know where she was headed—not only in the street, but with the mission. She'd always had a strong sense of purpose, and being directionless now frustrated her. And the future of her mission wasn't the only uncertainty. She glanced over at Sam, walking silent and tall beside her. This growing attraction between them created new mysteries.

Broadwell was on the move. She did not know where he headed. Communication with the Blades in Southampton had been severed. No one would be coming to her aid on this crucial mission. She had to plan her next step, and quickly. Every hour meant more distance between herself and Broadwell. But what her next step might be, she had no idea.

She and Sam walked without direction and without speaking. Yet she felt them both guided by an unknown force. When they passed a familiar storefront, they both stopped and stared at each other, recognizing something at the same time.

"This is the direction Broadwell went," she realized. "Last night, when he rode out of town."

"Pursuing him," Sam said, "without knowing it. I've been chasing him for what feels like an eternity. It's all I have, now." He studied her. "You're after him, too."

"I'm supposed to track him," she admitted. But after that, and without support from the other Blades, she didn't know what she was supposed to do.

"Why?" When she did not answer right away, he pressed, "The magic that created me—you said you knew about it."

"About magic of its kind, yes, but not whatever turned you into . . ." She searched for the appropriate word. "Into a zombie."

His mouth curved into a wry, but genuine, smile. "I prefer the term 'living dead.' Less ghoulish."

That smile made the kindled awareness within her flare higher.

She made herself concentrate on the topic at hand, not his extremely attractive smile. For half a moment, she debated whether to reveal the truth to Sam. Secrecy was always paramount. Yet if anyone could be trusted, and at any particular time, it was Sam, and it was now.

In silent agreement, they continued walking, tracing Broadwell's path.

"The object that turned you into the . . . living dead," she began, "there are more of its type. Not many of them can raise the dead, but they all possess magic. Some are stronger than others. Some are so powerful, they could destroy entire nations—or create them. They are known as Sources, and they are scattered across the globe. Wherever human civilization has taken root, you can find Sources."

He made a soft noise of incredulity. "If you'd said that to me three years ago, I would have demanded you give me a taste of whatever you'd been drinking, and then bought the bottle."

She smiled at that. "We both know the truth now."

They approached some steep, treacherous steps that had been washed moments earlier. A fine place for a person to slip and break their neck. Cassandra used to run at breakneck speeds up and down the hills around her home, but she had been barefoot or in Charlie's old boots then. Now, her dainty ladies' boots could send her crashing onto her bottom, or worse, her head.

Before she could debate the safest way down, Sam took her hand from the crook of his arm and laced their fingers together. Down the steps he guided her. When they reached the bottom of the stairs, he slowly surrendered his grip, as if reluctant to let her go, their palms sliding against one another.

She took his arm again, but everywhere within her reverberated with his touch, his care. They continued along the street like any ordinary man and woman on an early morning stroll— yet there wasn't anything ordinary about either of them.

"Unfortunately," she continued, somewhat breathlessly, "there are people who not only believe in the Sources, but seek to find and subjugate Sources for their own gains."

"Like Broadwell," growled Sam.

"He's a member of the Heirs of Albion."

"Pompous name."

She snorted in agreement. "And the Heirs only get worse from there. They spend their miserable lives plundering the world's magic to ensure England's primacy." Her voice turned to steel with long-standing hatred. Seeing the way Sam's jaw tightened at her words, he seemed immediately to share her loathing for the men and their objectives.

"How do you know about Broadwell, and these Heirs?"

"Magic, on its own, cannot defend itself. So there are people—a very few people—who try to protect it. They are called the Blades of the Rose. And I'm one of them."

If pride tinged her words, she felt somewhat justified. What the Blades sought to accomplish was nigh impossible, because there were always more greedy, cold-blooded men than altruistic ones, yet that was part of what made the work of the Blades so necessary. And, she acknowledged only in the innermost recesses of her self, she truly liked the challenge.

"And that's what you were doing outside the tavern last night." Sam's voice softened with wonder and, yes, a hint of admiration. "I'm not the only one hunting Broadwell."

"My orders were to track him after he'd been spotted in the area. I was supposed to wire headquarters as soon as I confirmed Broadwell's presence, and other Blades would head up to try and retrieve the Source he'd stolen. But the lines have been down for days." She frowned in consternation. "Which means I'm on my own."

Sam stopped midstride, bringing Cassandra up short. Yet he helped balance her before she could stumble. As she gazed up at him, she saw a new light in his eyes, one that had not been there an hour earlier.

"Even the most solitary wolf doesn't hunt alone," he said.

She stared at him, surprised yet again. This driven man was a hardened warrior. He also had carefully escorted her down steep stairs, yet did not treat her as if she were made of crystal. And he wasn't alive, yet he made her heart speed. A mass of contradictions. But she liked contradictions, for in those undefined spaces one was no longer beholden to any rule or preconception. A person could find their true self within contradiction.

"We're to find him together," she murmured, understanding.

"I've been chasing Broadwell for two years," he rumbled, "but now he won't escape me."

"You mean," she corrected, "he won't escape *us*."

"*Us*," he repeated. He tested the word in his mouth and

seemed to find it . . . not altogether unpleasant. "Been a long time since I've been part of an *us*."

Cassandra valued her independence, but—being a member of the Blades, and working for factory reform—she knew the value of having someone watching her back, gaining strength from others. Only a fool rushed into danger entirely unprotected and alone.

And perilous danger lay ahead. The cruel Broadwell had a fearsome Source in his possession, and she *must* get it away from him, secure it from further exploitation. Her only ally in this fight was Sam. An undead soldier who, for many years, had known only a thirst for vengeance. He could be trusted as a warrior, but could his need for retribution imperil the mission and the Source? Would he be an asset in this fight, or a liability? And could she separate herself from her dreams of the past in order to succeed in the present?

Cassandra suspected that the biggest uncertainty was her own heart.

Chapter Three

Considering that he was not only a veteran, but one of the living dead, Sam didn't think much could surprise him any more. He'd witnessed and fought in battles that would make most men curl into shivering, weeping heaps. He had been *raised from the dead*, and forced to engage in unspeakable acts. And he'd seen his share of beauty, too. Sunrise over the gleaming domes of Constantinople. A gypsy dancer covered in glittering coins, spinning in front of a fire as wild fiddles poured songs of dreams and desire.

Safe to say, Sam wasn't a boy anymore, with a boy's sense of wonder.

Yet Cassandra amazed him.

She walked beside him now, her hand securely tucked into his arm. He kept glancing down at her, waiting for her to suddenly realize that he was truly a monster and that she should run from him as fast as she was able.

She didn't do either of these things. She did not know precisely what he was—he couldn't disgorge that kind of wickedness to her, staining her with his corruption—but she had enough knowledge to deem him an unnatural fiend. He'd only sketched what he'd been made to do—even that should be enough to send her running far and fast. Despite all this, she looked into his eyes, *touched him*, and accepted. He could not even endure himself, yet Cassandra—the coltish, headstrong girl who'd grown into a slim, unconventionally pretty but still headstrong woman—accepted him. Not one woman, not one person, out of a thousand would do the same. And she was a member of these Blades of the Rose, protecting magic from bastards like Broadwell. Her strength awed and humbled him.

Just the same, she was still human, and as her footsteps dragged on the cobbled streets, Sam realized with a start that she'd been up all night and into the morning without sleep and without food. He needed neither. She did, however, and so he guided her into a tea shop. All his instincts roared at him to leave a place of such close habitation—people were sitting at tables, chatting over breakfast, reading their newspapers, the bustle of the servers—but Cassandra needed to eat, and the instinct to care for her overrode his demand for seclusion.

She smiled wearily at him as they sat down at a small table. "Exactly what I needed," she murmured.

He only nodded, strained by the warmly ordinary scene within the shop, at the simple pleasure of sitting with her at a little table and seeing her smile at him as if he was still the kind of man who could be in tea shops and receive her smiles.

When a female server hurried up to their table, Cassandra ordered a pot of tea and scones, "with lots and lots of jam," which made him chuckle. But he lost his humor when the server kept glancing at him uneasily, and seemed relieved to leave their table.

"What do people see when they look at you?" Cassandra muttered irritably.

"A monster," he answered. A simple statement of fact.

"You've no fangs," she said, surly. "Or fur. You look like an ordinary man. An extremely handsome man," and she blushed a little before rushing on, "but ordinary, not monstrous."

That blush intrigued him, and the fact that she found him extremely handsome. Yet he wouldn't be sidetracked by his need for her admiration.

"Look at them," he said, nodding toward some of the other patrons. "Truly look."

She followed his gaze, studying the people.

"You can see them breathing," he noted. "When they laugh, after they take a sip of tea or a bite to eat. You might not be fully aware of them breathing, but you sense it, nonetheless."

"Perhaps," Cassandra allowed.

"It's the same with everyone's pulse."

Her gaze flew back to him. "I can't see their pulses all the way from here."

"Maybe not in their wrists or their throats," he permitted, "but the movement of their blood through their veins . . . it creates a kind of . . . energy around them. An animation."

Frowning a little, she studied the people in the tea shop, trying to see what he meant.

"Now," he said, "look at me."

Cassandra turned to face him. Both a torture and a blessing to be the object of her frank study.

"I'm different, aren't I?" He watched, forcing himself to be indifferent as her eyes grew round with understanding. "No breathing, no pulse. You might not know any of that consciously, but you can feel it. So can they."

Sam waited. Terror would come into her gaze, a true comprehension that he was no longer alive, that he was a monster. Horror eventually emerged with everyone else who beheld him in full daylight. She would be the same.

Yet, as he waited, her fear never surfaced. She looked thoughtful, sad, a touch angry, but not fearful. Not of him.

He couldn't have been more amazed if she suddenly began levitating.

To hide his shock, he continued. "During the day, it's not so easy to hide. That's why I usually keep to the night, and away from places like this." He glanced out the shop window to the bustling street, full of sunshine and life. "Haven't been out this hour of the morning, with so many people, in almost three years." He turned back to her. "In three years, I haven't spoken to anyone as much as I have with you in the last few hours." The loneliness of that statement hit him like a fist of ice.

The sorrow for him in her amber eyes made him study the

tea-stained tabletop. He didn't know how to act, what to think, when she offered him true compassion. And he hated to think that she pitied him. He was a barely contained beast who could tear this shop and the people within it apart if he let slip his control.

All he wanted to do was bolt from this tea shop, this bastion of normalcy where he stood out like a bloodstained saber amongst butter knives. But Cassandra needed food, needed rest, so he forced himself to stay.

"My conversation isn't precisely the height of pleasant banter," she said with a wry quirk of her mouth. "Always scared off would-be beaux and horrified the matrons. My mother said I was *too forthright* with my opinions."

"No such thing," he said.

"That's what I believe! I can't help it if talking about lack of sanitation in factory towns gives some puff-brained swain the vapors."

In spite of himself, Sam felt a smile tug at his lips. He wished he could have seen Cassandra cut a swath through the polite ballrooms of London. "That might scare off a few lesser suitors."

"I don't suppose *you* might like to discuss sanitary conditions in factory towns?" she asked.

"We could try," he offered, "but I don't know anything about that topic. How about siege techniques?"

She grimaced. "I'm at a loss there. But," she brightened, "I recall you and Charlie could discuss horse racing for hours."

"Fishing, too," Sam added.

"And wenches," added Cassandra.

He sat up even straighter. "Little eavesdropping minx!"

She tilted up her chin with bravado, even as a fresh blush stained her cheeks. "I was curious what boys talked about on their own."

"I'm not talking to you about wenches—women," he corrected. Sitting with Cassandra at this little table reminded him that he hadn't touched a woman in those three years, either. He had thought that being undead meant all his physical needs would disappear. And they had—until now. Looking at her, the graceful curves of her shoulders, her slim neck and generous mouth, desires long buried now revived. Desires he had no right to feel. She may accept him as he was, but he would never pollute her with his touch. "We haven't time for horseflesh and angling. *Or* wen—women."

"Not with Broadwell at large." She switched immediately into clipped efficiency, which, as a soldier, he appreciated. "The Blades were alerted to his presence when it became known that he was traveling to England with a Source. That Source must be what changed you."

"He'll use it again, just as he did in Crimea." The idea that Broadwell planned on desecrating other men turned Sam's vision to a furious haze.

Cassandra placed a hand atop his, where he gripped the edge of the table. "Sam," she said quietly. "You must control yourself." She glanced quickly toward the other tea shop patrons, who were staring at Sam with agitation. Sam blinked, realizing that he held the table so tightly, it shook.

He forced his fingers to uncurl from their grip, to relax his body.

The server gingerly approached and set down a pot of tea, two cups, and a plateful of warm scones before scurrying away. Sam was grateful to see that Cassandra poured him a tiny amount of tea before filling her own cup, knowing without being told that she would have to perpetuate the illusion that he was a normal human. He pretended to sip from his cup—but the action sent a dart of ice through him. Playing at a world he could never have, and forcing her to help maintain the deception.

She started in on her breakfast with a good deal of eagerness. Just as she'd said, she did love jam, and often licked it from her fingers when she grew enthusiastic in its application.

The sight made him involuntarily groan.

She looked up at him with a mouthful of scone. Swallowing, she looked remorseful. "Does this bother you?" She waved her hand to his largely empty cup, then looked meaningfully at her breakfast.

He hated to see her ashamed, especially on his account. "No—I like watching you eat, your . . . eagerness."

She chuckled. "My manners are slightly better than a soldier's."

"Barely." When she made a small sound of outrage, he said, "You actually remind me of a mountain cat that was kept by a Prussian countess."

"*A pet?*" Her nose wrinkled.

"More than a pet. A fierce little creature that bent to no one and refused a chain. Clever and sleek."

Delicious color flooded her cheeks. He wanted to put his mouth there, to feel her skin warm against his own.

He couldn't act on that desire because of what Broadwell had done, which made Sam's need to find and punish that son of a bitch all the more demanding.

"I've been tracking Broadwell for two years," Sam said, curtly changing the topic, "and during that time, I've seen him make more . . . *things* like me. He'll do it again. Here, in England."

Cassandra's blush faded as she, too, considered Broadwell's next move. She moodily crumbled some scone between her fingers. "The question is, *where* is he heading?"

Frustration welled in Sam. He knew the bastard was close, but while Broadwell's agenda was clear, his whereabouts were elusive. Before Sam's anger could overwhelm him again, he calmed himself by watching Cassandra decimate a scone.

What agony. It was so like a typical morning, the kind he knew he would never have. Ignoring the pain, he indulged himself in imagining what it might have been like if, after he'd been wounded, he would have been shipped back home. Cassandra would be waiting for him. As he healed, he could have called on her, courted her, won her. They could have had mornings just like this one, following a night of fiery lovemaking. His cold body almost heated at the thought. To have Cassandra as his own, to give her children and watch them grow, together. A man's true life.

But Broadwell had stolen that from him, too. Just as he'd stolen from all the other men in Sam's company. Another reason why that bastard would pay, and pay in pain and blood.

Suddenly, Cassandra stiffened in her seat and gave a low cry, alarming him.

"What is it?" He sat up straight, alert.

Her eyes widened. "Only a few days ago, a transport ship full of Royal Marines sank just off the nearby coast. No one has been able to reach the wreck or the . . . the bodies. They're still out there."

Understanding hit Sam and Cassandra both, and, wordlessly, they stood. She'd lost all interest in her breakfast, but stared at him with horror, the same horror he felt like acid in his veins. They both knew what had to be done. Sam threw a handful of coins on the table, and they left the tea shop quickly.

"Horses," he gritted. "Have to hire some."

"The stable's back this way."

As they hurried down the street, Sam became aware that the tea shop patrons had followed them out and now trailed some thirty feet behind them. He took hold of Cassandra's arm and hustled her even more quickly, so that he practically carried her through the street. Confused, she started to glance over her shoulder, but he growled, "Don't."

"What's going on?"

More people joined the shop patrons, drifting away from their storefronts and wagons as Sam and Cassandra passed. They all wore matching expressions of distrust and a kind of bewildered antagonism. Some collected things as they joined the group—heavy boards, a poker iron—makeshift weapons.

"Arming themselves," she muttered. "I don't understand."

"*They* probably don't even know why," Sam rumbled. "Primal instinct. Something unnatural is in their home, and they want it out."

"But you haven't done anything!"

"Doesn't matter. You should run from me, get yourself to safety. They won't bother with you."

"Get it through your undead head," she gritted, "I'm not leaving you."

Without looking back, Sam knew that the crowd had grown even larger. He heard its restive muttering, the gathering consciousness of a mob. He'd felt this before, in armies turned loose to pillage. After his transformation, he also felt how he made the living uncomfortable. Yet he never truly believed their fear could lead to something like this. Something that could hurt Cassandra, because she insisted on staying with him.

The thought infuriated. He was angry, with the mob and with her. Why did she have to be so damned brave?

"Down here." He rounded a corner, then sidestepped into a niche between two buildings, pulling her with him.

In the narrow space, their bodies pressed tightly together. He felt her breath, the movement of her slender body wedged against his own. Deceptively fragile. Unmistakably female. She smelled of vetiver and warm oranges, and she stared up at him through long lashes, her soft pink lips parted.

Incredibly, for the first time in three years, Sam hardened. And she knew it, too, even with layers of clothing between them, for her eyes widened. But she didn't push away from him or edge farther into the niche. She stayed exactly where she stood. She even—he stifled a growl—moved closer still.

The mob surged past, not seeing them in their hiding spot.

Yet, even after the street was clear, Sam and Cassandra remained pressed against each other, bound by the close walls and a sudden, intoxicating desire. He forgot that he ever knew her as a girl, knowing her only as a woman. An astonishing, formidable woman with whiskey-colored eyes and unmistakable hunger—for him.

His hand came up as if obeying an unheard summons. He reached out and, with the very tips of his fingers, brushed along the column of her neck. The softness of her skin nearly made his knees buckle, and the quick flutter of her pulse let him know his touch excited her. Her lids lowered, and she tilted her head back, a gesture of acquiescence, of demand.

He let his palm touch her, stroking her neck more fully, then moving up so that he caressed along her jaw, up to her delicate ear, along the feathery wisps just at the base of her head, where she had pinned up her hair. He swallowed hard. Everything he touched was so goddamned silky, so incredibly tender, warm, and alive. He hadn't known sensations like this in many years, thought they were lost to him forever. The cold flame inside him blazed.

His other hand stroked her waist, and, though she wore a corset, he knew the slenderness of her waist was hers alone. Yet he wasn't content with this. He needed more, with the sudden hunger of a man who hadn't known he was starving until given a taste of nectar. Drawn up by a force greater than history, he traced up over the rise of her ribs, higher still, and then he palmed the curve of her breast. A perfect little breast, one he needed to touch beneath her corset and the fabric of her dress.

Her breathing hitched. And her hands moved, too. They slid up over his arms, testing the solidity of the muscles there, then played across his shoulders, his back. Wherever she touched, he came to life, the icy mist around him burning away under the sun of her caress. His cock ached, the concentration of all his needs. His body, his self. All wanted inside her.

He bent his head as she raised hers. For a bare second, he held himself back, allowing the tiniest space between them. Against his lips, her breath came quick and warm. Her eyes drifted shut. And he couldn't wait anymore. He kissed her, fully. Some part of him believed she needed gentleness, sweetness, but moments after their lips touched, she urged them closer, hotter. She opened to him, touching her tongue to his.

Lost. Her bold demand decimated his control, his sense of self. He wanted, wanted, and took. They came together in fierce need, lips and tongues and the liquid strokes of their hunger. She tasted of tea and jam and Cassandra, and she was unafraid, and he craved her, devouring. Her fingers wove into his hair, holding him tightly, as tightly as he gripped her, a cascade of light he'd somehow managed to grab and refused to surrender.

Sam pressed her into the wall, pushing his hips against hers. She met the rhythm of his body with her own, moaning softly into his mouth.

His hands shook with the need to lift up her skirts, to free his throbbing cock and sink into her. She would be wet, wanting. Silky hot. And, God, he needed Cassandra and her heat so badly. He never knew, not until that moment, how much he truly needed her.

His hand began to slide down to gather up her skirt. Then stopped. He broke the kiss, just enough to give him room to speak, even though he wanted her mouth back immediately.

"Keep going," she urged.

"Dangerous," he growled. "They're coming back—we have to get to the stables and get the hell out of here."

She nodded reluctantly. Yet, as she moved back, she brushed her fingertips against his mouth.

The ice around him shattered. His whole body ached as if thawing from a long freeze. And when he, too, stepped away, it was a wonder he didn't shout from the effort.

They disentangled themselves, a painful process, but when they stepped from the niche back into the street, their hands locked together, meshing as if by mutual instinct.

The stable owner counted out each coin as though personally responsible for the functioning of the national treasury. In the whole of this town, Sam now had to deal with the one man who didn't want to hurry from his sight. Yet Sam could hear the growing mob drawing closer, following a mob's intuitive need to find and destroy the strange.

Cassandra stood close by, watching the street vigilantly. Though she hadn't his heightened hearing, she knew the crowd was closing in, the crowd that grew increasingly dangerous. She didn't appear frightened, however. Only determined that she and Sam would be well gone before weapons were used, guns fired, or nooses fashioned.

Sam assessed their situation. The stable was located in the middle of a block, with a street running past its entrance. Which meant there were only two ways out: to the left or to the right. Two choices weren't enough for Sam. He wanted more options. He'd fought out of worse positions, but he didn't want a fight, not with Cassandra caught in the middle.

"Just take this," Sam growled, shoving a handful of banknotes into the stable owner's hand.

The man's eyes widened. "But, sir," he stammered, "it's too much."

Sam didn't care. "Are these our horses?" He nodded toward two saddled beasts tied to a hitching post. The animals looked to be in fine, rested condition. Good. He and Cassandra were going to push the horses hard, and they hadn't time for tired mounts.

"Yes, sir, but—"

Sam already strode toward the horses, Cassandra following. Without waiting, he lifted her up to the side saddle. He had an awareness of how slight she was, the narrowness of her waist, and how damned good it felt to touch her in such a proprietary, intimate way. But that awareness dimmed as both he and Cassandra heard the heated muttering of the mob.

Sam quickly mounted his horse.

The crowd appeared at the end of the street, to the left. They carried more makeshift weapons and some of the men had even grabbed firearms. Only a perfectly placed bullet could hurt Sam, but Cassandra was vulnerable to any wound. Or worse. He'd kill them all first.

"That's him," a burly laboring man at the front of the mob yelled, pointing.

"What the blazes *is* he?" hissed a respectable matron.

"Don't know," the laborer answered, barreling forward, "but he ain't one o' God's creatures."

The crowd muttered its agreement. As a single entity, possessing a rudimentary brain, it surged toward the stables.

Cassandra put heels to her horse before Sam had to utter a word. Together, they bolted from the stable yard, clattering over the cobblestones. The mob had blocked one end of the street, which left him and Cassandra the only other option. They steered their horses to the right as the crowd pushed closer.

"Block the road," someone behind him shouted.

A farmer ahead, bringing his crops to sell in town, shoved his laden cart into the street, directly in the path to escape.

"Can you jump?" Sam called to Cassandra.

She nodded.

She urged her horse up and over the cart in a faultless jump, just as he did. The farmer gaped at them as they soared over the intended obstacle. They rode on, and Sam heard the crowd jam up against the cart, thwarted by their own trap. People began yelling at the farmer to move the cart, but apparently the man wasn't fast enough, because the next sound was the groan of timber as the cart tipped onto its side. Pushed by the hands of the multitudes.

But by the time the mob had scrambled over the cart, Sam and Cassandra were already speeding toward the old town wall. The open country, and escape, lay just ahead.

Sam risked a look over his shoulder. And cursed. Several men had grabbed mounts from the stables and now pursued on horseback.

The gate to the old wall passed. He and Cassandra galloped down the road leading out of town, trees and pastures whipping past, the road lined with dense hedges. The men on horseback kept chase.

He considered the Colt pistol in his jacket, but discarded the idea. Shedding blood would only whip the mob into a greater frenzy. But, if he had to, he'd mow them all down if they tried to hurt Cassandra.

He glanced over at her and shook his head in admiration. She bent over her horse's neck, holding the reins with steady and certain hands. No one could fault her mettle or horsemanship. Even on a side saddle, she kept her seat well, though the same couldn't be said for the pins in her hair. They scattered like birds, causing her hair to stream behind her in chestnut waves that caught the sunlight. At any other time, Sam could have spent hours staring at the sight.

Now was definitely *not* the hour when he would marvel at Cassandra's hair. Now was the time to get her to safety.

He brought his horse alongside hers. "Ahead, to your left."

She looked and nodded. A tiny opening, almost invisible, in the hedge. They both veered off the road, Sam allowing her the lead. The gap in the hedge barely allowed their mounts through. Branches and brambles scratched and scraped their faces, their clothes. Pieces of Cassandra's cloak tore free. She didn't flinch, not even when a branch left an angry red welt across her cheek. The sight of her even slightly injured enraged him.

Clearing the hedge, they emerged in an open field. Startled cattle looked up from their grazing as Sam and Cassandra galloped past.

Sam chanced another look back. The pursuing men were struggling to get their horses through the hedge, but the animals balked.

"On the right, other side of that river."

Cassandra followed his direction with her gaze. "I don't see anything."

He forgot that she hadn't his sense of sight, either. A dubious gift from his resurrection. "Trust me." Nestled in a dense stand of trees was a dilapidated barn, barely standing, yet well concealed by the woods around it.

Without hesitation, Cassandra turned her horse toward where Sam indicated. They raced down the field, then across a shallow river and into the trees. Threading around the trees became an exercise in precision as the horses whipped through the copse. One wrong tug of the reins would send them crashing headlong into a low branch and certain devastating injury.

"Slow," Sam ordered, pulling up on the reins. "We don't want them hearing us."

Cassandra also slowed her mount, until they were both picking quietly through the grove. Dimly, Sam heard their pursuers finally clear the hedge, then shout in confusion and anger when they could not sight their targets.

"There," Sam said as the ramshackle barn emerged from the trees. It looked as though it had been built half a century earlier and abandoned a decade ago. Half the roof had collapsed, and the other half gaped to let in birds, wind, and everything else. The timbers were silver with age, traced with climbing vines that likely held the whole structure together. Without the vines, the barn might have been reduced to a pile of wood.

The door to the barn hung on precarious hinges, but enough stability remained for Sam and Cassandra to walk their horses into the decayed building. Inside, nature claimed what had once been the work of man. Grasses carpeted the floor, and what was left of the stalls became tiny forests, each abundant with overgrowth. A rusted wheelbarrow tilted in one corner. Roosting birds fluttered at the presence of the two mounted strangers in what had been an undisturbed haven.

Sam and Cassandra looked around. "What an odd, beautiful place," she whispered. Sunlight filtered through the roof, bright patches of color over her hair, her face, her shoulders.

"I'm beginning to find most odd things beautiful," he said, staring at her.

She laughed softly. "An insult or compliment—I can't decide." She peered through the open barn door. "How long should we wait?"

He frowned, also gazing through the door. He could see, but she could not, their pursuers riding across the field—away from the trees and the barn. No way to know how dogged the men would be in their hunt, but if they collected others, no place would be safe in the daylight.

In answer, he asked, "How far are we from where that transport ship went down?"

"About twenty miles."

The horse beneath him shifted, winded from its gallop. A few hours of rest would do both mounts good, in preparation for what lay ahead.

"We'll stay here until just before dusk." He swung out of the saddle. "Safer to travel. I can hide in darkness." The liability of his existence made every moment perilous for her. Little could kill him, but, despite her strength, she was as fragile as any living thing.

Cassandra also dismounted, moving with a smooth grace, then scowled toward the direction from where they had just come. "I wish I could smash those idiotic fools. You're different, but you didn't do anything wrong."

He glanced away, wounded anew by the anger in her voice, the hurt she felt on his behalf. So much easier when it was him alone, living not even a half life, barely human. Now Cassandra called forth a barrage of emotions, of feelings, he thought were forever lost. Pain wracked him, his heart a phantom limb that suffered even though it no longer existed, pierced by a bullet and amputated years ago.

"World's full of people just like them."

"You know from experience?"

"Soon after I broke free of Broadwell. I hadn't yet learned the boundaries of my prison. Tried to pretend that I was an ordinary man, live among them. And nearly got strung up or dismembered."

"And that can kill you."

"Beheading or a wound to the brain kills my kind. Otherwise, we're doomed to unrelenting existence."

She walked to him, leading her horse. From the corner of his eye, Sam watched her, willing himself immobile. When she stood only a foot away, she stopped, then reached out and placed her hand on his cheek. The sensation of her touch rocketed through him.

She lightly turned his face to her. He scowled down at her, yet she gazed up, unafraid.

"You're a fighter, Sam," she said, clear. "Always have been. Maybe that's why I followed you and Charlie everywhere. Because I knew that we were different from everyone else. We both challenged the world, that we couldn't be content without a struggle." Her voice took on a slight rasp. "I hate to think of you being shunned, dwelling in darkness. But . . . what you've been through . . . it hasn't destroyed who you really are."

"And you know who I really am?" His voice was gravel, hard with disbelief. He had to not believe her, to take the connection she offered. He was and would always be ruined. "Everything I am?"

"Perhaps not everything," she conceded. "Enough to know that you're a worthy man."

His jaw tightened under her hand. This slight woman would level him with merely a gentle touch and some soft words. He wondered what mercurial god he had crossed or pleased to put him in the path of the one woman who could accept him, whose character had the strength of giants—but he could never return what she offered, could never be restored. Truly dead, and also painfully alive.

Chapter Four

Sam wanted to rage, to tear down this decrepit barn and lay waste to everything in his path. He knew only one way to channel this anger, and it was destruction. But not of her. He vowed he would never hurt her.

Seeing his rising fury, she let her hand fall away. "If we stay here until dusk, won't that give Broadwell too much time? He might raise those soldiers long before we arrive."

He gladly seized the change of topic. "The living dead can only be created at night, at least two hours after complete darkness." He spoke from hard experience. The year Sam had been under Broadwell's control, and the years he'd chased him, he witnessed the colonel perform that same repulsive act over and over again. But Broadwell wouldn't do it ever again. Sam would make certain of that. "Something to do with the moon. And"—he glanced toward the direction from which he and Cassandra had just come—"our friends from town will still be out there searching for me."

"Then we'll wait," she said, decisive. Anger darkened her face. "I won't give those ignorant fools another chance to hurt you."

Her fierce protectiveness on his behalf stirred him, far too much.

Sam handed Cassandra the reins of his horse, then pulled off his jacket and laid it aside. He strode into one of the larger remaining stalls and, using his sword, cut down the overgrown grasses within. He glanced up to find Cassandra watching him with an unmistakable interest in her gaze.

"I like you better as a man than a boy," she said, approaching.

Though he often longed for the innocence of his youth, now was definitely not one of those times, not if his adult's body could produce such attention from her. "I'm not a man anymore."

"Oh, you most certainly are." Her eyes moved over him, and everywhere she lingered—legs, chest, shoulders—fire followed, heating his cold, numb body.

So, knowing very well that he was flaunting himself like a wolf strutting for a female, Sam went back to his task. He made a show of hacking at the grasses so that the fabric of his shirt clung and pulled. And when he bent down to gather up what he'd cut, she actually smacked her lips together, openly leering at his arse. A spontaneous laugh uncurled from inside him, his first in a long, long time.

He realized this was his first genuine laugh since his transformation. Every other laugh had been a mirthless approximation, a sardonic utterance that bore no resemblance to true laughter. But this—she brought it forth in him, the humanity and joy he'd lost. With it, the ice inside him began to melt.

"Feel like I'm up for auction," he rumbled.

"I'll outbid everyone," she answered, but she led the horses into the cleared stall. The two animals immediately began cropping at the remaining grasses, unconcerned that the barn holding them barely stood upright on its own.

Once the horses had been secured, Sam and Cassandra moved out into the open area of the barn. She turned to him, eyes warm in the filtered light. For the first time in many years, he was aware of himself, of his body, and that it could be more than a vessel for vengeance or destruction. When Cassandra looked at him, she saw someone she desired. Someone who could give and take pleasure. And he felt these things, too, seeing himself through her eyes.

She tempted him, with her slender curves and indomitable spirit. He couldn't remember wanting a woman more, not even when he was still alive. A new awareness stretched between Sam and Cassandra, heightened by their solitude, and the danger they had just escaped.

He had no heartbeat, no pulse, but if he did, he knew just then they would be racing.

Cassandra saw the change within Sam. The distant, bleak look that darkened his eyes and honed his face now subtly giving way to a true inhabitation of himself, as though slowly tugging on a close-fitting glove, living flesh within an inert article. Fingers flexing and stretching, warming the snug leather, until, at last, there seemed no differentiation between what was alive and what was an empty object.

Sam was *here*, within himself, and looking at her with desire so hot, so palpable, Cassandra grew light-headed.

"I'm glad you never looked at me like this when I was sixteen." A breathless admission.

"I should have," he rumbled.

"No—I wouldn't have known what to do with it. Probably climbed the roof and attempted to fly."

The corner of his mouth tilted. "And now?"

"Now . . . I have a very good idea what to do with such a look." She gave a tremulous laugh. "The trouble is, I don't know where to start."

He hesitated for the span of a moment, then moved because the momentum between them demanded it.

"Start with this." He closed the distance between them. His hands came up, cupping the back of her head and tilting her—she didn't need much urging—to meet his mouth.

Had she been an untried girl, Cassandra would have likely shuddered apart to be the recipient of such a heated, ravenous kiss. She wasn't an untried girl. So she met the demands of his lips, his mouth and tongue, with her own, taking him into her, learning him boldly with this most intimate exploration. But as much as she took, this kiss was his, his to lead and guide, because the need within him obliterated everything.

He stroked the inside of her mouth with velvet caresses of his tongue, and answering aches gathered in her breasts, between her legs. She pressed herself against him, seeking solace and also needing more. Her own desire quickly built into a devastating hunger she had never experienced before. It frightened her a little. But, like with most things that frightened her, she pushed onward, into the heart of the unknown.

He was a solid wall of muscle, tight and hard everywhere. Most especially against her abdomen, the unmistakable length of his arousal revealing his own dangerous need. When she urged herself against him, he groaned into her mouth.

Cassandra ran her hands up his arms, over the firmness of his shoulders. He felt marvelous, yet . . .

"Too many clothes," she murmured between kisses. And she shoved at his shirt, wanting his flesh against hers.

"*All* clothes are too many," he growled in assent.

Some moments of gracelessness as they tangled together, tugging on each other's garments, helping to remove their own. Her unfastened cloak slid down her back to land in a heap on the ground. His waistcoat shucked and tossed aside, then he shrugged out of his braces. The buttons down the front of her dress and his shirt became frustrations as both her hands and his, shaking with desire, grew clumsy.

His shirt opened, revealing his chest. Cassandra's hands and mouth stilled as she looked at the spot just over his heart. Sam glanced down, too, and his hands fell away as his jaw hardened.

A bullet wound, an almost perfect circle of torn flesh. Only hours before, Sam had been impaled upon an iron spike and showed not a single mark from that injury. But this wound remained. From her experience with target shooting, she knew that the shot had to have been fired at extremely close range. And that it would have been fatal.

Cassandra's fingers hovered over the wound. "Does it hurt?"

"No." His voice pulsed with anger. "I was lucky. Some of the others got their death wounds across the throat. And they never heal. Everything else . . . repairs . . . itself, but not the wound that kills us."

He stared at her, eyes sharp as blue ice. Daring her to turn away with this further evidence that he was no ordinary man, but an uncanny creature of darkest magic.

In response, she placed her hand over the wound in his chest.

"Can't bear to look at it," he said, and the mouth that had kissed her with such devastating hunger turned thin and hard.

"Can't bear to think of you hurting," she corrected. With her other hand, she wove her fingers into his hair and brought his lips back to hers. She made it clear: there was no pity in her kiss. She wanted him. With a ferocity that allowed no refusal.

He answered with a growl, wrapping an arm around her waist and holding her forcefully to him. They lost themselves in the kiss, until they both remembered that they were still partially clothed—a condition neither wanted.

They stopped long enough to finish undressing, though he was finished with his task far ahead of her. She paused in the process of stepping out of her dress to simply look at him. And, incredibly, tellingly, he let her. She saw how her gaze affected him. No woman had looked upon him in three years. Whether he trembled from desire or fear or a mixture of both, he stood with his shoulders back and his chin defiantly up.

She knew what it must take for him to do this, the courage he showed.

Her eyes moved over the breadth of his shoulders, the pure male form of his chest and stomach, precisely muscled, dusted with dark hair, that led in a trail to the glorious upright curve of his cock, and, even though the sight of his arousal enthralled, she looked lower, to the hewn muscles of his thighs and calves. Scars marked him, evidence that, before his transformation, he had been a soldier.

"You're not the first naked man I've ever seen," she whispered, "but, by God, you're the most beautiful."

His smile shot directly into her chest. But then it quickly turned into a scowl. "You've taken drawing lessons."

"With nude models? And that's my only experience? I've no aptitude for art." Cassandra curled her mouth wryly, yet she should have expected that even someone as extraordinary as Sam wasn't entirely beyond society's influence. "A man may explore his sensual appetites outside of marriage, but a woman may not?"

Naked, he stalked to her—a formidable sight. "Even if you had been married, I'd be—" He stopped abruptly. What was the next word he'd been about to say? *Jealous?* He continued, stormy. "The thought of *any* man touching you makes me want to kill."

As much as she considered herself a forward-thinking woman, his words oddly pleased her. "No killing," she said, tracing her fingertips over the ridged lines of his stomach. He sucked in a breath at her touch. "This is ours."

Her fingers drifted lower, along the pristine muscle that ran from his hip down toward his groin. Sam fought to hold himself still beneath her leisurely caress, fought to gather his thoughts, and she took it as a very promising sign that his voice came out a rasp and his hands were curled into fists. "How did . . . it . . . happen?"

She did not want to discuss this now, but he was intractable. "After word came that you and Charlie had died, I fell into a deep despondency. I had no interest in anything."

"I'm sorry," he said, gruff but genuine.

Her head bent as she thought of that dark time. "My parents sent me to the Continent to see if a change of scenery might help." Though images of her travels abroad flickered through her mind, all she could truly see was Sam's magnificent body standing before her now, submitting to her perusal. "Though it was a difficult course, eventually, I regained myself. When I reached Vienna, I felt I was ready to explore new things."

Sam's jaw tightened again, and a murderous blaze flared in his eyes.

"I discovered that without an emotional connection, the whole process felt quite . . . meaningless. The only person I ever thought about that way was—" Now it was her turn to cut her words short.

"Was who?" he pressed.

She saw his determination. He would not let her evade him.

She could produce some half truth, prevaricate. He'd gone away before she'd had her abbreviated Season. Perhaps she'd had a sweetheart or two during those few months in London. Of course, she hadn't, but Sam didn't know that.

But she couldn't lie to him. He deserved better than that—and so did she. And if her answer troubled him, if she left herself exposed and vulnerable, she knew she was strong enough to face the consequences. Whatever they might be.

"Was you," she finally answered.

There. She said it. Revealed herself completely to him. She made herself hold his gaze, saw the slight widening of his eyes as he absorbed her meaning. The tumultuous knocking of her heart against her ribs belied the calm with which she faced him.

Would he laugh at her and her youthful infatuation? Push her away? The cynical part of her mind said he wouldn't, because a nude man moments away from making love to a willing woman would say whatever he needed to ensure consummation. Another part of her mind believed that Sam had enough honor in him to step away, go no further, if he felt unable or unwilling to reciprocate her feelings. Which response did she fear most?

But when an expression of fierce, triumphant desire crossed his starkly handsome face, something else burst to life within her: hope.

He gripped her hips and pulled her to him, kissing her with an urgent demand, which she met in kind. An even greater resolve in him now, and if she hadn't detected any restraint on his part before, now, now, she thought she would be happily immolated in the heat he unleashed between them.

He continued to kiss her as he tugged impatiently on the re-
mainder of her clothes—her corset and petticoats, drawers
and chemise. Such a lot of ridiculous clothing women had to
wear. She thought she might lose her sanity entirely as both
she and Sam wrested with her garments. She unhooked and
kicked aside her boots.

As his long fingers yanked impatiently at the hooks of her
corset, and between kisses, he growled, "What a bloody idiot
I was, to enlist and leave you behind. I didn't know. Damn it, I
didn't know."

She smiled against his lips, rueful. "Would it have made a
difference, had you known? Charlie's skinny, funny-looking
sister pining for you?"

"You weren't funny looking." He snarled in triumph as her
corset finally gave way, and he tossed it aside without a thought.
Her own thoughts scattered when her chemise followed immediately after and he gathered her breasts in his large, calloused
hands.

God, but his touch inflamed her. He stroked her, running his
fingertips in circles over her tight nipples, and an answering pleasure gleamed through her, centering damply between her legs.
"Beautiful Cassandra," he said, hoarse, then bent and licked each
nipple, one, then the other, with the velvet rough of his tongue.

Her head tipped back, and if his hands weren't gripping her
waist, she would have tumbled backward into a trembling,
needy heap. She clutched at his head, urging him closer, even
as she tried to regain her thoughts. They were talking of something . . . weren't they? Did it matter at all when his sensual assault left her frenzied?

But still. . . . "Would it have mattered?" she managed to gasp.

He lifted his head slightly. "I don't know." He panted his
answer, and she was glad for his honesty. "Can't think about
the past. Nor the future. Only this, now. Only you."

It was enough. "Only you," she said. She wriggled out of
her petticoat and, in her impatience, broke the tie of her drawers, so that they all slithered down in a mass of cotton. And
then she was as naked as he.

Sam stared at her, raking her with his gaze. What he saw must have pleased him, because he sharpened like a knife, his features grew taut with desire, and his cock twitched, becoming even thicker, straighter, as if reaching for her. She'd never felt more beautiful, more seductive, than she did at that moment. He was not Sam, and she was not Cassandra. There were no Blades, no Heirs and Sources, no dead, no living. They were a man and a woman, and they wanted each other.

He moved too quickly for her to see. One moment, he stood before her, and in the next, he'd swept her up in his arms. He strode toward one shadowed corner of the barn, then laid her down upon a bed of soft green grass. He stretched out beside her, a sleek movement of muscle and intent.

When their naked skin touched, she gasped. His flesh was cool, like marble. But the sensation it produced against her own feverish skin was . . . exquisite. She rubbed her nipples over his chest, hissing in a breath of pleasure at the contrast of textures and temperatures. Hard male flesh, coarse hair, cool skin. She arched into him, trying to erase all boundaries between them.

When her hand wrapped around his cock, he swore, and pushed his hips into her touch. His eyes closed, rapturous, tortured. Up, down, he filled her hand and she gripped the way she wanted to grip him internally. As she stroked, heat bloomed in him. Beginning first in his penis, then radiating outward. In waves. His skin lost its coolness, turning, within moments, to burning satin.

"What's happening?" she breathed.

"Whatever it is," he gritted, "just . . . don't stop."

She didn't. She relished in touching him like this, pleasuring him, feeling her own power and pleasure in his response. His cock was beautiful and full in her hand, and she could hardly wait to have it, have *him*, inside her.

Sam ran his hands over her, caressed her clavicles, her breasts, the curve of her waist. Down her legs, and up again, lighting fires of his own wherever he touched. But he stopped himself from touching her more fully. His hand lightly rested on the curve of her belly.

He seemed to be deliberately holding himself back. "My luscious Cassandra," he murmured. "Did you think about me?"

Her eyes opened, though her vision remained blurred with desire. "What?"

"Did you think about me," he repeated, and now she knew it, he was indeed reining himself in, as if wary. But of what? Her? That couldn't be. "At night?"

"Y-yes," she gasped. Oh, Lord, why was he doing this? When all she wanted was for him to plunge his fingers or, better yet, his cock, into her. She made a sound of distress.

"And when you thought about me," he continued, "did you touch yourself?"

She turned and looked at him, saw his trepidation reflected in those bright azure eyes. He was just as aroused, just as hungry, as she. Yet almost . . . afraid. This man who had already faced death, this battle-scarred soldier.

Three years. She realized it had been three years since he'd been with a woman, and who knows how long before that. No wonder he was cautious. Perhaps he thought she would be repelled by him. Perhaps he feared unleashing his desire. So many reasons for his apprehension.

All she wanted was to show him pleasure—and receive it, as well. So she must show him the way.

"Yes," she answered. Even though she met his gaze steadily, a blush spread across her face, her body, to make this admission. "I would lie in my bed at night and think of you. I would touch myself, and pretend my hands were yours. On my breasts." She let her hands hover above her breasts. "On my sex." One hand drifted toward her delta, but rested lightly just above her slick, needy pussy.

"I pictured you over me, under me," she whispered. "Fucking me for hours. And it always made me come, to think of it."

He swallowed hard. "Bloody hell," he groaned, squeezing his eyes shut. "I wish I could have seen that."

She suddenly knew precisely what she had to do.

"Then open your eyes," she whispered, "and see it now."

* * *

His eyes flew open and burned her with their blue heat. Primal savagery darkened his features. She half believed he would take her now, simply lay his body atop hers and plunge into her. Instead, he levered himself up on one elbow—the better to watch.

A bare moment's hesitation. Could she do this? The most private act, always done in the shelter of night, within her solitary bed. Something for herself alone.

Yet she could share this with him, with Sam. For both of them. Show him the way. Conquer both of their fears.

So, holding his gaze, she took one trembling hand and ran it along the column of her throat. Then lower, over her collar bones, and then—a sigh slipped from her—over her breast. She imagined it was his hand touching her, and in this way, she felt the softness of her skin as if for the first time, and the pearl of her nipple tightened beneath her fingers. She arched up into her touch, and her other hand came up to stroke and toy with her other breast.

Sam stared down, watching. His jaw was held so tight, she thought it must ache, yet he moved not at all, watching her with an intensity that could reduce the barn, and them, to ashes.

She believed she would feel shy or awkward. Yet nothing felt more right than to have Sam here, seeing how the thought of him alone could arouse her. And to *show* him how he made her feel was . . . perfect.

She let one hand drift down from her breast, over the soft curve of her belly, until, with a moan, her fingers slipped into the slick, waiting heat of her pussy.

"I've never been this wet before," she gasped.

He growled.

Her excitement built, especially with him watching her as if nothing else in the world existed. Triumph thrilled her, knowing that she'd broken down some of the barriers Sam had put up around himself.

She rubbed along her cleft, at her opening, where she was most sensitive. Stroking the hard bud of her clit, bolts of pleasure shot through her. Her eyes began to shut.

"Look at me," he rasped.

She did, and nearly came, to see the blatant arousal etched in stark lines across his face as he watched her touch herself. He was not the soft and tender dream lover she once fantasized about. The real Sam was harder, devastating, verging on feral. And this understanding pushed her closer to climax.

This is how to touch me, she told him with her gaze. *This is how I want* you *to feel.* She managed to tear her gaze from his face, looking down at his cock. The hard length curved up Sam's stomach, nearly reaching his navel. It jerked and seemed to pulse as she stared at it. At the tip, a small bead of moisture gleamed.

He glanced down and started in surprise. "That hasn't happened since . . ."

Some change had been wrought in him, something profound. Yet all she knew at that moment was an overwhelming arousal to see his own.

"Touch yourself, too," she panted.

He shook his head. "Over too soon."

Her touch deepened, stroking the soaking flesh of her pussy more firmly. Her clit became the center of the solar system, glowing with heat and need. She pressed and kneaded. So close. She was so close.

A thick, hot presence delved into her. Sam's finger. One, then another. Driving into her. He braced himself over her, staring at her pussy as he plunged his fingers up, stretching her, filling her. He watched as if nothing fascinated him more. Their fingers brushed and tangled with each other, both seeking her pleasure.

The barriers had tumbled down. He no longer held himself back.

It slammed into her, her orgasm, tearing through her relentlessly. She bowed up, lost to everything, and the sound that ripped from her startled the horses and birds roosting in the eaves. But she couldn't notice, couldn't care. The world was this. Her climax engulfed all.

No sooner had the tremors wracked her body, than Sam

was over her, between her legs. He braced himself on his fore-arms, and gazed down at her with animal need. Of their own volition, her thighs widened for him, giving him access, and her legs twined around his waist. The broad, smooth head of his cock nestled at her opening. She and Sam both shook like wind-tossed trees.

"Please," she whispered.

He thrust into her. No hesitation now. She gasped, but rose to meet him further. Thick, so thick and full within her. His head tipped back, the cords of his neck tensing, his expression verging on pain.

"Cass . . . ," he growled. He tried to speak, but could only produce feral sounds, sounds that vibrated through her. And when he pulled back, then plunged forward again, they both lost themselves to incoherent growls. Language, words. All meaningless, when there was such primal pleasure.

She wrapped her arms around his wide shoulders, panting. Holding on, as he penetrated her, deep and thick, again and again. His whole body was taut muscle, working to drive them both to ecstasy. She was aware of nothing but him, and the release that already gathered within her as the speed of his hips against her own increased.

He pushed himself farther up on his arms, realigning their bodies, so that with each thrust, her clit blazed higher. She couldn't hold back.

"Sam, I'm—"

Release took her once more. Only this time, she contracted around Sam, deep within her, and this urged the climax on-ward, a seemingly endless succession of orgasms that deci-mated self.

Then it had him, too. He stiffened, muscles tensing, and he groaned—a sound of profound pleasure, of need and want and relief and . . . sorrow.

His climax went on, tearing from him as if tearing open the darkest places within. She felt him pulsing inside her, even after he could no longer hold himself upright, and collapsed atop her—though he was careful to keep from crushing her with his substantial weight. For some time, neither of them could move, but then he wrapped his arms around her, and took her with him when he rolled to his side.

"I haven't come in three years." He sounded awed. "Couldn't even get hard. But that . . . that was . . ." He shook his head, unable to find words to describe the sensation.

Even in the radiance following her own orgasm, a new pleasure engulfed her. "I'm glad I could give that to you."

They lay entwined, bodies slick and spent. A breeze passed through the open timbers of the barn. She shivered involuntarily.

Before she drew another breath, he'd risen and retrieved her cloak, which he spread over them both like a blanket.

Cassandra draped over him as he lay on his back. He stroked her hair, winding it around his fingers and letting the heavy tresses uncoil, over and over. Her ear pressed against the hard muscles of his chest, but he did not rise and fall with breathing, and she felt no heartbeat beneath her hand. As she leisurely brushed her fingers back and forth across his pectorals, raking her nails through the scattering of dark, curled hair, she carefully avoided his wound. They both knew a profound gulf separated them—his wound would only remind them of what neither wanted to acknowledge.

Despite this, she felt replete, almost content. Her eyes drifted closed, then opened again when he spoke.

"Tell me how you became a Blade of the Rose." His voice didn't sound sleepy at all, but his words were soft—out of consideration for her.

It took a few moments for her thoughts to cohere. "I'd been campaigning for years to obtain factory reform," she eventually murmured. "Showed up in a few newspapers. A gentleman's daughter appearing in public, fighting for change. I'd have thought the Grub Street hacks would have more important things to write about. But it seemed they didn't."

She fought a yawn. "And that's when the Blades recruited me. They'd been following me in the papers and thought I'd make a good operative in England. At first, it all seemed preposterous. Magic? In the modern nineteenth century?" She made a soft noise of disbelief, recalling her own skepticism from that first trip to Southampton.

"Yet I learned," she continued, "it was very real, and very powerful. Very easily used by corrupt people, and thus vulnerable. It was a cause I could not ignore. As a Blade, I could continue my work with the factories, but when the others needed me, I would obey the summons. And so I did—so I do."

"So you tell them you want to become a Blade of the Rose, and that's all." Even though she heard no heartbeat, she felt the vibrations of his deep voice, and this lulled her.

She shook her head. "You have to prove yourself in a field assignment. And before you ask," she added, "mine was in Scotland. I went with two other Blades to rescue a fairy of the Seelie Court. She'd been abducted by the Heirs and held for ransom. The ransom in this case being surrender of her magic. They had the poor thing for a week before we were able to get her free."

"No wonder Broadwell's one of the Heirs," he rumbled, stiffening. "They're just as foul as he is."

The world would intrude soon enough. For now, Cassandra wanted to give herself and Sam the brief illusion of peace. So, she steered the conversation away from the topic of their enemies. "The fairy was extremely grateful," she continued, "and shocked we'd managed to free her without benefit of magic. Yes," she said when Sam made a noise of surprise, "Blades ensure that we won't grow hungry for magic by not using it ourselves. If magic is ours by right or gift, then we may use it, but otherwise, we must rely on our strength and wits to protect Sources."

"A code of honor," Sam mused. "Such things are obsolete."

"Not so archaic. There's honor in most everyone." She snuggled closer to him, feeling the solidity of his body, his potency. How many nights had she dreamt of just this, lying entwined with Sam in the aftermath of lovemaking? Too many to recall. "Especially you."

He pressed a kiss to the top of her head, but she could tell he still did not agree with her on this matter. "And you and the other Blades fought the Heirs for the fairy's freedom."

"To be honest," she said, "I acted more in an observational capacity. The other Blades with me—Philippa Mallory and a young man named Catullus Graves—they did the actual fighting. But I helped," she added quickly. "Acted as a lookout and decoy."

"And your second field mission for the Blades?"

Now *she* was silent. She thought about feigning sleep, yet he was far too alert to believe that ruse. So she said, rather quietly, "*This* is my second field mission."

The veteran soldier had truly been caught off guard. His whole body tensed. "*What?*"

"This is my second—"

"I heard you." He disentangled himself from her as he sat up. She could only see his rigid, broad back, the muscles contracting as his hands curled and uncurled. For some time, he said nothing, yet she felt the waves of shock and anger roiling out from him. He swore under his breath. Yet she would not accept his anger toward her.

She, too, sat up, though her head still felt muzzy.

"The risks are mine to take." She spoke to the clean, hard line of his profile.

He stared at the wall of the barn with unseeing eyes. "Tell me where those damned Blades are. I'll ride down there right now and beat every one of them into oblivion." He turned to her, fury flaring in his eyes. "What the hell were those idiots thinking, to send you up against a dangerous bastard like Broadwell, on your own?"

"They didn't," she shot back. "Blades always work in teams. But with the telegraph lines down, and Broadwell on the move, I had to make a decision. Let him go, or pursue."

"Alone, you're no match for him," he snarled. "He'll kill you, Cassandra." His voice dropped until it was so deep she felt his words more than heard them. "Or worse." One of his hands came up of its own accord to hover above the wound in his chest. "I won't let what happened to me also doom you."

Cassandra's fury dropped away. She stroked the lean planes of his face, and, even though it had been many hours, he had no beard coming in. He was frozen in time at the moment of his death—yet only his body remained unchanging. Within, he could transform. The Sam she'd encountered in the stonemason's yard was not the Sam she touched now. He *could* move onward.

"I'm not facing Broadwell on my own," she said gently.

He stared into her eyes, holding her gaze as if staring into a well of secrets. She allowed Sam to see her as no one else ever had—all of her, withholding nothing. For *this* Sam, more so than the boy she'd known or the dream she had constructed, captivated and understood her in a way no man could. She'd just given him the gift of her body, now she gave him the gift of her mind. *Only you*, she told him with her eyes. *Only you are given this.*

And when he nodded slightly, leaned forward, and then took her mouth in a kiss of surpassing sweetness, her throat constricted and burned, even as she smiled against his lips.

Exhaustion flowed in, a breaking dam. He saw her eyes droop, and gently laid her down. He tucked the cloak around her, whispering, "I'll watch over you. Sleep now."

And she did just that.

Chapter Five

For hours, Sam watched Cassandra sleep. She'd fallen asleep with the speed of the exhausted, her body growing slack and still, and soon after, the delicate skin of her eyelids twitched as she began to dream. He envied her this. Years since he'd slept, since he'd dreamt, and now both were distant lands he knew he'd once visited but could no longer remember. His own life long ago turned into one long nightmare from which he could not wake.

What did she dream of? He hoped her dreams were beautiful and soft, comforting, because God knew how hard and cruel the waking world was.

Cassandra. Lightly, he brushed his fingertips over her face as if to learn her topography, carve it into his own unmoving heart. She'd made love to him as if he wasn't a monster, had given him wealth unsurpassed by any treasury. The way she'd responded to him—without reserve, entirely open—even now, he felt his icy blood heating. His flesh hadn't been warm for three years, and she changed that, stoking fires within him from cold ashes. Reminding him he was still a man, when he no longer believed it himself.

He could never grow weary of her. This fierce little creature of indomitable strength and generous heart. For just a moment,

Sam allowed himself the indulgence of picturing what their life could have been together. Not a typical domestic scene of hearth and children, for that was not her, but a series of battles, he and Cassandra against the world. They could shore each other up in defeat and celebrate victories. Endless passion. The promise of tomorrow. Love, at last.

Never to be. The undead claimed no future.

Restless, angry, Sam rose. He kept her covered with her cloak, ensuring her warmth, then threw on his clothes. He paced. Wanted to take his horse and ride. Do something with the energy and momentum of his mind and body. But he wouldn't leave her alone and unprotected. So he stayed, and gnawed upon his thoughts, all the while keeping watch over her small, slumbering form.

She looked so damned delicate. No denying her inner strength, but she'd been born and raised a gentlewoman. She might campaign for reform, but she'd never campaigned as a soldier. This was only her *second* mission for the Blades of the Rose. And in her first, she'd been more an observer than combatant.

Sam didn't fear death. He'd already died, and had been eagerly looking forward to finally achieving rest once Broadwell, and the magic that had transformed Sam, had been destroyed. Vengeance had driven Sam for the past three years. Now one goal rose above all others. No matter the cost—to himself or anyone else—he would protect Cassandra.

He could give her safety, though he could not give her a future.

Sunset, finally. Enough shelter in the dusk for Cassandra to go to the back of a farmhouse and buy some provisions for herself. Sam had no choice but to brood and pace in the shadows. If he went with her, he'd draw more hostile notice, just as he had before, and he wouldn't endanger Cassandra again. He watched her from the darkness as she talked to the wife of the house and made her purchases. They set off for the shore, and Cassandra ate as she rode. They had to reach the sunken ship and its drowned passengers before Broadwell could transform the men aboard. Sam knew the bastard was either already there, waiting for the right time, or would show soon. If Broadwell was at the ship by now, then Sam would make sure he couldn't transform the dead men. And if Broadwell wasn't there, then Sam would wait.

The transport ship had sunk along a part of the coast Sam knew well. His father had taken him and his two older brothers there every summer to learn to swim. A narrow beach, with a rocky promontory rising up from one side of the sand and jutting into the sea. Sam and his brothers always wanted to run off the promontory and jump into the water, but his father had forbidden them. The drop was too precarious. But that didn't stop Sam from trying to scramble up the rocky cliff the moment his father's back was turned. He never made it all the way to the top before his father caught him. But his father never thrashed him—only laughed and called him hellion before tossing him into the waves.

As he now rode toward the beach with Cassandra beside him, fond memories rose like the tide. But they would soon be replaced with others much less nostalgic.

Roars of pounding waves reached his ears before he sighted the water. When he and Cassandra drew up their horses at the edge of the sand, where numerous rocks marked the boundary of the beach, night turned the scene into a study of deepest blue, with moonlight painting the waves silver. Just as he remembered, the rocky cliff rose to the left, towering high before plunging into the frothing sea. The beach was deserted.

"I don't see Broadwell," Cassandra said quietly.

"Nor I." Sam scanned the beach, yet his heightened senses could not detect his former commanding officer. "There," he said, pointing out beyond the breaking waves.

"Broadwell?"

"The ship."

She peered through the darkness, then started at the dark shape over two hundred yards from the shore. "Good God."

An awful view. The stern of the transport ship jutted from

the water, and several shattered masts also projected out of the sea like compound fractures, their tattered sails flapping white and useless. Sam could well picture the scene—the ship foundering on the rocks, chaos and confusion above and below decks, so close to land but far enough to condemn everyone on board. The screams and pleas of men as icy seawater rushed in, bringing cold death. Soldiers whose losing battle was against indifferent nature.

Now he and Cassandra stared at the partially submerged tomb.

"Why hasn't anyone recovered the bodies?" he asked.

"Too dangerous," she answered. "All efforts have been beaten back by the waves. Everyone is waiting for low tide."

For someone who needn't fear drowning, none of that was a concern.

"Sam, look!" She rose in the saddle. "You see them? Men in the water!"

A few shadowy forms toiled to rise to the surface next to the sunken ship. From this distance, they looked to be dark insects, arms flailing, slowly crawling up the hull that rose above the water.

"Some of the Marines must have survived," Cassandra exclaimed.

Clammy dread slithered along his neck. "Look at their eyes."

She strained to see, then sank back down. "They're . . . glowing."

"Like mine."

She glanced over at him, then turned away with a stricken expression. He knew what she saw. The unearthly light shining from his eyes. The same light that appeared as pallid specks across the water, where the resurrected soldiers clambered to the surface. Sam knew what the men must be feeling at that moment—the pull of magic on their minds, dragging them from the tranquility of death, the confusion, the fear. He knew well they had good cause to be afraid.

"We're too late," she rasped. "Broadwell already transformed them."

Where that son of a bitch was, Sam didn't know, but he did know what he must do now. He swung down from the saddle.

"You have your pistol primed and ready?" he demanded.

She took the weapon from her pocket and rested it in her lap.

He gave her a clipped nod, hating that he was going to have to leave her alone. But he had to. If the undead soldiers reached the shore, she would be in even greater danger.

"Stay alert," he said. "If you see *anything* suspicious, there's to be no hesitation. Shoot whoever, whatever, you see. In the head and in the heart." He strode toward her and handed her both his own pistol and the reins of his horse. "Keep the hammer cocked and your eyes open."

"What are you going to do?" No trembling in her voice, and he admired her like hell. Few women, or men, could witness the resurrection of dozens of the living dead without screaming and fleeing in terror.

Sam cast a grim look toward the partially sunken ship and its unnatural compliment. "Don't know yet," he growled. "But I'll do them the kindness I never received. I'm going to destroy them."

He found several rocks and put them into his pockets. Then he turned to go, carrying his sword, but her voice stopped him before he took a step.

"Wait." She also alit from her horse, and crossed to him. In the moonlight, her upturned face was carved of creamy ivory, and her eyes gleamed, not with an uncanny fire like his own, but with emotion. For him.

She placed her hand upon his chest. "Come back, Sam," she whispered. "When you've done what you must, please come back. To me."

He went still. She had known, without him saying a word, what he'd been searching for ever since that night at the Redan, and that it tempted him even now. Release from the hell of his existence. Nothingness. Yet only one thing could call him back from oblivion.

Her.

He bent and kissed her, tasting her sweet strength, summoning the part of him that yearned for life. Yearned, though he knew it could never be given to him again. For now, he would give Cassandra what he could.

"I will," he said, then strode off into the surf.

Breaking waves churned around his legs as he pushed into the cold water. He hissed at the chill. Only a day earlier, he wouldn't have felt the water's temperature, but warmth still permeated his body after making love to Cassandra. His once-numb body sparked with new awareness and new pain. But he'd endure the agony of bitter cold or blistering fire to make love to her again.

As the water surged around his chest, he broke his own rule and looked back. She stood at the top of the beach, slim body straight and vigilant, while her cloak billowed about her and her hair whipped over her shoulders. Brave beyond measure, stubborn as hell, passionate. *Come back,* she had said. *To me.*

He said he would. He needed to return to her. She drew him back with the warmth and strength of her heart, as unexpected as a songbird on the battlefield.

After one last look, he turned back and moved onward. Farther into the sea, and it rose to his shoulders, then higher. In a moment, the heaving water was over his head. A brief vestige of fear as seawater flooded his nose, his mouth. Down his throat and into his lungs, chilling him from the inside out. He fought against his own impulse to struggle. Nothing to panic about. He couldn't drown.

But the water was dark, and it buffeted him as he slogged across the sea floor. The stones in his pockets kept him weighted enough to prevent being tossed around like flotsam. Walking along the sea floor took a long time, but trying to fight against the waves above would have been even more time consuming. Farther he strode, and the weight of the water increased, so each step onward became a colossal struggle against the whole of the ocean. Sand swirled, scraping his face and eyes. He glanced up to see the moon gleaming faintly far above the surface.

All around him, shapes of rocks loomed, and he threaded through them to reach the sunken ship. The ruined ship materialized from the darkness—a hulk of submerged wood and metal, its portholes like black sightless eyes. It lay in two pieces: the front of the ship rested on the sea floor, and jagged timbers marked where the ship had split upon the rocks. The aft, severed from the front, jutted up toward the surface. Floating amidst the wreckage were coils of rope, spectral yards of canvas swaying in underwater currents, articles of clothing.

All was not darkness on the ship. The glow of a hundred pairs of undead eyes dotted the vessel's remains. Some of the living dead were ensnared in the ropes above decks, writhing like eels, but most were below. Their hands pressed whitely against the portholes, their gleaming eyes peering between the shattered planks. The creatures wore dark blue Royal Marine Artillery uniforms—Sam had fought with Marines in Crimea, and they'd been stalwart fighters, but these Marines had been ripped from the peace of death to do far worse than simple combat.

God didn't know for what Broadwell meant to use these Marines, but the Devil surely did. And approved.

When the resurrected soldiers espied Sam trudging toward them over the sea floor, his own eyes aglow, they began to cry out and reach for him, recognizing him as a fellow member of the damned. A collective sound of outrage and confusion, carried in currents by the water.

As he neared the ship, he saw that nearly all of the Marines clustered in the central part of the vessel, blocked in by heavy fallen beams and cannon. The soldiers pushed at the hull the closer Sam got. The wood groaned at the pressure, but held. For now.

Another cabin held half a dozen men that watched Sam approach. They appeared more bewildered than hostile. None of them moved, until a force rocked through them. Sam, too, felt it. A hard tug on his mind, his control. Commanding the undead men, commanding him.

Broadwell. The bastard *was* nearby, but somehow, Sam hadn't been able to sense him.

Obey me, Broadwell now demanded. *My will overrides yours.*

Sam staggered as he fought Broadwell's control. He refused to give in. To lose his autonomy and be, once more, merely a pawn. But it had been years since Broadwell had tried to force his way into Sam's brain, and, like an unused muscle, his mental barricades against this manipulation had atrophied.

Grimacing, he saw the Marines sway as Broadwell's will overpowered their own. Sam's will shuddered and began to buckle under the pressure. A dark miasma crept through his mind, commandeering his limbs. He felt his legs move, driven into motion by an outside force. *Surrender to me. I made you and I always command you.*

Sam's control slipped even further. No! He had to fight, to resist, but he felt himself scrabbling along a steep embankment with nothing to hold to. Almost lost.

Then—a newfound source of strength. Something bright and fierce. Pushing back at the numbing darkness. Cassandra.

He pictured her lovely face, her amber eyes full of intelligence and humor. The sleek curves of her body. He thought of her stubbornness, her independence. And as Sam felt his will slipping away, her voice called him back. *Fight this, Sam. Hold strong, as I know you can.*

Three years had seen him cursed to this half existence. And for two of those years, he'd been utterly alone, using every ounce of his strength to survive another day, if only for the sake of vengeance. Yet he wasn't alone now. Cassandra's presence on the shore burned like a torch. He used her light to guide his path back to himself.

With a soundless roar, Sam shoved Broadwell from his mind. An exhausting effort that left him infuriatingly drained—but triumphant. Later, he would thank her.

If he survived until later. The six Marines in the upper cabin pushed against the hull. The wood split open, and the soldiers clambered out to stand on the sea floor. They wore officers' uniforms and swords. Sam saw now they'd been trapped within the officers' mess. But now they moved, en masse, toward Sam. Their faces were white and blank, but as they trudged toward him across the sea floor, Sam saw their intent. They drew their swords. Broadwell had commanded the undead soldiers to take Sam's head.

Sam pulled the rocks from his pockets and let them tumble to the sandy sea floor. Now able to swim, he kicked off, launching himself toward the stern of the ship. Leaving the men behind.

He glanced back as he swam, and saw the soldiers had turned back to the ship and were now climbing up its sides.

As he swam, he saw that there was no way into the vessel except through the large window of the captain's cabin at the rear. And that lay above the water's surface. He swam with hard, powerful strokes, heading upward, until he breached the surface. Above, out of the protective silence of the water, everything was a tumult of waves and spray. He couldn't see the shore, couldn't find Cassandra. And if Broadwell was out there, the bastard still kept himself hidden. Sam had to trust that Cassandra would be safe for the next few minutes while he found some way to thwart Broadwell's plans and end the Marines' suffering.

Sam coughed up lungfuls of water, then swam to the hull of the ship and pulled himself up onto it. Waves slapped him as he climbed up the vessel's side. With a groan, he hauled himself toward the row of windows running the length of the stern. A few panes had broken, but nothing was wide enough to accommodate him. He drew back a fist, then slammed it into the window, shattering glass. Sharp surfaces cut into the skin of his hands, and along his body and face as he lowered himself into the cabin.

He slid along the sharply tilted floorboards, then braced himself against a low half wall separating the cabin. What had once been the captain's luxurious quarters was now a sideways shambles—furniture in broken heaps, charts and maps sodden masses, and what had once been a prized silver tea service now nothing but dented trash.

Sam knew without looking that what he searched for wasn't to be found in the unlucky captain's quarters. He eased himself along the floor until he reached the door, which he wrested open.

More chaos in this part of the ship. Everything angled steeply, and it was nigh impossible to gain a sense of orientation. With his sword strapped to his back, he clung to whatever he could find, keeping himself from falling down into the water that filled the other end of the ship. The vessel echoed with the moans of the hundred undead Marines trapped in the hold. Through the water at the bottom of the passageway, Sam saw them, their glowing eyes, trying to pull themselves up toward him.

He needed to act fast. He crawled through the labyrinth of the ship's interior, searching. A grim smile curled the corner of his mouth when he spotted his goal. Powder kegs. Just beyond, he spotted the open door to the magazine, where more containers of gunpowder were jumbled.

He clambered toward the magazine, praying the powder in the kegs was still good. Demolitions didn't usually fall to the responsibility of a company's major, but Sam liked to know how every aspect of his army functioned, and had learned enough to light a charge, including a delayed charge.

Inside the magazine, he discovered a large hole in the bulkhead that he hadn't seen in his swim. It revealed the beach, a ghostly strand. Peering through the gaping timbers, he searched for Cassandra. No sign of her. He forced down his immediate fear. She could have gone for a better view elsewhere. Right now, he had to concentrate on his task. Those six officers had broken out of the wreckage, and it was only a matter of time before the rest of the soldiers in the hold also escaped.

A soldier's body draped limply across the magazine's floor, his head crushed by a fallen timber. No wonder he hadn't risen with the others.

Sam turned from the body and found not only enough dry powder to demolish the ship, but also lengths of treated cord for fuses. The small room that stored the munitions and power was dark as ink, yet Sam's enhanced vision enabled him to see enough. With hands shredded from the glass, he made fuses, attaching them to whatever gunpowder was dry enough to work.

The process took damned longer than he wanted—Cassandra was alone on the beach, and Broadwell lurked somewhere nearby. Sam had to get back, protect her. His cold blood turned even icier to think of her facing Broadwell on her own. If that son of a bitch even touched her while Sam was stuck in this waterlogged tomb, then Broadwell's only relief from Sam's vengeance would be death.

Done. He twisted the last of the fuse cord into the main fuse and adhered it to the final keg of dry powder. From his pocket, he pulled a flint, then struck it against his partially drawn sword. Sparks flared. They caught the main fuse as he sheathed his sword. Slowly, the fire crept up the cord, inching toward the gunpowder. Within minutes, this ship and everyone aboard it would disappear from the world, all blown to pieces.

And when that happened, Sam planned to be ashore, watching the explosion with Cassandra beside him.

Sparks from the fuses caught on the wooden bulkheads. Within moments, tongues of flame licked along any dry timber.

Satisfied with his work, he pulled himself from the magazine. He dangled for a moment as he hung on the open doorway, regaining his balance, readying himself for the difficult climb out of the ship.

Chill hands latched onto his legs.

Cassandra paced the beach. God, how long would this grim task take? Sam might not be able to drown—she doubted she'd ever forget the image of him walking into and beneath the waves like a returning sea god—but other dangers lurked below the water. He could be pinned by the treacherous rocks or trapped in the wreckage. There wasn't a damned thing she could do to help him, either. She'd learned to swim, but in a placid lake, not the angry sea. If she tried to swim out to him, she wouldn't last five minutes. And even if a rowboat was nearby, she and it would be dashed on the rocks as she attempted to row out to the ship.

Waiting passively on the beach while Sam endangered himself infuriated her. She needed to be useful, active.

In frustration, she picked up one of the small rocks at her feet and threw it toward the sea. It made a tiny splash just at the edge of the water. Rather than helping ease her exasperation, this sign of her lack of physical strength only annoyed her further.

"And I can't see a bloody thing," she snarled to herself. Her vantage on the beach only offered minimal visibility of the wrecked ship. Large rocks in the water blocked her view. She tried sitting in the saddle, but still didn't gain enough height.

The promontory. It rose up tall above the water, topped with a flat patch of earth. Had she been a smuggler, it would have made a perfect spot to look out to sea for approaching rum runner ships. She didn't care about illegal rum or silk or tea or any other cursed thing—she only needed to watch over Sam. And from atop the high bluff, she could do just that.

She hobbled the horses, removed her cloak, and put the guns into her pockets. Then she hurried across the sand to reach the promontory. Standing at its base, she gazed up at the rocky pinnacle. Its sides were sloped yet appeared easily scalable, but then, as they neared the top, they became almost perpendicular. Many years had passed since she'd last climbed a tree. She had to trust her strength to get her to the top of the promontory. At least hand- and footholds abounded.

She drew a deep breath, and ascended the steep incline. Thoughts of Sam urged her on, even as her legs began to burn, even as the incline gave way to a nearly vertical climb and she pushed and pulled herself up the side. Rocks bit into her hands and scraped her face as she clambered upward, and she scrabbled a few times when the rocks under her feet tumbled loose. Only once did she make the mistake of looking down. Thank God night veiled distance, so that she was only aware of the pale beach *somewhere* below her.

At last, her whole body shaking with effort, she dragged

herself up and over the top. For a moment, she sprawled on her stomach, panting. Then she rose to her feet.

And found herself face-to-face with Colonel Kenneth Broadwell.

A space of ten feet separated them. They stared at each other, both still, as her mind whirled. She hadn't seen him standing here from the beach—darkness must have hidden him. He'd been expecting her, because he stood, relaxed but ready. Cassandra saw in his posture a similarity to Sam, the presence of military bearing, but Broadwell was wiry and lean where Sam was prolific with muscle. Moonlight turned Broadwell's graying hair silver, yet, despite the fact that he was at least fifteen years older than Sam, he was fit and capable, lethal as a coiled snake.

She wondered how he could see her, though, since he wore spectacles with dark lenses.

"My congratulations," Broadwell murmured. "I didn't think you could make it all the way up. I thought that certainly you'd fall and split that pretty head of yours wide open."

"Tenacity has its rewards," she answered.

He laughed, a remote, metallic sound. "Well answered, Miss." His geniality disappeared, cold calculation taking its place. "Now who the hell are you and what are you doing here with Samuel Reed?"

He didn't know she was a Blade. And somewhere on his person was the Source that created the undead. But how to get it? Her hands drifted toward her pockets. Blades couldn't use magic, but firearms were most definitely allowed when it came to recovering Sources.

"You wouldn't be reaching for those pistols, would you?" His own pistol came up quickly. "If so, I suggest you stop."

Blast. Her hands froze.

Broadwell took a step closer, smirking. "What an intriguing puzzle you are. Obviously a lady, but you're climbing promontories in the middle of night with guns in your pockets. And keeping company with Sam Reed. Do you have any idea what kind of monster he is?"

Anger flared. "I know *exactly* who and what Sam is. He's no monster, but *you* have tried to make him one."

Broadwell's brows rose in surprise. "You know everything?" Before she could answer, he drew nearer, peering at her. "Hold— you've a familiar look about you." He came closer, so that only a foot separated them. "A resemblance to someone."

She turned her face away, but his icy fingers pinched her chin and forced her head back to look at him. She tried to slap his hand from her, but her hands bounced off him uselessly. His dark spectacles were soulless voids, his face sharp and predatory.

"Fielding," he said. "Charlie Fielding."

"My brother," she bit out. Hatred seethed through her. She thought about going for his pistol, but the odds were too good that it would fire in the process. Possibly wounding her.

Another arctic laugh from Broadwell. "That's right. Fielding had a sister. Always crowed about you when your letters came. His clever little sister."

Cassandra finally was able to jerk her chin free of his grasp. "I thank God Charlie wasn't transformed after he died. Sam and the other men weren't as fortunate."

"Oh, Fielding would've been a perfect zombie." Broadwell grinned sardonically. "So strong. He could have done some wonderful work—just like Reed did after I changed him. Pity there wasn't enough of your brother left to make the spell function."

Fury swept through Cassandra, obliterating everything, even fear. She launched herself at Broadwell, hands curved into claws. Her nails raked down his face before he grabbed her wrists, his grip an iron vise. His pistol fell to the ground.

"What an adorable hellcat you are," he chuckled.

Maddened, she wrenched and pulled but could not free herself. "And you're a disgusting worm," she snarled. "Killing and enslaving men through the perversion of Sources."

"Sources?" he repeated. She felt the wintry knife of his gaze, even through his dark glasses. "You're a Blade of the Rose."

He sneered. "Those idealistic fools let a *woman* into their ranks."
He twisted his arms, turning Cassandra around so that her
back pressed tight against his chest. His arms formed an im-
penetrable cage around her.

"But where are your friends, the Blades, now?" he hissed in
her ear. "You can't fight me on your own."

As much as she wanted to deny this, she knew it was true.
She simply hadn't the physical strength necessary to battle
Broadwell by herself.

He turned them both so they faced the sunken vessel. "Your
only ally is Reed. And my zombies are tearing him apart this
very moment."

She saw him through a gaping wound in the side of the
ship—Sam, backlit by flames, as he fought against several undead soldiers below him. They cast dark shapes against the fires,
a seething mass of combat. As she watched, two of the undead
grabbed Sam by the legs.

Terror and rage flooded her—no, please don't let anything
happen to Sam—but logic gleamed beneath. Stay focused, she
told herself. She had to get the Source. Her mission for the
Blades demanded this, and if she took the Source away from
Broadwell, she could try and stop the undead Marines from
destroying Sam. Surely the Blades would forgive her use of
magic if it was for a good reason. And no better reason existed
than protecting Sam.

The demons of hell tried to drag him under. Not demons,
he amended, staring down at the chalky faces of the undead
officers. Monsters—like him.

Half a dozen of them reached up from the passageway below,
their expressions utterly blank, eyes glowing in the darkness,
but their searching hands relentless. Two of them grabbed at
Sam's legs, fastening to his ankles, pulling. Other Marines joined
in, clutching the soldiers that held Sam and tugging hard so
that the force of six men weighed on Sam's legs.

Sam, gripping the doorway of the magazine, kicked out.

The fingers of one Marine slackened, yet the other held tightly. Sam's own grip on the door began to loosen.

"Fight it," Sam growled at the Marines. "Fight his control."

But the soldiers' eyes remained empty. They were only husks obeying Broadwell's commands. And they would continue to do so, their minds trapped within their undead bodies, witnessing the horrors they would be forced to commit.

Sam would make sure that didn't happen.

With a groan, he freed his legs and climbed back into the magazine. Flames engulfed two of the remaining bulkheads, and the fuse slowly burned. The flame inched closer to the kegs of gunpowder. He cursed. If the Marines didn't tear his limbs from his body, the explosion would turn them all into pulp staining the water. Once, Sam believed all he wanted was an end to this existence. Now, with Cassandra's face glittering in his mind, he fought for survival.

Impassive faces of the undead appeared in the doorway. Hands clawed at the door frame.

Sam drew his sword. He slashed at the forearms of the officers. One grunted as the sword cut cleanly through his arm, severing the limb just above the wrist. No blood spouted from the wound, but the amputated hand fell away, tumbling into darkness.

The soldier's hand would regenerate, but the explosion would happen long before. And nothing could regenerate after that. Not even Sam.

Obeying a silent directive, the Marines clambered over each other, trying to reach Sam. They had no regard for the men they used as leverage, nor did the soldiers yelp in pain as boots smashed into their backs and faces. Pain meant almost nothing to their kind. Yet Sam felt it now—not as much as if he were still alive—but he'd changed since making love with Cassandra, so that his arms and legs burned with regained awareness.

The officers pulled themselves into the magazine.

Sam did not wait. He swept out with his sword. A soldier's head toppled from his shoulders. His body pitched back, through the open doorway. The other Marines paid no attention, but kept advancing with their own drawn swords.

Again and again, Sam's sword sliced through the air, hacking at the advancing soldiers and dodging their own blades. They ignored the numerous cuts they took to their faces and bodies, as he did. But when Sam plowed his sword into their heads, grisly magic no longer animated their bodies. They fell like the corpses they were, knocking against the wooden floors and bulkheads until they were swallowed by the sea below.

Only two Marines attacked him now. And the fuse burned even closer to the powder kegs. With a roar and burst of strength, Sam lunged, severing one's head and then driving the tip of his sword through the eye of the other. Both officers fell to the ground, immobile. Sam was free.

He wasted no time, climbing back through the groaning, burning carcass of the ship toward the stern. He disregarded the pain in his limbs as he went up. There wasn't time to marvel at the new wonder of pain.

At last, he reached the remains of the captain's quarters and hauled himself through the cabin. The indigo night sky shone through the broken windows, stars like distant dreams, perfectly indifferent to everything beneath.

Sam grasped the casement and dragged himself upward, until he stood on the edge of the window. Waves battered the hull.

He sent one glance below him into the ruined ship. In the wreckage within the dark sea, a hundred undead men had been resurrected, torn from the solace of death for an unholy purpose. If they made it to the surface, Broadwell would use them to commit atrocities until a merciful blade removed their heads.

It could have been Sam. It *had* been Sam.

"I'm sorry," he whispered to the men and all those within the ship. Then, with his sword strapped to his back, he stood. He looked back at the shore and could still see no sign of Cassandra, then movement higher above caught his eye. Rage decimated every other thought. There, atop the promontory, she struggled. Against Broadwell.

Get to her, his every instinct screamed. *Protect her*. Sam dove into the water.

The ship exploded.

Chapter Six

A massive detonation tore the night open. The partially submerged wreckage of the transport ship erupted into a colossal ball of fire. The sound of the crashing waves disappeared beneath a roaring explosion—the force of which rocked both Cassandra and Broadwell as they struggled on the promontory.

One thought screamed in Cassandra's mind: *Sam*. Had he escaped the ship before the explosion? Or was he lost, destroyed with the ship and the undead soldiers?

God, she couldn't let herself think of that now. She must believe he had survived and stay focused on her goal: retrieve the Source.

Broadwell's grip on her loosened as another detonation burst from the wreckage. She immediately freed one of her hands. She had to take the lead, deliberately and definitively. She wasn't Broadwell's passive victim. Her thumb reached beneath Broadwell's dark spectacles and jammed hard into his eye.

He howled, reeling back. As he clutched at his face, Cassandra took advantage of his confused, weakened state. She leapt onto him.

They struggled as she frantically searched Broadwell. Her hands delved into his pockets, the gaps in his clothing, concentrating on finding the Source. The water and sky formed a luridly glowing backdrop, flames from the destroyed ship reaching high into the darkness. Nothing and no one could have survived such an explosion.

No—think only of the Source, whatever it might be.

Broadwell began to shake off the effects of her attack. Still somewhat clumsy, he pushed at her as she searched through his clothes. A powder horn, a folding knife, coins. No Source. Where was it?

"Get off me, you stupid whore," he slurred.

She refused to answer him, even as his shoving grew stronger. He dug his elbow into her spine and she winced in pain. But she wouldn't stop her search.

Wait—there! An inside pocket of his coat. Her hand touched a small pouch of coarse fabric. Sewn to the outside of the pouch were what felt like feathers and beads. She couldn't tell what was within the small bag, though it felt like dried plants and pebbles. Energy radiated from it, a palpable sensation of power that ran all the way up her arm to resonate throughout her body. The resounding, dark connection that delineated the boundaries between life and death. Most assuredly this was the Source.

Just as her fingers closed around the pouch, Broadwell's crushing grip encircled her wrist.

She stared up at his enraged face, his mouth contorted in a snarl. He'd recovered from her attack and looked ready to smash his other fist into her face. Cassandra braced herself for the blow, but wouldn't release the Source. He'd have to knock her out cold before she let it go.

As Broadwell raised his hand to strike, someone behind her slammed a fist right into his jaw. Broadwell stumbled to the edge of the promontory, away from Cassandra. She glanced down at her hand. In her tight grip nestled the pouch.

She whirled around to face Broadwell's attacker. She couldn't contain her gasp of astonishment and profound relief.

"Sam," she breathed.

He stood, clothes torn, soaking wet, tall and lethal as he

glowered at Broadwell. His sword glinted on his back. In the moonlight, his eyes glowed with merciless fury, his shoulders broad and bunching with unleashed rage. If she did not know that Sam was her ally, Cassandra would have been terrified by the sight he made. Yet, even understanding that he was her friend, she took an involuntary step backward.

"Did he hurt you?" he growled at her.

"Not much," she answered. She held out her hand. "I have the Source."

He gave a curt nod, less concerned with the magical object than with her. Reaching out, he wrapped one arm around Cassandra and pulled her close. "You truly all right?" he rumbled.

"Yes, yes." She clutched the Source to her chest but stared up at him, an avenging spirit from the depths of the sea, as he glared at Broadwell, who straightened as he stood at the edge of the promontory. "The son of a bitch didn't get the opportunity. And you're alive."

"Not alive," Sam corrected with a wry quirk of his mouth. "But here with you." His attention fixed on Broadwell. "Those men are at rest now," he snarled at his former commanding officer. "And you won't desecrate anyone else."

Broadwell straightened as he recovered. "Should have left you dead," he sneered.

"I'd agree," Sam replied, "but then I wouldn't get the chance to do this."

Sam pulled a gun from Cassandra's pocket with a motion so fast, she barely saw it. He leveled the pistol at Broadwell. Then shot him directly through the heart. As he'd been shot and killed three years before.

Instead of toppling over, Broadwell simply looked down at the smoking wound in his chest. No blood stained the fabric of his now-torn waistcoat. He glanced back up at Sam and Cassandra with a smirk.

"What—?" she gasped.

Broadwell pulled the dark spectacles from his face and tucked them neatly into an inside pocket. His eyes glowed, white and otherworldly.

Sam cursed, lowering the pistol.

"Come now," Broadwell chuckled. "Why should you undead chaps get all the fun?"

"Fun?" Sam growled. "*Fun?*"

"Was that your scheme, all along?" Cassandra demanded. "Turn yourself into . . . into . . ."

"A zombie," Broadwell finished, verging on cheerful. "No, that wasn't part of my plan. But after Reed here broke away from me and the others, there was a skirmish with some Russians and I took a mortal wound." He pulled at his high collar to reveal a huge, jagged gash running across his throat.

"So I transformed myself." He grinned, a death's head. Cassandra shuddered at the sight, and the vicious glee in Broadwell's voice. "Don't know what all your fuss was about, Reed. All this strength and power. Indestructibility. Bloody wonderful."

"Not without free will," Sam gritted back. "And not at the cost of a normal life."

Broadwell snorted. "Who wants normal when the world is ours for the taking? And it can be ours, Reed. Ours, and the Heirs of Albion." His tone took on a wheedling note. He took a step closer and pointed at the pouch still gripped in Cassandra's hand. "With us both in possession of the Source, there's nothing we cannot do, nothing we can't have."

Sam stared at him, the only sounds emanating from the burning ship and waves crashing against the shore.

A brief panic from Cassandra. Could Sam be tempted by Broadwell's offer? Many other men would.

Sam drew his sword, the blade hissing as it slid from the scabbard.

"I want my goddamned life back." He glanced down at Cassandra, and pain flashed across the hard lines of his face. "I want what I can't have."

Broadwell sighed and shook his head. "Never figured you for the sentimental type, Major Reed."

"When your head's decorating my mantel," Sam said as he

pushed Cassandra behind him, "I won't feel very sentimental." He raised his sword.

Broadwell stepped back, keeping his distance. "Tonight isn't the end, Reed." He turned his glowing eyes to Cassandra. "The next time we meet, I won't be alone. The Heirs *will* retake the Source. And I think," he added with a grin, "you'll make a marvelous zombie, Miss Fielding. You'll have *so many* uses."

Sam lunged forward with a growl.

Broadwell took another step backward. He disappeared over the lip of the promontory.

As Cassandra and Sam rushed to the edge, all they saw was Broadwell vanishing into the waves far below. They watched as swift currents carried him away, along the coastline. He'd escaped. For now.

More cursing grated from Sam. "The bastard keeps slipping away."

"But the Source is ours." She tucked the pouch into her pocket, then turned to him and pressed her hands against his chest, feeling the solid strength of him. "And you survived. I saw you fighting with those soldiers, and then, when the ship went, I didn't know . . ." All the fear she hadn't allowed herself to feel came hastening back, until she felt dizzy and sick with it.

She leaned her head against him, and his wet fingers wove into her hair, gently easing it to one side. He pressed his lips to the bared nape of her neck. "A hell of a fight," he murmured. "Only thoughts of you kept me from defeat."

Her heart pounded thickly in her throat. She felt herself overwhelmed. Too many emotions collided within her. Turning her head slightly, she watched the burning wreckage of the ship as it and its blighted passengers turned to sodden ash.

"Those poor souls," she whispered.

Straightening to his full height, he kept his hand softly cupped around her nape. "Not 'poor souls,'" he said, his voice oddly muted. "The fortunate ones. They now have the peace I long for."

Sudden anger roared through her. She shoved him back. "Damn you, Sam Reed."

He jolted in surprise, staring down at her with puzzlement.

Once the slightest trickle of emotion escaped from the dam of her control, Cassandra could not stop the flood. Everything she had felt that night but suppressed—fear, rage, relief, despair, joy—all seethed and spiraled within her so that she no longer could distinguish one feeling from the other. They merged into a roiling miasma.

She didn't know what to think, what to feel. She knew only the sensation of her blood pounding through her body, an awareness of her flesh—and a swift sensual hunger that stole her breath.

On this isolated promontory, she and Sam existed outside of time and space. Nothing—the burning ship, Broadwell—could touch them, harm them. They were far above everything, enclosed within the safety and danger of desire.

She breached the distance she'd put between her and Sam, striding up to him as he watched her, wary. When she plunged her fingers into his slick, wet hair and tugged his head down to hers, he was too surprised to resist. And for only a moment, he was motionless as she pulled his cool, firm lips to her own for a demanding kiss.

Only a moment's stillness. Then he met her savagery with his own. They plundered each other's mouths, a hungry consuming of growing heat and humid desire. A challenge and affirmation, each struggling to dominate and be dominated. Her arms twined around his neck. He must have sheathed his sword, because his broad hands came up to grip her waist, hauling her tight against him.

His skin and clothing were soaking wet, yet she didn't care. She felt only the hard, unyielding strength of his body snug against hers, a firm wall of muscle against which she gladly battered herself. In an instant, her own garments clung damply to her body, along her thighs, her belly and breasts.

Against her stomach rose the insistent, thick press of his arousal. She pushed her hips into his, urged on by a need that robbed her of everything but desire. They growled into each other's mouths.

When his hand came up to cup her swollen breast, her nipple tightening, she moaned her approval. Yet, even with her clothing wet and clinging, revealing nearly everything, too much separated her and Sam. She pulled back enough to undo the buttons of her bodice. His impatient fingers helped, and in short order, she'd bared herself from the waist up.

His glowing gaze fastened hungrily on her naked breasts. She'd forgone her corset when dressing earlier, and now blessed that decision.

"I want you everywhere," she rasped. She hardly recognized her own voice, low and throaty, but she did not care. "On me, inside me. *Now.*" In this, she refused denial.

Sam stared down into her eyes, warming himself with the heat and demand he found there. The amber depths gleamed with such desire, he almost believed she had a magic of her own. She *did* have magic—calling forth from him the needs of his long-numb body and heart.

He'd spoken without thinking before. He had said the now-destroyed Marines finally achieved the peace he wanted. Once, that was all he craved. Now—he wanted her. Only her. However he could.

The Cassandra he once knew had been a headstrong girl. And the woman he'd come to desire possessed an intractable will. But *this* woman looking up at him with undisguised sexual hunger tolerated nothing but complete submission.

Sam stood taller than her. He easily outweighed her and could, if he so desired, toss her aside like so much thistledown. They both knew this. Yet the prospect of yielding to her, giving her his body and everything else for her pleasure, excited him tremendously. At her bold words, his cock thickened, straining to give her exactly what she wanted.

"I'm yours," he growled.

She drew in a sharp breath, then tugged his head toward her breasts. At once, he took a silky stiff nipple into his mouth.

His tongue lapped and circled, drawing on her, and she hissed with pleasure as she pulled him even closer. He stroked her other breast with his hand, feeling the perfect, satiny weight, teasing her to writhing.

"Touch me, Sam," she gasped.

They sank down to their knees, neither noticing the hard ground, aware of nothing but each other. He gathered up her skirts, the fabric bunching as his hand delved beneath. At the feel of her smooth, slim leg, he rumbled his praise. He drew his palm up, along the length of her thigh. With a grateful snarl, he realized she wore no drawers. Beneath her skirts, she was entirely bare.

He filled his hands with the luscious curves of her arse, then trailed one palm across her belly before sliding through her damp, hot pussy. The moment his fingers dipped between her folds, she tipped her head back and moaned. She abandoned herself utterly. Up and down she moved as he stroked her, her breath coming in short, harsh pants.

The pressure in his cock was a sweet agony. He wanted only to plunge into her. But delaying his hunger made it all the sweeter. He would take her through one orgasm, and another, and another, until they both dissolved entirely from pleasure.

And she was so close, riding nearer and nearer to climax. Suddenly, she wasn't. She shoved his hand away.

He frowned. Did she not enjoy his touch?

Yet as she leaned back, bracing herself on her elbows, her gaze smoldered. She was a predatory cat. "You've seen me," she breathed. "Now it's my turn." Her eyes strayed to the huge ridge along the front of his trousers.

"This?" He ran one hand down the length of his cock, and groaned.

"Yes." Her voice was smoke and honey. "More. Unfasten your trousers and I'll watch you stroke yourself."

He nearly came at just her words. Summoning all his control, he pried open the buttons of his pants and groaned again when his stiff shaft sprang free. Already at the tip, moisture gleamed.

Cassandra licked her lips. "Let me see. I want to see your cock in your hand."

Once more, he nearly spilled at merely words. Hell—to hear her soft voice say such exquisitely crude things to him— no man could bear it. But he would. For himself, and her.

He grasped his cock tightly, learning his own sex again. As an adolescent, touching himself had been one of his favorite pastimes. Private moments had seen him enthusiastically— though quickly—bringing himself to climax. As soon as he'd been old enough to have a woman, however, one hobby fast gave way to another. Then war arrived and he'd been reduced to infrequent, furtive wanking in the middle of the night to dull the edge of his substantial appetite. And, once he'd been transformed, he and his cock had no relationship at all. They were both dead and cold.

So it was with a newfound pleasure that he stroked himself now. Not only because he relished the sensation, but because Cassandra watched him with lust etched sharply in her face.

"Slower," she commanded as he ran his fist up and down his shaft. When he complied, she ran one of her fingers over the peak of her breast, her eyelids drooping with need.

She followed with her gaze each movement of his hand on his cock. His balls tightened. Sensation built. He ground his teeth, fighting his release, even as he continued stroking himself.

"I didn't say you could stop," she panted when his hand dropped away.

"Can't continue. Or I'll spend."

"I want you to."

"Only inside of you."

Pursing her lips, she levered herself up to walk on her knees until little space separated them. He let her push him down so that now he lay back with his legs stretched out in front of him, his weight on his forearms. When she began to straddle him, holding her gathered skirts in her arms, he reached for her.

She edged from his touch, and he understood. This moment

was hers to control and command. So he lay back and watched as she grasped his cock and guided it to her waiting entrance. Feral noises clawed from his chest as she sank down onto him, his cock disappearing into her in torturous inches.

God. *God.* She was so hot, so snug, impossibly wet. His hips jerked up of their own accord, wanting him in as deep as he could go.

She rose up and slid down. He clenched his hands into rock-hard fists to keep from gripping her hips and helping her ride him. He'd never seen or experienced anything as potent as the sight of her moving on him, finding her rhythm, discovering her pleasure. Her expression both soft and sharp with bliss.

I'm hers, hers alone. He was the means to her ecstasy, and it was all he wanted.

"Take me, Cass," he growled. "Hard as you want. Take everything."

At his urging, she began to move faster, grinding against him, gripping his cock in the perfection of her body. She caressed her breasts, and it was as if she touched him, too, for he felt her pleasure resounding in him.

Building, climbing. They both threw themselves toward completion. His climax gathered, unwilling to wait for his permission.

"Can't hold off," he gritted.

"Sam." She gasped. "Be with me now." And then she stilled, tightening around him. Tremors racked her body, one after the other. Her head tipped forward as she cried out noiselessly, too enrapt to make a sound.

He erupted, his release tearing through him with an intensity that stole every other sense. A climax without cessation. Fiery. Harrowing. Wonderful.

She collapsed on top of him, panting, as the last of her orgasm shuddered through her.

When his arms came up to hold her, she didn't protest that he'd disobeyed her commandment. Instead, she sighed and burrowed closer, nuzzling his neck.

Just then, he didn't care that, within his chest, there was no movement or beat of his heart. Hers was strong enough for them both.

On slightly shaking legs, they descended the promontory. He suggested he jump down first, unconcerned about injuring himself, and he would catch her as she leapt. This, she flatly refused.

"I don't doubt you can catch me," she said. "But until I grow a pair of wings, I'm not leaping off a cliff."

She'd been so damned fearless up to that point, he couldn't fault her for a little caution.

So they made their way slowly down. He did go first, but stayed close, in case she should slip. Along the way, neither spoke, but stopped sometimes to watch as the burning wreckage gradually reduced to floating charcoal.

Once back on the beach, they returned to their horses. The animals looked up from grazing on spindly grasses and snorted in recognition. Cassandra took one look at the waiting saddles, and sat down heavily in the sand.

He immediately crouched beside her, concerned. "Tell me what's wrong," he demanded.

She gave him a weary smile. "Just give me a minute before we go tearing off again."

Nodding, relieved, Sam sat next to her. He could not sense Broadwell nearby, so Sam allowed this pause. He enfolded her small hand within his, and they both gazed at the waves breaking against the shore. The moon curved back toward the horizon. With the flames extinguished, the stars reemerged, arrayed in patterns both careful and haphazard across the velvet night.

"Never thought I'd have this," he murmured. "A beautiful woman beside me on a moonlit beach. Some other man's dream now my reality." He brought her hand up to his lips.

She smiled again, tenderly. "Even as an infatuated girl, I could never image this much."

Then, because he discovered himself bound to her in a way he could not truly fathom, he offered a confession. "I don't know what to do. About . . . about this." He glanced at their interwoven hands and felt the frown gather between his brows. "I can't give you anything, Cass." His growl of frustration was for himself. "I'm a monster."

"You're not—"

Heated, he turned to her. "There's no future with me. You know that. As I do. I can't be part of the normal world."

"I never said I wanted normal," she shot back. "Good God, Sam, if I desired an ordinary life, I wouldn't have become a Blade of the Rose."

"On your *second* mission."

She made a dismissive noise. "Second or hundredth, it doesn't matter. All that matters is now. This moment." She leaned forward and kissed him sweetly, and he found himself falling deeper into an emotion even he, a battle-scarred soldier who had already died, was afraid to name.

She rested her forehead against his. "I don't know what the future holds for you and I, either," she admitted. "Two things I do know—you have beguiled me so that all I desire is making love with you again and again until we're both utterly exhausted."

"And the other?" he growled, hardening at her words.

"The other." She sighed, and moved back. "We must take care of the Source. Broadwell will return with other Heirs, and they'll want it back." From her pocket, she produced what appeared to be a tatty little pouch of hempen fabric. Crude beads and scraggly feathers adorned its surface.

His immediate desire retreated, though he suspected that from now on, whenever he was in her presence, he would want her. For the moment, he let the demands of his body be supplanted by the sword of duty hanging over his head.

Sam plucked the little bag from her hand and studied it. "Looks old, but it seems fairly shabby." Despite its plain appearance, the moment he touched the pouch, currents of dark energy moved through him. A rush of power that stirred him almost as much as Cassandra—but in a different way. With her, he felt himself wanting only her. This magical object he now held made him hungry for more power, more strength. More everything. It engendered greed.

"The Blades say that Sources are very seldom impressive objects. Most of them are ancient and homely. Fashioned of things that belong to the common people. Because magic belongs to *everyone*—rich, poor, male, female, the elderly and the young. All races. All faiths."

He started to untie the cord that kept the pouch closed, but she laid her hand over his. "We should know what's inside," he said.

She shook her head. "Whatever's in there, it must be kept undisturbed. Or else we risk catastrophic danger."

"Then we destroy it. Without this," he hefted the small pouch in his hand, "Broadwell and the Heirs of Albion can't create more things like me. And no one else can, either."

"You're not a *thing*," she said at once, and he almost smiled at the temper in her voice, as if she'd do battle with anyone who opposed her feelings about him. "And Sources cannot be destroyed. Without the physical object enclosing the magic, it is unleashed upon the world. Becomes volatile and unpredictable."

He stared down at the pouch in his hand. "Seems so ordinary." His fingers closed around it. "But I can feel its power. It's . . . captivating."

Smiling wryly, Cassandra said, "If it wasn't, then there would be no need for the Blades."

"If we can't destroy this thing, what *can* we do with it? Take it back to the Blades in Southampton?" Broadwell would attack long before then.

"The only way to safely contain a Source's magic is to secure it through the people to whom the magic belongs." She gnawed on her lower lip as she considered this. "But I don't know where this Source originated from."

Sam thought back to what he knew of such magic—which was practically nothing. "Broadwell used to speak to me and the others, after he'd changed us. To amuse himself. He thought none of us listened, but I did. And he said that zombies came from the Caribbean. Haiti."

Her eyes lit with understanding. "Yes! *Vodou* magic has its roots in West Africa, but it migrated with the people who were taken to be slaves in the French Caribbean. That's where *vodou* truly took shape. The Source must have come from Haiti."

"So we take this thing all the way across the ocean?" His mouth twisted to consider the demands and complications of a long sea voyage. So many opportunities for danger. His own safety didn't matter, but, strong as Cassandra proved herself to be, she still was vulnerable. He'd rather die a thousand times over than allow anything to happen to her. But he knew she'd refuse to be left behind while he undertook the journey alone.

Yet she didn't frown with concern at this prospect. In fact, she smiled.

"We needn't go so far," she said.

Down a dark road they cantered. Through sleeping villages and past farms. Sam kept himself constantly alert, ready for the inevitable moment when Broadwell attacked. That bastard would be back. It was only a matter of when.

From the scent of fresh dew upon the grass, the subtle changes in the sounds of nocturnal animals, Sam could tell dawn was close at hand. A quick glance at Cassandra showed her shoulders still straight, her posture alert. But he realized she had to be exhausted. An eventful night.

She pushed herself, though, to reach their destination. Wherever that might be.

"Tell me who we're going to see," he said above the pounding of the horses' hooves.

"Blades do not permit themselves the use of magic in their mission," she answered. "Yet that doesn't mean we're without resources. For several generations, one family has provided . . . I suppose you might call it 'mechanical assistance.'"

He frowned, puzzled. "They build things."

"Not mere 'things,'" she corrected with a grin. "The most incredible devices. Contraptions and mechanisms that defy logic and yet also harness scientific principles. If the human mind can conceive of something, the Graves family can construct it." She shrugged. "The only way to truly understand is to see their work in action."

"And these Graves people, they have a means of containing the Source."

"Unfortunately, no. Magic seldom obeys scientific rules. But the Graves *do* come from the Caribbean. It's my hope that if anyone can help us with this Source, it's them." She tilted her chin, indicating the road ahead. "One member of the Graves family retired a few years ago, and she lives nearby."

The whole thing sounded damned improbable to Sam, but no other course presented itself. Strange, when he'd spent so many years entirely focused on one thing—finding and punishing Broadwell—and now he dwelt in the midst of uncertainty. Even before his transformation, he'd been a man who demanded precise, straightforward goals. A problem presented itself, and he found the quickest way to solve it. But this ambiguity chafed.

Another ambiguity pained more than all the rest. He gazed at Cassandra. Something much more than lust roared through him whenever he was near her, when he looked at her or touched her. His miserable existence had changed utterly since he found her again, and sick dread filled him to think about what that existence would be like without her. But he'd spoken honestly before. He could give her nothing. He was a doomed creature whose presence in her life would only bring her isolation and misery.

When the Source was finally contained, he'd have to let her go.

The thought sent a bolt of gleaming white pain through him.

The sun chose that moment to crest the horizon. Overhead, the sky paled with daybreak, and the very tops of the trees were edged with golden light. Morning birds called to each other, trilling. A fair, crisp dawn, utterly indifferent to the wrenching decision Sam had made.

As he and Cassandra rounded a bend in the road, they came upon a tidy, two-storied house. Cheerful smoke curled up from the chimney, proving that someone inside already left their bed. It seemed like any other well-kept country house, though its lush garden would make any gardener bilious with envy.

"This is it," Cassandra said.

They drew up on the other side of the fence enclosing the garden. And that's when Sam saw it: snaking through the garden, a gleaming network of pipes, spigots, and valves. The mechanism dispensed water throughout the garden, and Sam heard a clicking sound, indicating a timed device regulating the hydration.

"I'm no farmer," he muttered, "but that is bloody genius."

A woman stepped from behind the shelter of an abundant rose bush. Though her hair was snowy white, her chocolate-brown skin showed no lines and her jet eyes gleamed with intelligence. Sam had never seen a more regal-looking woman.

"Of course it's genius," she said. "*I* made it."

Chapter Seven

The inside of Honoria Graves's home proved as remarkable as its exterior. A system of clockwork mechanisms regulated each room, so that Honoria had only to turn a small key located by the door, and the curtains lowered all over the house while the lamps seemed to light themselves.

"You're being pursued, I expect," she said as she guided them through her astonishing home, "so we'll need some privacy." She spun on her heel, surprising Cassandra, and fixed her with a sharp stare. "Heirs of Albion, yes? Which ones?"

"Kenneth Broadwell," Cassandra answered at once. She felt as though she was back at Miss Delafield's Academy for Young Ladies. But none of the teachers there possessed an ounce of Honoria Graves's intellect. Or were nearly as disquieting. "Others will be following."

Honoria's mouth thinned. "Broadwell. A despicable character. The worst kind of military man."

"How do you know him?" Sam asked from behind Cassandra.

The stately older woman fastened her piercing gaze on Sam. She did not seem at all intimidated by his height, the breadth of his shoulders, the deadly sword he wore with ease, his sharply handsome face—or indeed anything about him.

Cassandra smothered a laugh when tall, commanding Sam

actually straightened his shoulders and smoothed his wind-blown hair as if being inspected by a senior officer.

"It is my *business* to know my enemy," Honoria answered crisply. "The Graves family has been the foundation of the Blade of the Rose for generations. We would each of us be remiss if we did not know precisely *who* and *what* we are dealing with." She took a step closer as she peered more intently at Sam, forcing Cassandra to edge backward. "And you, sir? What *are* you?"

Sam's awe of the older woman disappeared, replaced by cool distance. His jaw hardened, his eyes turning glacial. "Undead, madam." He pulled at the front of his shirt, revealing the wound in his chest.

As Honoria donned a pair of spectacles and studied the wound, Cassandra reached out and took Sam's hand. His fingers lay unmoving in her own, but she gave them a squeeze. If Honoria Graves shunned Sam, or feared him and put her from her home, then Cassandra would leave, as well. No longer would Sam have to face his outcast status alone.

Honoria straightened and tucked her spectacles into the pocket of her pristine apron. Her face was unreadable. "Broadwell did that to you," she said.

Sam gave a clipped nod.

"With this," Cassandra added, holding up the Source. By the infinitesimal widening of Honoria's eyes, Cassandra understood that she recognized the little pouch for what it was: a wellspring of powerful magic.

Then the regal older woman did something Cassandra didn't expect. She cursed. Profanely. And, truth be told, rather well. Even Sam looked admiring, and he'd been a soldier, where foul language was as common as bedbugs.

"Come into my kitchen," Honoria said, turning and walking briskly down the hall. "The young woman needs food and rest, and I need both of you to tell me everything that's happened." She paused at the entrance to the kitchen. "And, by God, it will be my greatest pleasure to help send Broadwell straight to hell."

Cassandra and Sam stood precisely where they were, gaping.

"Come on, then," Honoria clipped. "The kettle's already on." She disappeared into the kitchen.

Sam and Cassandra knew better than to disobey a direct order. They followed at once.

It was an ordinary kitchen, to Cassandra's surprise. No diabolical mechanisms that turned the roast or rolled crusts for pie or swept the floor. Everything was as typical as it was in her own family's kitchen. Hearth, stove, larder. Honoria saw Cassandra's astonishment.

"Aside from gardening, domestic issues have never held much interest, yet I have some measure of aptitude," Honoria explained. "So I have a village woman cook and clean for me, though she keeps requesting a device to help with the washing. I may consider such a project." She made an elegant shrug. "But retirement isn't nearly as restful as one supposes it to be." At Cassandra's look of contrition, she made a gesture of dismissal. "No, I'll take no apologies for disturbing my retirement. Frankly, no Blade ever truly leaves, and certainly no Graves ever stopped inventing."

She waved Cassandra and Sam to sit at the homey wooden table. In short order, a plate of eggs, toast, sausages, and broiled tomatoes was set before Cassandra, along with a steaming cup of tea. Sam subtly braced himself for his own plate of food which he would have to refuse, but, to his quiet relief, Honoria pressed no food on him, nor demanded explanations.

Honoria poured herself a cup of tea, seated herself, and then said, "So, out with it. Tell me everything, and spare no details."

So they did, as Cassandra ate ravenously. Defying death had a peculiar way of sharpening the appetite. She and Sam went back and forth, recounting all that had transpired, not only since their meeting in the stonemason yard, but the history before it, including Sam's transformation. They both opted not to discuss making love, though there was something in the way Honoria looked at them that made Cassandra think the older woman knew, anyway. Again Cassandra waited for condemnation or disgust from Honoria that a living woman would make love with an undead man—but there was no judgment, only intellectual curiosity. Thankfully, Honoria did not ask questions about the logistics or significance of having an undead lover.

She did, however, ask many direct and pointed questions about everything else, even about what appeared to be trivial.

"You smile, Miss Fielding," Honoria noted. "Are you amused by something?"

Cassandra forced down her smile. "No, Mrs. Graves. Only, there is a very strong familial resemblance between you and your grandson."

"You know Catullus?" One eyebrow arched.

"I accompanied him and Philippa Mallory on my first mission. Catullus was . . . is . . . quite extraordinary." And only a few years younger than Cassandra, yet absurdly accomplished. He'd finished his course of study at university in only two years, and became a full-fledged Blade by his eighteenth birthday.

Sam scowled at her description, and it secretly pleased her that he might be jealous. But she was no coquette, playing one man against another for her own gratification, so she sent Sam a quick, speaking glance indicating that *he* was her only desire.

The smallest of maternal smiles appeared in the corners of Honoria's mouth. "I do believe that boy might be the most talented Graves yet born." Then the smile disappeared. "But don't tell him I said so. He might grow abominably conceited."

Knowing Catullus as Cassandra did, that event seemed unlikely. He was, in fact, a little shy. Still, she replied solemnly, "Of course, Mrs. Graves."

"But this is not Catullus's mission," Honoria continued. "It is up to us to determine what to do with this Source." She considered the small pouch that now sat in the middle of the kitchen table, then gingerly poked it with the tip of one finger.

"After being a Blade for nigh on decades, I'm still baffled how so much power can be contained within such a small space. Defies all scientific principles."

"And moral ones," Sam growled.

"Magic, in and of itself, has no morality, no alignment." Honoria nodded toward the pouch as she sat back. "It is simply a by-product of the human imagination. How it is used, however, rests solely on whomever wields it, for good or for evil. In your case," her gaze gentled slightly, "you were sorely wronged by magic, and though I was not responsible, I *am* sorry."

He frowned, taken aback by her genuine contrition. Cassandra felt her own heart ache, thinking how hard life—or the lack of life—had been for Sam for so long. No one deserved his fate, especially not him.

Could it be undone? The Source's transformation of him? She had never heard of such a thing. True life couldn't be restored once it had been taken away. Nothing had that power.

She gazed down at the remains of her breakfast so he wouldn't see the gathering dampness in her eyes. It wasn't pity she felt, but loss. Of what might have been. But she forced the incipient tears away. It didn't matter what the future held, despite what Sam had said. In whatever form, she would seize her chance to be with him.

"We need to contain this Source's magic," she said, lifting her head and turning to Honoria. "Can you do it?"

She held her breath, expectant.

But Honoria shook her head, remorseful. "The Graves family came from Jamaica and Barbados, not Haiti. *Vodou* arose when the beliefs of slaves taken from West Africa merged with the Catholic faith of their French owners. Similar beliefs are found in Hispaniola, Cuba, and parts of the Southern United States, but not Jamaica and Barbados."

Cassandra's stomach plummeted with disappointment. She wanted to secure the Source and perform her duty to the Blades. And she wanted to have done with Broadwell and his wickedness, see him punished for his sins, so that she and Sam might move on to the next chapter of their lives, whatever that might be. Yet here was another stumbling block.

"That's good enough," Sam said. "It's all in the Caribbean."

"My Jamaican and Barbadian ancestors would twist your ears for that." However, Honoria did not seem overly cross at his assumption. "Where Sources are concerned, furthermore, location is extremely important. A symbiotic relationship exists between the land and its people, each fashioning the other. Each crucial to the formation of magic."

"So, in this case," Cassandra offered, "only someone from Haiti and entrenched within the realm of *vodou* would have a direct link to the Source. Only they could secure it."

"Exactly," Honoria said with an approving nod.

Cassandra tried not to beam as if she'd won the headmistress's prize. Sobering understanding lay beneath her deduction. "Then we *do* have to go to Haiti." A million thoughts scrambled for attention in her mind, not the least of which was how to explain her unchaperoned absence of a few months to her parents. Right now, they believed she was attending a week-long labor rally with friends in Birmingham, and even with this excuse, her parents had held serious misgivings.

She would find a way, though, to get her and Sam to Haiti. She had to. She saw the grim resolve in Sam's face, as well. Truthfully, she could think of few things better than spending weeks alone in a ship's cabin with him. The circumstances could be better, of course, but she couldn't complain about the result.

Yet Honoria Graves's next words both dismayed and heartened Cassandra. "Not so, Miss Fielding. The Graves family is not merely famed for our staggering intelligence. We are also," she smiled, "*extremely* well connected."

Being well-connected, in Honoria Graves's case, meant not exchanging correspondence with the Secretary of the Exchequer, nor did it mean having the local gentry over for games of euchre. It *did* mean knowing an actual Haitian sorcerer, however.

"Fortunately, Achille Voisin lives half a day's ride from me," Honoria informed an astonished Cassandra and Sam, "so you can settle the situation with this Source and *still* be home for tea."

"And this Voisin," Sam said, rising to his feet, "he'll know what to do with the Source."

Both Honoria and Cassandra watched as Sam began to pace the small kitchen, energy and intent emanating out from him in powerful waves.

"If anyone can contain and secure the Source," Honoria answered, "it's Achille. He emigrated from Haiti fifteen years ago, but he's never given up his practice of *vodou*."

Cassandra also got to her feet. "Then we have to leave at once." She shared a nod with Sam and started for the door. "Thank you for breakfast and the information, Mrs. Graves," she said, "and if you'll point us in the right direction—"

"Absolutely not."

Cassandra jerked to a surprised stop and turned to face the older woman, who continued to sit. Yet her tone had been precise and definitive.

Sam took a warning step toward Mrs. Graves. "Tell us where to find Voisin," he rumbled.

With a reproachful glance at Sam and Cassandra's clothing, Honoria sniffed, "I refuse to let you out my front door in that disgraceful condition. You're both covered in grime from the road and you," she said, fixing Sam with her sharp gaze, "are not only encrusted with seawater, but your clothes are on the verge of disintegrating entirely."

Too long familiar with a disapproving mother or governess, Cassandra fidgeted under Honoria's censure. But Sam scowled.

"Haven't given thought to trifles," he gritted.

Shocked disapproval crossed Honoria's regal features. She smoothed her spotless apron over her quietly stylish morning gown. "Major Reed, one's appearance is *never* a trifle. And, as Achille is a good friend of mine, *your* appearance matters to *me*." She elegantly rose to standing.

"But Broadwell, the Heirs—" Cassandra began.

One look from Honoria silenced her. "A matter of a few minutes will not signify. Now, Major Reed, you may use the bedroom on the ground floor, and Miss Fielding, if you'll just follow me upstairs. There are full pitchers and washbasins for the both of you."

Without another word, Honoria sailed past Sam and Cassandra and out of the room.

Cassandra gazed at Sam. He seemed slightly befuddled, this man who fought in a terrible war and faced some of the worst and most daunting conditions ever known. Bewildered by a single woman of advanced years.

"We could just leave," Cassandra suggested.

"Better to have our bearings," he answered. "In the end, we'll save time by waiting a little longer." Then he shook his head, yet seemed admiring. "She should've been an officer. No one would've dared defy her. She could have done wonders."

Cassandra glanced toward the rest of the house, where, even now, the small whirrs and clicks of a hundred precise mechanisms monitored the functioning of Honoria Graves's home. "I think she has," she said.

"*Now*, children," Honoria's voice commanded from the hallway.

By the time they made it out into the hall, Honoria was already climbing the stairs. "To your left, Major Reed," she directed Sam. "Up here, Miss Fielding." Then she strode up the staircase.

Cassandra started to follow, but then stopped when she reached the step that brought her level to Sam. Resting her hands on the banister, she gazed at him, a peculiar reluctance tugging on her heart. Sam stepped close to the railing, so that only a few inches separated their faces.

"Strange," she murmured. "I'm only going upstairs, but I find it hard to separate . . ." A little smile touched her lips, more rueful than amused. "I'm as foolish as a girl again."

Yet the crystalline blue fire in Sam's eyes told her she was not foolish. In them she saw a barely suppressed blaze of hunger and need and something more. His hands covered hers on the banister, and she realized suddenly that the chill had left his body long ago. Even when he'd emerged from the sea, he'd retained his warmth.

She had done that. Warmed him. He was not the icy monster he believed himself to be, not anymore.

He brought his mouth to hers, kissed her softly, until her eyes drifted shut with the sweet pleasure of it.

"I'll be just downstairs," he whispered against her lips. "Waiting for you." Then he stepped back with a flattering amount of reluctance. "Now, go, before General Graves flogs you for insubordination."

Cassandra gave him a salute with a jauntiness she didn't feel. An unnamed fear began to grow inside her—not of Broadwell or the Heirs or the Source—but something shapeless and uncertain. As though she tried to clutch at the rain. Time, she realized, was fleeting. She raced against an unknown adversary. But who? What?

She ascended the stairs. At the top, she felt that strange fear again, and quickly looked back. Sam still stood there, looking up at her with the kind of attention with which a man watched his last sunrise. And then, deliberately, he pushed away from the banister and retreated somewhere into the house.

Inside a sunny, immaculate bedroom, Honoria motioned toward a washstand that held a pitcher, a basin, a cake of soap, and several clean cloths. Also occupying the bedroom was, unsurprisingly, a bed, made up tidily with a homespun quilt and fresh pillows. Only when she saw that bed did Cassandra discover she was exhausted. It looked like a distant paradise, one from which she was barred.

Snapping her attention away from the bed, Cassandra moved toward the washstand.

"You're a grown woman," Honoria said, "so I assume you need no directives here."

"Thank you for your kindness." Cassandra solemnly looked at the other woman, who, in the more direct light of day, revealed more of her age by the fine lines radiating at the corners of her eyes.

Honoria waved her hand airily. "This is what Blades do. We protect Sources. We look out for each other."

"Yes," agreed Cassandra. "But thank you for . . . for Sam." She swallowed hard against a rising knot of emotion. "For treating him like a man,"

"Why shouldn't I?"

"Most people do not."

"Most people are silly creatures who want to destroy what they don't understand. People like *us*," she added with a restrained smile, "are decidedly different. I think," she continued, "it takes someone rather extraordinary to see beyond limitations. To see. And to love."

Cassandra faced Honoria, not allowing herself to shrink from the other woman's close perusal. She confronted not only Honoria Graves, but the truth of her own heart, now given a voice. It had been there all along. She understood that now.

"I do love him," she said. Simple as a vow, just as binding.

Again, the minute gentling of Honoria's face. "I know, child. It doesn't take a scientific genius to see that."

Saying no more, Honoria swept out of the room, shutting the door behind her.

Alone. Outside, birds sang and wind brushed through tree branches. The curtains in this room had not been drawn, so that the room was full of warm yellow sunlight. The first moment in what felt like a lifetime that Cassandra wasn't in the midst of some maelstrom. Yes, Broadwell was somewhere out there, and the Source had to be protected, but in this little bedroom, bathed in light, peaceful morning sounds enveloping the house, she allowed herself a moment's respite.

Slowly, Cassandra peeled down the bodice of her gown, then pushed her chemise to her waist. She poured water into the basin, then dipped a cloth into the water. Over the washstand hung a mirror, and she looked at herself for a moment, the cloth in her hand.

Her hair was a mess—a tangled mass that would require mowing, much less brushing. Purple circles of fatigue rested beneath her eyes. Her skin looked ashen. And yet . . . Sam looked at her as though she was beautiful. More than beautiful. Precious. But not fragile.

Staring at herself, Cassandra saw a new strength in her face. Her fatigue came from fighting important battles, from loving a tragic, courageous man, from proving to herself that she was every bit the woman she wanted to be.

But she couldn't grow complacent. They had to move on. Nothing was certain.

As quickly as she could, Cassandra cleaned herself, rubbing the cloth briskly to reawaken herself. Then she reassembled her clothes.

Once the last button was fastened on the front of her bodice, Cassandra glanced into the mirror again to check her appearance. She piled her hair into something resembling a chignon and used some borrowed pins to hold it in place. Well, she wasn't a French fashion plate, but she wouldn't embarrass Honoria Graves too much.

In the mirror, Cassandra saw the bed's beckoning reflection. She sighed, turning to face it, then found herself drifting closer and closer as if drawn by the siren song of its soft expanse. Without realizing it, she sank down to sit upon its edge and sighed again. Oh, it felt truly wonderful after punishing hours on horseback.

She couldn't help it. She leaned over and rested her head upon the quilt, her eyes growing heavy. Just for a moment, she promised herself. She'd let herself rest here like this for one minute, and then she'd get up, join Sam downstairs, and they'd be off to find the Haitian sorcerer. Soon.

She opened her eyes to find Sam gazing down at her, unmistakable tenderness in his eyes. The sight fanned delicious heat through her. Of its own volition, her hand drifted up to run along the straight, even line of his jaw. He caught her hand and pressed it to his mouth.

"You've had a good rest." His voice was warm and low, an intimate voice reserved for bedrooms.

She blinked at him as hazy details began filtering into her mind. She was now lying on her back, rather than sitting on the edge of the bed. A square of sunlight illuminated the floor—when she'd put her head down, the light had been on the wall and had since moved.

Hell. She'd fallen asleep.

A gasp flew from her mouth. She tried to sit up, but Sam's large hands on her shoulders gently urged her back down.

"Easy," he murmured. "Go slowly or you'll set your head to spinning."

"What time is it? Why did you let me sleep? Oh, damn it, I'm so sor—"

"No apologies." His tone allowed not a single argument. "You were exhausted. Even soldiers need their sleep. Otherwise, they hurt themselves or someone else."

She nodded, even as embarrassment heated her face. She doubted any of Sam's men had dared to fall asleep under his command. As she gathered her thoughts, rousing herself from slumber, she glanced down.

"Your clothes," she said with a trace of wonder.

Sam also looked down at himself, and a self-conscious smile quirked. "Mrs. Graves was appalled by the condition of my clothing. These belong to her grandson. He and I must be of a size. But that's all we share. A bit of a dandy, this Catullus Graves."

Not dandyish, Cassandra would have corrected, had she the means of speaking. She remembered now that Catullus had been rather splendidly dressed over the course of their mission together. But to see the expanse of superbly tailored black wool mold to Sam's broad shoulders, the snowy white shirt and burgundy silk neck cloth, and dark gray trousers—tucked into Sam's scuffed boots, since that size was something the men didn't share—and his dark hair damp and combed back. The sight was mesmerizing. A gorgeously arrayed, lethal animal. In society, Sam would have devastated. Female and male alike. No one would be able to resist him.

She surely could not.

"That is a phenomenal waistcoat," she said instead of blurting out that she loved him. The feeling was too new, too raw, in the midst of uncertainty, and she cradled it against herself as one might shield a young, green bud.

Sam passed a hand down the front of the silver vest that perfectly displayed his muscular torso. The surface of the waistcoat was covered with silk Florentine embroidery, as opulent as a Medici palace but infinitely more inviting. All Cassandra wanted to do was pluck open the silver buttons running down the front of the waistcoat and run her hands all over him.

"Told Mrs. Graves not to lend me such fine clothing," he muttered. "Clothes have a tendency to be destroyed when I wear them. But she wouldn't accept anything but acquiescence. I feel . . . ridiculous." He grimaced.

She interlaced her fingers behind his neck and tugged him down. They came together in a heated, open kiss.

A marvelous torment—kissing him while lying on a bed. They hadn't had the privilege of a bed, yet. She could see them losing days, weeks, and months in bed together. Nothing but time and soft mattresses as they explored their passion.

"When all this is over," she gasped, pulling back, "I will buy you a suit of clothes just like this one and demand you make love to me while fully dressed. You are *delicious*. In these clothes. And out of them."

His chuckle was part laughter, part animal growl. Then it trailed away as a darker thought occurred to them both simultaneously.

There might not be a time for them when this mission was over. They might not survive the inevitable clash with Broadwell. And if, by some miracle, they did defeat him, and secure the Source. . . . That nameless fear came back to her in a rush, the sense that something was slipping away.

They unwillingly disentangled, and Cassandra sat up with Sam's help. For a moment, the room tilted as she regained her balance, but then she felt herself steady enough to stand. The clock on the mantle showed that she'd been asleep for four hours. Not nearly enough, but it would have to do, for now.

Together, they made their way downstairs. Honoria waited for them outside, on the front walkway, with a little basket.

"More food," she said. "And I've changed your horses. Always thought keeping two was a needless expense, but it's proven itself worthwhile today." When both Sam and Cassandra started to thank her, Honoria held up a hand. "Please. No unnecessary protestations of gratitude. I find such sentiment excessively wearisome."

She then gave them directions to Achille Voisin's cottage, with brisk advisement to stay off the main roads. "But I'm sure you already know that, Major Reed."

"Yes, madam." Sam gave her a crisp military bow, then took her hand and brought it to his lips. "Your servant, Mrs. Graves."

Even Honoria Graves could not entirely resist the sight of a darkly handsome, beautifully dressed Sam gallantly kissing her hand. She actually blushed.

"Yes . . . well . . ." She recovered enough to say, "That's enough of that." Then pulled her hand away, clearing her throat at the same time.

Smiling enigmatically, Sam strode off to see to the horses, leaving Cassandra alone with Honoria.

From a pocket in her apron, Honoria produced a small vial, stopped with red wax. Pale green liquid filled the vial.

"Take this." She pressed the vial into Cassandra's hand. "For future battles. Should you find yourself in a difficult situation, throw the vial at your aggressors. And, for God's sake, stay out of the way."

Cassandra took the vial and slipped it into her pocket, wondering what effect it might have. She was both curious and afraid to find out. "I won't thank you again. But I understand now why the Graves family has been the cornerstone of the Blades of the Rose. And not only for their technological contributions."

Honoria studied her for a moment, moving over Cassandra's face with her assessing gaze that missed nothing. Then she nodded. "You'll go far, child. If you hold on to your courage. For you and him, both."

Cassandra sank into a curtsey, absorbing Honoria's words. When she rose, the older woman handed her the basket of food and glided into the house without a backward glance.

Drawing a deep breath, Cassandra turned and followed Sam. Each step away from Honoria Graves's home brought her closer to what she knew would be a final reckoning.

Chapter Eight

Honoria Graves's warnings only confirmed what Sam already knew. As he and Cassandra rode toward the *vodou* sorcerer, they stayed on bridle paths and dirt tracks crossing fields and wooded glades. The day was sunny and mild, heralding the oncoming summer and its lush abundance. Hay grasses scented the air. Sheep bleated to one another. A lovely English pastoral.

To Sam, the warm afternoon sun only indicated time of day and position. Hay grasses and sheep meant that somewhere nearby was a farm, and the likelihood of being noted and followed by whomever might dwell there. He scanned the trees and fields constantly, vigilant for any signs of Broadwell, the Heirs of Albion, or anyone else who meant to take the Source and hurt Cassandra.

"Give me the Source," he said to her now. They were proceeding through a stand of trees.

"I've already said no." She didn't glance over at him as they rode side-by-side, but her hand strayed to the pocket in her skirt that held the Source.

"You'll be safer if I'm carrying it."

"I am a Blade, which means that the responsibility of protecting the Source belongs to *me*."

"And the responsibility of protecting *you* belongs to *me*," he growled.

She did look at him then, and he saw it in her eyes, the flash of emotion that she quickly tried to hide. Ever since they'd left Honoria Graves, a shawl of unease hung about Cassandra's shoulders, which would make sense. Broadwell lurked, his threat ever present. Yet it seemed as if more troubled Cassandra than the danger of the Heirs of Albion. Whenever she gazed at Sam, he saw it.

"No it doesn't," she answered, so softly he hardly heard her above the beat of the horses' hooves.

He understood—it was *him*. *He* troubled her. She must have come to the realization that they had no hope together, and sought a way to distance herself from him. He'd come to the same conclusion, himself, vowing that once the Source had been secured, he'd make certain to disappear from her life so she might have some kind of future.

Having her decide to leave him, however, hurt like a son of a bitch.

One couldn't feel noble and self-sacrificing without the object of one's sacrifice giving a damn.

Sam was nobody's hero—not Cassandra's, and sure as hell not his own. He'd almost believed he wasn't the monster he knew himself to be. Brief delusion and stupidity.

But he still meant to protect Cassandra, whether she wanted his protection or not. No matter what she felt for him, she meant *everything* to him.

They emerged from the trees into a shaded, open glade. "Cass," he began.

Something large and heavy flew at him from the shelter of the trees surrounding the glade. Sam drew his pistol, but it slammed into Sam before he could turn and fire, knocking him off his horse. Both he and the *thing* smashed into the ground. The smell of stagnant, musty water assailed him.

Dimly, he heard Cassandra shouting, sounds of men approaching on horseback, but he could do nothing but tumble over and over, locked in combat with . . . with . . .

A monster. Sam shoved his hands against its throat, forcing its head back as it raked his face with its claws. The creature snarled and snapped with jagged, greenish teeth, its eyes the size and color of yellow lamps. It had a vaguely human female form, only enormous and covered with skin like gray India rubber. Its long green hair tangled around them both like sentient weeds, wrapping about Sam's arms and legs.

He twisted to get free. Extracting himself from the damp, clinging hair, he pushed back, knocking the creature away and gaining his feet. For his trouble, he received a gash across his shoulder and down his arm. The beast rolled down a small hill and splashed into a rocky creek.

A foul curse ripped from Sam as he stood. He'd been pulled to the far side of the glade. Cassandra was on foot, thirty yards away, surrounded by three men.

One of the men was Broadwell.

The bastard advanced toward her while his companions looked on, jeering. She had her pistol drawn, even though she knew it wouldn't do her much good.

The two other men were ordinary mortals, expensively dressed, with the refined looks that came from painstaking breeding among the wealthy and elite. Still, they were also armed with guns and looked more than eager to use them.

"You've one chance to save yourself and Reed," Broadwell rasped. "Give me the Source."

"Go to hell," Cassandra replied.

"Not for a long time." Broadwell grinned. The other men laughed.

Sam drew his sword. He charged across the glade toward Broadwell, closing the distance.

Nearly halfway there. Something grabbed his ankle and he pitched forward, then was dragged back. He darted a look behind him. The monster had climbed up from the creek, scrabbling after him, and reached out with arms twelve feet long, twice as long as its body. It clutched his ankle with webbed, arachnid fingers. Sam cursed and swung with his sword, but the blade only glanced off the creature's thick hide.

Broadwell's taunt cut across the glade. "Enjoy playing with

Nellie Long-Arms, Reed. She has a taste for flesh, even if it isn't alive."

"Sam!" Cassandra shouted. Not with fear, but anger. She started toward him, but was forced back by Broadwell and his cronies closing on her.

Sam clawed at the ground as the creature pulled him closer. A flash of remembrance, nursery stories about boggarts that dwelt in ponds and lakes, waiting to grab hold of unwary boys and girls and drag them down to watery deaths. He'd dismissed those stories as tales to keep adventurous children away from the water. But, somehow, the Heirs had conjured a real water boggart. And if Sam didn't break away from it, he'd never be able to protect Cassandra.

Closer to those jagged, mossy teeth and ravening mouth. The undead could be killed either by beheading or a direct wound to the brain. But dismemberment and digestion probably had the same effect. He didn't want to give that a test.

His sword proved useless. And he'd lost his pistol when the monster tackled him.

He threw another glance at Cassandra, growing smaller as the monster dragged him away. He'd fight his way back to her, through hell if he had to. And, judging by the creature's gaping, stench-filled maw opening to receive him, he just might.

"Call that beast off," Cassandra hissed, "or I'll—"

"*What*, Miss Fielding?" Broadwell gloated as he eyed her pistol. "That can't hurt me."

"Not *you*." She spun and fired at one of the other Heirs, a thin sandy-haired man. Just as she did, Broadwell leapt toward her, knocking her pistol up. The bullet grazed the shoulder of her intended target.

"The bitch shot me," the thin man whined, clutching his shoulder.

"Just a scratch, Purley," snapped Broadwell.

Scratch or no, it gave Cassandra enough of a distraction to dart between Broadwell and the second Heir, a thickset man with dark, bushy mutton-chop whiskers. She ran across the glade toward Sam.

She had to help him, however she could. She hadn't seen much magic during her short tenure with the Blades, certainly no creature like that slimy, grotesque beast attacking Sam. As he tried to beat the thing back with his fists and the butt of his officer's sword, she thought frantically of all the things she'd been taught when first initiated into the Blades.

Magical creatures usually had some kind of a weakness. One tiny thing that could bring them down. But the possibilities were endless.

Think, *think*. Some faerie beings feared iron. Cassandra had none on her. What else?

She thanked her foresight that she had forgone layers of petticoats as she sped across the glade. Bullets from the Heirs' guns sped past her, chipping into the ground while she ran. As she neared, she saw the monster grappling with Sam, tearing at him. Its attention was focused only on him.

Thus distracted, Cassandra ran up directly behind the thing. The closer she got, the uglier and more terrifying it appeared. Yet she did not hesitate to grab hold of its hair, pulling with every ounce of strength, tugging so hard her arms shook. The smell of dank water inundated her, nearly making her gag.

More shots rang out. Cassandra ducked as bullets bounced off the boggart's rubbery skin.

Cassandra pulled harder on the creature's hair. It shrieked in pain. One of its long arms shot out and knocked into her, sending her tumbling. Pebbles scraped across her cheek. Cassandra held onto its hair, however, and felt a satisfying rip. The monster shrieked again as a chunk of its scalp tore free.

Sam had sufficient opening to leap to his feet. He started toward Cassandra, but the beast blocked him. He swung his sword, avoiding the creature's flailing arms, and aiming for its eyes. "Get the hell out of here!" he snarled at Cassandra.

"Don't be an ass!" she shouted back. She tossed aside the clump of writhing hair, then aimed her pistol at the creature.

"Nothing penetrates its skin," Sam yelled. "Hold your fire!"

Fire. That was it!

"You have a powder horn?" she called.

He frowned, dodging the now-upright creature's thrashing arms and gnashing teeth. "Yes."

"Throw it!"

"What?" He nimbly leapt to the side as the beast swiped at him.

"Throw your powder horn at its feet!" She saw he was about to argue more, just as she saw Broadwell and the other Heirs running toward them. "Do it *now!*"

Still frowning, Sam dug the powder horn out of his coat and lobbed it so that it landed between the beast's long, claw-tipped feet.

"Get back!" Cassandra shouted.

He saw what she meant to do, and started backing up. But the beast still wanted him. It surged forward, moving away from the powder horn. Cassandra cursed. If the creature wasn't immediately over the gunpowder, the chances of her plan working shrank to nothing.

The Heirs jogged toward them and readied their pistols.

Two threats converging—the monster and the Heirs. She and Sam couldn't fight them at the same time. Something would have to be dealt with first, but what? And how?

Sam took all of this in within an instant. He immediately launched into an attack on the monster. His sword slashed out in a series of expert strikes. The creature reared back under the assault, bellowing.

Forcing the monster backward, Sam continued his attack, evading its retaliatory swipes. With consummate skill, Sam maneuvered the thing until it stood once more directly above the powder horn.

"Fire!" he shouted.

She hesitated, fearing that she'd hurt him.

"Do it," Sam yelled.

Drawing back the gun's hammer, Cassandra aimed her pistol at the dropped powder horn. When she had purchased her gun, she'd practiced shooting with a paper target and hadn't had the best luck controlling the weapon's aim and recoil. A small container holding gunpowder between the feet of an enraged water beast was a far cry from a large paper target on a hay bale. A quick prayer went up to whatever deity chose to listen. She let out her breath, then held it in the middle of her exhalation.

And fired.

The kick of the pistol pushed her back. But she regained her footing just as the bullet pierced the powder horn. At that same moment, Sam dove to the side. The monster took its huge, sulfurous eyes from him and looked down. It opened its enormous mouth to scream.

Cassandra rocked back again as the horn detonated. Bright flame radiated outward in an explosion.

The creature exploded at the same time.

It blew apart wetly, chunks of gray flesh and green hair flying in all directions.

But Sam, Sam was safe.

Everyone—Sam, Cassandra, even the Heirs—shielded themselves from the rain of viscera and limbs. If Cassandra hadn't been so pleased by the result, she might have cast up her breakfast. But the creature was dead and couldn't hurt her or Sam, or anyone else, so she swallowed her disgust.

To give herself something more pleasant to focus on, she gazed at Sam as he picked himself up off the ground. True to his word, his borrowed finery was now torn, stained with bits of water monster; the knees of his trousers bore grass stains. Cuts and slashes covered him. But, to her, he couldn't have been more handsome.

He stared at the powder burn on the ground, then looked over at her, wearing an expression of amazement and admiration. And . . . desire.

Her blood immediately heated in response. She loved that a show of her strength aroused him, so unlike most men.

Broadwell and the other Heirs gaped at the remains of what once had been their unfair advantage. When Sam turned and gave them a feral grin, the two men standing beside Broadwell visibly blanched.

Sam leapt between the Heirs and Cassandra, his drawn sword gleaming in the afternoon sunlight. "Let's try this again."

Broadwell hadn't his cronies' fear. Sam would grant the bastard that much. His former commanding officer barreled toward him, sword upraised. Sam moved to protect Cassandra, shielding her from Broadwell's attack and bringing up his own sword in a defensive block.

The force of their swords clashing against each other brought sparks. Gritting his teeth fiercely, Sam disengaged from Broadwell's block and swung again. This time, his blade hit home. A gaping wound slashed from Broadwell's throat down to his abdomen.

Had Broadwell been a mortal man, such a wound would've dropped him where he stood and he would bleed to death. But he wasn't. Through the tear in Broadwell's clothing, Sam saw the enormous cut already begin to close.

Broadwell spun and stabbed Sam straight through the thigh. Unlike a living man, Sam didn't spray blood or buckle from the pain. Instead, his blade sliced across the side of Broadwell's head.

His opponent made a guttural sound as his left ear and a goodly chunk of his face dropped to the ground. Within minutes, Sam knew, the ear and skin would regenerate while the severed flesh in the grass would turn to dust.

Sam would make sure that Broadwell's lifeless body also crumbled to dust—before this day was through.

He and Broadwell slammed together, crossing swords, both snarling.

"A losing fight, Reed," Broadwell rasped. "The Heirs always win."

"Not today."

Sam broke away to slice at Broadwell's arm, but his move was parried. They fell back, then came together again, the sound of ringing steel sharp in the glade.

"Yes, let's play a little longer," Broadwell sneered. "While my friends take the Source from your whore. I think they're enjoying themselves," he added idly, glancing over Sam's shoulder.

He's trying to get into my mind again, Sam thought. *Break my concentration*. But, damn it, it worked.

Sam cast a quick look behind him. Fury shot through him. The two other Heirs closed in on Cassandra, and the looks on the men's faces left no doubt as to what they planned on doing with her once the Source was theirs.

Bellowing in rage, Sam started toward her. Then stopped and looked down when he felt Broadwell's sword pierce his shoulder straight through, right above the collarbone. He was skewered, but could only think of Cassandra, facing two enemies on her own.

Had to get to her. Had to protect her. No matter what.

"Damn," Broadwell muttered, drawing his sword out of Sam's body. "Just a little higher." And he swung again.

Perhaps she'd led something of a sheltered life. Yet Cassandra could not imagine anything more horrible than the sight of Sam and Broadwell slashing at each other in vicious combat, absorbing wounds that would have killed a living man.

Only decapitation could kill Sam, she reminded herself, but she couldn't stop her wincing in agony every time Broadwell cut deeply into Sam. At least Sam gave as brutally as he received.

As the two other Heirs stalked her, both with pistols drawn, she backed toward the trees surrounding the glade. When the men drew nearer, she darted between the tree trunks. A bullet whizzed past her, but she kept on running farther into the shelter of the forest, with the Heirs in fast pursuit. She ducked behind a tree in time to dodge another shot. Splinters of wood pelted her as a bullet slammed into the trunk.

She leaned around the tree long enough to fire back. Her shot went wide, but it forced the Heirs back so that they had to take their own cover.

Her heart throbbed in her throat. No one had ever shot at her before. Yet she couldn't lose herself to fear.

Bullets whined through the forest as she and the Heirs exchanged gunfire. Cassandra winced when the thin Heir, the one called Purley, shot at her and she actually felt the heat of the bullet speed past her face. Two of them—twice as many guns—and only one of her.

"I've my own score to settle," snarled Purley. He gripped his injured shoulder. "No woman hurts me without getting something worse in return. Just watch me destroy this bitch, Tolland."

He darted forward and Cassandra shot. But her aim was no good, and he was too fast, because her bullet slammed uselessly into the ground. As he sped toward her, narrowing the two dozen feet between them, he aimed and fired.

A blur darted forward, intercepting the bullet.

Cassandra clapped a hand over her mouth. Sam. He'd run between her and Purley's gun. The bullet pierced right below Sam's ribs, yet he only grunted slightly from the impact.

"Hurt?" he demanded, whirling to face her.

Stunned, she shook her head. Then found her voice in time to cry out, "Behind you!"

Sam ducked just as Broadwell's sword slashed out. The blade narrowly missed the top of Sam's head and lodged itself into a nearby tree. Broadwell swore violently as he pried his sword from the trunk.

With one final, fierce glance in her direction, Sam charged toward Broadwell. The two undead men plunged back into their battle. They continued trading strikes and crossing swords, edging out of the woods and into the clearing.

Purley had ducked behind a tree to avoid Sam, but now the Heir crept toward her again. She fired, but her aim still wanted. So she shot again—or tried to. A clicking sound told her that her pistol was now empty and useless. There wasn't time to reload.

Her head whipped up to see that the other Heir, Tolland, had used the distraction of Purley's gunfire to come around and flank her. Tolland raised his pistol.

Cassandra dove down to the ground, but instead of gunfire,

she heard another click. Peering up, she saw Tolland scowling at his empty pistol.

She shoved herself back to her feet, then fumbled in her pocket. Her hand clenched around a small vial. With all her strength, she threw the vial at the Heir.

It shattered against his chest, splattering him with green liquid. Hissing, he looked down at the large, sticky stain. He plucked at his clothing.

"What is this? An acid?"

If it was, it wasn't very effective. His clothes and skin did not dissolve. In fact, nothing happened.

Both Heirs began to laugh. Cassandra's heart sank. Damn! Whatever Honoria's concoction was supposed to do, it hadn't worked.

Now Purley came forward as an emboldened Tolland produced a long, wicked knife. He brandished it with a grin. "Mine, now, little Blade slut." He stalked toward her.

Cassandra scurried around the tree at her back. The Heirs' laughter ceased abruptly as buzzing filled the air. The sound came faintly at first, but then grew louder and louder, growing in intensity, until the noise deafened. Cassandra fought the urge to cover her ears, even though it felt as though the piercing sound went straight through her head.

"What the blazes is that?" demanded Purley.

"Oh, hell," said Tolland weakly.

From deeper in the woods emerged a thick black cloud. It shot straight toward Tolland.

He started pulling at his clothing. Too late. The cloud descended on him, and he screamed. "Jesus! Bees!"

Both Cassandra and Purley backed off as thousands and thousands of bees alit all over Tolland, stinging him. The Heir opened his mouth to scream, and more bees flew in, stinging the inside of his mouth. Tolland dropped his knife as he waved his arms maniacally, but the bees continued to attack, clinging to the attractant covering his clothes and skin. Through the haze of thronging bees, Cassandra could just make out Tolland's red swelling face and hands. He could barely open his eyes.

Shrieking, dancing about in a frenzy, Tolland broke into a run. The swarming bees pursued, even as he dashed farther into the trees. His screams and the buzzing died off into the distance.

Well—Cassandra would have to report back to Honoria that her invention was a roaring success.

Purley watched Tolland go with a look of horror combined with a flicker of relief that it wasn't *him* being attacked by a countless multitude of bees. Then he turned to Cassandra with hate in his eyes.

"You don't fight fair, bitch," he spat.

"But using water monsters and exploiting Sources is altogether sporting," she answered.

"Fine. We'll do this sportingly."

He aimed his pistol between her eyes.

Sam feinted, catching the tip of Broadwell's sword just across his throat. He resisted the urge to touch his fingertips to the cut. So close . . .

A curse from Broadwell. And a redoubling of effort. Met with equal intensity.

Under the shade of the trees, they fought, each swinging their weapons in purposeful, ruthless arcs. Cold fury gleamed in Broadwell's eyes as he and Sam clashed.

"Always *you*," Broadwell snarled between blows. "Even before I changed you. Challenging me at every turn, questioning my command."

"You were never fit to be an officer," Sam said. "The men meant nothing to you."

Broadwell scoffed. "Why should they? Pawns on the chessboard. Only victory for England matters."

"They had *lives*. You took that from them. From us."

Broadwell bared his teeth. "You were ever a sodding thorn in my side."

"Just a brief pain in your neck," Sam said. "Then it'll all be over."

Broadwell's retort was lost in a thunderous buzzing. Both

their swords paused as the most enormous, angry swarm of bees Sam had ever seen came hurtling through the trees. It engulfed one of the Heirs close to Cassandra.

Broadwell gaped as his comrade screeched and ran, the bees in close pursuit.

Sam had no idea what Cassandra had done to call forth the bees and whip them into a stinging frenzy, but whatever she'd done, he wanted to call out his praise to her. Broadwell didn't share Sam's pleasure. Seeing the ignominious defeat of his fellow Heir, Broadwell grew even more enraged. Yet nothing could top the hate Sam felt for this bastard, who'd stolen everything, ruined hundreds of lives, including Sam's own.

He and Broadwell smashed together. One of them, Sam knew without doubt, would not leave this glade.

Cassandra faced the Heir, Purley, staring down the barrel of his gun. Her mind churned as time both slowed and sped.

"Give me the Source," Purley barked, "and I'll kill you quickly."

"Not much of an inducement."

"Then I'll take it from you and make you beg for death."

Without moving her head, she glanced around quickly. There had to be something . . . something. She could try for the knife Tolland had dropped, but that was risky, since the knife lay midway between her and Purley. Attempting to grab the knife would bring her too close, only increasing the likelihood that he'd shoot her at close range. "I'll take the third option."

"There is no third option," retorted the Heir.

But there *was* something. The very thing she needed to protect could give her precisely what she needed.

"As you wish." With a sigh and bent head, she took the Source from her pocket and showed it to Purley. "This is what you want."

His eyes lit greedily as he swayed closer. "Yes."

"Come, then, and take it."

She held the Source out, stepping closer. Purley narrowed the distance.

Cassandra threw the Source into the air.

"Bitch!" He looked up, stretching an arm overhead to reach the Source, the gun in his other hand momentarily forgotten.

She ran forward and, interlacing her fingers, brought her hands up as hard as she could into the underside of Purley's chin. A sharp pain rattled her, but it was nothing like the jolt that ran through Purley. His whole body shuddered. He stumbled, trying to regain his footing, and Cassandra plowed her fists right into his nose.

Blood shot from his nostrils as his bones crunched. Then he fell to the ground, unmoving.

"That's the third option," she said.

Cassandra stared down at him while shaking out her aching hands. She thought of the teasing Charlie made her endure, the dirty fighting techniques she'd had to learn as a result, and she silently thanked her brother for being such a nuisance throughout their childhood.

Even in death, he'd helped to save her life.

She quickly grabbed the Source from where it had fallen in the grass, then retrieved the knife and plucked the pistol from the unconscious man's hand. For a moment, she wavered. A seasoned soldier would put a bullet through his brain, but she was not a seasoned soldier. She couldn't kill in cold blood—not even a man who would have readily done the same to her.

A nudge from her boot proved Purley was truly unconscious. She would have to think what to do with him. Throwing him off a cliff sounded extremely appealing.

The glade filled with the sound of steel against steel. Cassandra hurried to the edge of the woods and gulped with true terror to see Sam and Broadwell battle back and forth, trading blows without mercy. Both men were swathed in cuts and lacerations, their clothing barely held together. A sickly nub was all that marked where Broadwell's left ear should be, and his cheek was a grotesque expanse of unformed flesh. The wounds enveloping Sam all showed to be in different stages of repair, including the one across Sam's throat.

She saw in the way Sam fought that this was more than a simple duel—it was three years of vengeance. This was everything or nothing.

Though she wanted to call out to him, Cassandra knew Sam needed all his concentration focused on this one goal. *Yet she could help.*

Cassandra raised Purley's gun and aimed.

Neither Sam nor Broadwell could tire. Nothing short of decapitation could kill them. Sam had an endless supply of rage fueling him. Broadwell hungered covetously for power.

This battle could stretch on forever.

Another kind of hell, locked eternally in combat with Sam's most hated enemy. Broadwell had taken Sam's life, but Sam wouldn't allow him to steal anything more. He refused to surrender. Not only for the demands of justice, but because, if anything happened to Sam, Cassandra would be alone and vulnerable.

As their swords met again and again, Broadwell noticed Sam's quick glance toward Cassandra emerging from the forest. A rapacious smile twisted his mouth.

"Never thought you a fool, Reed," he sneered. "You could have immortality, unlimited power. Instead, your lusts have made you weak."

"Not lust." Sam blocked a strike and spun to make his own, which Broadwell barely countered. "Something better than that. And it's made me stronger."

Broadwell's laugh was a hard bark. "Doubt it. When I finally take your head, I think I'll keep your whore for myself, transform her. Then she'll do *exactly* as I desire." He licked his lips.

Though rage nearly blinded Sam, he fought it back as strongly as he battled his enemy. Broadwell counted on manipulating him through his feelings for Cassandra—just as he'd commanded him to perform unspeakable acts years ago. But Cassandra had shown Sam he was more than a thing to be controlled, more than a puppet pulled on the strings of revenge.

What remained of his life belonged to *him*.

Sam pushed himself, intensifying his attack until Broadwell had no choice but to begin defensively edging away.

A bullet slammed into Broadwell's neck. The force caused him to stumble.

Sam whipped his head around to see Cassandra standing at the edge of the woods with a smoking pistol in her hands. She held his gaze.

Taking advantage of the distraction, Sam lunged and struck against the backs of Broadwell's legs, severing the muscles. They'd regenerate, but not immediately, and Broadwell stumbled as his legs collapsed beneath him.

Broadwell cursed foully. From a kneeling position, he swung his sword in wild, frenetic arcs, knowing he'd lost parity.

Stepping forward, Sam neatly deflected the strikes. He felt himself grow suddenly very calm as he raised his own sword. A strange, profound stillness.

Broadwell looked up at Sam, at Sam's blade glinting in the sunlight. His eyes widened, and a look of true fear distorted his face.

"You'll have a lot to answer for, where you're going," said Sam. "Tell them who sent you." And he brought his sword down.

Broadwell's head rolled across the grass, the expression of terror still on his face. His body dropped to the ground with a thud.

Moving back, Sam gazed down at his enemy's body. He felt no sense of relief, completion, or triumph. It was over. The nightmare of the last three years was done. And he felt numb and cold.

"Sam!"

He looked up to see Cassandra dashing toward him. She was a little scraped, a bit fatigued, her hair coming down and dust covering her clothes. And so beautiful, running to his opening arms.

That's when it came, like a hawk breaking free of its jesses. The realization hit that vengeance brought him nothing. But there was another burst of emotion so powerful, it nearly made him stagger. Sam saw this new emotion for what it was.

Love.

She raced toward him, needing to feel his solid, true presence, his arms around her, her own entwined around him. All she saw was Sam, tall and straight and eager for her.

Yet as she neared, he suddenly darted to one side. He leapt right past her, his sword upraised, icy fury etched across his handsome face.

Cassandra spun around. She couldn't stop her gasp of surprise.

Purley stood only feet behind her, his hands upraised as if to grab her, gaping in shock as he saw Sam's blade plunged directly into his heart. A growing red stain spread across his chest. Then he slid off the steel and onto the ground.

Sam withdrew his sword and dispassionately wiped it on the grass. He sheathed it before turning to her.

She found herself pulled fiercely into his strong arms, and she gripped him just as tightly.

After a moment, they silently moved away from the bodies of Purley and Broadwell to a patch of sunlit, clean grass, untouched by violence.

In this small island of light, Cassandra and Sam wrapped their arms around each other—a hold so tight, they nearly fused into one being. They each absorbed what had just happened, how close they'd come to losing one another, and how they had *both* come to each other's aid.

"Sam," she breathed. Just saying his name was a balm to her heart. "My courageous soldier."

"Cass. My fearless lady."

He tipped her head back and kissed her deeply. She wasn't certain if he trembled, or she did, or if they both shook. It didn't matter. They were here together and the sensation of each being held by the other overrode all delineations of self.

Vicious water monsters. Swarming bees. Murderous Heirs. None of that shook her as profoundly, as completely, as this man. Her warrior. Her lover. *Hers.*

Chapter Nine

She felt herself suspended in a dream, and yet she never felt more alive, more awake, than she was at that moment. As she and Sam continued riding on toward the sorcerer Voisin, her mind drifted miles back to the glade. It had been a pleasant patch of sun-dappled grass; it became a place of vengeance, a proving ground.

Both she and Sam had emerged safely. The Source rested in her pocket, and soon, no one would be able to exploit or misuse it again. Her second mission for the Blades of the Rose was almost complete.

With that nearing goal, resolution took hold.

They cantered down a lonely road into increasingly isolated stretches of country. Voisin had selected for himself a place of seclusion, far from railroad lines, and, in truth, other human habitation. Tall trees lined the road—more of a slight depression in the earth than a road—and the setting sun threw a veil of purple shadow across the land. Night would follow soon.

Cassandra pulled up on the reins of her horse, slowing. Sam, with a puzzled frown, did the same.

"What is it?" He looked around, immediately on alert. "More Heirs?"

She shook her head. Saying nothing, she guided her horse off the road, into the dense forest. Trusting Sam to follow her.

He did. Almost as if he understood what she wanted, what she meant to do. Energy thrummed through her body as she picked her way through the woods and heard Sam behind her. She did not know precisely where she was going, only that she would know her destination when she reached it.

Instinct told her when and where to dismount. Somewhere deep in the forest. A trickling stream chimed nearby. Soft bracken covered the ground. She tied her horse to a sapling and waited as Sam did the same. Her heart raced, its pace matching in intensity how she'd felt during the battle with the Heirs.

This wasn't battle, but the stakes were just as high.

Sam finished tethering his horse and unslinging his sword from his back, then turned to face her. Almost cautious—such a contrast from the bold warrior he'd been less than an hour earlier. Yet something about *her* caused him to hesitate, as if he doubted the reception he would receive.

She let her eyes move over him in a bold perusal. No dissembling. She wanted him, and let her face show this truth.

Registering this, he strode to her with an expression of dark hunger. She saw that his numerous wounds were repaired, with only a few faint lines indicating where they had been. His clothes, however, hadn't the same power. They hung on him in tatters, but it provided her with glimpses of his skin, his sculpted muscles that she wanted to touch and lick and learn as intimately as she knew her own self.

They met in a devastating kiss, both ferocious and tender. His hands journeyed all over her back, then lower, cupping the curves of her arse and hauling her close to him. She let her own hands roam over him, savoring his taut muscles, the need that vibrated through his tight body.

"Wild woman," he murmured into her mouth. His deep voice sent waves of desire through her. "Danger excites you."

She realized this was true. Once the fear dissipated, arousal took its place. "No wonder I was never suited to being a gentleman's wife. Nothing dangerous or exciting about planning a dinner party."

"Depends on the guests."

"And what you're serving." She slid her hand down his broad chest, then lower to stroke his hard length through his trousers. He hissed in appreciation. "*This* will be delicious."

She drew her hand away, and his lust-glazed eyes tried to focus on her. "But it's more than the aftermath of danger that makes me want you now."

He struggled to clear his mind, gazing down at her. A growing understanding sharpened his attention, and he looked wary but intrigued. "More," he said.

"Sam." She stared into his eyes, knowing her own were unreserved, unguarded. "I love you."

For a bare moment, hope and need flared in his gaze, before he glanced away. His whole body tensed, and a muscle in his jaw tightened. "You shouldn't."

This was not precisely the response she'd been hoping for, nor was it entirely surprising. She gripped his chin and turned him back to look at her. "I will say this one more time. *I don't care what you are.*"

"An undead monster."

She resisted the impulse to scream in frustration. "All that matters to me is *who* you are. Sam Reed. Not the boy I chased after. Not the fantasy of a lover. Not the living dead. *You.* Honorable. Courageous. Passionate. The only man who has ever fully accepted me for who I am."

"You deserve someone who accepts you." Azure fire lit his gaze. His voice deepened further to a low rumble. "Had I been anything else, I would have claimed you for my own."

Heat flooded her. "I want to be yours. And I want you to belong to me, and me alone."

"Damn it, I can't do that to you." He broke from their embrace to stalk away. "You say you don't care what I am—"

"I don't."

He went on, shouldering her words aside. "But the rest of the world does. You've seen it yourself. I terrify people. They don't even have to know that I'm undead—they hate and fear me. I can't stay anywhere for too long. I have to live in darkness. I've no home. No family. Not even a goddamned heart-beat." He rounded on her, savage. "And I bloody well *refuse* to subject you to that kind of life. You need better than that."

She marched up to him. "Presumptuous bastard! Don't *dare* tell me what I need. That is *my* choice. Not anyone's. Including yours."

"Stubborn," he growled.

"And honest," she countered. "Good thing, too. When I say that I love you and want us to belong to each other, then *I sure as hell mean it*."

They glared at each other, panting with anger and . . . desire.

She shook her head. Leading Sam to this remote corner of the forest was not about anger or self-denial.

Her black humor fell away as she might cast aside a brittle husk. He saw this, and his own expression cleared to something waiting, marveling.

Sliding her arms around his neck, rising up onto the tips of her toes, she whispered, "Let me show you."

He held himself back. Only a moment, then his hands came up to stroke along her arms, reverent. At his touch, her desire grew yet stronger, gathering within.

Drawn together by mutual need, they kissed. Not the ravenous consuming of earlier, but slowly, savoring each other's tastes and textures. A leisurely exploration, yet no less hungry. Lingering, thorough discovery, and she felt in herself and him the demands to let their mouths and hands and bodies demonstrate precisely how much they needed, wanted, each other.

They pulled and pushed at one another's clothing. The sensation of bare skin to skin became essential. Each layer fell away, dropping to the ground in whispered folds, and, as garments disappeared and flesh emerged, she touched and caressed Sam everywhere, just as he ran his hands over her body. Exalting and carnal.

Together, they stood naked in the forest.

"I love the feel of you," he growled, gathering her uncovered breasts in his hands. He bent his head and licked the peak. She felt his wet touch all the way down between her legs. "I love the taste of you." His tongue swirled over her nipple.

Her fingers threaded into his thick, dark hair, drawing him closer, ablaze with pleasure. As he continued to tease and lap at her breasts, she became both languorous and demanding. Her hands played over the bunching muscles in his shoulders, down his back, even stroking the tight curves of his buttocks. He was hard and satiny, and everywhere she touched him, he warmed further, just as she heated.

Against her stomach, his cock curved, firm and full. Answering slickness grew within her. He could do that to her— call forth her richest arousal, the likes of which she'd known only with him.

He'd given her more than arousal. He had awakened the fullest essence of who she was meant to be, and her heart ached with abundance.

She gently moved him back from her breasts. "I will taste you, too." And when she knelt before him, the bright blue fire of his gaze told her how much he needed, wanted.

Cassandra gazed at his cock, thick and reaching upward, and a smile of appreciation curved her mouth. She had touched it with her hand, felt it within her body, and knew it—Sam— gave her the most profound pleasure she'd ever experienced. She loved this part of him, as she loved all his body, but this distillation of his most masculine self made her want to worship him like a pagan, celebrate the flesh and all the life it represented.

She looked up at him. He was all things hard and hungry, male. And hers. *Hers.*

When she grasped him in her hand, he groaned. And when she took him in her mouth, hoarse, guttural sounds broke from him. He shook. She dipped her head lower, taking more of him into her mouth, stroking her tongue along his shaft, and the feel was exquisite. He tasted luscious, the best kind of sweet. Unlike sweets, however, her appetite grew the more she consumed.

His large hands cupped the back of her head as she licked and sucked him. He couldn't seem to stop his hips from moving, plunging his cock into her mouth as he watched her, and this sent her own arousal into a fever. She lavished him with her tongue, gentle and greedy at the same time.

She tasted the salty beginnings of his release, and sucked harder, wanting that. But he pulled her back almost roughly.

"Not yet," he growled. "Want to last . . . forever."

The forest floor was cool and soft on her back as Sam gently pressed her down. Then he knelt between her legs, his expression verging on feral. Yet beneath the animal desire, he gazed at her as though nothing in the world mattered more.

Fierce—and tender.

Then he bent to her. He held her thighs, spreading them slightly, and lowered his mouth with a growl. Her breath caught in her throat. The first lick made her arch up with a cry. Another. And another. Learning her. He traced her with tongue and fingers, and both he and Cassandra groaned. Awareness ebbed so that she knew only the feel of his mouth on her, adoring her, decimating her. The pleasure was so sharp and exquisite, it couldn't be borne. Yet she did, because he demanded it of her.

She bowed up again as she came, the contractions wracking her, her thighs locking around him. He pushed her further, continuing his sensual onslaught. Her climax rose and fell in waves, then built and exploded once more until she was dimly amazed she did not simply shatter apart to lie in trembling shards across the bracken.

"*Now*, Sam."

He covered her in less than a second. His lean, strong body shook, and his face was a study of tortured desire. Along her soaking folds, he ran the length of his cock, drenching himself in her need. Then, with one sure plunge forward, he sank into her.

Her legs wrapped around his waist as she pulled him fully within, her arms around his shoulders. For a moment, he held himself utterly still. He drew back, slow, slow, then just as slowly thrust back into her. She felt every slide, every inch. He filled her completely.

She bucked against him, wanting. Faster, harder. Throw her right over the edge with the speed and heat of a falling star. Yet he held back, taking her in deliberate strokes that, she saw through hazy eyes, cost him as much as her. He shuddered as he thrust deeply, and hoarse rumblings climbed from his chest.

"Take us over," she pleaded.

But he clenched his jaw. "More . . . pleasure for . . . you. As much as you . . . can take . . ."

He would kill her with pleasure, because it possessed her entirely. And she understood with gem-bright clarity what he was doing. Giving her this ecstasy with his body because he felt it was all he could provide.

With this bittersweet realization, another climax overwhelmed her. A scream ripped from her throat. She dug her nails into his back as she arched upward, lost. This was the beginning of the world and its end.

Her climax pushed him into a frenzy. His strokes drove even deeper, his pace quickening. A groan, a curse, and a blessing. Then he froze as he came in hard, wringing pulses. Her name tumbled from his lips as if the word encapsulated everything that ever could, and should, be said. Then he sank down, wholly depleted.

Murmurs and kisses as they stroked each other's faces, brushing back strands of hair. They rolled to their sides, but he remained within her, and they lay like that for a long time. Overhead, the sky turned lilac, then a deeper violet. Stars began to emerge. A cool evening breeze danced across her damp skin and she shivered.

Gradually, unwillingly, they disentangled and dressed. Neither spoke, though they stopped often during the process to kiss and touch one another. When they finally rode out of the forest and were back on the lane that led to the sorcerer, Cassandra understood that he'd given her the pleasure of his body. Yet his soul remained as remote as a distant dream.

*   *   *

Achille Voisin's cottage sat at the very edge of a windblown moor. By the time Cassandra and Sam reached it, the moon had risen, so that the roof seemed thatched with silver. A light gleamed in one of the small windows.

As they approached, what had been a faint tinkling sound grew in volume. Cowrie shells hung in strands from the eaves, and ribbons fluttered beside them.

Cassandra placed her hand over her pocket. "I feel the Source stirring." It gave off pulses of energy, sensing kinship magic close at hand.

Grim-faced, Sam dismounted and then, when she did the same, strode up to the front door.

It opened before he could knock.

Standing at the threshold was a dark-skinned man of indeterminate age. Candlelight behind him limned him in gold, and he stared at his visitors with eyes both clear and ancient. He drew on a pipe then exhaled fragrant smoke.

"Monsieur Voisin—" Cassandra began.

"You have it with you?" His voice was also ageless, yet musical.

When she nodded, the man waved them in. Once inside, she saw that the little cottage abounded in color—small shrines of brightly painted pictures, candles, and offerings covered every surface.

"How did you know we were coming?" Cassandra asked. "Honoria told you, somehow?"

The man tipped his head toward a bowl of water sitting in the middle of a table. Black candles surrounded the bowl, and their flames reflected in the water's surface. "The *loa* tell me what I need to know."

"You're a sorcerer," Sam noted.

"Men such as me, we are *bokor*," corrected Voisin. "We serve the *loa*—spirits, you call them—with both hands. The dark and the light. Some of us make the *zombi*." He glanced at Sam. "No *bokor* made you. Some other, stealing the power of the *loa*."

"He's dead now," Sam answered flatly. "I killed him."

Voisin looked at him with surprise. "You were able to break the chains of the one who created you? Freed yourself?"

Sam gave a curt nod.

The sorcerer plainly marveled. "No one, in all the lore, has ever done the same. I think you must be a man of great strength." When Sam did not respond, Voisin nodded, approving. "It is just that it is you and this fierce woman should put right the *loa*'s magic." He turned to Cassandra. "Show it to me."

She took from her pocket the little pouch and set it on the table. As soon as she produced it, Voisin inhaled sharply, then whispered a string of French as he gestured over himself. The candles beside the bowl of water flickered, the flames changing from yellow to green.

"The Dark Gift of Baron Samedi," he breathed. Reaching forward with one shaking hand, he brushed the tips of his gnarled fingers just above the top of the pouch. "He is a *loa* of the dead. A great and powerful magician, a judge of excellent wisdom, a fearsome spirit of sex and resurrection." Voisin pointed toward one of the shrines.

Cassandra looked, and shivered. Baron Samedi was depicted as a skeletal man in funereal clothing, yet he grinned with shadowy knowledge as he clutched a gravedigger's shovel. Black candles surrounded his shrine, as well as plugs of tobacco and a bottle of some kind of liquor. Offerings to the terrible spirit. She edged closer to Sam, whose arm came up to wrap around her shoulders.

"Long ago, the Dark Gift was taken from a priestess of the *vodou*." Voisin's voice hardened. "A white man took it, stole it away, and no one knew where to find it. Since then, the balance has been disturbed. Too many *zombi* made. *Bokor*, priests, and priestesses have all tried to reset the balance, but, without the Dark Gift, our efforts were in vain. Until now." He smiled at Sam and Cassandra, though she felt little comfort in it.

"You can make things right." Sam glanced intently back and forth between the pouch and the sorcerer.

"Yes—I will send the Dark Gift back to its homeland, back to Haiti and Baron Samedi."

"Will it be safe then?" Cassandra pressed. "The men who took it, they might try again."

Voisin bustled around the cottage, gathering objects: several figurines, more candles, vials of liquids that Cassandra could not, and did not want to, identify. "The Dark Gift shall never again be abused. Not by the white men, not by anyone. All will be put to rights."

As the sorcerer collected what he needed to perform his magic, Cassandra's heart began to pound. A strange sensation of dread crept over her, but she could not understand why. She was so close to completing her mission for the Blades, so near the achievement of what she and Sam both pursued.

She reached down and gripped Sam's hand. His grip was just as strong, and, as she chanced a look up at him, she saw his brow lower, his expression grim.

"Now, we have all that we need." Voisin surveyed his gathered items and then placed them in specific patterns around the shrine to Baron Samedi. He uncorked the bottle of liquor and poured it into a tin cup. The smell of rum wafted through the air.

"Is there anything we can do to help?" Cassandra hoped it did not involve making sacrifices or offerings of blood.

Voisin chuckled. "Ah, this is for the *bokor*, *petite fille*. You do nothing but watch." Then he sobered. "But, *mes enfants*, I must tell you about part of the spell."

Now Cassandra's heart threatened to rip from her chest, it beat so hard. "What?"

"I know." Sam's deep voice startled her.

She looked back and forth between the nodding sorcerer and Sam. "What?" she demanded. "What the hell is it that you know?"

"The balance, it must be restored," said Voisin. He directed a pointed gaze at Sam, who just nodded darkly.

Understanding pierced her like a knife to the heart. She felt dizzy, sick, despairing. And furious.

"You have to die." Her eyes burned. "*Truly* die."

He turned to her, his jaw tight. "Thought that might happen, when we returned the Source."

"You didn't say anything."

"Wasn't certain."

"But you knew."

He made a clipped nod. She'd never seen him look so bleak, yet his expression matched the sudden desolation that carved her hollow. She realized that when they had made love in the forest, he knew it was to be the last time. He'd given her everything he could.

Her hand tried to clench into a fist, but he held it firm within his own.

"No," she choked. "No, I won't let you."

"It has to happen, Cass." His voice rasped. "The Source needs to be secured, and if it means I have to finally die, then . . ." He tightened his jaw again.

"Then you're happy to do it," she filled in, bitterness lacing her words.

His gaze burned down at her. "Like hell," he snarled. He forced down his anger, so that, when he next spoke, awe and tenderness abraded his voice. "Even dead, I never felt more alive than when I'm with you."

Hot tears rolled down her cheeks as she stared up at him, his starkly handsome face. She had no idea how to go on living without him. He was essential. Existence without him couldn't be comprehended.

"I don't want to give that up," he rumbled. His hand came up to trace along her cheek. She leaned into his touch. "But there's more at stake here than what either of us wants. We both know that."

There was no denying the truth of what he said, even as she railed against it. Yet, as he said, neither of them truly had a choice. It was simply a matter of how they faced the inevitable.

"I love you, Sam." She stretched onto the tips of her toes to press her lips against his. "All my life, it's only been you. And I'll go on loving only you until the end of my days."

He claimed her mouth, branding her with his heat, his essence, and she clung to him desperately as he enfolded her. "I love you, Cass. I wish . . . I wish . . ."

But that was too much. "I know," she whispered. They held each other, trying to prolong these moments into lifetimes.

"Pardon, mes enfants," Voisin interrupted quietly. "We must do this now, when the moon is high."

They broke apart, and the sensation of him stepping back felt as though her own limbs were being torn off. She refused to surrender her grip on his hand, however. She would touch him for as long as she was able, so that, at the very last, he could feel her with him.

Sam straightened to his full height, drawing back his shoulders. A proud soldier. He nodded at the sorcerer. "Begin."

Voisin doused all the candles in the cottage, save for the black ones in front of Baron Samedi's shrine. The Source was also set before the shrine. Voisin began chanting in a language Cassandra could not recognize—a mixture of English, French, and some older, distant tongue that recalled a far away shore, primal forests. As Voisin chanted, his voice changed, turning sharp and nasal. He waved his hands above the shrine. The candles sputtered, then flared higher.

A green light uncoiled from the picture of the death *loa*. It swirled around the shrine, touching on the offerings, lingering over the pouch. Then it grew, reaching out in widening circles. For a moment, it hovered around the sorcerer before moving on. The light snaked through the cottage, heading toward Cassandra and Sam.

When it reached her, she stiffened to feel its cold burn. Sam immediately hauled her behind him, shielding her. The green light spiraled around him, beginning at his feet, then winding its way up his body, lingering for several moments over the wound in his chest. He tensed but did not try to pull away.

Voisin chanted louder and louder, until Cassandra's ears

rang. She felt a powerful force drawing on the cottage, a vacuum, stealing the air from her lungs and chilling her skin. But she would not let go of Sam's hand.

Suddenly, Voisin shouted. The candles gutted, went out. At the same time, the green light flared, blinding her, then it, too, extinguished.

The next moment, Sam collapsed.

Chapter Ten

Cassandra fell to her knees beside Sam. She'd known it was coming, yet, even so, to kneel next to him and touch his lifeless body—she heard a strange sound, like a wounded animal, and realized it came from her.

Light flared. Voisin came forward with a lamp, staring down at Sam's body with a puzzled frown.

She barely looked at the sorcerer when he said, "The Dark Gift has been returned. It is safe. The balance restores itself."

It didn't matter. Nothing mattered. Her hands moved over Sam's face, tracing the shape of his features, the handsome face she'd grown to love in all its expressions. Only stillness now. His skin already began to cool, losing the warmth she had brought out in him. When Sam had beheaded Broadwell, the Heir's corpse almost immediately began to decompose, as if years of death finally caught up.

She couldn't bear to watch Sam decay, though she knew it had to happen. No matter how hard she tried, however, she couldn't make herself rise up from the floor and leave him, even to prepare a grave. He'd have to be buried quickly.

"*Petite fille,*" Voisin murmured, placing a hand on her shoulder. "There is more to be done."

She shook Voisin's hand away, fierce as a flame. "Not yet."

Cupping Sam's still face, she bent over him. One last kiss.

She would have to content herself with that—as her heart broke and the emptiness within her howled like a cave of ice.

Shaking, she pressed her mouth to Sam's. He didn't kiss her back. Beneath her lips, his own were cold and motionless. But she stayed there, trying to imbue this final kiss with all the love she would never feel again.

A rattling. The sound of a storm, a wind. Something drew at her breath, pulling it from her.

Sam's motionless body suddenly arced up in a spasm, nearly throwing her back.

She clung to him. With wild eyes, she looked at the sorcerer. "What is this?" she demanded. Nothing like this had happened to Broadwell.

The sorcerer gazed back at her, unreadable.

Cassandra tried to force Sam's body back down to the ground, but whatever power gripped him now, she couldn't fight it. He shook and convulsed.

He suddenly gasped. Dragged in air in long, shuddering breaths. His eyes flew open. At his sides, his hands knotted into fists.

"Sam?"

He didn't hear her. Some force clutched him. He took in another breath, and then another, the sound harsh and loud in the quiet cottage.

Cassandra held onto him. Under her hands, she felt movement, a growing energy. She parted the torn fabric of his shirt, then gasped.

The death wound . . . it was closing. Healing. And then— she could scarcely believe it—she lay her hand over his chest. Beneath her palm, his heart beat. Once. Then again. And then its rhythm steadied, became regular.

His body stopped shaking. He breathed.

"Sam?" She brushed damp hair back from his forehead, then realized with a start that he was sweating. He'd never done that before.

A hesitant joy began to expand within her. She dared not

believe, yet wanted to so badly that she held herself in suspension midway between despair and elation.

Slowly, he turned to look at her. He blinked his azure eyes, confused, disoriented. The first time he tried to speak, his voice croaked. After swallowing—*swallowing!*—he tried again. "Dead?" he rasped. "Heaven or . . . hell?"

"Yorkshire," she answered, smiling though tears soaked her cheeks. "You're *alive.*"

His eyes widened. He struggled to sit up, and she helped him, wrapping her arms around him and cradling him to her. He fumbled at his chest, then sucked in a shocked breath when his hand found no wound, only a circular scar marking where a bullet once pierced and killed him. Then he started again when he realized he actually breathed.

He held up his wrist. Sure enough, his pulse beat just beneath the surface of his skin.

"My heart." He tilted his head as if to catch a sound. "It's beating." A small, wondering smile tilted in the corner of his mouth. "Loud." Then he gazed at her, and euphoria lit his face, transforming him from merely handsome to extraordinarily beautiful, until uncertainty crept in. "Cass—is this real?"

"It is real," answered Voisin. When Sam and Cassandra looked at the sorcerer, he continued, "When the Dark Gift was stolen, too many *zombi* were made. One life had to be returned to restore the balance."

"So I'm . . . mortal again?"

"Yes." Voisin glanced at Sam's tattered clothes. "You must be more careful from now on."

"Gladly."

Sam's strength must have returned, because Cassandra found herself suddenly pulled tight against him in an embrace. She threw her own arms around him, and for some moments all they could do was hold one another, feeling their hearts beat against each other and the soft warmth of their mingled breaths.

When they kissed, she tasted the living essence of him, and

wasn't entirely certain whether the tears on her face were his or hers. But it didn't matter. Sam was alive.

She faintly heard Voisin slip from the cottage.

"Cass," Sam rasped. "Beautiful Cass. I thought . . . I thought you were an angel."

"I am no angel."

He chuckled. "I know that now."

"How do you feel?"

He frowned, assessing himself. "Hungry." He laughed.

"Anything you want," she vowed. "Dozens of roast chickens. Towers of meat pies. Strawberries. Turnips."

"You." His expression heated.

Warmth surged through her body. "Always."

He turned fierce as he cupped the back of her head. "Not letting you go again. I learned something from death—to seize hold of life and love. And that means you, Cass. I love you."

"I love you, Sam." She stroked his face, his throat, reveling in the warmth of him. "And I'm sure as hell not letting go of you."

He pulled her closer, so that their foreheads touched. "I'm alive."

"Thanks to the magic of Baron Samedi."

But he shook his head and pulled back just enough to hold her gaze with his own. Her breath caught at the depth of emotion there.

"No, Cass," he whispered. "It was you. *You* brought me back to life." He took her hand and pressed it against his solid chest. "And this beating heart will always be yours."

Simon Says

BIANCA D'ARC

Prologue

"Bravo one. Echo delta niner." Simon repeated the pre-arranged code for extraction. His small team was mostly gone, decimated by an enemy for which they'd had no way to prepare adequately. They'd been briefed, but nothing could match encountering the walking dead for real for the first time.

"Sitrep," someone barked over the radio. He knew that voice. It was Matt Sykes, an old friend, comrade in arms, and the officer in charge of this little fiasco.

"Jenkins and Bradley are dead. Hsu has gone over to the dark side. Wally and me are the only ones left." That was more than enough reason to get the hell out of Dodge.

Simon wasn't about to mention his own injury. The eggheads on base said one bite from the creatures they were hunting brought instant death. Simon had been lucky so far. He'd been scratched up by their claws, but not bitten. The claws were probably harmless as far as spreading the contagion went. Maybe they had to get a good hard bite of you in order to spread their infection.

That was something the doctors could puzzle out later. Right now, Simon needed to get himself and Wally out of the hot zone so they could regroup and come back stronger with reinforcements. Lots of reinforcements.

"A helo is coming to get you. ETA ten minutes. Hang tight,

Si." Matt's voice was reassuring but Simon caught sight of movement in the trees.

They had to get to the rendezvous but they were being pursued. They could move faster than their pursuers, but the creatures had the advantage of numbers. If they managed to box him and Wally in, they'd be toast. Or rather, a tasty snack for these ghouls who liked to eat human flesh.

"We're on the move," Simon reported. "Being pursued. Tell the helo to come in hot and be ready to fly. We'll most likely have company on our six. We won't have time to stop and chat."

"Simon . . ." Matt sounded ready to read him the riot act, but Simon didn't have time to listen. The enemy had found them. He could see the creatures maneuvering through the trees to flank them.

"Gotta go, commander. We'll be at the LZ in ten. Blackwell out."

Wally, otherwise known as Ensign Rob Wallace, the newest member of the team, came crashing through the underbrush. So much for stealth.

"They're flanking us. Bradley and Jenkins are with them."

"Shit." Their former teammates had risen from the dead and were now playing for the other team. Could this day get any worse?

They'd been sent into a horror movie with inadequate intel, inappropriate weaponry and not a chance in hell of winning. Bullets didn't stop these things. They were already dead. Nothing short of a block of well-placed C4 that could blow the bastards to smithereens would stop them. Simon had lost three friends already to this menace, not to mention the Marines that had been sent in before they'd called in Special Forces.

"Stay with me, Wally." Simon could see fear in the young man's eyes. "Helo's coming. We just need to keep it together until they get here. I don't want to enter the LZ until the last minute. Otherwise, we'll be forced to make a stand in the clearing or fall back. Neither one of those things is an option." Simon talked fast as he moved with Wally to a better position. "We don't stand a chance if we try to take them on head to head. The ammo we have doesn't work against them. The only thing that seems to do any good are grenades, but they have to be close enough to blow them apart. Just hitting them with shrapnel won't stop them, so use your remaining grenades sparingly. How many you got left?"

Wally did a quick check of his utility belt. "Just one, sir."

"Better than me. I used all mine. I'm out." They'd each been issued five grenades back at base before this mission. When they'd set out on this journey, it had seemed like more than enough to take down a few tangos in the woods. Now Simon knew differently. A whole crate of grenades might not be sufficient to take out these nightmare creatures.

Simon held up one hand for silence. He listened hard to the surrounding forest. All the wildlife had long since vanished. Critters knew better than to stick around when there was a predator in the area. The leaves rustled as the undead moved through the forest, brushing against the foliage.

"They're on the move. We need to go." Simon stood. Wally followed behind. "We have five minutes to kill before the helo gets to the clearing."

Near as Simon could tell, the walking dead no longer comprehended language. They could still hear though, and small sounds would give away Simon and Wally's location. Simon whispered, keeping his voice as low as possible.

The creatures seemed to retain some of the training they'd had in life. They were good at stealth for one thing. The Marines were good at moving silently when they chose. The members of Simon's team who had been lost to the enemy, only to rise from the dead, were even better.

Maybe that's why Simon fell into their trap. One minute he was making plans with Wally under cover of a big maple tree, the next, claws ripped into his shoulder and teeth sank into his flesh.

The fucker had bitten him!

Wally kicked the creature away from Simon, but not in time. Blood welled and Simon knew he'd fall fast if the deaths of his teammates were anything to go by.

Still, the instinct for self-preservation pushed him onward. He ran alongside Wally to the circle of trees that marked the clearing. The helicopter would land in a few minutes but Simon would probably be dead by then.

He'd seen Hsu drop about twenty seconds after he'd been bitten, and beefy Beau Bradley had taken only ten seconds more than that. The poison would course through his body, felling him like one of the mighty trees in this idyllic forest turned horror show. Any second now.

Creatures surrounded them. They were coming across the clearing and up from behind. Not much chance of escape from this mess now and Simon was already dead.

"Get out of here, Wally. I'm done. Save yourself."

At that precise moment, they both heard the sound of helicopter blades in the distance, growing closer.

"Get into the clearing," Simon ordered the younger man. "Use the grenade if you have to. Your ride's almost here."

"I'm not going without you, sir." Wally dragged Simon toward the line of undead Marines standing between them and the Landing Zone.

"I'll take 'em down if I can. You run for the chopper."

Wally reluctantly agreed to the plan. Both of them knew Simon was living on borrowed time. The least he could do was get young Wally to safety before his time ran out.

"Tell Matt Sykes I'll see him in hell." Simon grinned, thinking of his old comrade and the good friends he'd lost along the way.

"It's been an honor serving with you, sir." Wally spared Simon one long look before they both turned to face the enemy.

They could see the helicopter now. It was coming in for a landing. If they timed it just right, they could make a hole through the mass of creatures for Wally to run through and jump onto the chopper. It was his only shot.

"You know, sir, it's been more than a minute and you're

still standing," Wally observed as they waited for the opportune moment to launch their offensive.

Simon stopped breathing for a split second, thinking about what Wally had said. "Yeah, you're right."

"Could be the science guys were wrong. You might live." Wally shrugged but Simon could feel the air vibrate around him as the helicopter came closer. It was almost time. "I think you should come with me, sir." Wally had to shout to be heard above the roar of the helicopter's blades.

"I think you're right, Wallace," Simon shouted back, a grin splitting his face as the helo descended toward the grassy clearing. "We'll both get out of this mess." Almost there. They had to time this right as the monsters tightened the noose around them. "On three. One. Two . . . Three!" Simon gave a war cry as he ran toward the enemy, hoping like hell that brute force would allow him and Wally to muscle their way past the armada facing them.

He pushed past the first row of stinking flesh easily. The second line was a little harder. He looked over at Wally, but the kid was holding his own. This was like an evil game of football where the stakes were life or death. Simon fought through the secondary line, dodging grasping hands and shouldering through the ranks of dead Marines.

He made it to the open door of the helicopter and looked back to see Wally, in the grip of Lieutenant Hsu. Simon turned to go back and help Wally but hands from inside the chopper grabbed him, tugging him forcefully aboard. He fought against them, but there were too many people gripping him in too many places, pulling him into the hovering helicopter.

The last Simon saw of Wally, he was surrounded by zombies, their teeth ripping into his living flesh. Then Wally pulled the pin on his last remaining grenade.

Chapter One

He watched from the bushes, gauging the woman's reactions as she peered up at the full moon from her back porch. She wasn't wary, and that was a dangerous thing. For her.

Dark things prowled the night. Things out of nightmares. Things a woman like her should never encounter.

If he had his way, she never would. It was his job to see that she remained in ignorance of the creatures that stalked the forest behind her home. He was her silent protector, though she would never know it.

If things went as planned.

A few hours later, Simon cursed his bad luck. His plan had gone right out the proverbial window, but he was a hell of an improviser. His fast actions and lightning reflexes had saved his life more than once in the past. This time, however, he might've cut things just a little too close. Only the dawn pinkening the eastern sky had saved him tonight, sending the creatures he hunted to ground.

In the night, the hunter had become the hunted and now he was injured. Blood drew the undead creatures like moths to a flame. Simon had left a blood trail through the forest that would have the zombies in a frenzy when they rose again.

Thankfully, the day was sunny and he knew the reanimated corpses shunned the sun's cleansing rays. They'd be in hiding until sunset. Or until storm clouds showed up. Cloudy days were the worst, because then he had no respite from hunting the creatures that should never have been let loose in the first place.

Simon headed for the deep woods that would take him eventually to Quantico, the Marine base from which he was currently operating. He had been recruited to eradicate the threat in the woods surrounding the base before it could spread any further.

Ostensibly, he was a civilian contractor doing some unspecified work on base. Only a select few high up in the command structure knew his true identity and his real mission. One man against a potential army of the undead wasn't great odds. Simon's training, unique skill set, covert operations experience, and immunity to the contagion that had created these monsters tipped the scales in his favor.

Until today. Today he would be lucky to make it back to base without passing out. He would head straight for the small clinic that served as an infirmary for men in the field. He would go there even though he'd been avoiding that one particular place for weeks now. Not the place really. In truth, it was the woman who worked there he had been trying so hard to avoid. He'd guarded her. He'd watched over her from afar, but he'd been avoiding a face-to-face confrontation with the woman out of his past. The one he'd let get away.

Now, if his rotten luck held, he would be unable to avoid her.

Dr. Mariana Daniels arrived at the base infirmary early, as was her habit. She had only a few more weeks left as a naval officer before she finally returned to civilian life. It had been a long time since she had first put on the uniform. At one time, she had thought to make the military her life's work. Now, over a decade later, she was ready to start a new adventure in the civilian world.

She opened the door to her office and set her coffee cup

down on the cluttered desk. A commotion from the front of the clinic made her turn. Usually, she had a good half hour alone before the rest of the staff started reporting for duty in the small infirmary that was just a field branch of the larger medical facility on base. She retraced her steps, curious to see who was early.

She rounded a corner and stopped short in the hall, face to face with a man she'd thought never to see again.

"Simon?" Shock colored her voice.

"Damn."

Three years and the first word out of his mouth was a curse. She shouldn't have expected anything different. Her time with Simon Blackwell had been a low point in her life from which she was still recovering. To be fair, he had also been a high point. Their short-lived relationship had made her happier than she had ever been. Then he'd left with little fanfare. One day he was there, the next he was gone, leaving her to pick up the pieces.

She shouldn't have been surprised. That's what special forces guys were like. When they got called up for a mission, they had to leave and couldn't say where they were going or when they would be back. At first she had waited. Only when she'd run into one of his teammates a few months later had she finally realized he wasn't coming back. At least not back to her. He was alive according to his friend, but the prolonged silence where she was concerned told her all she needed to know.

He still looked as handsome as ever, those twinkling blue eyes all too serious and clouded with . . . pain? She looked him over and realized he was holding his arm abnormally close to his chest and leaving a faint blood trail down the crisp white corridor.

"You're hurt."

He nodded, still apparently a man of few words. "I wouldn't have come here otherwise."

Now that hurt. She tried not to flinch, but Simon had always been a little too perceptive.

"I didn't mean it that way, Mari. I figured it would be better for you if you didn't know I was here, on base."

She ushered him into a curtained treatment area and watched as he sat unsteadily on the paper-draped table. She didn't like the pale look of his tanned skin.

"What happened to you?"

"Field exercise. Training accident." His clipped words told her there was a lot more to the story than met the eye. His tone told her not to pry.

She'd known going into their relationship that he was a special operations guy. What he'd been doing in the years since she had last seen him was a mystery. Simon Blackwell lived much of his life on a need to know basis. It had been hard to deal with while they'd been dating, but she had always understood duty and honor. She had even admired him for his devotion to both.

Mariana stepped closer and started examining his injuries. There were multiple gashes running along one side of his body and some of them looked deep. A few would probably require stitches.

"Well, your field exercise seems to have put you in the path of . . . are these claw marks?"

"Ran into a badger. Got scratched up."

"Ah, I see. A badger . . . with what looks like a serrated edged weapon in addition to some very nasty claws."

She gasped as he grabbed her hand, stilling her motions. "Don't push, Mari." His tone was both familiar and forbidding.

Silence passed between them as she regarded him. He had always had an intensity about him that made her want to swoon. A badass vibe that turned her on like nothing else. He had locked eyes with her a couple of times while they were making love and she'd thought she'd seen her future in his bottomless blue gaze.

She'd been wrong.

"All right. I won't ask any more questions. Other than medical questions, of course. You're up to date on your tetanus, right?"

He nodded, letting go of her hand and she relaxed fractionally.

She took a closer look at his wounds. The slashes and claw marks extended over his biceps and onto his chest. The shirt had to go.

He wore a dark green camouflage Battle Dress Uniform shirt. They were called BDUs for short, and the shirt was more properly called a blouse, but that had always sounded a little too feminine to Mariana. It buttoned up the front, which would make it easy to get off him.

With deft movements, she began unbuttoning the heavy weight cotton shirt. She was surprised when he stilled her hands as she worked her way down his muscled abdomen.

"I'll get the rest."

She nodded tightly and turned to locate the scissors. They were on the instrument tray kept ready in every treatment area. Simon's olive drab undershirt would have to be cut off him. It was torn and tattered already, as was the heavier cotton of the BDU shirt. The undershirt would be easy to cut through to clean and dress his wounds, while the BDU top would be too much for her little scissors.

Turning back to him, scissors in hand, she got her first good look at his physique, clad only in the form-fitting undershirt. It had been three years since she had last seen him. Damn, the man still had the power to push the breath from her lungs. He followed her movements with a guarded expression as she drew closer. She tried desperately not to betray the unwanted attraction that still flowed through her body for him.

Simon had always been a bad boy she should have known to stay away from in the first place. Unfortunately for her heart, he was also too compelling to resist. He had never been overly talkative. Of course, when they'd been together, the furthest thing from her mind had been conversation. Theirs had been an explosive passion. Even memories of their time together were enough to get her hot and bothered.

So she tried her best not to think about him. It worked,

more now than it had in the beginning. It had gotten so that now she could go whole days without something triggering a memory of their short time as a couple. She'd given her heart to the man, though she'd never said it to him in so many words. She'd been afraid of scaring him off.

Simon had always been the strong, silent type. A man of few words, he was all about action, and all of his action was devastating. He had just about ruined her for other men, though he'd never done anything to deliberately hurt her. Except leave and not come back.

She kept reminding herself that they'd made no promises to each other. Mariana had been rudely awakened when he didn't return. She realized then that any emotional attachments in their relationship had been totally on her side. Simon hadn't led her on. She didn't blame him for toying with her affections. She had done the hatchet job on her own heart.

And now, here he was, bleeding and in need of help in her clinic. He still didn't talk much, and she could see a new wariness that hadn't been there before. Those pretty blue eyes were truly the mirrors of his soul. He didn't betray much in his expression, but she had often thought she could tell what was going on in his active brain by watching the subtle nuances in his stunning baby blues.

Maybe that was self-delusion as well.

She shrugged off the thoughts of what had been and what could have been. He held his BDU shirt in one hand. She took it from him and tossed it onto the counter.

"That shirt is ruined."

"I have a few things in the top pockets I'd like to get before we chuck it in the trash."

She turned back to him, armed with her small scissors. "I'll leave it here for now. Let's get you fixed up and then we'll deal with everything else."

"Sounds like a good plan to me."

She went to work on his undershirt, cutting it away a little at a time. The gashes on his arm and chest were deeper than she had originally thought and they got worse the more they were revealed.

"How long ago did this happen?" She was all business now. He had to be in serious pain, but nothing showed on his face.

"About oh four hundred."

"And you walked all the way in?" She consulted the clock on the wall. "It took you three hours to get here?" Damn, the man had a will of iron. Any normal guy would have collapsed by now.

"About that." He shrugged his uninjured shoulder as if walking three hours through rough terrain while seriously wounded and dripping blood was no big deal. Perhaps to him, it wasn't. The thought was chilling.

"All right. I'm going to start an IV to replace some of your fluids." She reached for a blood pressure cuff and wrapped it efficiently around his uninjured arm. The slashes and scratches were on his left side, leaving his right arm relatively unscathed. She knew he was right handed, so at least he would have the use of his dominant arm as he healed.

She heard the front door open and the chatter of two of her nurses arriving. Thank goodness. She shouted to get their attention and in short order she had them bustling around Simon. His blood pressure was lower than it should be and she monitored him closely as the IV began to do its work.

Simon lay back on the padded table at a slight incline, watching Mariana as the three women bustled around him. He was out of it. The blood loss had been worse than he had expected. He was so light-headed at this point, it felt like the small treatment room was spinning around him. Luckily, his own personal guardian angel knew what to do. She would save his miserable hide so he could go on protecting her from afar.

The situation was truly fucked up. If he'd had a choice he would have stayed far away from Mariana. He was no good for her. A guy with his baggage could only drag her down.

He'd glimpsed it during their brief affair. He'd seen the way she looked at him, with forever in her eyes, and he knew he couldn't be that guy. He couldn't be the guy who would make her life the fairy tale it was supposed to be.

No, all his fairy tales ended in death. There was no happily ever after in his world. Never had been. And now there never would be. All chance of changing his luck had been taken away on that last mission. The mission that had changed his life and put Mari forever out of his reach.

When duty had called him away from her addictive presence, at first he'd had every intention to return. Then things had happened—changes had been made to his very being—and he knew he would have to stay away from her. Far away. He had kept tabs on her from afar though. He hadn't been able to help himself. And when he'd been tasked with clearing the woods near Quantico, he'd been unable to keep himself from watching her. The woman mesmerized him and made him yearn for things he could no longer have.

Then a moment of miscalculation last night and here he was, lying on a thinly padded examination table while she fussed over him. She touched him with gentle fingers, even while she probed and cleaned the deepest of his wounds. Her warm breath breezed over his skin as she put a few stitches across the worst of the cuts and his gut clenched in reaction. If those nurses hadn't been in the room, he didn't know what he would have done. It was all he could do to control himself when Mariana was this close.

She smelled as good as he remembered. A little hint of gardenia mixed with her own delicate scent. It was intoxicating.

But she wasn't for him. He had to keep reminding himself of that sad fact. He could only screw up her life with the weirdness that had taken over his world. Mariana was better off without the likes of him. Too bad her big brown eyes made him want to forget all his damned good reasons for staying away.

"Almost done," she promised as she went to work on the

last of the deep gouges on his chest. Her touch was soft and gentle, but being stitched up hurt, regardless of the topical anesthetic she had applied. "How are you feeling?"

"Better." His head was clearing and he noted the way she glanced at her assistants—particularly the nurse who still had his right arm in the blood pressure cuff.

The nurse reported some numbers that sounded markedly better than his last reading and deflated the cuff. Simon clenched his fist a few times to dissipate the tingling sensation in his arm. He found himself unable to look away from Mariana. She was still just as beautiful as she had been three long years ago. More beautiful, in fact, with more character in the gentle lines of her face and a slight roundness to her cheeks, and the soft curves of her body made his mouth water. She had filled out in all the right places.

He knew medical school and residency had taken a lot out of her. She had been just a little too skinny, in his opinion, when they'd been dating. He was glad to see she'd recovered from those early stresses in her life and had the womanly curves to prove it. Just looking at her now made his mouth water. He did his best to suppress any outward display of interest, knowing it probably wouldn't be welcome. He'd left her. He'd hurt her. There was no doubt in his mind that was the case. She was too soft-hearted not to be hurt by his complete lack of communication.

He had taken the coward's way out by not saying goodbye. At the time, it had seemed the best thing to do. He hadn't been sure he would be strong enough to end it if he had to see her again. She was as addictive as any drug. At least to him. Though she probably hadn't known it. Simon had been careful to hide his feelings. He hadn't wanted to lead her on.

"Who's your CO, Si?" She surprised him with the gently voiced question about his commanding officer. His thoughts had drifted so far, he almost jumped when her question brought him back to Earth, but his training held him in check.

"I'm a civilian now, Mari."

She looked at him in surprise as she finished with the last of his stitches. "A contractor? Don't tell me you're working for those black ops guys in the swamp."

He should have known she would jump to the right conclusion. She had a quick mind and a wide knowledge of military and political things one wouldn't necessarily expect of a medical doctor.

"You know I can't tell you, Mari. Everything about my presence here is on a need to know basis."

"Well, right now I need to know who to report your injury to. You must have a CO on base."

She was right, but he didn't really want her any more involved than she already was. "Give me the phone and I'll report in."

She stared at him for a moment, probably deciding whether to argue, then finally turned toward the wall phone, snatching up the handset. She handed it to him and he sent a pointed look at the two nurses, who were busy with various tasks in the small space.

"Oh, for heaven's sake," she grumbled, sending the two ladies on their way, giving them errands to run in other parts of the infirmary. It wasn't truly private, of course. Still, it was good enough for him to report his location and condition. He wouldn't get into any incriminating details of his mission while on a public phone line anyway. Mariana turned back to him as the other two women bustled off. "What number?"

He couldn't reach the wall mounted keypad from where he sat. He would rather she didn't know who he called, but there was no other choice. He gave her the commander's extension number and a raised eyebrow was her only response. She dialed for him, then turned to leave the enclosure, giving him the illusion of privacy.

Soon after he ended the call, Mari returned, taking the handset and hanging it up for him. He had no doubt she had heard every word of his brief conversation, but no comments on the call were forthcoming. She didn't speak at all, in fact, as she continued to monitor his vital signs and work on the less severe of his wounds. She had taken care of the most serious first. All that were left were a few shallow scratches and bruises.

The silent treatment was driving him nuts. He knew he owed her an apology at the very least, for the way he had ended their relationship. He had never been the most eloquent of men and still didn't know how to make her understand his reasoning, all these years later. A bare bones apology would have to do. It was a good place to start anyway.

"I'm sorry, Mari." The words spilled out as she bent near, tending a smaller slash on his upper chest, just below the collar bone. Her startled gaze flew upward to meet his. He had her attention, he only wished he knew what to say to make things right. "I'm sorry for not saying good-bye. I should have made a clean break rather than leave you hanging."

"Why did you?" The echoes of remembered pain in her unguarded expression sent a wave of sorrow through his heart. He had hurt her worse than he'd thought.

Simon sighed. "It wasn't anything you did, sweetheart. I just . . . I thought it was best to end things. I guess I hoped you would move on as soon as I shipped out."

Silence met his statement and he saw anger begin to simmer in her expression. "I waited for you, Simon. When you said you had to go, I thought you'd be back after your mission ended. Remember how I didn't ask any questions about where you were going or when you'd be back? I knew better than to ask, but then when you didn't return, I thought maybe you'd taken my silence as lack of interest."

Oh, he'd known she was interested. It had nearly killed him to leave her, but he hadn't seen any other choice at the time. Not after he'd recovered from that last mission. Everything had changed too much by then. He could never go back. Not then and not now.

"I'm sorry." It was too little, too late. The apology was all he had to offer and he knew it wasn't enough.

She turned away. "Yeah, me, too. Sorry I ever met you."

Her words were pitched low, but he heard them . . . and felt them, like a knife to his gut.

He didn't know what he would have said in reply because at that moment the curtain of his cubicle was swept summarily aside and a Navy commander swept in. Not just any Navy commander, this man was an old friend and the commander he had been tasked to work under on his current mission.

"Where are your weapons, Si?" Commander Matthew Sykes didn't pull his punches. He was a man on a mission and all business while danger was a possibility. And they both knew Simon's weapons were more than run of the mill and highly classified. That was precisely why he hadn't brought them inside the clinic.

"Stashed in the bushes outside the good doctor's office window." Simon nodded toward Mariana, one raised eyebrow making Matt aware of her presence and the need to be circumspect in front of her.

Matt snapped a look at his aide who had followed close behind, and the young seaman scurried off to secure the top secret darts. The creatures Simon was hunting could only be destroyed by a special, super strong toxin, and it was kept under lock and key except when he was in the field.

"Sorry for the intrusion, Doctor," Matt spoke to Mariana for the first time, and Simon didn't like the interest in his old buddy's expression.

"No problem, sir."

"How is he?" Matt asked Mariana about his status rather than talk to Simon directly, which annoyed him to no end. He had spent too many weeks being talked over by medical personnel to have any patience with it now.

"He lost a lot of blood and required a few stitches. His prognosis is good. I believe he'll be good as new in a few days. I'd like him to go to the base hospital for observation. He may still need a transfusion, though he's responding well."

"No hospital," Simon said quickly. Matt, thankfully, agreed with him.

"Only if it's absolutely necessary, Doctor. I'd prefer to keep this quiet. In fact, I'd prefer you didn't discuss his treatment with anyone else, and make no record of his visit to your clinic, if possible. His position here on base is—"

"Classified." Mariana dared to cut off the superior officer, a bored expression on her face. "I understand, sir. Simon and I know each other from his spec op days. He told me he's a civilian now and I can extrapolate from that."

Matt's eyes narrowed. "Then you understand his presence here is on a need to know basis."

"And I don't need to know. Got it, sir. I'll keep him here and observe him myself, then send him on his way if there are no complications."

Again Matt watched her, an uncertain expression on his face. They had been friends too long for Simon not to realize Matt was intrigued by her.

"I'd like a verbal report on his condition this evening, Doctor. Call my office and speak to no one except me. Understood?"

"Yes, sir."

"And Simon, I want you to stay here as long as necessary. I'll have Johnson bring over your kit before dark, just in case. In the meantime, get some rest."

"Sure thing, Matt." They'd been friends too long for Simon to be awed by Matt's rank. If Simon had stayed in the service, no doubt they would be equals at this point, having come up together through the ranks.

The commander left without further ado and Simon was left with Mariana once more.

"Want to tell me what that was all about?" A raised eyebrow dared him.

"Honey, you know I can't." The easy smile on her face said she was just teasing him and the idea that she would deal so easily when confronted by the very real secrecy he had to live with was surprising. He wouldn't have thought she'd take it so well.

"Fair enough. How are you feeling? Still light-headed?"

"I never said I was light-headed."

"You didn't have to say it, Simon. You were pale as a sheet when you wobbled onto that table. If you can walk, I have a more comfortable berth for you in back. You can catch some sleep and I'll check on you during the day to be sure you're bouncing back the way I expect. Sound good?"

"I've slept on some pretty hard ground over the years. Still, I wouldn't turn down a soft mattress if one is available." He levered himself upward with her assistance. He was still a touch dizzy, but he wouldn't let that stop him. She held his arm and his other hand went to the rolling IV pole as she guided him down the short corridor to a back room.

"We use this cot when we need to work late or do double shifts when there are large numbers of men in the field. It doesn't happen often, but it's there if we need it and right now, I think you need it most. Nobody will disturb you back here. The head is just down the hall. You should probably wait for one of us to assist you before you decide to walk any distances. Just in case."

"You'll have to tell your nurses not to discuss my presence. My mission is top secret, Mari."

He stopped just inside the door to gaze down at her. She was a head shorter than him but somehow they'd always managed to fit together like matching jigsaw pieces. When they'd made love, the experience had been transformational. Transcendent, even. Like nothing he had ever experienced before, and probably would never experience again.

"I'll take care of it. Don't worry. Margaret and Nancy are trustworthy. These days, medical professionals are held to a very high standard of patient privacy. Your treatment falls under that category."

He nodded, unable to look away from her beautiful face. The moment stretched. He had one hand on the IV pole and his uninjured arm resting on her shoulder. It took very little effort to pull her unresisting body closer, until they were only a breath apart.

God, how he'd missed the feel of her, the touch and scent of her. He needed . . . just one taste. That's all. One taste to hold against the future without her. Simon dipped his head, her lips so close to his own.

And then he kissed her. He did the thing he had promised himself he would never do again. He kissed her, getting lost in the magic of her, her soft sighs, her delicate flavor, her luscious curves that fit so tightly against him.

For a moment, time stopped. She was in his arms and all was right with his world—for just a second out of time. Then reality came crashing back as voices came down the hall. More staff arriving for their shift made a racket as they sought their desks, just beyond the wall that separated this back room from the rest of the small infirmary.

Mariana drew back, out of his arms, and he had to let her go. He hated to do it, but he knew damned well he had overstepped. The condemnation he feared he would see on her face would undo him. Instead of anger, he read the same startled deer-in-the-headlight response he was feeling. She would get mad later, he supposed, but for now, she was just as affected by their kiss as he was.

They'd never lacked chemistry. They'd had that going for them, at least. Still, there was too much else wrong with the relationship—with him—for there to be any possibility of a future together. Simon knew he would die a single man. No way would he subject any woman to the uncertainty that loomed in his future.

Mariana backed away from Simon, shocked nearly senseless by his kiss. It had always been that way with him. Explosive, almost mindless passion that sent her to the moon and back with nearly instantaneous motion. God, that man could kiss. And make love. She had dreamed about his lovemaking in the years since they'd parted.

He'd hurt her by leaving without a word and she didn't know if she could ever forgive him. By his actions and words, she didn't even know if he wanted to be forgiven. She didn't know what this kiss was all about. Was it impulse? Or was it some deeper overture? Did he want to get back together? Or did he merely want to tease her again, work her up into a frenzy of need, want, and desire, only to leave her without a backward glance again?

The bastard.

He had disappeared once. He would do it again in a heartbeat. She knew that like she knew the back of her hand. He was a spec ops soldier, now a civilian contractor, which was a polite term for a soldier of fortune. A good, old-fashioned mercenary. Likely he was even worse now about commitment than he had been when he'd still been officially employed by Uncle Sam.

She needed to be wary. And she needed to stay away from him. No more kisses. No more tantalizing glimpses into what could have been . . . if only he'd returned to her.

This wasn't a return. It was a matter of coincidence that he needed medical help and she was the nearest doctor. If not for his injury, she suspected he never would have revealed his presence. He had probably done all he could to avoid running into her.

"How long have you been here at Quantico, Simon?"

He stepped back farther, in clear retreat. "About four months."

She should have known. Mariana just looked at him for a long moment, shaking her head as she mentally called herself all kinds of fool.

"Well." She had to get out of this room and he needed to lay down before he fell down. She took charge of his rolling IV stand and ushered him into the bed. It wasn't grand. More of a cot, really. But it would do. She arranged his arm and helped him find a comfortable position, tucking a sheet over his legs and up to his waist. He could tug it higher if he was cold. The infirmary was usually a little warmer than most of the other offices on base. "I'll check on you every half hour until I'm sure you're out of the woods. Try to sleep. If you need anything, just call. My office is next door. I'll hear you."

He grabbed her hand before she could bolt for the door.

"I won't apologize for kissing you, Mari. I will admit I was wrong to do it, though. I won't touch you again. Okay?"

He seemed to be seeking absolution. It was the least she could do for him so he would rest easy. And if he kept his word and didn't throw her into a tizzy again, it'd be worth it. He was too dangerous to her peace of mind.

"Okay. Get some rest, Si. I'll be back in a bit to see how you're doing."

Chapter Two

Simon's eyes snapped open the moment she walked into the room about twenty-five minutes later. He had always been a light sleeper. Spec ops guys trained for that sort of thing.

"Feeling any better?" She kept her voice deliberately low, in deference to his awakening senses. She also didn't want any of the other clinic workers to realize he was back here, per the commander's orders.

"Much better, thanks. You don't need to check on me. All I need now is sleep and I'll be fine."

She gave him a teasing smile as she advanced into the room. "Oh, I guess I thought I was the doctor here. Just let me take a quick look at your stitches and I'll leave you to sleep."

She reached for the edge of his bandages, but he caught her wrist in a firm grip, shocking her gaze upward to meet his.

"I'm fine, Mari. Seriously."

"Well, seriously, Si. I need to check your condition. By rights, I should've sent you to the hospital for observation at the very least." He stared her down, apparently unwilling to let go of her hand. She recognized a brick wall when she met one. Mariana sighed and relaxed her stance. "Come on, Simon. You know you can trust me. What's up with you? Why won't you let me take care of you?"

"You already did, Mari." His whispered words reach right

into her heart. "And I do trust you. It's why I came here last night instead of heading for the base hospital. I knew you'd patch me up and not ask too many questions."

"Oh, so that's your angle." She gave him a cunning smile as she perched on the side of his cot. "Buttering me up won't make me drop the subject. I *will* check your stitches and I *will* read your vitals. I'm the doctor here, Simon, lest you forget. *You* came to *me* for help. I'm not going to leave my job half done." He still hadn't let go of her wrist, making for close quarters as she sat next to him. "And it should go without saying that doctor-patient privilege holds. I won't discuss anything private about your condition or treatment with anyone. The only one I'm authorized to discuss your fitness with is your CO and I've already promised to call him tonight with an update. If you trust me enough to treat you, you should trust my discretion as well."

Simon seemed to think about it for a long moment, then finally let go of her wrist and lay back, flat on the small bed. The cot was barely large enough to hold his muscular frame, but she recognized the signs of intense fatigue. A man could sleep just about anywhere when they were as tired as he was. She had seen it before in troops undergoing combat training.

Simon's circumstances puzzled her. He seemed to be working alone and was no longer an official member of the military. A lone former special forces soldier, working clandestinely on one of the nation's most high-profile military bases, showing all the signs of having been living in the field and working hard on whatever mission he'd been given. It didn't make a lot of sense.

Even more troubling was Commander Sykes's unusual interest and the prohibitions he had given her against speaking about Simon's presence or condition. Something was definitely up, but it looked like she was the only one, aside from the commander and Simon, who had any idea that something was going on. What it was, she had no clue.

When Simon didn't make any more objections, she reached over and flicked on the bedside light so she could see him better. A few of the minor cuts had been left uncovered and they looked remarkably good. In fact, as she took a closer look, most of them seemed completely healed.

Impossible.

She adjusted the light closer and looked again. The minor scratches were gone.

Mariana felt chills run down her spine as she reached for the bandages that covered the worst of his wounds. She felt Simon's attention focus on her as she lifted the edge of the largest gauze pad. The stitches were still there, but the gaping gash beneath was now only a thin red line.

Mariana sat back, pulling the bandages completely off.

"What's going on here, Simon?"

"Mari, I . . ." He grimaced as if not sure what to say. He took his time deciding how to explain what she was looking at. "I was changed."

Her gaze shot to his, searching for meaning in his vague words. "Changed how? Did you volunteer for some kind of experiment? I've heard rumors about accelerated healing projects, but I've never seen anything like this."

"I didn't volunteer. I was affected by an injury on a mission. I nearly died. It was a close thing for a while, from what they told me later. I pulled through and this is one of the side effects. I heal really fast now."

"When?" Facts were spinning and colliding in her mind. "When did this happen to you?"

"On the mission right after I left you. I was sick for a long time and when I was finally well again, I . . . I thought you'd be better off without dealing with something like this. There's still a lot of uncertainty surrounding my condition."

"Oh, God, Simon." She was devastated by his words. He had left her without a backward glance—or so she'd thought. Now perhaps, she understood why he'd never said good-bye.

"You can't talk about this, Mari."

There he went with that need to know garbage again. Sometimes she really hated the fact that he was a covert operator. The secrecy in his life was maddening.

She had to think. She had to regroup. She had to check his vitals and reassure herself that he truly was in as good condition as he seemed. She wouldn't let him leave later today if there was any danger of internal bleeding or complications from the blood loss he's sustained earlier. He looked really good on the surface, but she needed hard facts and numbers to be sure he was as healthy on the inside as he looked on the outside.

"All right." She rested her palms on her thighs and took stock, breathing deeply to regain some measure of sanity. "Let me take your vitals and then I'll get out of your way so you can get more sleep. You were beat when you showed up on my doorstep and I'll be damned if I let you go until you've caught up at least a little on your beauty rest."

He smiled at that. Just a small smile. It touched her deeply nonetheless. Simon's rare smiles had always had that effect on her, which was why she had tried so hard to earn them.

She reached for the blood pressure cuff and thermometer she had brought in with her and proceeded to take his readings. She occupied herself for the next few minutes with routine chores that told her what she needed to know about his inner condition.

"I hardly believe it. Your numbers are good, Si." She watched him with near disbelief as he bunched a pillow behind him and sat up to face her.

"I told you it would be okay. Please don't freak out on me, Mari."

"If I haven't freaked out yet, I'm not going to, but I won't lie to you. This is just plain weird. Have you had any other complications from that injury?"

He closed up. "I can't talk about it. I shouldn't have told you this much."

Damn, there was that secrecy again. Ultimately, she realized only now, it was the clandestine nature of his work and experiences that had driven them apart more than anything. She cursed it. Yet in the same moment she knew that without his commitment to duty he wouldn't have been the same man she had grown to love. He was an elite soldier who lived by a sacred code of honor that she respected as much as she respected him.

And she still admired his commitment, honor, loyalty, and service, even though it had come between them. Knowing what she knew now, her heart thawed. He had left her for her own good. Or what he perceived as being for her own good. He had always put her welfare first. It was maddening at times, as well as being incredibly sweet.

"So I guess my next question is, do you want me to take out the stitches now so you can sleep easier, or wait and do it tonight? Fair warning, it'll be easier now, while the wounds are still healing. I'm afraid if we wait it might hurt more."

"Then now it is." Simon gave her another tiny lift of one corner of his mouth. The man didn't fear pain, but he also wasn't stupid. The mixture of cunning and bravery had drawn her to him from the beginning and it was no less potent now.

"I'll just get a few things and be right back. Do you want me to bring back anything? Maybe some juice or water?"

"Juice would be good."

Or a seven-course meal with her luscious body for dessert. Simon kept that thought carefully to himself. Being around Mariana again was playing havoc with his control. He'd thought he could handle it, but he'd been wrong. Mari was his Achilles' heel. She got to him like no other woman ever had, or likely ever would.

He'd just shared one of his deepest secrets with her and she had barely blinked an eye. In all the scenarios he'd run in his mind, he never would've expected her relatively calm acceptance of the freak he'd become. She was made of even stronger stuff than he had thought.

She returned a few minutes later. She had a big bottle of orange juice in one hand and a small pan full of instruments, gauze, and what looked like small bottles of liquid in the other. He guessed the medicine bottles probably contained a topical anesthetic of some kind and a disinfectant. Mari was a thorough and careful physician with a truly healing touch. He had always admired her skill and way with people.

She handed him the juice wordlessly, then adjusted the bedside light before sitting once more on the edge of his temporary bed. There wasn't much room on the small cot, so her thigh and hip pressed against his side.

He longed to stroke her skin with no barriers of cloth between them, but knew it was impossible. He'd made his choice when he'd left her. There would be no second chances for them. Not after what had happened to him.

Still the heat of her body pressing against his, even in this innocent way, brought back memories and longings best forgotten. How she had moved under him. How she had cried out when he made her come. How beautiful she always was when they made love and after, with her dark hair spread out over his pillow.

She was the most feminine, graceful woman he had ever known. Yet he knew her as a capable officer, brilliant doctor, and cunning opponent whenever they battled wits. Her tastes in music and films ran parallel to his, though she did tend to like the odd chick flick. Still, she didn't object to his penchant for horror movies too strenuously, so they'd rubbed along well together.

Then his life had actually *become* a horror movie and he knew he couldn't subject her to any of it. He would die before he saw her in danger. Especially danger he brought to her doorstep because of his work. No, she was better off without him in her life. Nothing would convince him otherwise, no matter how badly he wanted to take her in his arms and wish the world away.

He opened the juice bottle, busying his hands while she worked. She bathed the area in a liquid that tingled and then began snipping and tugging at the neat stitches she had put in him just an hour before. By tonight, if precedent held, he would be good as new, with not a scar in sight. Freak that he now was.

"This may hurt a little. Let me know if you want some more anesthetic."

"Just do it, baby. I've had worse."

Damn, his voice sounded rough. He needed to get a grip here. Her nearness was wreaking havoc with his libido . . . and his control. He hadn't bedded a woman since her. None since the attack that had made him what he was now.

A zombie hunter. A damned zombie magnet. The only thing that stood between the real world and the world of nightmares.

"I'd rather not hurt you if I can help it." She sounded more than a little annoyed. "No matter how much of a tough guy you are. You have nothing to prove here, Simon."

Oh yeah, she was annoyed. He'd always thought she was cute when she got uptight about something, which only annoyed her more of course. Simon wisely kept silent but damn if she wasn't still the most complex, engaging, and attractive woman he had ever known. Even when she was pissed off at him.

"How does that feel?" She'd finished with one row of stitches and was on to the next.

"Fine, doc. Just keep going. I'll let you know if there's a problem."

She shot him a disgusted look. Still, he could see the worry that tightened the tiny lines around her eyes. It touched him that even after the way he had left her, without even saying good-bye, she still cared. At least a little. At least enough not to want to cause him unnecessary pain.

Of course, she was a doctor. It might have something to do with her Hippocratic oath. She would probably do the same for anyone. Even her worst enemy. Even the man who'd left her without a word.

Simon tried to live his life without regrets but the way he had dealt with Mariana was one of his biggest. He felt guilty about what he'd done—or rather what he hadn't done. Not saying good-bye was a cowardly move and he wasn't proud of his past actions.

Maybe this was his chance to finally make it right. When he'd first been hired to do this job, he had scoped out what he would do if he was hurt. The base hospital was out of the question. Once a military doctor saw what his body could do now, Simon would never be free of them. He wouldn't go down that road if he could help it.

When he'd learned of Mariana's clinic he knew that was his only option. One he wouldn't take unless there was no other alternative. Last night, his choice had been taken away and now he had to make the best of it.

That he could trust her went without question. He knew her to be a woman of deep integrity. Even after what he'd done, she wouldn't betray him. Now, perhaps, was his chance to apologize for his cowardly actions and help her heal from the injury he'd dealt.

As she finished with the last of the stitches, he captured her hand. "How have you been, Mari?"

She seemed surprised by his question, but less annoyed than she had been a moment ago. "Better than you, from what I've just seen."

He had to laugh at her wry humor. The tightness around her eyes eased some more.

"You've got me there." He let go of her hand. "I meant what I said before. I'm sorry for the way I left without a word. It was wrong."

"It was," she agreed readily as she collected her things back into that curved pan. "I think I understand why you did it a little better now. I just wish . . ."

"What?" He wasn't sure he really wanted to know, but had to ask.

"I wish you'd trusted me. I don't know—maybe I could have helped. I'm a pretty good researcher. Maybe I could have found something to help you."

Her words surprised him, though on reflection, they shouldn't have. She had been part of a military led research study when they'd met. She had a brilliant mind and a stellar reputation as a medical professional. She probably would have done all she could to help him, had he told her the true nature of his condition.

The military didn't even know everything about the changes to his body, and he was careful to keep it that way. As far as they knew, he'd gained immunity to the contagion only. They didn't know about the other side effect of his run-in with the monsters they had created. He'd been lucky up to this point. He hadn't learned of the super fast healing until after he was out of the service and being treated by a civilian doctor.

"I'm okay, Mari. Really. I have a doctor I trust and he says I'm stable for the moment."

"For the moment?" She sounded suspicious and a little annoyed. He could tell she didn't like that last part at all.

"It's the best he could do given what happened to me. We're breaking new ground here, Mari. For what it's worth, I prefer to do it on my own, without being a lab rat."

"Si, you know I would never—" She looked so affronted it was actually cute. He cut her off by placing one finger over her luscious lips.

"I trust you with my life, Mari. That's why I came here when I got hurt and didn't trek over to the base hospital. I figured if I could trust anyone on this base, it was you, even after what I'd done. I'm gratified to know I was right, but I can't say I'm surprised." For once, he hoped his expression conveyed what he was feeling. "You've always had my utmost respect."

She tilted her head, considering him for a long moment. "And you will always have mine, Simon." Her low voice sent shivers down his spine all out of proportion with the conversation, but then all Mariana had to do was breathe to turn him on. She stood and gathered her supplies. "Get some rest. I'll check on you in a few hours and bring you some food. How does roast beef on rye sound?"

"Delicious. You remembered." He still remembered all her favorite things, too. Like her favorite positions for making love, her favorite places to be touched, and her favorite techniques for making him absolutely crazy with need. But those were better left alone for now. He didn't deserve her. He had never deserved her. All he had now were memories and he would have to be content with them.

"I remember a lot of things, Simon." The heat that flared in her dark eyes told him her agile mind might be tracking along the same path as his.

That was a danger zone, fraught with trouble for them both. He backed off, yawning to break the sudden sexual tension that lay thick in the air. He was drained both physically and emotionally after the physical rigors of the night before and the confrontation with Mari he had put off too long. He wasn't really faking the yawn. His body needed to recharge in a big way.

She let it slide, backing away and heading for the door. "Sleep well, Simon. I'll be back in a couple of hours."

Knowing he would see her again, Simon followed orders and sank into a dreamless sleep on the almost-comfortable cot.

Chapter Three

As it turned out, the clinic was a madhouse for the rest of the day. Mariana was able to sneak in back a few times to peek in and make sure Simon was okay, but that was all she had time for. When one of the nurses went out to get food, she asked her to bring back the roast beef on rye with all the works, plus a salad.

The sandwich was for Simon, the salad for herself. She took a half hour to go in back around two o'clock in the afternoon to find Simon dozing lightly. He was the next thing to ravenous as they ate together, talking about commonplace things and old times. It was light conversation. With the noise from the clinic in the distance, she was just as glad not to get into anything too heavy with him while they ate.

She looked at his wounds once more, shocked by the clear flesh that met her inspection. Not even a scratch marred his skin. Chills went down her spine as she realized how radically his body chemistry must have been altered by whatever had happened to him. He was right to stay clear of any doctor who might not have his best interests at heart. At least for the moment.

Simon could all too easily become some selfish doctor's lab rat. If the changes in his body could be studied—if the healing power he possessed could be harnessed—well, it would make someone very rich indeed. It could also be something the military establishment could use to make their soldiers nearly invulnerable. It could be something huge. And something very dangerous for Simon, since he was the only one in the world to possess such power at the moment.

He was much better off keeping it a secret for now. For all she knew, it could be a temporary condition. It might dissipate on its own. Or it might morph yet again into something that could kill him.

She wished he had come to her in the beginning. She wished he would let her help him more than by just patching up his cuts. But it was his life. His decision. She wouldn't pressure him. She just wanted him to know she would be there if he ever needed her help.

"I'm going to call Commander Sykes and tell him you're much improved and will be on your way after the clinic closes for the day."

"That sounds about right. After this most excellent lunch, I'll probably sleep a few more hours. If Matt Sykes sends over his guy with my stuff, I can duck out of here right after your staff leaves for the night."

She wished he'd stay, but knew her reasons were purely selfish. "I'll call him this afternoon then."

"Mari," his tone grew serious as he drew her attention. "Matt doesn't know about the healing. If you could avoid telling him everything . . ."

"Never fear. I, of all people, can see the potential problems for you if news of your condition got out. I'll tell the commander that you're good to go and that's all he needs to know."

"You're a peach, Mari." The grin her sent her reminded her of their dating days. It was too close to flirting for her comfort.

Mariana stood, gathering up the trash. "I'll let you rest. If you need anything, you know where to find me."

"Thanks, Mari. For everything." The moment stretched and felt just a little too serious. Then he grinned again. "And especially for remembering my favorite sandwich. I've been living off field rations for a few weeks. That roast beef tasted like a little slice of heaven."

He rubbed his stomach with a silly expression on his face and she knew he'd done it to make her laugh. She couldn't help herself. Simon was his most charming when he didn't take himself too seriously. It hadn't happened often, but once in a while he'd unbent enough to act the clown. Just for her.

She left him, still chuckling, and headed for her office to make the promised call to Commander Sykes. She was careful to give the commander the bare facts, not delving into the details of Simon's physical condition, only assuring Sykes that he was fit for duty and would be leaving the clinic that night after closing time. Sykes seemed satisfied with that and Mariana breathed a sigh of relief.

Sykes reminded her there were to be no records of Simon's treatment or even his presence. For once, Mariana was grateful for the clandestine nature of Simon's work. No one would hear of his healing abilities from her—or even know he'd been in her clinic. She trusted her nurses not to say anything, so Simon was in the clear for this incident. She only hoped he would be as lucky the next time he got hurt.

He slept the afternoon away while Mariana finished up her day of duty in the clinic. It had been a busier day than usual and more upsetting by far. She locked the clinic door behind the last nurse to leave and went back to see how Simon fared. A young officer had come over a half hour earlier to drop off a big black duffel full of stuff for Simon's eyes only. She'd directed the man to the back and he had come and gone without much more ado.

Mariana tapped on the door frame, hearing movement from within. "Simon?"

"Come on in, Mari." She heard rustling as she entered and realized he was stuffing his old clothing into the duffel. He had changed into fresh camo BDUs and managed a quick shave. Damn, the man looked good enough to eat.

She'd been down that road before. No matter how much she missed him, and though she knew now why he had left without a word, she wasn't sure she was ready to risk her heart again. He'd broken it once already.

"I just locked up. Everyone's gone for the night."

"Then I'll be going, too. There's not much time before sunset."

She wondered why that mattered. Then again, he'd been on night duty when he'd gotten hurt. Whatever he was doing out there in the woods, it was a nighttime thing. Maybe he had a squad he had to get back to, waiting for him in the trees. She wouldn't ask, no matter how curious she was.

"I can drop you off wherever you want." She thought she would at least make the offer, though he wasn't likely to take her up on it.

"Are you heading right home? No errands to run or places to go tonight?"

She was puzzled by his question, though she saw no harm in answering him truthfully. "No place to go tonight. I'm heading home to do laundry actually."

He lifted the bulging duffel bag as she watched him from near the door. "That's good. Mari"—he stepped close to her, his expression intent—"until my mission is complete, stay close to home at night. It's safer."

"Is there something I should worry about?"

"Just trust me. I can't say more. Just stay inside while the sun's down."

Frankly, she was surprised he'd gone that far. Whatever he was doing in the woods at night, it was dangerous. Dangerous enough for him to warn her when he was probably sworn to secrecy. Now *that* gave her pause.

"All right, Simon. I'll be more cautious after dark."

He prowled over to her in that silent way of his. He moved into her personal space before she could say another word and one of his big hands touched her cheek. He towered over her and something infinitesimal in his eyes made her feel . . . odd.

Not quite the way she used to feel in his presence—totally overwhelmed and as if he was her past, present and future—but protected . . . cherished . . . and regretted.

It was bittersweet.

He didn't say a word as his head dipped and his mouth claimed hers in a poignant farewell. Tears started behind her eyes. She wasn't sure if she would ever see him again after this and the kiss he gave her had a sense of heartbreaking finality in it.

Her hands went to the lapels of his shirt as she pressed herself against his muscular chest. He hadn't changed much since she'd last seen him. Not in any outward way. It was the internal changes that gave her pause.

Simon drew back, holding her gaze. There was something indefinable in his eyes that touched her deeply. The silence stretched as he looked at her and she wondered what thoughts passed through that agile brain of his.

"Stay safe, Mari."

The moment ended and she stepped back. "I'll be fine, Simon. Watch yourself when you're out there. If you need anything, you know where to find me."

"I need a lot of things, Mari." His expression smoldered. "Most of which I can't have."

"Can't you?"

"No." The word hung between them for a timeless moment, then he moved, breaking the spell.

Simon opened the door and held it open for Mariana to precede him. They walked the short distance to the clinic entrance before they both paused once more while she unlocked the door.

"Will I see you again?" Damn, she hadn't meant to ask. She cringed inwardly at how needy she sounded.

"It's not a good idea." His eyes clouded with an emotion she couldn't interpret as the moment dragged.

"I understand." She didn't really, but it seemed the thing to say.

"No you don't." His smile was almost her undoing. "And I

can't tell you any more than I already have. You'll just have to trust me."

"I do. I've always trusted your judgment as far as my safety goes, Simon. I think you're wrong about other things. In particular, I think you're wrong about us."

Their eyes locked. "You don't know how much I wish I were."

He gave her one last, hard kiss, then left her standing in the empty doorway. She saw the sun hanging low in the sky as he walked off, into the setting sun. It was sort of poetic, in a way.

In all other ways, it just plain sucked.

Simon was gone within moments, walking straight into the tree line until he disappeared and she doubted she would ever see him again. Her breath caught in her throat as that realization struck home.

It had been an upsetting day all the way around. She'd discovered things about him—about what had happened to him—that made her want to cry. For him. For the things he'd been through. The uncertainty about his condition, the threat to his life. She hated that he'd had to go through that alone and longed to be let into his life so she could help in whatever way possible.

Simon was a tough guy though. He had rarely opened up to her during their brief affair and now wasn't any different.

At the very least, she'd achieved some closure. Seeing him again and gaining insight into why he had disappeared before helped a little. It would take time to put everything in perspective but at least she wasn't left wondering.

Not about his abandonment anyway. No, now she would wonder about his health, his safety, whether or not he was alive or dead. She would wonder and worry for him. The man she had never gotten over. The lover she missed every single day.

She sighed heavily and left the clinic, heading for her car. The sun was sinking behind the trees and she'd promised him she would stay in tonight. She didn't understand why it was so important to him, but she had felt the urgency in his words, in his stare. So she would go home and do this last thing for him.

It was little enough. This one last thing and then she would do her best to put Simon Blackwell behind her. Forever.

Walking away from Mariana again was one of the hardest things he had ever done. Of course, he didn't see any other way to keep her truly safe. He faded into the trees, then doubled back, watching as she made her way out of the clinic and into her car. When she pulled out and headed for home, he headed back into the woods and began a jogging pace. He decided to head for the woods near her house.

He would check that she made it home safely, then begin his nightly patrol. The search area had grown closer and closer to her backyard lately as the creatures started to go farther and farther afield. That wasn't good. He vowed to contain them. Failure was not an option. Especially not with Mariana's safety in question.

A little more than an hour later, Simon peered through the trees at Mariana's home, watching her move around behind the windows. She was home. Safe for now.

It was time to go hunting.

Mariana tried her best to put the disturbing thoughts of her encounter with Simon out of her head as she ate dinner, but found it impossible. He was never far from her mind. She had learned so much today. Still, she knew so little. His healing was nothing short of miraculous. He had hinted at something horrific that had brought it about and she wanted to know more. She also knew he would never tell. Not unless there was no other choice.

She would either have to be read into the program—which was as likely as a snowball in hell right about now—or she would have to discover what had happened to him on her own somehow. Another fat chance. In all likelihood, she would never know what had brought about his amazing change. She might not ever see him again either. It was that last thought that brought a tear to her eye.

She had loved him so deeply. He had taken up residence in her soul and she realized only now, after seeing him again, that he'd never quite left. She still loved him and cared about what happened to him. Even if they could never be together, she wanted to be sure he was safe. And she wanted him to be happy.

He hadn't looked all that happy today. Dark shadows filled his eyes—even darker than they had been before. His face had been leaner, harder than she remembered, though his physique hadn't suffered. He was still built like a Greek god with a casual attitude about his body that made her mouth water. He used his body as a tool in his work. He didn't perfect that physique by standing in front of a mirror in a gym somewhere. To her, that was a plus. Simon was unconsciously sexy, a warrior first, whose body was a honed weapon.

Just remembering what he could do with that killer bod made her quiver. They had been together far too short a time, in her opinion. She could have spent years making love to him and still not be satisfied. He had ruined her for anyone else.

With a sigh, Mariana finished her lonely dinner and began cleaning up. She spent some time by the sink, washing the dishes that had stacked up over the past few days. She lived alone, so she could afford to be a little lax on the household chores if her work schedule interfered.

Her cabin was rustic, but she loved it. She had taken her time choosing it, wanting something closer to nature than she had ever had before. Hers was the only house on the lane, with her nearest neighbors out of sight over a small hill. The neighbors were quiet, an elderly lady and her granddaughter who took care of her. Mariana had visited them a few times since moving in, but mostly they kept to themselves.

Mariana's backyard was small compared to other places she had lived. It bordered the woods so it felt like the whole forest was her backyard at times. Deer often came out of the woods to nibble on her lawn and there were all kinds of birds and little furry creatures that visited from time to time.

There was a small window over the sink and as dusk turned to deep night, she watched the woods as she worked, noting the appearance of a few small woodland creatures. An owl hooted and she thought she caught the flash of its eyes in one tall pine, but couldn't be certain.

Turning back to her task, she concentrated on the dishes for a while. When she looked up again, the woods were dark, mysterious, and silent. Not a single creature stirred. A predator of some kind must be nearby. The smaller animals always knew when something bigger and badder was around.

She shut off the water and wiped her hands, raising her gaze to take one last look out the window.

She froze, a scream stuck in her throat as a face—a gruesome face—reflected back at her from the other side of the window.

Was it a trick of the light? Was she looking at her own reflection, somehow distorted into a grotesque mask? Or was there someone—or some *thing*—out there, looking back at her?

She dropped to a crouch, using the kitchen counter for cover as her breathing spiked in panic. What to do? Her cell phone was plugged in to the charger in the other room. Her rifle was in the hall closet, unloaded. She had a few kitchen carving knives in the drawer behind her, but she wasn't much of a hand-to-hand fighter. She'd had the training early in her career with the Navy, of course, but had only done enough to pass, never excelled.

She cursed her own inability and laziness. She had meant to better her skills. She'd just never gotten around to it. Something always had seemed to get in the way or be more important. Now she saw the folly in her delay. She would go tomorrow and sign up for a self-defense course. It was stupid to live way out here on her own with no real way to defend herself should someone try something.

If someone was really out there, she was a sitting duck. The more she thought about what she had seen in that flash of time, the more convinced she was that something really was out there. A person or maybe a few kids playing a trick of some kind, trying to scare the shit out of her. Well, they'd succeeded, if that was their aim. If not, what was up with the guy she'd seen?

And what was with that face? The quick glimpse she'd gotten looked like something had gnawed off parts of that horribly misshapen face. She was so frightened, yet felt silly. She didn't know if she had really seen what she thought she'd seen. Second guessing her senses, she still wasn't quite brave enough to stand up and take another look outside.

Instead, she listened carefully, every sense extended as she cowered behind the sink. Was that a creak? Did something just brush against the exterior of the house?

Oh, God.

This was ridiculous. Cowering there by the sink like a ninny was getting her no place. It was time to man up and go see what was really going on. For all she knew, it could really just be some local kids prowling around, hoping to scare the bejeezus out of someone. She'd be damned if she would be the one they snickered over in the woods.

Crawling forward, she plotted a path out of the kitchen that wouldn't expose her to view from the window. It involved climbing under the kitchen table, but she was okay with that. She could stand to lose a little dignity in exchange for safety— just in case it wasn't kids and there really was some sort of trespassing Peeping Tom outside her window.

Mariana headed for the hall closet first. Better to be armed and the phone was farther away. She felt marginally better with the rifle cradled in her arms, fully loaded and ready for action. Next, she grabbed her phone, dialing the emergency number as she moved toward the back door that faced the woods. She approached it at an oblique angle, trying to peer out the small window set into the door.

The phone seemed to work at first, then petered out and died. Not enough juice. Damn. She'd have to go back into the other room to get the charging cord and she didn't want to take the time. The more time that passed, the more she became convinced that she had to have been seeing things. No suspicious sounds came from outside and she couldn't see anything, or anyone, in her backyard. Maybe it had all been just a trick of the light. Or if it was kids, they were gone now that they'd succeeded in their prank.

Cautiously, she opened the back door and stepped onto the porch.

A second later she saw it, coming from the woods. It looked like a man in tattered camo fatigues, but its face . . . its face was . . . horrible.

Streaked with grime that didn't look like camo paint, bits of flesh hung off his jaw and gouges were taken out of his hollow cheeks. His eyes were vacant, staring. His jaw locked in position, seemingly unable to move.

Mariana stared. Her rifle lay in her arms, but she was unable to lift it—or even to think—as the thing came toward her.

"Get in the house!"

She knew that voice. Or rather, that shout. It was coming from the woods.

"Simon?" She peered into the darkness, looking for him. He broke through the cover of the trees a moment later. He ran toward her and the creature, weapons in hand.

"In the house, now!"

She didn't need further urging. Her body responded to the order in his tone, the urgency of his command. She fled, locking the door behind her and racing through the house, rifle in hand, to make sure all the other entrances were shut tight.

The windows were vulnerable, of course, but they were small enough that a full-grown man would have to shimmy through them carefully, if he even fit at all. It was a trade-off she'd made for safety, living alone out here in the woods. Smaller windows meant less light and a reduced view. When she had first seen the house and the tiny windows, she'd thought the decrease in light was worth the increase in protection, and that compromise was paying off now.

House as secure as she could make it, Mariana returned to the kitchen. She peeked out the window. No sign of the monster that had taken the form of a man. She gasped as a camo green covered chest filled her vision.

Simon was on her porch, in front of her door. Thank God.

"Is it clear?" she asked through the door.

"For the moment. Open up, Mari."

She did, flinging her arms around him as he stepped over the threshold. She heard him kick the door shut behind him and the dead bolt snick into place. Thankfully he didn't let her go, even as he saw to their safety. She was shaking from head to foot and he was a solid, comforting presence.

Rifle barrel gripped tight in one hand, she clung to him, reaction setting in. After a moment she felt his arms settle around her shoulders, stroking her back as she shook.

"It's all right now, sweetheart. I took care of the problem. He won't trouble you again." His deep voice crooned to her, calming her further. At length, she stepped back.

Damn, he looked good. Whole and healthy once more. She never would have believed he'd be in such good shape after the way she had seen him, broken and bleeding only hours ago. His color was good, though his face was darkened in places with camo paint. He was all hunter, lean and alert, clearly on a mission.

"What was that? What did you do with him?"

"He's gone. That's all you need to know."

"More secrecy, Simon?" She hated the way her voice broke, her blood still running high with emotion. "I can't take much more, you know. Not now. Not after that guy scared the living shit out of me!"

"Whoa," he reached for her, tugging her into his arms again. "Calm down, honey. You're okay. He's gone and I'm here. I'll watch over you."

That sounded awfully possessive to her. "How did you know where I live?" His expression shuttered as she looked up at him, pulling out of his arms. "You've been watching my house, haven't you?"

She had her answer when he looked away. His face never betrayed his thoughts, but his eyes told stories. At least to her. She had always been able to uncover his feelings just by looking into his eyes.

"Damn it, Simon. Am I in danger out here?"

"Yes." Well, he certainly didn't pull his punches. She would give him that. "You should think hard about moving onto the base until this is all over. As you saw firsthand tonight, it isn't safe to be out here in the woods all by yourself."

"What the hell was that, Simon? I saw his face. He looked like . . . like some kind of monster. Like something had been eating his face!"

She'd seen more than he'd thought. More than he'd hoped. More than she should have.

"Come clean with me, Simon. You know I won't share classified information or blow your mission. I need to know what that was and . . . if there are more." The crack in her unsteady voice moved him.

He shouldn't tell her anything more. She had seen too much already. On the other hand, she was an experienced Naval officer with a distinguished record. He knew her personally, and knew she could be trusted. Furthermore, he knew her personality and that she was likely to try digging for answers on her own. That path could only lead to trouble.

For her sake, he would give her a little more information. It was a judgment call on his part, and he trusted her to be circumspect.

"There are more, Mari. That's why you need to get out of here. They come out at night. The sun makes them hide. Clouds and twilight are their friends. Whatever you do, don't go out in the woods when it's overcast, or at night. If they bite you, you're dead."

"What about if they bite *you*? God, Simon! Your mission is to take out these things, isn't it? That's why you're here and why everything is so hush-hush."

"You always were quick, Mari. And now you know way more than you should."

"But not nearly everything, I'll bet."

"I've said too much already."

"Who am I going to tell? You know I would never put you

or your career in danger, Simon. I'll keep your secrets, but I'm worried for you and scared to death of what I just saw." She was still trembling. He hated seeing her in such a state. "You've been living in the woods, hunting these things, haven't you?"

He couldn't deny that. His bivouac was very close to her house, in fact. "I've been nearby," he hedged.

She crumpled, sinking into one of the kitchen chairs. "Then you might as well stay here during the day. This house is practically in the woods and after that injury, even with your new superpowers, you should be sleeping in a bed, not on the ground in the elements." He heard the sarcasm and the very real concern for his well-being in her voice.

He weighed his options. Her plan had merit, loath as he was to admit it. She worked during the day and wouldn't be in the cabin except on her days off. He worked nights on this mission and the cabin was convenient to his hunting grounds. The only thing that stopped him from accepting her offer was the possibility that he might bring more of the zombies to her door.

Of course, at least one of them seemed to have found her on his own. That was a troubling development. If they were ranging closer to the few houses that dotted this area, they were getting more adventurous. Not a good sign at all. He had to work fast before the infection spread any further.

"All right. I'll camp out on your porch during the day. At night, I'll expect you to either hole up tight inside or stay on base for your own safety. As you saw tonight, I can't be everywhere at once. This one slipped past me. I'm sorry, Mari." He hated to think what had almost happened. "If I'd been any later—"

"You weren't." She cut off his words with a gentle touch of one hand on his forearm. His compassionate lover was back, comforting him when she was the one truly in need of comfort. His Mari had a heart as big as the world. "Thank you for coming to my rescue."

"If one of them ever gets that close to you again, I want you to promise me you'll run, Mari. Regular bullets don't work on these guys. If they bite you, you'll die. Then you'll become one of them." Unspoken went the thought that he would have to destroy her if the worst happened. It would kill him.

"They're infectious?"

"Highly. The contagion is in their bite. And they really like to bite."

"You got bitten." Understanding dawned in her eyes. "That's what happened to you, isn't it?"

Grimly, he nodded. "I'm a one in a million case. I survived. And I'm not a carrier. I'm not contagious and can't give it to anyone."

"That's why they sent you after these things."

"The virus doesn't work on me. Something in my system gives me immunity, though it did make me very sick the first time. Since then, well, you saw the changes in my healing. That's what the virus was designed to do, but . . ." He trailed off, realizing he was saying too much.

"But something went horribly wrong. Simon, this is terrible. Truly awful."

"You won't get an argument from me." He leaned back against the kitchen counter. "Look, I have to get back out there. I was tracking two more of them when I heard the commotion over here. They can't be far and I want to get them before they go to ground for the day."

"You've been doing this every night for the past four months?" He read the disbelief and horror on her beautiful face.

"I spent the first month scouting. These guys were once Marines. They still retain some of their knowledge and training, as far as I can tell. They know how to evade capture and hide in the woods."

"How many more are there?"

"Near as we can figure, just a few more. We've accounted for all but a handful of missing Marines. A few more weeks and I'll be done laying them to rest."

That made her pause. Those . . . things . . . had once been men. Marines, from what Simon had said.

"Did they volunteer for the initial experiment?" She was almost afraid of his answer—if he'd answer at all. He'd been surprisingly forthcoming so far, but she knew he hadn't told her everything. She also knew there were limits on how far he would go in briefing her.

"The initial group was made up of Marines who had fallen in battle with no family other than the Corps. They left their bodies to science and one of your colleagues in the medical world used them for the initial round of tests."

"They were reanimated after death?" The horror of that didn't bear thinking about, yet it had been done.

"An unintended consequence of what was supposed to have been a much simpler test. Something to do with cellular response. I'm no expert on the science part. I guess they figured there wasn't a need for any security on the lab. No need to protect a few dead bodies, right?" He paused and shivers coursed down her spine. "Then the corpses got up and walked out of the lab in the middle of the night. Being good soldiers, they headed for cover in the woods. Soon after, the first attacks began. A platoon of Marines was sent after them and only a few made it back. The rest became what you saw tonight. Me and my men were called in and we learned how to fight them. The science team came up with a toxin that disrupts the bioelectric connections that keep them going. They sort of disintegrate as their cells lose cohesion. It's the only thing that stops them. Regular bullets don't even slow them down. They feel no pain and can't really die. Because they're already dead." He straightened and checked his weapons. "I'm going to leave this with you." He handed her a pistol loaded with what looked like a dart. "Only use it if absolutely necessary. Aim for any exposed skin. The toxin works fast once delivered, but stay clear until the zombie disintegrates. That's the only way to be certain it's finished."

"Zombie? You're calling them that?" She was appalled.

He shrugged. "It seemed to fit. They're dead. They're walking around trying to eat people. Sounds just like one of those old horror movies to me."

"Good Lord." She took the weapon gingerly, checking the safety automatically. She noted his approving nod.

"Be very careful with the darts. The substance inside can kill you as easily as it does the zombies. It's highly classified and usually kept under lock and key unless I'm out hunting."

"That's why Commander Sykes was so keen to take control of your weapons while you were in the clinic."

"And why only his staff has access to the vault where my ammo is kept. I'm probably breaking a half dozen rules giving this to you." He impressed her with his serious mien. "I figure you're a doctor, you probably know how to handle this stuff without hurting yourself, and as we just saw, you're in the line of fire. If you won't agree to leave, you should at least have some protection."

"I'm not leaving."

"We'll argue more about that later." The slight roll of his eyes and lift of his lips told her he was taking her refusal better than she had expected. Simon could be very autocratic at times. Luckily, those times were rare.

"I'm not driving anywhere in the dark tonight with more of those things nearby. I think I'm safer here, for the time being at least."

"Fair enough. For now. Look, I've got to go. Lock everything. Barricade what can't be sealed any other way. Hunker down and lay low. I'll be back at dawn when they go to ground for the day. If you have any problems before then, call this number." He scribbled on a pad she kept on the counter near the door. "Put that in your speed dial. I have a cell phone set on vibrate. I'll feel it, even if I can't answer, and come running. Be vigilant." He paused by the door. "I don't like leaving you alone here."

"Go do your job, Si. I'll be all right until you get back. And I do know how to shoot. Remember?" Once upon a time, they'd shared a memorable afternoon at the shooting range followed by a spectacular night of lovemaking. It had been their third date and the first time they'd made love.

"I remember, Mari." In a lightning quick move he pulled her

into his arms for a quick kiss that left her weak kneed. He let her go all too soon, while her world was still spinning. "Lock this after me and stay out of view of the windows. If they see you, they'll coming looking."

"Aye, aye, sir." She tried to hide how scared she really was. Scared, but she was staying in her house. She wouldn't abandon ship when Simon was out there, in danger. She would wait for him. Just like she had been waiting for him since he left the last time. Only this time, he'd promised to come back. She didn't know how long he would stay this time, but for at least one more day, he'd be in her world.

She was beginning to think any time with him was better than forever without him.

It was a dangerous path she was on, in more ways than one. He had broken her heart once already. More than likely, she was already setting herself up for another fall, and putting herself in harm's way just to be near him. If he didn't break her, the zombies just might.

Chapter Four

Simon returned just after dawn. Mariana hadn't been able to sleep a wink, but it didn't matter. She wasn't on duty today and didn't have to go anywhere.

She'd spent the night making a fortress out of her little cabin in the woods, barricading windows and covering them with curtains, blankets, and any kind of dark fabric she could find. She didn't want to be seen from outside as she moved around in the house. All the while, she had kept watch on the woods, dreading seeing another one of those monsters staring back at her. Or worse, seeing Simon emerge, covered in blood the way he had been the day before in the infirmary.

When he finally did show up, he looked tired. Tired and unharmed. Thank heaven. She let him in, surreptitiously looking him over to be sure he was truly all right.

"You're a sight for sore eyes," she admitted as he walked past her shouldering a small pack.

"Miss me?" He looked tense and a little grim even as he teased her.

"What's wrong?"

He paused, lowering his pack to the floor. "You always could read me like a book. Nobody else can, Mari. It's a little unnerving."

She was surprised by the moment of candor and decided to repay it in kind. "Nothing shows on your face, Simon. It's your eyes . . . I can read a whole story from the way they sparkle at me. It's subtle and it took me a while to figure out your secret code." She gave him a lopsided smile. "I doubt a casual acquaintance would be able to read you at all. Never fear." He regarded her for a minute more, then turned away. He was clearly uncomfortable with her words. It wasn't the first time she'd said something that made him wary and it likely wouldn't be the last. Not if he stuck around for any length of time. "Did you get your man?"

His lips tightened. "I got them both. It's . . . not easy to end them. They were Marines. They shouldn't have died that way."

She realized he was dealing with some serious emotional issues on this mission in addition to the danger and sheer weirdness factor. Mariana had thought about it all night while she had been cowering like a mouse in her cabin. She felt a certain amount of sympathy for the Marines who'd died only to become monsters, but the zombies themselves freaked her out. Big time.

"From the little I saw last night, it has to be done, Simon. They're lucky to have someone like you on the job." His compassion and insight didn't surprise her. She'd long suspected he had a sensitive soul hidden under that tough as nails exterior.

"Did you have any trouble here?"

He was changing the subject again. Her cue to let it go. For now, she would let him have his way.

"No trouble after you left. I took your advice and shored up the cabin. I made a place for you in the spare room."

"I'm happy on the porch. I don't need anything fancy."

"It's not fancy. It's just a bed, Simon. Why sleep outside on the porch when you can be more comfortable in a real bed just a few yards away?"

She motioned him toward the short hall off the kitchen and he followed with his pack.

"So you're not leaving, I take it?"

"I've been thinking about it and I'm staying. From what you said, those things have been out in the woods for months now and I've never seen one until last night. Chances are, I'll be fine out here, right?" She opened the door to the small guest room and preceded him into the tightly furnished space. The bed took up most of the area, with a little room to squeeze by to get to the chest of drawers and small table in one corner.

"I'd feel better if you stayed on base until this is over, Mari." He had stopped in the doorway, crowding her into the small room with just his presence. She'd forgotten how huge he really was in comparison to her. He was overwhelming . . . in the most deliciously masculine way, of course.

"I'll consider it if there are further problems, but for right now, I'm staying put. I've barricaded the doors and covered the windows. This place is sealed up tight and unless they have access to C4 or other high explosives, I doubt anyone will be able to get in here once I've shut it up tight for the night."

"The fact that you saw one of the zombies at all means they're getting more adventurous, ranging farther afield. It's not a good sign, Mari."

She couldn't respond to the appeal in his voice. She needed to be here, to be sure he came back every morning, to see him and talk to him. Maybe it was foolish, but she'd gone for months without seeing him and this might be her last chance to store up memories of Simon before he left again. If memories were all she could have of him, she wanted as many as possible to hold against the long, lonely future ahead.

"Don't ask me to leave, Si." Her voice whispered through the space between them, making the moment more intimate. Simon moved closer, holding her gaze.

"Mari, I didn't want you involved in this." She saw the caring in his expression, for once unguarded and open. "I worry for your safety. I'd die if anything happened to you."

He cupped her cheek as he moved closer still. Those were some pretty serious words and she knew he meant every syllable. They warmed her, as did the longing in his eyes.

"I could say the same for you, Simon. I worry about you. I don't ever want to see you covered in blood the way you were the other day." This time, she stepped closer, bridging the gap between their yearning bodies. She stepped right into his arms and pressed herself against him as his hands slipped around her waist and shoulders, drawing her close.

"Mari . . ." He whispered her name with need in his voice as she raised her lips to his.

The kiss was uncontainable. She felt the strength of his arms, the passion in his embrace and the undeniable hardness of him pressing against her. It was intoxicating. *He* was intoxicating. As he always had been. She was swept away as he walked her two steps backward until her calves came in contact with the edge of the bed.

When he eased her downward, she didn't demur. She wanted every second, every moment she could grab in his arms. His tongue worshiped her, sweeping into her mouth in stark possession. His hands caressed her, carrying her down to the bed as gently as his passion would allow.

When the kiss ended, he only took her deeper, settling over her on the bed that was barely big enough for the two of them. Her legs parted, cradling his hips and she despaired of the fabric that lay between them. She wanted to feel the rough skin of his thighs, the smooth, muscled contours of his abs and buttocks under her hands, the way she remembered.

His lips trailed kisses down her neck and onto the small expanse of skin accessible in the vee neck of her shirt. Then the nuisance became too much and she tugged at the hem of her top, wanting it gone. He helped, pulling it off over her head and throwing it aside. He made short work of the front clasp on her bra and then her breasts were in his big hands, her nipples kissed by his possessive lips, then licked, then sucked in the most delicious way. Simon had always known how to touch her, from the first time they'd been together.

They'd made love many times in the comparatively few short weeks they'd been together, but each time had been special and unique. Simon was an inventive lover and the most satisfying of any of the men she had bedded in her admittedly limited experience. She hadn't been able to bear another man's touch since he had left. She hadn't dated, she hadn't even flirted. She'd felt no desire to attract any other man's attention and worried that she would end up alone with only memories of Simon to comfort her in her old age.

That could still happen. In fact, it was more likely now than ever. Simon hadn't said anything about wanting to get back together. He'd told her why he'd left and that reason seemed to continue to plague him. There were too many questions surrounding the future to know what it might hold for the two of them.

But none of that mattered now. Not with Simon's knowing hands on her body, lowering the zipper on her jeans and sliding inside her panties. No, when Simon touched her, all coherent thought slipped from her mind.

She pushed at his shirt, hearing the sound of tearing fabric as she struggled with his clothing. He slid her jeans down her legs along with her panties and then his capable hands took over the task of removing his own clothes. Thank heavens. Within moments, he was as bare as she, lying over her, his muscular thighs in the space between her legs, his cock hard and waiting only for her to be ready to take him.

Simon always sought her pleasure before his own. He was a considerate and expert lover and even in their haste to come together after so long apart, he was careful of her. His hands stroked down over her rib cage as he watched her reactions, then into the vee of her thighs, spreading, parting. His fingers dipped within the wet folds, teasing and making her squirm.

"Don't make me wait, Simon. I need you now!"

"This is going to be so good. Let me make it good for you, Mari." He slid one thick finger into her core, his thumb circling her clit, heightening her pleasure. Bending over her, he placed licking kisses up her abdomen, pausing at her breasts to suck and nibble gently, all the while stroking into her depths with that maddening finger.

"Are you close, sweetheart? Are you going to come?"

"Simon!" She panted, raising her head to watch him as he teased her. He had kept her on the knife's edge of pleasure before but she couldn't take that kind of play tonight. She wanted him more than she'd ever wanted him before. She had to have him.

"That close, eh?" His knowing grin was almost her undoing. "Come for me then, baby. Come on my hand."

As if in response to his wicked words, her inner core clenched hard on his invading fingers. She cried out at the climax that hit her from out of nowhere. It had been fast and not nearly satisfying enough. With Simon though, she knew there was more to come. Only with Simon had she ever achieved multiple orgasms and this promised to be one of those encounters.

He held her gaze as her body quaked around his hand. She was so open to him, so willing to give him everything, anything he asked. She knew it was written all over her face but only his glittering eyes told her how much he hungered for her at that moment, how much he wanted to be inside her. He removed his hand from her body and reached over to grab his pants off the floor.

She followed his movements, glad to see at least one of them was still thinking clearly. Simon grabbed a condom out of his pants pocket, opened the foil packet, and rolled it over himself with efficient movements. Only the slight trembling of his hands told her how much he wanted to be inside her. As much as she wanted him, she guessed.

When he came back to her, she made room for him between her legs and he grinned. An unguarded, sexy grin that took her breath away and made her insides clench.

"I've been dreaming about this, Mari. So many dreams," he whispered. Levering himself into just the right position, he held her gaze as he slid into her.

For Simon, it was like coming home after an eternity away.

Her wet heat surrounded him, gloved him in her warmth, like no other woman had ever done. There hadn't been anyone since Mariana, and with all that had happened to him in the interim, he very much doubted any other woman could ever take her place.

She would never know that, of course. He couldn't tell her. It was bad enough he had succumbed now, when she was still in danger from the creatures he hunted. By all rights, he should have left her alone, but circumstances had conspired to bring them together one last time. One last time to hold her, to worship her body with his own and feel . . . complete.

Simon paused deep within her, savoring the feeling. The forbidden feeling of being one with the only woman who had ever really mattered to him. He wouldn't call it love, thought it was something just as big and scary. She completed him in a way no one else ever had. She was funny, smart, and so beautiful. He cared for her more deeply than he had ever cared for anyone.

Pain lanced through his heart as he thought of having to leave her. Again. For inevitably, he would have to go. He would have to let her get on with her life.

But not today. No, today was a moment out of time. A moment for them to steal. A moment for him to spend making love with the most magical woman he'd ever met.

Simon began to move, each thrust rocking his world. Making love with Mari had always been like that, from the very beginning. It was good to see that hadn't changed in the years since they'd been together last.

"You're beautiful, baby. And so tight. Damn." He tried to hold on to his excitement but it was slipping through his fingers. This first time was going to be fast. He only prayed Mari was with him. He didn't know if he could wait for her this time. It had been too long. Much too long.

"Simon!" She breathed in excited gasps, the evidence of her renewed arousal pushing his own higher. "Simon, I'm so close." She grasped his hips and urged him to move faster, wrapping

SIMON SAYS / 209

her luscious legs around him. Little keening moans issued from her lips with his every thrust. He remembered the signs. Thank God, she was as close to oblivion as he was.

Able to let go at last, Simon pounded into her, giving her the slightly rough fuck that he knew she liked. He liked it, too. Almost too much. He had never been able to completely let go like this with another woman. Mari was like no one else. She matched him in every way. Her heels locked around the small of his back, her body stretching beautifully to accommodate him as if she were made to take him, made to receive his passion.

And perhaps she was. There was no doubt he had never found a more perfect bed partner. If he was the type to believe in happily ever after, he would certainly put Mariana at the top of his very short list of possible life mates. In fact, she was the only one on his list.

If he believed in that sort of thing.

But all of that didn't matter as he felt his climax building, ready to release. He touched her, to be certain she would be with him at the last. He wanted her with him . . . always.

That crazy thought haunting his mind, Simon's orgasm hit him like a fifty-caliber round, punching him skyward in a blinding rush of light and pleasure so intense, he nearly blacked out. He heard her cry out under him and knew she had found the same shuddering release as he spasmed within her tight depths.

She was magic, pure and simple. His Mari. His love.

They spent the day in bed, sleeping only to make love again and again. Mariana had given herself permission to enjoy this time without worrying about the future. It was the only way she could deal with this whole messed-up situation.

Zombies running around in the woods. Simon, back in her life, in her bed. It was all too bizarre and almost too much to take in.

They'd moved to her bedroom in the afterglow of their first climax together in years. Her bed was bigger and more comfortable than the one in the spare room. Simon had carried her in his arms from the spare room to her room and planted her in her big, fluffy bed. Then they'd lazed there all day, making love and chatting about commonplace things when they weren't dozing in each other's arms. Those were hours out of time, floating in some utopian world.

She had gone into the kitchen once or twice to get them sustenance, but other than that, they'd either been sleeping or making love since sunrise. By sunset, she was sore in places that hadn't been sore since Simon left, and in desperate need of a shower. She soaked in the hot stream of water until Simon came in to fish her out.

That led to a slippery encounter in the shower that almost landed them both on their backsides. Simon's sheer brute strength saved them from more than one potential fall that could have cracked both the porcelain bathroom fixtures and Mari's bones. She was also delighted to discover his inventiveness was back in full force. He had taken her in every position she could think of and a few she had never even contemplated throughout the day. She'd loved every minute of his possession, his passion, his desire.

Only one thing was missing, as it had been during their halcyon days years before. He had never uttered those three little words she longed to hear. She'd always thought and hoped he had felt the same way about her as she had about him, but he'd never said it in so many words. Mariana thought she'd be beyond the need to hear it now, yet the niggling thought remained with her while she dressed and headed for the kitchen where Simon had promised to prepare a meal before he went out on patrol.

They hadn't talked much about anything serious during the day, spending their time either sleeping or making love. All in all, she'd had worse days, but she didn't think she'd ever had better. Her body was deliciously sore and even with her mind in a whirl, she was looking forward to spending as much time with Simon as she could . . . before he left her again.

She resolved not to think about that now. She might be deluding herself, but she wanted whatever time she could get with him. For however long it lasted.

Entering the kitchen, she saw he had pulled out all the stops. Chicken breasts from her freezer had been thawed and marinated and were now cooking nicely on the stove. He had made rice and green beans, too. He was fairly well domesticated for a man. Of course, special ops guys were trained to survive in many different kinds of situations. The kitchen training though, had to have come from his mother, or some other nurturing influence in his life. This was too much like a family dinner not to have been something from out of his past.

"Where'd you learn to cook?"

He turned, spatula in hand, and leaned down to give her a quick kiss. Before it could turn into something more, she scooted away from the stove.

"Now is that any way to greet your chef?" He shook the spatula at her in mock chastisement, then turned back to turn the chicken.

"If I let you *greet* me any more, our dinner would end up burnt to a crisp."

He tilted his head as if considering. "You may have a point there."

"So where did you learn to cook like this? It looks and smells wonderful."

"My mother believed her boys should at least know their way around a kitchen. As it happened, I enjoyed helping her. More than my brothers, at least."

This was the first time he had talked about his family with her. When they'd been together before, he'd been very reticent. He had never talked about his past or where he'd come from beyond the basic vital statistics. Something had subtly changed within him in the years since.

It wasn't noticeable at first glance. Only now that some of the barriers between them had broken down, little by little, she was seeing new facets to him that hadn't been visible before. Anytime she had tried to ask about his past before, he'd managed to steer the conversation back to her. He probably knew more about her family than anyone except maybe her family members themselves. He was as adept at evading questions as he was at evading the enemy.

"How many brothers do you have?"

"Two. One older and one younger. All three of us can cook if we have to, but Jeremy and Bobby don't enjoy it half as much as I do. They used to joke that I should become a chef and wear one of those poufy white hats. Then I'd pound some sense into their heads and they'd drop the subject. I still like to cook when I get a chance."

"Lucky me." She smiled at him as he plated the chicken and brought it to the table. He'd already set out the steaming rice and green beans. It was a simple and hearty dinner that both looked and smelled delicious.

"Did they join the military, too?" They served themselves and began to eat.

"I followed Jeremy in, but he went in for jets in a big way. He's a test pilot now, the crazy bastard. Bobby got accepted to Annapolis and is on the fast track to the admiralty if my mother is to be believed. The family is really proud of him. He was always a smart, sort of nerdy kid, and he's grown into a fine officer."

"He's still in?"

Simon nodded as he ate a bite of chicken. "Stationed at the Pentagon right now."

"This is really delicious, by the way. Thanks for cooking. I don't think a man has ever cooked dinner for me before. It's nice."

"Just my way of saying thanks. For letting me stay here and for this afternoon." His expression shuttered. "Mari, I—"

"Don't." She cut him off, unwilling to hear him say it had all been some kind of big mistake. "Let's just say it was for old time's sake and leave it at that."

An uncomfortable silence greeted her words. Not daring to

look at him, she applied herself to her dinner and refused to meet his eyes. She was afraid of what she might find there.

"It was more than just old time's sake, Mari." His low words forced her gaze upward to meet his. His eyes glittered with something she didn't know how to interpret. Strange, when she'd thought she'd known every nuance of his subtle communication. "Thank you for today."

It sounded so formal. She didn't really know what to say, so she nodded tightly and returned her attention to her plate.

"Are you going back out tonight?" She already knew the answer, but desperately needed to change the subject.

"I hunt every night, and will continue to do so until this is finally over."

"It won't be long now though, right? I mean, you said you thought there weren't too many left."

"There were probably about six left, near as we can figure. I got three last night, so that leaves three more. Once they're accounted for, I'll patrol for a few more nights, just to be certain. Then my job will be done."

"And then you'll leave."

"Then I'll leave," he agreed.

"Where will you go? You're not military anymore, so where do you go between assignments?"

"I have a place in southeastern Pennsylvania, near my folks. It's a small farm, actually. I don't have any livestock for it yet. That's in the works. As soon as I get some time to set things up the way I want them, I figured I'd keep a horse or two, maybe some chickens. Later, when I'm not working for hire anymore."

"Sounds like heaven."

"Your dad owned a big spread in Kansas, didn't he?"

"Yeah, I grew up on the farm. It belongs to my brothers now." She was surprised he'd remembered, but then, he had managed to get her entire life's story out of her back when they had been dating.

"You sound like you miss it."

"I didn't think I would, but as I get older, I find myself longing for the simple things. A little place to plant a vegetable garden and live in peace with nature sounds like heaven to me now."

"What about your medical practice? I thought you wanted the bright lights and the big city after your stint in the Navy was up."

"I guess I did at one time, although I thought I'd stay in the service a lot longer. Things changed as I got older and my priorities realigned. My time in the Navy is almost over. I didn't re-up. I'll be a civilian again in just a few short weeks." She was surprised to hear the almost wistful tone in her voice. "I've been thinking about my options a lot. I've had enough of the hustle and bustle while I was in the Navy. It wasn't what I really thought it would be when I was younger. Now a quiet life appeals to me much more. That's why I opted for this cabin way out here in the woods rather than stay on base or in town. I like the quiet."

"That's quite a change from the way you used to talk." He sat back, finished with his meal, and just watched her.

She shrugged, uncomfortable with his scrutiny. "I've changed in the past few years. My priorities have shifted a bit. That's all."

Unspoken went the thought that the failure of her relationship with him had changed her on a basic level. His leaving and his lack of communication after had made her rethink her priorities in a big way. She had spent a lot of time reevaluating her life and her goals. What had seemed so important when she was younger wasn't nearly as crucial now. No, now the things she had shunned when she left the farm were what mattered most. Family, familiar surroundings, a home to nest in and make her own . . . and love.

She didn't know if she'd ever really find it, but she wouldn't give up hoping that somehow, she would have love in her life. The love of family, of friends, and if she was really lucky . . . the love of one special man.

The man sitting across the table from her right now, in fact.

But he was a tough nut to crack. She'd tried, and he'd left. She didn't think she had a chance to convince him now. It was probably too late for them to start over. She would have to settle for what she could get now, because the day spent in his arms had only brought home how much her feelings were still engaged. She loved him with all her heart.

Chapter Five

Simon went out the door after a lingering kiss. He had made her promise to stay inside and he'd also left the specially loaded dart pistol with her again, just in case. As the night deepened, so did her fear for both his safety and of the creatures that stalked the night with him, evading and possibly lying in wait for him.

She wasn't foolish enough to go out there, thinking she could be some sort of GI Jane with guns blazing by his side. She knew her limitations, and while she could defend herself if necessary, she was nobody's idea of a warrior. She could hit what she aimed at and had passed the required self-defense tests, but she was a doctor first and foremost. Her calling was to heal, not to tear apart.

And if Simon was to be believed, those fallen Marines out there were really into tearing people apart and sentencing them to join their sinister brotherhood. The thought sent chills down her spine.

Around four in the morning, Mariana heard a noise outside and peeked out the windows to see if she could see anything. Sure enough, in back of the house, she caught a glimpse of light fabric as someone walked through the woods.

The Marines wore camo or dark green. The figure she saw

looked small, possibly female. Could it be little Becky Sue McGillicuddy, the twenty-something girl who lived just over the hill with her elderly grandmother?

If so, the girl was in big trouble. The locals had most definitely not been warned about the danger in the woods. It was unusual to see the girl walking alone this early in the morning, but then, Becky Sue had always struck Mariana as a little odd on the few occasions they did chance to meet.

She had to be warned.

Gathering her courage, Mariana opened the back door and stepped onto the porch. Simon's specially loaded pistol was in her hand and her heart was in her throat. She could see more clearly now and it was the girl from the neighboring house, walking calmly along the edge of the trees.

"Becky Sue!" She whispered loudly, hoping to get the girl's attention.

It must not have been loud enough because Becky Sue kept walking at a steady pace, looking neither left nor right. Her path took her nearer to Mariana's house, but the girl was still in the woods, walking almost parallel to Mariana's backyard.

"Becky Sue." She tried again, louder this time.

The girl paused and slowly turned.

Half her face was missing.

Mariana jumped back, her raised hand hitting the frame of the doorway in her haste. She held on to the pistol out of sheer desperation. Becky Sue was one of them. She wasn't *in* danger. She *was* the danger.

The girl changed paths and began walking directly toward Mariana. She didn't hurry. She didn't run. She just walked relentlessly closer as Mariana trembled in fear.

She raised the gun, knowing what she had to do. Now she fully understood Simon's dilemma. Could she shoot a young girl who'd had her whole life ahead of her?

As a doctor, Mariana had dedicated her life to helping people. She had never deliberately shot at someone, even with a dart gun. Especially not a dart gun loaded with a highly dangerous top secret toxin that had to be kept under lock and key. Mariana's hand shook as she took aim. She had to steady both the gun and her nerves. Becky Sue got closer and Mariana could see her more clearly with every step.

She realized she couldn't kill the girl. Becky Sue was already dead. Nobody could survive the kind of injuries she displayed and her pale skin appeared to be completely bloodless. She was a zombie. Like something out of a horror movie.

Praying silently, Mariana pulled the trigger.

A dart flew from the business end of the pistol and landed square in Becky Sue's chest. She didn't even flinch, just kept coming. No pain at all registered on what was left of her once lovely face.

Mariana fired again. The dart hit lower, in Becky Sue's abdomen. She was closer now, out of the tree line and halfway across the grassy yard. A sound traveled on the wind. It was an eerie kind of high pitched moan that sent shivers down Mariana's spine.

She fired once more, backing into the doorway already planning her next move. She would slam the door shut and call Simon's cell number. If he was nearby, he would come help her. The third dart hit Becky Sue midthigh and her steps slowed. The shock of pain was still missing from her ruined face, but her eyes looked queer for just a moment, then she . . . disintegrated.

She melted from the top down. In less than sixty seconds, she disappeared. All that was left was a dark pile of . . . something . . . in Mariana's backyard. She wasn't about to go out to see exactly what it was. Whether the girl had been turned to dust or goo was really beside the point. The toxin had done its job and the once vibrant young girl was now gone forever.

Mariana felt awful about what she'd had to do, yet breathed a huge sigh of relief. She looked around at the woods in case there were any more of them, and seeing none, shut the door, locking it tight behind her. She was safe for now.

She said a prayer for poor Becky Sue McGillicuddy, and one for Simon while she was at it. Now more than ever, she understood how hard this mission was for him. He wasn't made of stone, no matter what anyone thought. He had a compassionate heart under all that macho bravado. He had to feel something for those fallen soldiers he had to lay to rest. He had to have some feelings about the experiment gone so terribly wrong for those first fallen comrades, and for the later victims, and the horrific way they had died.

Mariana touched her face, not really surprised to find tears running down her cheeks. She felt sick to her stomach, but muscled through, ignoring the nausea as best she could, keeping vigilant watch on the woods from the corners of her windows. If there were any more of them out there, she now knew what to expect. Of course, Becky Sue hadn't been a highly trained soldier in life. The others, if they truly retained some of their life's skills, would be much harder to deal with than the innocent young girl from down the road.

Although she kept watch until dawn, no more of the nightmare creatures came to call. Simon marched in from the tree line as the sun rose fully, looking tired. He paused at the pile of rubbish that used to be Becky Sue McGillicuddy and his jaw tightened. After a moment, he continued toward Mariana's back porch, a little more energy in his step.

Mariana flung open the door and reached for him as he climbed her back steps.

"Thank heaven you're all right." She kissed his stubbly cheek, then his waiting lips.

"What's this? You're shaking. And what was that I saw in your yard?" He held her away from him, his expression grim.

"That was Becky Sue, from next door. I saw her in the woods around four this morning and tried to warn her, but . . ." Her gaze trailed to the lump of dirty clothing and organic debris in her yard. "Simon, half her face was missing. I used the darts you left but she didn't go down right away. I fired three times. Hit her three times. It seemed to take forever. Just when I was going into panic mode, she . . . dissolved. Melted, right in front of my eyes."

Simon tugged her into his chest, placing one big hand on her hair as he hugged her, offering comfort. He felt so good. Whole and unharmed by the terrors of the night. He was her rock of comfort in a sea of confusion. Her body trembled in remembered fear and he calmed her with gentle touches.

Somehow, he had walked her inside and kicked the door shut behind them. She didn't remember him doing it, but she felt the play of his muscles when he reached behind his back to lock the dead bolt on the back door. He maneuvered her toward a kitchen chair and helped her sit.

"I'm going to make you some coffee. Okay?" She nodded as he moved toward the automatic coffeemaker. He put the water in and added more grounds than she normally used to the filter cup, then switched the thing on and turned back to her. The sound of perking and the strong scent of brewing coffee filled the small kitchen within moments. It felt oddly comforting. Commonplace and routine, it brought sanity back to her life faster than she would have believed possible.

Simon leaned against the kitchen counter and regarded her with concern. "Better now?" She nodded again. "You'll be steadier once you get some coffee in you. Now, tell me about this neighbor. Does she live alone?"

"Oh, no." She realized what he was getting at. If Becky Sue had been attacked, more than likely, so had the sweet little old lady that was her grandmother.

Simon cursed and turned to the coffeepot, removing the carafe and filling a mug directly from the stream of freshly brewed coffee. When it was half full, he replaced the carafe and handed the mug to her.

"Drink this. It'll perk you up and steady your nerves." She did as ordered, though she usually didn't go for such strong, black coffee. "I take it from your reaction, the girl didn't live alone?"

Mariana clung to the mug for strength even as the strong brew started to permeate her body. Surprisingly, it helped her focus as the caffeine hit her system.

"She lived with her grandmother. Just the two of them."

Simon's expression grew even grimmer. "How close is their place?"

"Just over the hill. They're my nearest neighbors."

"I know the house. I've scouted it before. Damn." He filled a cup for himself from the coffee maker. "How old is the grandmother? Can she get around okay?"

"She's pretty old and suffers from arthritis. Becky Sue pretty much took care of her. I visited them once or twice, but they mostly kept to themselves."

"I'll need to go check on the grandmother and their house."

"You don't think . . ." Her words trailed off when he turned to her. She could see he did indeed think the worst. "If she was crippled in life and unable to get around much, would she still be that way under the influence of this contagion?"

"I truly have no idea. The only people I've seen infected were fit young Marines. But I guess I'm going to find out."

"I'm going with you. If she wasn't infected, she'll be frightened and may need help. There's no way of knowing how long ago Becky Sue was attacked. Her grandmother could have been alone for days. She'll be disoriented and frightened if you show up on her doorstep. At least she knows me, if only in passing. Plus, I'm a doctor. Mrs. McGillicuddy knows that." Simon seemed unconvinced by her argument. "It's daylight and it's supposed to be sunny all day. Didn't you tell me the others hide from the sun? It should be safe to take a quick drive over to their house, check things out, and come back. It'll only take a few minutes, and you'll be with me the entire time, right? What could go wrong?"

Grim faced, Simon relented. "All right, but we do this my way. I'll approach the house first and check things out. If the old lady is still alive, I'll signal you in. If not, you stay clear. Got it?"

"Aye, aye, sir." She gave him a salute and a smile, glad to see his expression soften just the tiniest bit.

"Take the pistol with you. How many rounds do you have left?"

Mariana checked the specially crafted handgun. It could hold up to six dart rounds in an oversized, rotating cylinder. She'd only used three on Becky Sue.

"Three left. How many does it usually take to disintegrate one of those creatures?"

Some of the grimness returned to his eyes. "Theoretically, it should only take one, or so the experts tell me. As you probably saw, I've learned it actually takes awhile for the toxin to spread and do its work. Multiple rounds help the process along. I usually use at least two if possible—one in the upper body and one in the lower. The key is to hit them while they're still some distance away, or when you're in a position to retreat quickly to a safe distance."

"Good to know." She hated to think how hard won his knowledge was.

"Finish up your coffee and we'll get on the road. I want to do this, then report in before I go down for the day." He rubbed his unshaven face in a rare outward show of fatigue. He was unbending more and more around her, showing that he was, indeed, human, after all. That was something he had never really done during their previous involvement.

"How'd you do last night?" She watched his expression as she sipped the strong coffee.

"I got two more. By our counts, there should be only one left, but if they've infected civilians, the problem has spread."

"That's not good," she observed, stating the obvious.

"No, not good at all." He swallowed the last of his coffee and placed his mug in the sink.

She grabbed her jacket, stowed the pistol within easy reach in one pocket, and headed for the front door, next to which was her car, a small, sturdy SUV. Simon said nothing when she made for the driver's seat, though he did open her door for her as soon as she chirped the locks open. He was a gentleman, after all.

She noticed him looking into the back before opening the door, probably checking to be certain the spacious vehicle was indeed empty before they got in. She would have to remember to do that herself. She wasn't used to living under near constant threat. Until this situation was fully resolved, she would have to be more cautious.

"I meant to tell you before," he said as he got in on the passenger's side and shut the door. "I like your choice of vehicle. My little brother has one of these and I borrowed it the last time I moved. It holds a lot more than I expected."

She guessed he was making small talk as a way to defuse her fear. It wasn't working, but she loved him for trying. She was wound tighter than a top and wouldn't rest until they knew one way or the other if that sweet, crippled old woman had been attacked by something out of a nightmare.

"I appreciate what you're trying to do." She turned to look at him as she started the car.

"What?"

"Come on, Simon. You're not exactly the chatty type. Thank you for trying to take my mind off it, but I'll never forget what I saw—what I did—tonight."

"And you never should," Simon agreed, surprising her. "If it helps, try to remember that girl was already dead. You helped put her soul to rest. You didn't kill her. She was dead a long time before the creature she'd become tried to attack and kill you. It was both self-defense and an act of mercy."

"Will the courts see it that way?" A dreadful thought entered her mind. "Simon, I never even thought about the legal ramifications of this. Becky Sue was a civilian. Do we have the right to do what I did to civilians? What about the law?"

"I'm operating under the highest authority, Mari. Orders from the president himself, cosigned by the director of the Centers for Disease Control. This contagion has to be stopped at all costs and I'm authorized to use any and all means necessary to end it wherever it spreads, be it to military or civilian personnel. When I make my report to Commander Sykes tonight, I'm going to mention the continued problems you've had on your land, but otherwise I'm keeping you out of this, Mari. They'll know you're aware of the contagion and the creatures. That's it. Anything else, let it be on my head."

"But Simon—"

"No. Trust me on this. Everything surrounding this experiment has been screwed up from day one. I don't want your name all over some top secret dossier somewhere. It's bad enough that as it is, you'll be a footnote in the file. I don't want this to come back to haunt you at a later date." His jaw set in a stubborn line even as his words struck fear in her heart.

"Do you expect more trouble?"

"Honey, I always expect trouble. It's the only thing that's kept me alive this long." He let out a heavy sigh, his stance relenting just a bit. "I've been walking a tightrope here. They know I'm immune. Already the research team wants to know why. I only have Matt Sykes to thank for the fact that the researchers don't know my name or how to find me. I trust Matt. After this is over, I'm going to fade away where those mad scientists will never find me."

"But won't they know who did the job of cleaning up the base?"

"That's where the mercs come in. All the paperwork is run through them. Some creative paper shuffling should keep my name far from Quantico for many years to come." He shrugged. "It helps to have friends in interesting places. As for you, I want any record of your involvement as limited as we can make it. The locations of all the kills are being recorded by the cleanup team. There's no way around that. They'll know about the action on your land. You'll be listed as a witness in the reports. That's as far as I want it to go."

She was uncomfortable with the idea of lying, even by omission. Simon was so serious though, he convinced her of the need for secrecy. And really, what could it hurt for the reports to say Simon took the shots that disintegrated poor Becky Sue? Mariana would always know the truth. She would always remember what she'd done.

"So what about the McGillicuddys? Becky Sue, and possibly her grandmother? How will their disappearance be explained? People do check on them and visit from time to time."

"When I call Matt, he'll help square things. He's good at that sort of thing. I imagine there'll be some sort of cover-up to explain the girl's disappearance and satisfy the locals. Don't worry." He reached out to take her hand. "I won't let anything bad happen to you. I promise."

The seriousness of his vow took her by surprise. She had known he cared on some level, but what she saw in his expression—more open to her now than he had ever been before—floored her. He'd never made her any promises before. This could be a breakthrough moment, if she was foolish enough to believe he would let her into his life after this crisis was over.

Only time would tell.

She squeezed his hand and gave him a sad smile. "Thank you, Simon. That means a lot to me."

"Mari," he tugged on her hand, leaning over the small console to meet her lips in a soft, gentle kiss. "You mean a lot to me. I never told you before, but I don't think I could survive if something happened to you on my watch."

Simon kissed her once more and let go, turning away to gaze out the window. He'd almost revealed too much there. The sad, scared look on her beautiful face had made him want to ease her hurt and fear. She had looked so lost. It tugged on his heart and made him want to comfort her.

If the situation wasn't so urgent, he would march her right back into the house and make love to her until her eyes lost that shadow of apprehension. She was dealing well with a situation in which she was totally out of her depth. He was damned proud of her, but he also wanted to protect her. Make her go back into her house and batten down the hatches until it was safe again. Or better yet, go get a room on base until the terror was over. He wanted her safe. He wanted her happy. He wanted her. Period.

Mariana put the SUV in gear and headed for the gravel lane that led to the neighboring house. He had done reconnaissance on the entire area and was familiar with the layout of each house and outbuilding where the creatures might possibly try to hide. He had found more than one making use of someone's garden shed in the first few weeks. After he'd dispatched those, the others seemed to have steered clear of such places. They apparently had the capacity to learn from mistakes, which made them even tougher to deal with in the long run.

The one Marine that was left was one he'd been hunting for a long time. This one had been part of a sniper-spotter team. He had been an expert at stealth in life and had demonstrated a propensity for the same now that he was . . . something else. He'd also been one of the original test subjects. He'd died honorably in battle, only to have his body experimented on after death to become a thing of nightmares. Nobody deserved that.

As they made their way down the lane, Simon decided to share a little more information with Mariana. She had already faced two of the creatures, and they might be walking into the lair of a third. She deserved to know what he'd learned and observed during his time in the field hunting these creatures. Plus, it would help him organize his thoughts to bounce them off her. She had always challenged him intellectually, and he respected her knowledge and ability to reason things out.

"They're able to learn simple things." He could tell he had surprised her by speaking. She listened attentively even as she navigated the narrow gravel lane. "Luckily, the more complex operations, like using firearms, seem to be beyond them."

"Thank heaven for that, at least. I can only imagine a platoon of zombie Marines able to use Uncle Sam's artillery against an unsuspecting populace. Talk about a nightmare."

She caught on quick. He really enjoyed that about her. "They can use simple weapons like sticks and such. The knowledge of anything more mechanical than opening a door seems to have disappeared along with their humanity. They don't move fast but they can sneak up on you if you're not careful. They don't talk either. Sometimes they make a sort of moaning sound."

"I heard that when Becky Sue got close. It was horrible. Like she was begging for help or something. I've had a few patients make similar sounds while they were delirious, but Becky Sue's vocalizations sounded like a wounded animal. It was inhuman."

"She wasn't human. Not any longer, Mari. Try not to let it get to you. You did the right thing. You put the girl out of her misery and let her soul finally rest in peace."

"I didn't know you had a spiritual side, Simon." She raised one eyebrow in his direction as she slowed the vehicle. They were close to the neighbor's house. He saw no problem with parking in the old lady's drive and knocking on the door. There was bright sunshine in the sky and the zombies shunned the light. If the worst had happened and the old lady had been turned, she should be cowering inside. If she was still alive, she would probably welcome a visit from Mariana after not seeing her granddaughter for a day or two.

Simon shrugged off Mariana's interest in his spiritual beliefs. "Like most soldiers, I have faith in a higher power. I've seen too many weird things and too much death not to believe the spirit lives on."

They arrived at the neighbor's house and Mariana parked in the drive. There was an open space between the car and the house, which suited him just fine. He felt the weight of her stare.

"That's deep," she commented when he finally looked at her.

He had to laugh. His Mari always managed to surprise him with her reactions. She'd managed to take a very serious situation and make it light without discounting the innermost thoughts he'd just revealed.

"Look, I want you to stay here. Keep the car doors locked, and the windows rolled up. I'm going to do some recon around the house. I'll make one circuit of the perimeter and then come back to you. If I don't see anything suspicious, we can go knock on the door together, just in case your neighbor is all right. She would probably be alarmed to see a strange man at her door, but like you said, she knows you. If she's been turned, I'll take care of her. I want you to stand clear. Run back to the car and lock yourself inside. There's still one Marine unaccounted for and he's the smartest of the bunch that I've faced. He could be hiding around here somewhere. Especially if he's the one who attacked Becky Sue."

He hated the fear that reentered her eyes. Unfortunately, she had to know the truth about what they could be facing.

"If you see anything bad while I'm gone, honk the horn. A short tap for something suspicious. Two taps if you see one of them in the distance. Lay on the horn if you need immediate help. I'll come running."

She visibly gulped and he took her hand, leaning in to kiss the fear away. She warmed to him, but this wasn't the time or place. Why couldn't he keep his hands off her? Why couldn't he get enough of her? And why was he tormenting them both this way—letting them both glimpse something that could never be?

No doubt about it, he was a glutton for punishment. Still, his duty was clear. She had been dragged into this mess and he had to stay by her side and protect her until the situation was resolved. He owed her that much at least. He would do the same for anyone, but knowing it was Mari who was in danger made it all that much more disturbing to his psyche, his deeply buried emotions . . . and his heart.

"Be good while I'm gone." He gave her a lopsided smile as he drew back, liking the way her eyes dilated in pleasure even under such dire circumstances. For that short moment in time, she wasn't scared anymore. He had given her that respite. It made him feel proud and even more protective.

"Be careful, Simon." She touched his sleeve as he opened the car door.

"Don't worry. I do this for a living." He winked at her and slipped out of the SUV, waiting by the door until she locked it behind him. With a parting grin, he left her to do a circuit of the house.

Chapter Six

Mariana watched him go with her heart in her throat. She hated seeing him in danger. She knew intellectually that in his profession, he often put himself in harm's way, but actually seeing it—participating in it, even to a small degree—was something very different. Watching every tree branch for movement, she did her best to stay vigilant, biting her lip when the sun dipped behind a scudding cloud for a long minute.

She watched what she could see of the sky through her moon roof. It looked like clouds were gathering, which could mean trouble.

Mariana didn't breathe easy until she saw Simon rounding the corner of the house, moving at ease though obviously alert. He ambled up to the driver's side window and she rolled it down to talk to him.

"It looks clear. Clouds could pose a problem later, but it's still a little too bright for them to be very active. Come on out and let's check on the old lady."

She popped the locks and Simon opened her door for her, his head swiveling to check all directions before he stepped back to let her out. She was careful to chirp the doors locked behind her as she walked at Simon's side up to the front porch. The place looked welcoming, with bright pink petunias in the flower boxes and a profusion of red and white impatiens lining the walk.

There was no sound from within though, which was troubling. Mrs. McGillicuddy couldn't get around much, but she loved her television. From sunrise to sunset that old TV was usually blaring some game show or soap opera. Now it was eerily silent.

She looked up at Simon with apprehension. "Something's wrong. She usually has the TV turned up loud all day long."

Simon immediately took point. "Stay behind me. I'll knock, you get ready to run if this goes bad."

She nodded, knowing he was the only one who could really face these monsters. He had already been bitten and lived to tell the tale. Nobody else had been so lucky. It was likely she would face the same fate as Becky Sue if she got stupid and got bitten.

Simon walked up to the door and knocked loudly. "Call out to her," he instructed.

"Mrs. McGillicuddy. It's Mariana, from next door. I came to see if you were all right." She spoke as loudly as she could, given the lump in her throat. "Mrs. McGillicuddy, are you there, ma'am?"

A shuffling sound came from within the house and then she heard that distinctive, inhuman moaning sound. The sun was swallowed for the moment by a thick cloud, casting a pall over the landscape. Mariana cringed, shuddering as she realized her worst fears had come true. Becky Sue's grandmother—that sweet, crippled old lady—had been turned into a zombie.

"Get back to the car. I'll handle it." Simon's words were clipped as he braced himself to kick in the old wooden door. "Stay alert. There could be more. Run. Now!"

She pulled out the pistol and held it ready as she flew back down the porch steps, looking wildly all around as she made a beeline for her SUV. Behind her she heard an ominous crack as Simon broke through the door with one solid kick. Then she heard the faint report of the rifle as he shot twice in quick succession. His boots hit the wooden boards of the porch steps with loud, hurried steps as she unlocked her car door. She pushed inside, barely remembering to check the backseat before she got in and locked the doors tight.

Turning, she watched in horror as poor old Mrs. McGillicuddy made her way down her porch steps. The plump old lady was walking stiffly and her head looked misshapen. Mariana realized why as she drew closer. Her skull had been bashed in and it looked like something—or someone—had been gnawing on her brain.

Mariana had to stifle the urge to vomit. She had seen a lot of things as a doctor but never anything as truly horrific as this.

Simon reached the car and she unlocked the passenger side door for him. He hopped inside with little fanfare and slammed the door shut.

"Back up to the end of the lane. She should go any second now."

Mariana didn't have to be told twice. The gruesome specter of Mrs. McGillicuddy advanced steadily, the flailing ends of Simon's darts sticking out of her neck and hip. He'd hit cleanly and if their luck held, she would disintegrate any minute now.

Mariana backed the SUV to the end of the gravel drive and waited. The old woman advanced a few more steps, reaching out as if for help, making that high pitched moaning sound. But there was nothing more they could do for the poor old thing.

Mrs. McGillicuddy took one more step and then began to dissolve, melting from the sites of the darts, inward. It was all over in a matter of seconds. Mariana gripped her steering wheel, shaken to the core. It was one thing to see it happen in the dark of night. It was quite another to watch a sweet old lady turned monster melt before her eyes in the harsh light of day.

"Sweet Lord," she whispered.

Simon's hand on her thigh snapped her attention to him. "It's better this way, Mari."

"I know you're right, but . . . damn, Si. This isn't something they prepared me for in medical school, or even in boot camp. This is a nightmare come to life."

"Welcome to my world. I've been living with this for months now. I'm only sorry you got dragged into it." He removed his hand and turned to scan the trees. "The only good thing is that it will all be over soon."

"But it's spread to civilians."

"Yeah, that is a problem. Luckily, there are only the two houses in this area—this one, and yours. You're safe, and the two occupants of this place are now accounted for. With any luck, it hasn't spread any further. Now if I can just get that last Marine, we can call this done. Frankly, it'll be a relief."

"I can understand that." Yes, she understood it, but feared the end of his mission would spell the end of their renewed affair. It was an agonizing thought. She wasn't ready to give him up yet.

"Drive back up to the old lady's house. I have to check inside, to make sure she was alone."

She hated the thought of him going back in there, but knew he had to be certain. This contagion was too dangerous to allow to spread any further. She pulled up next to the house again and left the car running. If they had to make a quick escape, she would be ready.

"Remember the signal?"

"Tap my horn once for something suspicious. Twice if I see one of them far away. Lean on it if I've got a serious problem."

"Good girl." He smiled as he leaned close to give her a peck on the cheek.

Simon was out of the car and in the house before she could tell him to be careful again. She watched the surroundings, her eyes straying to the destroyed front door of the house every few seconds, willing Simon to reappear, safe and sound.

She thought she saw something flicker through the woods,

but wasn't certain enough to sound the horn. A few minutes later, Simon appeared at the door. His expression was closed as usual. There was no real urgency in his movements, which she took as a very good sign. Likely, the rest of the house was clear.

He made a few hand signals that she interpreted to mean he was going to scout the grounds again. He disappeared around the side of the house and she went back to waiting. If this is what his life was like in the special forces, he could keep it. Moments of blind panic interspersed with what felt like hours of tense waiting. All in all, her medical job was easier on the nerves. Even her stint in the Emergency Room a few years back had been less nerve wracking than this.

Simon appeared again a few minutes later. He stopped by the pile of debris that had been Mrs. McGillicuddy and dropped a small object onto the ground. He gave the area another searching look, then ambled up to the passenger side door. She unlocked it for him and he climbed in. She could see the weariness of the long night in every move of his muscular body. The man needed sleep and a few hours away from the tension of his mission.

"As your doctor, I'm prescribing bed rest for the next six hours, at least." She always enjoyed the challenge of making him smile and was rewarded when one side of his lips quirked upward.

"I'll be glad to follow your orders, ma'am, as soon as I report in. Commander Sykes has to get the cleanup team to sanitize this area as well as your backyard ASAP. It's standard operating procedure for this mission sent down from the CDC. I mark all the kill sites and the hazmat guys come in and do their thing. You didn't see them, but they were out behind your house yesterday."

"When?" She was shocked by the idea that a group of soldiers had been on her property and she'd never even known about it.

"When I was keeping you otherwise occupied." His eyes heated with remembered desire and her stomach clenched.

"Damn, Simon. Is that what had you so eager to keep me in bed all day?" She put the SUV in gear and backed out of the driveway again, turning onto the gravel road.

"No, sweetheart, that was just a fringe benefit. I didn't want you worrying."

"So what changed?" She began the short drive back to her place.

"The girl was bad enough, but now her grandmother. You're involved now, Mari, more than you should be. I didn't want you in this at all, but you're in it now, up to your neck. You have a right to know the full parameters of the op and what happens next. You're a doctor, after all. I bet you were already speculating about what happened to the remains after I did my part of the job. Weren't you?"

She shook her head. "You know me too well. I just didn't think you'd tell me so much about the operation, Simon. I know it's probably all top secret, right?"

"It is. And you'll be held to that top secret classification. Which means you don't talk about any of this to anyone except me. You've already seen and done too much to be kept out of the loop. I talked to Matt Sykes last night, while you were in the shower, and he agreed."

"You already talked to Commander Sykes about me?" That was a surprise.

"He needed to know where I've been. He's keeping close tabs on me since I'm the only thing standing between the base, the surrounding populace, and . . . well . . . what you saw happen to your neighbors."

She thought about that. "A lot of responsibility is riding on your shoulders, Simon."

"It's what I do." He shrugged. The casual attitude didn't fool her. She knew he was feeling every bit of that responsibility. Simon always took important things, like his duty, very seriously indeed.

She would have said more but a flash of white at the side of the road caught her eye. She slammed on the brakes.

"What?" he asked, instantly alert.

"I thought I saw something." She backed up the SUV carefully. "Look over there." She pointed to a dense patch of greenery. It was ripped up and torn now that she looked closely, with obvious tire tracks leading away from the gravel road bed and onto the dirt and grass at the side of the road.

Simon hefted his weapon and slid out of the vehicle. "Stay here and keep the engine running." She didn't have to be told to lock the doors behind him as her heart crept into her throat yet again.

Simon approached the vehicle. It was small, boxy and white, with the distinctive stripes and logo of the Postal Service. Even from several yards out he could see the smashed windows and deep red streaks of blood all over the interior of the crashed Jeep. Mail was strewn all around, but the postman was nowhere to be seen.

No doubt he'd been attacked and was likely already dead.

Another fatality in a string of deaths that had gone on far too long. And another target to add to his list. Simon dropped a transmitter tag in the vehicle, did a quick sweep of the area, and headed back to Mariana's SUV.

She waited for him with the world in her smile. The relief on her face as he broke from the cover of trees warmed him from the inside out. God, she was good to come home to. These past days had teased him with a glimpse of how good life could be.

But not for him.

He was weakening, though. His resolve to stay detached was on the wane. Would he be strong enough to resist the allure of her? Would he be able to do the right thing when this was all over? Would he have the strength to leave her again? He wasn't so sure. And that thought was even scarier than the zombies.

He didn't want to hurt her. He didn't want to ruin her life. Right now, he was still firmly convinced that his continued presence in her life could only accomplish both of those things. He just didn't see how being with him could spell anything but disaster for her.

For one thing, there was his . . . affliction, for lack of a better word. He had been changed by the attack on a cellular level. Nobody could tell him for certain what that would mean for him in the long term. For another, there was his job. Although he was no longer at Uncle Sam's beck and call, he was still employed in the same line of work. He had to pick up and go when he got the call. Nowadays he could either accept or pass on jobs, at his discretion. That was different, but if he wanted to get paid, he had to work. It was that simple.

Still, he knew he couldn't do mercenary work forever. At some point he would be too slow to be good in the field and that day grew nearer with every passing moment. Younger, faster guys would take his place in the field, and he would either have to find a new line of work, or find a way to utilize his hard won skills as a training officer or operations manager of some kind. He'd been thinking a lot about it since the attack that had left him in the hospital for weeks. He still hadn't arrived at any conclusive decisions.

Crossing paths with Mariana had started those thoughts of retirement up again in his mind. If he found a less dangerous way to earn a living, could he somehow convince her to share his future? However long that lasted? Would it be fair to her? He still didn't have an answer.

He approached her vehicle, careful to look everywhere before signaling her to pop the locks. He slid into the passenger seat and dreaded giving her the news. She was strong and had been a real trooper up to this point. He hated to lay even more on her, but she needed to know what they were up against, so she would be wary.

"It was a postal vehicle. The driver is gone, probably dead. The claw marks on the sides of the Jeep look like they were made by our target. Probably in the last few hours. It's dark under the trees and the clouds have been hiding the sun off and on."

"Jeff Humbolt is the postman on this route. He lives alone out on Webster Road. You think he's turned into one of them?"

He nodded, thinking through the possibilities. He knew where Webster Road was. It wasn't too far from here, in fact, out near the edge of the woods and very isolated. Up to this point, the zombies hadn't strayed far from this patch of woods, bordering the base. But if the postman retained some affinity for his home area, he might try to make it back home tonight, after the contagion ran its course and he rose from the dead.

"Let's go back to your place. I need to report in and get some sleep. Tonight is soon enough to go after the wayward mailman. The contagion takes awhile to take over its host."

"Poor Jeff. He was a sweet old coot. A widower. He used to flirt with me for fun, not in a serious way." He saw Mariana try to hide a tear as she surreptitiously wiped her cheek.

Simon was touched by the sadness on her face and in her voice as she put the SUV in gear and started off toward her house once more. She had lost people she knew to this horrific contagion and had been attacked and threatened herself. Most women would be a blubbering mess right about now, but not his Mari. No, she was soldiering on, even though he knew she was having a hard time dealing with all of this.

Hell, he had a hard time dealing with it, too. Of course, he'd had a lot longer to get used to the idea of the walking dead. Of zombies running around trying to eat their victims' faces.

"I'm sorry, Mariana."

"It's not your fault, Simon. If anyone's to blame, it's the scientists and doctors who unleashed this thing on an unsuspecting world. My profession has a lot to answer for this time. I hope they came down hard on the person or persons responsible for this tragedy."

"I heard the entire science team was being held incommunicado pending the resolution of my mission. They were allowed to develop the toxin to stop the zombies, but they've been effectively put into custody awaiting judgment. Someone else is gathering the data on where and when I tracked and killed the creatures. Hopefully a new, more ethical group of doctors will be appointed to figure out what went wrong and how to prevent it from ever happening again."

"I suppose the fact that the original team came up with an effective way to stop their creations will count in their favor." Mari's tone was grudging and he knew she was angry, thinking about her defenseless neighbors and the postman who had been murdered in such a heinous way.

"You could probably testify as to what you saw. It might make a difference when their fates are decided. The proceedings will be top secret, of course. Sykes could get you an interview with counsel, I suppose, if you want to go that far."

"I'll have to think about it. It's not a bad idea. At the very least, I could submit an affidavit of some kind so the judge will know the true extent of the civilian consequences. Someone should speak up for Becky Sue, her grandmother, and Mr. Humbolt, the postman. They didn't deserve to die that way. The people responsible should be made aware of the human consequences of their actions, as should those who will decide their punishment and whether or not they get to practice medicine or conduct experiments in the future."

"It couldn't hurt." Simon admired her desire to see justice done on behalf of her neighbors.

"Can I ask you a question about the zombies' condition? You may not know the answer, but I've been wondering why they have claws. They didn't die that way. Most human beings keep their nails trimmed and they're not that thick."

"Yeah, that surprised me at first too. The geeks tell me it has to do with the contagion's effect on dead tissue. It reanimates it, and with older tissue, it seems to have slight regenerative properties. It makes the nails on both hands and feet thicker and longer. They seem to keep getting longer up to the point where the dead body rises. Once that happens, the contagion has run its course in the host and it doesn't reactivate until it finds a new body to kill, then bring back."

"That's really sinister, when you stop to think about it." She looked appalled, as well she should.

"You can say that again." They pulled into the driveway leading to her cabin. "Those claws threw us all for a loop the first time we saw them. It took the scientists about a week to figure out why that happened to their original test subjects. I've been reporting my observations through Sykes. Even though this experiment is a total bust, at least someone is learning something from it. For one thing, the toxin to destroy the creatures is a brand-new and useful discovery."

"Necessity is the mother of invention yet again, I suppose." Mariana sighed and he knew she was upset by the horrific deaths her unknown colleagues had caused.

They pulled up in front of her house and Simon turned to her.

"Stay put for a minute while I check the perimeter, okay?" He waited for her nod of agreement before he set off. He couldn't be too careful with her safety. She had already been stalked by these creatures twice. That was twice too many times as far as he was concerned. He shuddered to think how he would have felt if she'd been infected and he'd had the grim task of ending her.

He frankly didn't know if he could survive it.

When he was satisfied the perimeter around the cabin was clear, he motioned for her to leave her vehicle. She joined him by the front entry and he continued to scan the area as she unlocked the door.

He went in first, just to be certain the house remained undisturbed since their departure. Everything was as it should be and he ushered her inside, locking the door tight behind them. He breathed easy for the first time that morning.

"I have to call Sykes."

"I'll make a bite for us to eat. I don't know about you, but I need fuel and then sleep."

"Sounds like the perfect plan." He pulled her close for a quick hug and kissed the top of her head before letting her go.

He needed to touch her, to be sure she was really there and really all right. It was a need in his blood that grew stronger with every passing minute.

He went into the living room to make his call while she headed for the kitchen.

Chapter Seven

Mariana could hear Simon's deep murmuring voice coming from the living room, though she couldn't tell what he was saying. She liked having him in her house. He made her feel safe, even in this horrific situation.

She put together a few sandwiches for them, unwilling and unable to spend a lot of energy on cooking anything more complex at the moment. They needed something to eat and they needed sleep. Both of them had been up all night, and while Mariana had gotten used to pulling all-nighters and double shifts as a young intern, it had been a while since she'd been called upon to stretch her endurance to the limit. She had been running on adrenaline for the past few hours and desperately needed some real, deep, healing sleep.

She figured Simon was only a little better off than she was. While he'd trained himself to run on little to no sleep, at some point the human body needed to crash and recharge. They'd spent all day yesterday sleeping in short snatches between furious bouts of lovemaking. While she felt more relaxed than she had in years, neither of them had really gotten any deep, restorative sleep. They both had to be running on fumes today.

"Sykes is up to date. He's going to send the cleanup team to the neighbors' house first, then they'll fix up your yard." Simon came into the kitchen and snagged one of the sandwiches she was about to place on a serving platter. He ate half of it before she could even blink an eye.

He took the platter out of her hands and ushered her to the table, setting the plate of sandwiches between them as they both sat. She grabbed a sandwich and ate mechanically, knowing she needed the nutrition but not really tasting the food at all. She was just too tired. She was aware of Simon watching her as the silence dragged. Looking at him, she had to catch her breath at the glitter of emotion in his eyes. There was a mixture of longing, care, and a hint of possession that made her feel oddly cherished.

"Eat up, Mari." He tipped the platter toward her and urged her to take another of the sandwich halves she had prepared. After she took another, he got up and fished two tall glasses out of a cupboard and filled them both with ice cold milk from her refrigerator.

"How did your talk go with the commander?" she asked as he placed one of the glasses in front of her and sat back down.

"He wasn't thrilled that you'd been stalked twice. There will be some top secret paperwork added to your file, and the op file, that will cover you with the brass should they get wind of this operation at some point in the future. For now, everything is being kept need-to-know and will likely remain so for many years to come. Nobody wants a repeat of this. What really concerns me is that if the limited success in my case was known, some moron somewhere would try this again. Only five people know what really happened to me and all the written and electronic records of my treatment have been wiped. It was one of the conditions I put on taking this mission. I didn't want to become a lab rat they would poke at until they figured out how I survived. This thing is just too dangerous."

"Smart thinking." Simon had always been brilliant. He was right to realize that the scientists wouldn't leave him alone if they knew about his survival and his new healing abilities. He was in a dangerous situation, even without the creatures he was hunting. If the wrong kind of person knew what his body could do, he might just be in a world of trouble. "Who are the five people that know about you?"

"Matt Sykes, the civilian doctor, and two nurses that treated me when I was sick, and now you."

"Are you sure you can trust them all?"

"I trust you without question." She liked the way he put her at the head of the list. His trust was something she knew wasn't easily given. "Matt Sykes and I go way back. He's one of my oldest and best friends. He won't betray me. The civilian doctor was an older fellow. After I was bitten, I didn't report it. The op was over and I went to my apartment off base to crash. I don't remember anything until two days later when I dragged myself to a local clinic. I felt too sick to make it to the base hospital, but as it turned out, that was probably the best move for me. The man who runs the clinic, Doctor Shepard, is like an old-fashioned country doctor. He was trained by the best, and moved to the small town outside the base when his oldest boy was killed in action a few years back. He said I reminded him of his son. Doc Shepard was the first to point out what a problem I'd have if that science team learned what happened to me. He gave me the original records that would've betrayed anything about my rapid healing, and destroyed the rest. He thought I might need them down the road if something went wrong, but felt nobody else should know unless I wanted them to."

"Sounds like a smart man." Mariana began to think maybe Simon was in the clear—as much as possible—from being turned into a human guinea pig. "Who were the nurses?"

"One was Doctor Shepard's wife, Matilda. The other was Jenny Shepard, the doctor's daughter-in-law. It was her husband who'd been killed in action. I don't think either of those ladies would betray me. They watched over me for weeks in their clinic. After I dragged myself to his office, I pretty much collapsed. He took me in and those women nursed me while I was out of it. I owe them my life."

"You got really lucky, Simon."

"I know. Things could have gone a lot worse for me, especially early on, if the military science team had known what happened. Doctor Shepard helped me clear things with the military doctors. He told them I had pneumonia and I used up all my accumulated leave. I went back, finished the few weeks on my tour, and retired as planned. I contacted Matt Sykes and told him what had happened because I knew he still had a big problem on his hands, and I was the only one who could safely go in and solve it."

"So you volunteered for this duty?" It didn't really surprise her. Simon wasn't the type to sit idle when he knew there was something he could do to help.

"I knew if they sent others, they'd most likely die and become zombies, exacerbating the problem. I knew the score about the creatures and I'd already figured out a little about hunting them from that first op." He shrugged as if it was no big deal. "I knew I could do this without risking too much and save other guys' lives in the bargain. What choice did I have?"

It went without saying that he could have chosen to stay out of it. He wasn't in the military anymore. He didn't have to follow orders unless he chose to.

"So you were going to retire even before you got bitten?"

He nodded. "It was all arranged. A job was all lined up for me with the mercs. That came in handy when Sykes wanted to hire me. Everything's being run through the merc company in the swamp. In reality, I'm an independent contractor for both the merc group and Sykes. Having the mercs as middle man helps keep the paperwork muddled enough so nobody will ever figure out what exactly Uncle Sam hired me to do or where I'm doing it."

"Convenient." She finished her sandwich and reached for her glass of milk, finishing that, too. There was a holder with paper napkins on the table and she took one to rid herself of crumbs.

"That's a specialty of theirs. When a job is too distasteful to run through official channels, the independent contractors ride to the rescue. Or so their recruiters say. Personally, I wasn't convinced until it happened to me."

"Do you plan to stay with the mercenary group after this mission is over?" She tried not to show how much that worried her.

"Frankly, with what they're paying me, I could retire tomorrow and be well off for the rest of my life. It pays well to be the only person in the world who can safely hunt zombies." He winked at her comically and even through her exhaustion, she had to laugh. "Honestly, I don't know. I'll no doubt take some time off. Preferably on some tropical island with an umbrella drink in my hand and warm waves lapping at my toes." He ate silently for a moment, polishing off the last of the sandwiches. "What about you, Mari? You're retiring in a few weeks. What plans have you made? Nobody on base seems to know where you'll go next."

"You've been asking around about me?" She was just sleepy enough to tease him with more candor than she would've otherwise used.

"A good soldier always does detailed recon." His smug expression prompted her to throw her balled-up napkin at him. He ducked with a grin. "So what are your plans? Got a job waiting?"

She pretended to fume for a moment more before relenting. "Actually, I was going to take some time off myself. I've had a few offers, from private practice to a big city hospital, but I haven't made up my mind yet. I thought I deserved a long vacation before I jump back in with both feet. In fact, your tropical paradise sounds like just the ticket."

"Great minds think alike." He saluted her with his glass and drained it. "Now what are your feelings about bed? I need to crash and all I can think about is your nice soft sheets, that comfortable mattress, and you tucked close in my arms. My own personal hot water bottle."

If she'd had another napkin in her hand, she would've thrown that, too, as he got up and put their dishes in the sink. She loved his teasing. When he teased, he was truly comfortable. It was when he was tense that he became the serious soldier she had known for the first few weeks of their courtship. When he relaxed was when he was at his most charming, and most desirable. At least to her.

"I don't like being called a hot water bottle, Simon. That's not exactly a compliment." She pretended to be annoyed by his unflattering comparison.

"To me it is." He grabbed her around the waist as she stood, drawing her back against his chest, nuzzling her neck playfully. "I dream about hot water bottles when I'm stuck on the cold ground in a bivouac. I've even fantasized about hot water bottles a time or two when I was doing cold weather training in Alaska. Mariana-shaped hot water bottles, who called my name as I made them come."

"You have a very kinky imagination." Mock outrage filled her breathless words as he cupped her breasts through the thin fabric of her T-shirt.

"You love my kinky imagination, Mari. Come on, admit it." He nipped her earlobe and she squirmed in his arms. Damn, the man still knew just how to touch her to make her burn.

"I plead the Fifth." She reached back to tangle her hands in the short hairs at the back of his neck, pushing her breasts more fully into his grasp. His hands went up under her T-shirt and right to the front clasp of her bra, parting it so he could touch her skin. Mariana whimpered and moaned.

"Then admit this, Mari. Admit you want me." He whispered in her ear, his warm breath sliding past her defenses to fan the flame of arousal in her blood.

"Yes, Simon. I want you. I always want you."

His low chuckle made her squirm. "Now that's the kind of thing I like to hear."

He turned with her in his arms and walked them both out of the kitchen toward the bedroom. Her shirt was tossed off along the way, as was her bra. Her jeans ended up in a heap next to his at the door to her bedroom.

She pushed at his shirt until he, too, was naked and they tumbled onto the bed together. Their limbs tangled and twined as he sought and captured her mouth with his. The kiss was tempestuous, like nothing that had come before. They rolled until she was on top, her thighs spread on either side of his hips, ready in an instant to take him and ride him to oblivion. Simon had always been able to flip her switch with a single touch.

Mariana slowed down, a moment of sanity prevailing. Protection first.

Reaching for her nightstand drawer, she fished out a condom from her dwindling emergency supply and ripped the package open. Sliding down his thighs, she took her time about covering him, enjoying the way he watched her, his eyes half lidded and oh so sexy.

"Don't tease, Mari. Come back up here."

"In good time." She leaned in closer to use her tongue on his exposed skin. She liked the way he twitched in her hands.

"No time like the present." His words were strained and his fists were clenched at his sides. Oh yeah, she was getting to him.

A grin spread across her face as she prowled up his body, trailing her lips and tongue over his abdomen and chest. He was hot, hard, and ridged in all the right places and she relished the opportunity to discover him all over again. It had been years since they'd been together and the previous day had been a blur of urgent need. There hadn't really been a chance for her to study him in detail.

"You've aged well, Simon. I think you're even more muscular than you were before. Have you been working out?"

The half-teasing question startled a laugh out of him. He reached for her, sliding his hands under her arms and lifting her over him. Yes, indeed, he must have been working out. At least, he was a lot stronger than she remembered.

"I've lived in interesting times since I last saw you, Mari." His expression clouded just for a second and she realized there was more truth to his words than he wanted to let on. "It makes a man hard." He realized his double entendre and gave her a lopsided grin. "Scratch that. *You* make me hard. You always have, sweetheart. Now what are you going to do about it?"

She straddled him, sliding over his hardness with teasing intensity. His eyes followed her movements, half lidded and sexy.

"I believe you deserve a reward for all that hard living." She teased as she took the tip of him inside. Little by little, she lowered over him, enjoying the feel of him stretching her. She was still just a little sore from the marathon they'd engaged in the day before but she went at a slow pace, allowing her body time to adjust.

"I like your rewards, ma'am." Simon lifted his hips gently, joining them fully.

"If you're good, I may have to reward you again, soldier." She gasped as she settled over him, taking him fully. She loved the way he felt inside her. For just a moment, she held position, cataloging the feel of him, the width and breadth of him, the way they fit so perfectly together. Nothing and no one had ever felt as right as Simon did.

"Oh, I plan to be very, very good." His teasing tone made her laugh and the moment was lost. She had to move. It was a biological and spiritual imperative.

Mariana repositioned herself, arranging her legs to give her better purchase, then began a slow, sliding rhythm. She shimmied her hips to get his full attention and his sleepy gaze rose from watching the place where they joined, pausing at her bouncing breasts momentarily and then finally to meet her gaze. She licked her lips, offering him a sinful smile.

"Like what you see?" Her head tilted to one side playfully.

"More than like, as I'm sure you can tell." He winked at her and moved his hands to her hips, guiding her into a faster rhythm. "Lean down here and I'll show you how much."

She did as he asked and his hands rose to cup her breasts. He knew just how to touch her to make her whimper with need. Just how much pressure to use to draw out her most explosive response.

"That much, eh?" She leaned into him, trying for a sexy grin. She must've succeeded because his fingers contracted, just slightly, and she saw his eyes darken with even deeper desire.

"Play time's over." In a split second, he moved his hands to her back, supporting her as he rolled them over so that she was flat on her back on the bed and he rose over her. "Now let me show you just how good I can be." He nipped her neck before drawing back, kneeling between her spread thighs as he began a rough, urgent pace that grew in intensity with each long stroke.

All coherent thought fled as he possessed her, pushed her higher, lost all control in the glorious union of their bodies. She surrendered all to him and felt his surrender in return. At least, that's what it felt like. That's what she thought she read in his eyes. What she felt in every touch of his body, every stroke that claimed her, pleasured her and turned her inside out.

"Come for me now, Mari. Come with me." His deep voice spurred her on, ordering her desire, commanding her pleasure. She could do nothing but comply, her body responding to his mastery as she had never responded to any other man.

Mariana shuddered as he pounded into her in short digs. Her climax hit her all at once, rocketing her to the sky and back down, only to climb even higher on the next wave. She screamed his name as he groaned. She felt him surge into her one last time as they both came hard. Together.

Dare she hope it could last forever?

Chapter Eight

Simon realized he must've slept far longer than he had intended. The sun was low in the sky, but there was still time to eat and make love to his woman once more before he had to go out and hunt.

His woman. Man, that sounded right, though it was a problem all the way around. He hadn't intended to get mixed up with Mari again. He knew he'd hurt her the last time. In fact, it was kind of amazing she had forgiven him so easily. Regardless of her reasons, he was thankful for the past two days spent with her. It was a glimpse of Eden. Of what could have been if circumstances were different.

Mariana was such a special woman. If he had the luxury of planning for a lifetime, he would want to spend it with someone just like her. Who was he fooling? He wanted to spend it with *her*. No one else. Only Mariana.

She was the perfect woman for him. She matched him in every way. In fact, she far outclassed him in many ways. If she could put up with some of his more barbaric inclinations—which she had already demonstrated she could—then as a life partner, she would be perfect.

Too bad his life was totally fucked up at present. The zombie attack had changed him in fundamental ways. He didn't know how long the changes would last or if at some point in

the future, they'd become fatal to him. He shouldn't be thinking about the lonely decades possibly to come. He shouldn't be
dreaming about a life with Mariana in it. Not even a little.

But he couldn't help himself. Just like he couldn't help touching her, wanting her, making love to her. When she was near,
all his best intentions went right out the window. And when
she was in danger, all his protective instincts went on high
alert. Nothing would happen to her on his watch. Nothing.

What happened after this crisis was over, well, that was up
in the air. Right now, he would enjoy the days in her company
and keep watch by night. He'd left her once and it had almost
destroyed him. Only the thought that he'd done it for her own
good had allowed him to stay away after his miraculous recovery from the zombie bite.

He didn't even have a scar to show for that horrific attack.
In fact, he hadn't scarred since, and the scars he'd already carried on his body from his life before, faded more with each
passing day. He'd become like something out of a comic book
and the only doctor he trusted, aside from Mariana, didn't
know how long the effect would last, or even if it wouldn't
somehow turn dangerous later.

There were too many questions surrounding his condition.
Too many variables in his life. Too much danger to drag Mariana into it again. No matter how badly he wanted her there,
next to him, in his home and in his bed. For as long as he lived.
However long that might be.

"What time is it?" Mariana's morning-rough voice greeted
him from the other side of her bed.

"About six, I think." He pulled her into his arms, spooning
her from behind and gave her a smacking kiss on the temple.
"You can sleep in, if you want."

She turned in his embrace, nibbling her way down his jaw
to a particularly sensitive spot on his neck. "What if I don't
want to sleep?"

"Well then, my mother taught me never to argue with a
lady." He let his hands roam, cupping her softness and exploring the wet heat between her legs.

"What if I'm not a lady?" One of his hands tightened on her breast, rubbing the nipple between thumb and forefinger until she squirmed in pleasure.

"You're always a lady, Mari, even when you're a siren, luring men to your bed." He dipped his head and licked her nipple, soothing her and driving her higher. Sucking her in deep, he didn't let up until he heard her moan.

"Men?" Her voice was a breathy, teasing taunt. "There's only one man I'm interested in."

"Good thing." He lifted his head and turned her so she lay on her stomach. He then raised her hips and stuffed a pillow beneath to support her. Leaning close, he whispered in her ear. "Because I don't share." Finishing his possessive statement with a playful nip to her earlobe, he drew back, hovering over her, admiring the line of her sinuous back. Her skin glowed, enticing him. She truly was the siren he'd named her.

"Is that a promise?" She grinned at him over her shoulder, ever the coquette, and he felt his body tighten even more. She knew just what to say, just what to do, to make him want to explode.

The thing was, if he had his way, she would never know another man's touch again. He would never share her. He would keep her all to himself. But that was a dream for another time.

One hand drifted down her spine to her core, testing her readiness. She was warm, wet, and if her wiggling was any indication, more than willing.

Reaching into the open drawer in her nightstand, he fished out another condom and made short work of slipping it on. Then he bent over her, surrounding her with his larger frame to whisper in her ear.

"Do you want me, Mari?"

"Yes." Her breath caught as he moved into position behind her. He liked that. Oh, yes, he liked that very much, indeed.

"How much?" He teased her wet folds with the tip of his cock. She was quivering, just slightly, around him.

"Simon! I want you more than anything. Please. Oh, please."

She gasped as he slid into her from behind. She was morning soft and wet with arousal, making his way easy.

"That's my girl." He tried to keep his rhythm slow and easy but she was too much for him. She always had been. No other woman could make him so hot so fast or keep him on the knife's edge longer. Only his Mari.

He stroked into her deep, hard, and long, just the way he knew she liked it. He guided her hips as she began to move back against him, urging him onward, into an ever increasing rhythm.

"Faster, Simon!" Her voice became hoarse with reaction as her head thrashed.

"Your wish," he panted as he sped his thrusts, "is my command."

Before long, she was making those little sounds of arousal on every inward glide and he felt her inner muscles clench around him. The grip of her body gave him that little extra edge of sensation that only she had ever given him.

"Are you with me, baby?" His hands cupped her hips, gripping hard as he pressed within her.

"Simon." His name was drawn from her lips as two separate, long syllables. Yeah, his little tigress was with him. "Simon! I'm so close."

So was he. It wouldn't take much more. All he wanted was for her to come hard, and she would take him with her. Reaching under her with one hand, he teased her clit with his fingers. She clenched hotly around him and screamed his name. Music to his ears.

Oh yeah. She was coming and he wasn't far behind.

"Do it, baby. Do it for me."

She cried out and her body shook beautifully around him. A second later, he followed her over, into the void where only pleasure existed. The two of them and the greatest pleasure he'd ever known, or would ever know. The pleasure of Mari. His Mari. His woman.

It took a long time for them to recover. Eventually the glow of the setting sun, just visible around the edges of Mariana's bedroom curtains, roused them both to action. Simon got up and grabbed a five-minute shower, then left the bathroom to Mariana while he put together a simple meal in her kitchen for them to share.

"Mmm, what did you cook? It smells good." Mariana took him by storm, coming up behind him and enveloping him in that wonderful scent that was hers alone. He turned and took her into his arms for a lazy kiss. She was warm and her hair was still a bit damp from her shower. She felt like heaven to him.

"I raided your cupboards. Hope you don't mind."

"I don't mind a bit. What's mine is yours."

Including her heart? He wasn't sure he really wanted to know. One part of him wanted her love, another part—the more sensible part—knew no good could come of it. He'd hurt her before and would likely hurt her again. He hoped, for her sake, she hadn't fallen in love with him. It was bad enough to leave her hurt. He would hate to leave her heartbroken as well.

"Let's eat, then I have to get out there. I want you safely locked in before dark."

They ate, making easy conversation. She told him about her life since they'd parted and amused him with funny stories from the research project she had been involved with until a few months ago.

"So you continued in research? I knew that's what you'd hoped to do."

"It took some time, but eventually a space opened up for me on a more advanced project. I was working on a live trial of dietary supplements, charting how different natural substances like vitamins and certain enzymes affected the performance of soldiers in the field. It was interesting work and the leader of the project, Doctor Amelia Jones, is a brilliant scientist. She promised to give me a sterling recommendation should I decide to try for a research post in civilian life. She doesn't do that often, so I guess I impressed her. She has a bit of a hard-nosed reputation, but she's a truly gifted scientist. That grants her a lot of leeway."

"I have no doubt you wowed her with your brilliance." He meant every word. Mariana possessed one of the brightest minds he had ever encountered. "So how did you end up manning the clinic?"

"Since I'm leaving the Navy shortly, they wanted to give me time to train my replacement on the research team. They managed to get him early, so I wound up with a little overlapping time. The clinic needed staffing after the last rotation. I've been here for a few months working out the rest of my time. Lucky for you."

"Very lucky for me, indeed." He toasted her with his water glass as they finished their meal of canned soup, vegetables, and salad from Mariana's refrigerator.

Simon would have said more, but just then his phone came to life, vibrating urgently in his pocket.

He stood and moved into the living room for a few minutes to take the call. When he returned, he had his pack over his shoulder and was fishing out a clip of darts. He handed it to Mariana with a grim twist to his lips.

"Sykes was doing a flyover and spotted the mailman walking out in the open on Webster Road. He didn't look good." His expression darkened. "I'm going over there. You stay here and hunker down. I'll be back to check on you after I take care of this, before I go out again. That Marine is still out there and he gets cleverer by the day."

He drew her in for a quick hug and she kissed him with all the emotion she couldn't put into words. "Be careful, Simon."

"Always. You know how to reload the pistol, right?" He pressed the clip of darts into her hand as she nodded. "I'll be back as soon as I can. Lock the door after me and stay out of sight."

He paused for one last kiss at the door and then he was gone, melting into the woods in the direction of Webster Road. He could've taken her SUV, but she knew Simon could get there in half the time by cutting through the woods, rather than taking the meandering backcountry roads.

Mariana reloaded the pistol first thing. She would have the full six shots if anything tried to get in. She had already barricaded the largest of the windows and locked the dead bolts on both doors. She decided to close off the bedroom and spare room and spend her time in the kitchen and living room. Those were the largest rooms in the house and both had doors to the outside. If anything sent her into retreat, she could always get out of the house and make a run for it, barring unforeseen circumstances.

About fifteen minutes after Simon left, she heard a noise outside, on the far side of the house. Tiptoeing into the spare room she took a look out the window. That room had a good vantage point for that side of the house.

Her skittering pulse pounded in her ears when she saw the shape of a man walking steadily toward the house from the woods. His face was intact, but his skin looked a ghastly gray and his eyes were menacingly vacant. He was wearing blood spattered fatigues. This was the last missing Marine and he was heading straight for her house.

Mariana dialed Simon's number and prayed while the phone rang. He picked up on the second ring.

"Simon, he's here! The Marine. He just walked out of the woods and he's heading for the house."

"Hold tight, Mari. I'm on my way. The mailman was a diversion. I got him, but he led me on quite a chase. I'm out past Webster Road and will have to double back. Stay hidden if you can."

She heard a scratching sound against the side of the house and saw the Marine round the corner. He was heading for the front.

"He's going around front," she whispered, desperate fear edging into her voice.

"Stay out of sight, Mari." It sounded like he was running and his voice was breathy.

She headed for the front of the house, wanting to keep tabs on where the zombie was, so she could avoid him. She heard a bang and her heart leapt into her throat.

As she entered the living room, the small window nearest her smashed and a fist opened just feet from her head. Long, yellow claws tipped the fingers on a hand that had once been human. She still didn't really understand what it was about the contagion that made their nails grow to hard claws after death, but thought it was probably as part of the semipetrifaction process. The thought came out of the part of her mind that could still reason, the part that observed the unfolding events in a sort of calm horror.

The rest of her was scared shitless and trembling in fear.

She screamed as the clawed hand rent the air in front of her face.

"What's going on?" Simon demanded, his voice a tinny shout from the tiny speaker in the phone.

"He broke through the window in the living room, but it's too small. He can't get in that way."

Apparently the zombie realized that at around the same time. The arm retreated from the broken window and the creature moved to the front door. Running, Mariana threw whatever furniture she could in front of it, barring the way. The couch, the small bookcase, a chair, and whatever else she could scrounge went in front of the wooden door.

Just in time, as it turned out. The creature began pounding against the door. It sounded like he was throwing all his weight against it and she watched in terror as the pile of furniture began to move—just slightly—inward.

"Hold on, Mari. I'm—"

The call disconnected. She'd lost contact with Simon!

The phone was dead in her hand and she didn't dare spare the time to redial. She had to take care of herself until he could get here. She had the pistol and if she could get a clear shot, she'd take it.

Maneuvering around to the side, she watched the gap between the broken door and the pile of furniture widen by slow degrees. When the arm reached through again she aimed and fired. She tried to hit the fleshy part of his upper arm, but missed.

This one was faster than the others she'd seen. He'd pulled his arm back hastily when the pistol went off, ruining her shot.

She still had five darts loaded and a few more in the kitchen if it came to that. The eerie sort of moaning sound the others had made transformed into loud groaning and grunting sounds with this one. He was stronger, too. He looked as if he had been in the prime of life when he'd died, at the peak of his physical strength and stamina.

Mariana was in trouble. This one wouldn't go down as easy as Becky Sue. He was no soft civilian. This was a highly trained soldier. She wasn't sure if it made any difference, but this guy had to be one of the first zombies created in the lab. His face was still intact from what she'd seen, though oddly discolored, as was the rest of his skin.

He was probably responsible for making others like him—for killing innocent civilians, including Becky Sue, her grandmother, and the poor postman. This was a killing machine spawning horror in its wake.

He shouldered through the widening opening in the door and she fired again.

"Shit!" She missed again as he jerked back. She was down to four rounds in her pistol. She had to make them count.

The pile of furniture moved again; the gap between door and barricade widened an inch more. Mariana eyed the furniture pile. In another two or three inches, the couch would wedge up against where the closet wall jutted out from the far wall. It would be nearly impossible to move after that unless something in the pile of furniture shifted or broke under the creature's weight.

But he would also be a few more inches into the house. Would that be enough for him to squeeze inside? She said a quick prayer that it wouldn't.

Just in case, she backed toward the kitchen door. She could barricade herself in there if she had to and still be able to flee through the back door if he managed to get into the living room and made inroads on the door leading from there into the kitchen. It was a sound plan. Too bad she was shaking like a leaf contemplating her retreat.

She just had to buy time until Simon could get here. He had been after this creature for weeks now. He would put an end to this thing once and for all, as was only fitting.

Unless she got a clear shot in the meantime, of course. The zombie shouldered farther into her living room and she took another shot. Another miss. She cursed herself. She was better than this but panic was making her take chances she shouldn't be taking.

Three darts left in the pistol. The couch bumped up against the closet wall and stuck. Ominous snapping sounds told her some of the furniture pile wasn't holding up and the barricade moved a lot farther inward than she expected. Time to retreat.

Mariana saw the creature. He actually made eye contact. His eyes were narrowed as if in anger, but otherwise blank. He saw her, but there wasn't any real sign of life in his gaze, only a vapid intentness that sent chills down her spine.

She fired one last shot and retreated through the kitchen door. He flinched, but she couldn't be sure if it was from being hit by her dart, or a quick move that saved him from it. Either way, he was too close. She had to retreat.

She scrambled into the kitchen and moved the refrigerator, table, chairs, and anything else she could in front of the door that led from the living room to the kitchen. The zombie might get into the living room. She had conceded that ground. If he tried to get in here, though, she would be able to retreat through the door leading to her backyard. It was locked, of course, but she could flip the dead bolt and be through it in a matter of seconds, if necessary.

Increasingly loud noises from the other room told her he had gained entrance to the living room. Loud crashes made her cringe and shiver in fear as she heard things being thrown around and breaking. Then it got quiet. These creatures didn't make a whole lot of sound unless they were pounding on something or making those pathetic moaning sounds that were almost subvocal. You had to be close to hear them.

"Come on, Simon," she whispered, urging him to get here soon.

She needed help. She wasn't afraid to admit it. She was a doctor, not a highly trained special ops warrior used to dealing with the worst of the worst although she had been getting plenty of real world experience the last few days. More than she had ever expected and certainly more than she'd ever wanted. She would gladly trade in all this excitement for a nice, normal, hectic day treating patients. She wouldn't have wanted to give up her time with Simon, but she would happily trade in the zombies for a bunch of unruly patients any day.

The sounds from the other room died down, and she tiptoed toward the back door to see if she could find out what was going on. Where the heck was Simon?

Mariana approached the window in the back door from an oblique angle, just in case, but she couldn't see much. Little by little, she edged more fully toward the small window. Everything looked clear, so she faced the small pane fully—and came face to face with the zombie.

She screamed and lunged away from the window, back toward the countertop where she had left the extra darts. She still had two in her pistol and she intended to make them count.

Her close-up look at the Marine's face gave her details she wished she hadn't seen. His flesh was gray. The area all around his mouth and between his yellowed teeth was stained brown with dried blood. Simon had told her they liked to bite and undoubtedly this one had done his share of chewing on his victims.

The man reared back and then his fist punched inward, breaking through the thick security glass of the little window as if it were nothing. When she saw him reaching inward, looking for the doorknob, she knew she was in serious trouble. This one was way smarter than the others.

His fingers found the knob for the dead bolt and turned it. Then he reached farther down toward the small dimpled lever on the doorknob itself. If he turned that, the door would be fully unlocked and all he would have to do then . . .

Mariana steadied her shaking arm as best she could and took careful aim. Firing, she hit the thing's arm, up near the biceps. The dart stuck and held, but the creature didn't slow. He turned the final lock and then the doorknob, dragging his arm out of the small window, dislodging the dart as he pulled it through the tight space.

She watched the dart clatter to the floor with a sinking heart. Had he gotten enough of the toxin? Had the dart been stuck in him long enough to deliver its full dose? How long before the toxin took full effect? Would she have enough time before he cornered her?

Her thoughts raced as she backed as far away as she could. She pulled the kitchen table and chairs off the pile barricading the inner door and threw them between herself and the zombie at the back door. She could never get everything moved out of the way in time, but she preferred to die fighting if she had to, not fleeing, her back to the danger. No, she would face it head on.

She only wished Simon knew what he truly meant to her. She wished she had told him how much she loved him. How much she always had . . . and always would.

Regrets. She had so many where he was concerned. Through the fear that rode her, she knew her regrets were best saved for another time. Now was the time for action. Her fate would be decided in the next few minutes.

The door opened, slamming back against its frame as the Marine pushed inside. He moved faster than the other zombies she'd seen, but she wouldn't give up without a fight. Mariana squeezed off her remaining round, lodging it squarely in his chest.

She knew the toxin took time to work. Would she make it? Did she have enough time? She pulled out two darts from the spares—one for each hand. She would stab the son of a bitch with them if he got too close. She would go down fighting if it was the last thing she did.

He stalked closer, moving quickly now, picking up her

kitchen chairs and throwing them aside. Only the table stood between her and the zombie.

And then he began to dissolve.

His legs fell out from under him, stopping his forward motion, then his torso disintegrated, falling to the floor in a shower of organic matter. Then she saw the large darts from Simon's rifle.

He had to have shot the zombie in the back while it was still out in the yard. His rifle had a much longer range than her small pistol. He'd taken the shots from far out, maybe while running to her rescue. Her darts hadn't had enough time to work. Simon's darts had been there first, in the creature's back, doing their job in the nick of time. Thank heaven.

A second later, Simon burst through her back door. She was never more grateful to see him. He'd saved her life.

"Mari? Did he touch you?"

"No, Simon. Oh, God, it's so good to see you."

She flew into his arms, climbing over the table and jumping the pile of debris that had been the zombie. She almost knocked Simon backward, but he steadied her, his powerful arms coming around her and holding her tight while he rained kisses down over her face.

"God, baby, I thought I'd lost you. I can't, Mari. I can't ever lose you." His whispered words were music to her ears.

"I love you, Simon. I wanted you to know. My one regret when I thought I was going to die was that I'd never told you. I've loved you for a long time. Since we were first dating. And I never stopped loving you, even when you left."

"Oh, Mari. I need you so much." He kissed her then, a long, lingering kiss. Mariana was beside herself with relief and joy. She had finally admitted the love that had never waned in her heart for him.

She wrapped herself around him in both delight and relief. He'd saved her life, no doubt about that. There hadn't been enough time for her darts to do the job. Simon's longer-range rifle darts had saved her.

Now that the danger was past, she was free to let her emotions take over. Tears mixed with the joy in her heart, sliding down her face and into their kiss. Simon pulled back, concern in his gaze. His expression was completely open to her for the first time and she could see the love shining in his eyes, the care in every beloved line of his face.

"You're all right, Mari. You're safe."

"I know. I'm just feeling a little overwhelmed. That's the last one, right? You're through with hunting them?"

"As far as I know, he was the last and the most difficult to catch. He's been evading me for months."

"He seemed smarter than the others."

"He was. He set the mailman up as a distraction, near as I can tell. He waited for me to go after that poor soul before attacking you here. None of the others showed that much initiative or cognitive ability."

"I'll freely admit, he scared the bejeezus out of me. I don't ever want to go through anything remotely like that again."

He hugged her close, stroking her back. "It's over, Mari. I think that's the last of them, but I'll probably be prowling around for the next few nights, just to make sure."

"And where will you be spending your days?" She challenged him, daring to hope his declaration meant he would be willing to stay with her this time, to see where their relationship might lead.

"I'll spend my days making love with you, if you're available." He winked at her, a devilish grin on his face.

"I'll see what I can arrange," she teased back. "I do have a bit of leave left that I really should use up."

"I'd be honored to help you find something to do with all your free time, Doctor." He lowered his head again and kissed her deeply, but all too briefly. He straightened. "Hold that thought. I need to report this to Sykes so he can get containment on Webster Road before any civilians go through there. Then I'm taking you to the nearest hotel so they can scrub this place and put it back to rights. Go pack a few things while I make the call."

She did as he asked, glad to have a task to occupy her hands and her mind. She was still dizzy from fright and from the amazing turn of events. Simon had saved her life and he'd admitted some pretty deep feelings for her. She didn't know which event was more amazing.

She had gone from stark terror to utter despair to grim resolution and then to blessed relief, all in the space of an hour or two. Her emotions were definitely on overload and spending what was left of the night at a hotel sounded like an awesome idea.

Chapter Nine

"Let me get that for you." Simon made short work of moving the refrigerator and other pieces of her make-shift barricade out of the way so she could get into the rest of the house.

He preceded her into the living room, to assess the damage and make certain everything was truly safe. He hated seeing the devastation on her pretty face when she looked at the ruin of her living room.

"Oh, boy." She sighed sadly. "This place is a disaster."

The monster had trashed the living room. Many of her ornaments and knickknacks were broken, as was a lot of her furniture. Otherwise, it was safe enough. The zombie hadn't left any nasty surprises that he could find.

"Let's check out the rest of the house before I make my call."

"Thanks, Simon." She tugged on his sleeve, her little hand stealing into his for a quick squeeze.

He leaned down to place a quick, reassuring kiss on her lips. He wanted to make love to her, but safety, duty, and security had to come first. There would be plenty of time to get her mind off the horrific events of the night. The rest of their lives, if he had his way.

"Come on, sweetheart. The sooner we do this, the sooner we can get out of here."

She seemed to gather herself before turning to the small hallway that led to the rest of the house. She had locked her bedroom, bathroom, and the door to the spare room. All were still locked. The creature hadn't even ventured down the hall from what Simon could see.

She unlocked all three doors one at a time at his signal and he checked each of the rooms out before he would let her enter. They were untouched, thankfully, and he watched as she grabbed a satchel and began tossing things in. He grabbed his bag, which he had left by the door to her bedroom, and went into the living room to make his call. Despite the late hour, Matt Sykes picked up on the first ring.

"It's done. We just got the last one at Mari's house. It was close. Bastard came right for her. That's the third time she's been in the line of fire with these things, Matt."

"She okay?" Sykes asked. Simon heard the concern in his buddy's voice. Matt Sykes was a good guy who truly cared about the people under his command, even if he seemed tough as nails on the outside.

"She's shaken, but she's a trouper. I want to get her out of here though. The guy trashed her living room and cornered her in the kitchen. What's left of him is in there. I'll tag it on the way out. There's also another down on Webster Road. The mailman. The one that attacked Mari set the mailman up as a distraction."

Matt Sykes whistled on the other end of the line. "I didn't think they were capable of that kind of forethought and planning."

"Neither did I. This last one's been a thorn in my side for weeks. He was a lot cannier than the others."

"You got him. That's all that matters. Good work, Si. By the numbers, that should be the end of it, but I want you to stay in position for another week or two, just to be sure."

"Roger that. But I'm done for tonight. I'm taking Mari to a hotel. She's been through a lot."

"Good idea. Put it on the tab. We'll spring for the accommodations while we put her house to rights. The containment team will be there shortly. When they're done I'll send a carpenter out to fix her place up good as new."

"Thanks, Matt. I'll let her know. I'm sure she'll appreciate it."

They spoke a few more minutes about the mission and what came next. By the time they ended the call, Mari was ready. She stood in the hall, waiting for him, the packed satchel in her hands. He took the bag from her and slung it over his shoulder along with his own.

They had to go out through the kitchen because the front door was still mostly blocked. Simon dropped a small transmitter on the debris that had once been a Marine. He had been a hell of an adversary but all in all, it was better that he was now gone. Simon pitied the man who had come to such an untimely and unnatural fate.

The sky was turning gray in the east as they walked together around the house, a sure sign of the dawn to come.

"Give me your keys, sweetheart. I'll drive."

She didn't argue, just handed the keys over. Her hands were trembling, and he knew she was still dealing with the residue of the adrenaline surges that had helped save her life.

He opened her door, checked the interior of the SUV, and ushered her in. Stowing his gear and the two packs in back, he then claimed the driver's seat. They rode in silence for a while as Simon negotiated the gravel lane that led to the larger paved road. He hadn't driven in this area much, but he knew the layout from both map study and reconnaissance. He knew just where to head to find the nicest hotel in town.

"I'm glad that's over." Mariana shut her eyes as she collapsed back against the headrest.

"Me, too." He reached over and took her hand.

"You're out of a job now." Her attempt at humor warmed him.

"Can't say I'm sorry about it." He took the turn toward the highway. There were a series of hotels out toward the city at a variety of price points. The one he had in mind was top of the line and luxurious. Mari deserved a little pampering after what she had experienced over the past few days.

She dozed on the way and Simon understood the adrenaline that had been keeping her going had also caused her to bottom out. Her body was crashing after the hell she had been through that night. He pulled in to the circular drive of the upscale hotel and despite the hour, a bellman and a valet were ready for them.

Simon touched her cheek. "Wake up, love. We're here. Just a few more minutes and you can go to sleep in a big, comfy, king-size bed. What do you say?"

"Is that a promise?" She didn't even open her eyes and her voice was sleepy.

"Scout's honor."

She propped one eyelid open. "Were you ever a scout?"

"Not a boy scout. But I took scout training. I'm the real deal," he teased.

"I have no doubt about that, Simon." She straightened, stretching as she came more fully awake. Her expression was serious when she turned to him in the dim interior of the car. "If I never said it before, I've always admired your skills in the field, even if I never really experienced them until the past few days. You saved my life more than once and I'll always be grateful."

"I don't want your gratitude, Mari." The conversation turned serious real fast.

"It's way more than gratitude, Simon." Her eyes met his and the moment stretched.

She had said she loved him. He hugged those words close to his battered heart. He wanted to reach out and grab onto her with both hands and just hold her for the rest of their lives.

But how could he take a chance with her future? How could he not? Simon moved closer, on the verge of declaring himself.

There was a noise by the driver's side door.

He mentally cursed the valet who chose that moment to walk up to his window. Her gaze flickered to the intrusive presence at the window, and the mood was broken.

Simon wasn't sure if he was more annoyed or grateful. In that moment he'd been tempted to throw all caution to the wind. Now, saner thoughts prevailed. Any more insanity on his part would have to wait until they were inside.

"Come on, let's get checked in."

He hopped out of the SUV and dealt with the valet while she exited the car and stretched some more. She was about to get their bags when he stopped her, utilizing the bellman's services. This sojourn was all about pampering her. Starting right now, he wouldn't let her lift a finger.

He checked them in using the company credit account, and within minutes they were ensconced in a luxury suite with a lovely view of the city far below. She hadn't said much on the way up in the elevator and was yawning a lot. The poor woman was beat. Simon's first priority had to be her comfort—getting her settled in a warm bed with nothing to do but sleep until she woke naturally.

Simon was used to the letdown after an extreme adrenaline rush and was better able to deal with it. Poor Mari was trying hard to keep her eyes open, but was losing the battle when he ushered the bellman out with a hefty tip.

"Alone at last." He leaned back against the closed door and couldn't help the grin that spread across his face. She was tousled and adorably sleepy, perched on the foot of the king-size bed.

"I'm sorry, Simon. I seem to be dead on my feet." She made a face. "Sorry. Bad choice of words there."

He laughed in spite of himself. It was a good sign that she was already able to joke about what they'd just been through.

"How about you just relax and I'll take care of you for a change?" He pushed away from the door and walked toward her.

"That sounds interesting." She perked up a little.

"Do you feel up to a hot bath? There's a Jacuzzi in there." He jerked his chin toward the door to the spacious bathroom. "There's also a bottle of wine in the cooler. After a glass or two, you should be mellow enough to sleep straight through."

"After a glass of wine and a hot bath I'll be comatose, Simon." She laughed and the sound warmed his heart.

"That's okay. Your only job now is to sleep until you can sleep no more."

"What about the clinic? I have to go back on duty tomorrow—or rather, today. What time is it?" She searched for the clock on the nightstand next to the big bed.

"Don't worry, it's all arranged. Commander Sykes is going to square things. You're off duty for the next three days at least. More if you need it. All we have to do is let him know."

"I'm impressed. It must be nice to have friends in high places." She gave him a teasing smile as he took her hand and helped her rise to her feet.

"You've earned a rest after what you've been through the past few days. Matt Sykes agreed. He also wanted me to thank you for pitching in on my mission." He walked her toward the bathroom door, ushering her through into the white wonderland of porcelain and steel.

"Oh, this looks like heaven." She ran her hand over the gleaming countertop as they passed on their way to the tub. Simon reached down to start the taps then returned to help her undress.

"My version of heaven is right here." He cupped her shoulders and looked down into her sleepy eyes. His words came out in a rough whisper, clogged with emotion. He knew he shouldn't speak of his feelings, but found he couldn't help himself.

"Do you really mean that, Simon?" She looked so hopeful as she stared up at him, searching his gaze.

"More than anything, Mari. You've always been it for me. Since the moment I first met you, I haven't wanted anyone but you in my life." She looked responsive so he dared a little more. "For always."

"Always?" Her whisper sounded full of anxious hope, sparking the same feeling in him.

He nodded. "I know I don't have any right to ask . . ." He trailed off, uncertain, then started again. "I want to be with you, Mari. I want to try again, and I promise I won't leave this time. You'll have to kick me out of your life if you want me gone, because I don't think I can give you up. It nearly killed me the first time and I'm not strong enough to put myself through that again. Even though I'm asking you to deal with the uncertainty I'm facing. I mean, they don't really know what the contagion did to me. I could have complications later—"

She stilled his tumbling words by placing one of her fingers over his lips, but the beatific smile on her lovely face reassured him.

"I want you in my life, too, Simon." Her voice was laced with tears. They looked like happy tears, judging by the delicate smile on her face. "Your condition doesn't bother me. I'll take you any way I can get you. Remember, I'm a doctor, and not a bad researcher. If you're willing, I'd be happy to see what I can discover about what happened to you and what could happen in the future. I want to help in any way I can, Simon. You mean a lot to me."

"You mean a lot to me, too, Mari."

It wasn't a declaration of love but it would do for now, Simon thought. He had to work his way up to saying the words. He wanted to hear her say them again first. He didn't want to be the only one out there on that most fragile of limbs. He had gone pretty far up the tree already. That final gamble would be better saved for another time when they were both rested and able to think more clearly.

* * *

The Jacuzzi really was heaven. Mariana felt boneless between the warm, gushing water and Simon's hands stroking over her. The tub was big enough for them both and Simon had brought in the wine and two glasses shortly after he'd helped her into the full tub. Then he'd undressed and climbed in behind her, spooning her from behind.

The combination of the wine, the warm water, and the hot man behind her had her in a state of relaxation she hadn't felt in a long time. In fact, she didn't think she had ever felt so good. At least not in recent memory. Probably not since the last time she and Simon had been together.

"This is nice," she said, trailing her fingers through the water.

"More than nice," Simon agreed from behind her.

"Someday I'm going to get one of these tubs for my house."

"In that little cabin? I don't think it'd fit. You'd have to add on a room."

"No, the cabin is a rental. I mean, when I buy a house. I'll probably be moving out of the area once I'm out of the Navy, depending on what job I take next, and . . . where you'll be."

She felt his muscles tense behind her and waited with held breath for his response.

"Would you come live with me if I promised to put in a Jacuzzi?" The words were teasing, but she thought the sentiment was very real. It made her warm all over. He was asking her to live with him. Hopefully that was a first step toward a lifetime together and she would take it—she would take *him*— any way she could get him.

"With an enticement like that, how could I refuse?" She reached behind her, twisting to pull his head down for a tender kiss. The warm water and his strong arms combined to make her forget all her troubles, all the fear and worry that had gone before.

"I think you'll like my place in the country. How do you feel about chickens?"

"We had chickens when I was a kid. And a couple of geese. I could never eat the ones we raised and wouldn't let anybody near them if butchering had been mentioned. My family used to laugh at me, but those birds were like pets."

"Duly noted." He chuckled at her, as she'd known he would. "How about if we get a few hens for eggs and let them live out their lives on the farm? No hen stew."

"You'd do that for me?"

"For you, I'd move mountains."

He sounded so calm about them living together and she could picture his little farm in her mind. It was like a fairy tale. A dream come true. She hugged the image to her heart, daring to hope for the first time that it might really come to pass.

They languished in the tub for a few more minutes. She would have loved to make love to him, but she just didn't have the energy. The steam made her sleepy and the feeling of security and happiness that only Simon gave her lulled her into a dreamlike state.

She was half asleep when he coaxed her out of the bath, dried her off, and ushered her toward the bed. He had been so good to her. She'd been able to banish the horrors of the past few days almost completely from her mind while he pampered her. She would have loved to do the same for him but she was too tired, too drained after the trip here and the night they'd just passed. She would make it up to him later. When they woke up. For now, she reveled in the feel of him lying next to her as he tucked them both into the huge, fluffy bed. She hugged the thought of living with him close to her heart. It was a start. He wasn't pushing her out of his life. He wasn't pushing her away anymore. They'd live together, and wherever life took them, they'd face it as a team.

He spooned with her, tucking her close against his warm body, making her feel safe. For the first time in days, she felt truly safe. She could let down the guard she'd developed and let go, trusting to Simon to protect her. For always. That's what he'd said.

She hugged the memory of their conversation to her heart.

Simon wasn't the most eloquent of men at the best of times, but he had come closer than he ever had to expressing some pretty powerful feelings. Feelings she returned fully.

"I love you, Simon," she whispered as she drifted to sleep in his arms.

Chapter Ten

Mariana woke shivering in reaction to a nightmare she couldn't really remember. It wasn't hard to guess what she had been dreaming about. Her life for the past few days had been the stuff of horror movies.

"You okay?" Simon's gravelly voice came to her in the dim room. She turned to find him watching her, concern in his expression.

"Man, that was a doozy. Sorry I woke you." She wiped her face, not surprised to find tears on her cheeks. Her hand was shaking as faint tremors wracked her body. Adrenaline still coursed through her veins making her long to flee . . . somewhere. It made no sense, but nightmares never really did.

Simon tugged her into his arms, letting her nestle her head below his chin. One strong hand circled her waist while the other stroked gently over her hair in soothing motions. She felt cocooned in his warmth, in his protection.

"Listen to my heartbeat, Mari. Let it steady you. Breathe deep and let the adrenaline dissipate. You'll crash in a few minutes if you let go of the fear."

"Have some experience with this, do you?" She tried for calm despite the way her heart still raced. It was embarrassing to be so vulnerable, so afraid and trembling in his presence.

Simon was a modern-day warrior of iron will who didn't

show fear. He probably didn't even feel it anymore. Not after all he'd been through. He had faced down zombies for the past few months as a matter of course. She felt like a fool for the unreasonable fear that had snuck up on her when she was most vulnerable. In her sleep. When all her defenses were down.

"I've learned to deal with the ups and downs of the adrenaline fog." Simon's husky voice touched her, drawing her away from the fright that still rode her body.

"You?" She moved back a few inches to look up at him. "I seriously doubt you ever feel fear."

"Oh, I feel it." His hand cupped her cheek, his thumb stroking her skin with a light touch. "Maybe not as easily as I used to after all I've seen, but believe me, it's there. I just don't show it like most people. I've learned to channel the adrenaline rush, to use it to make me stronger instead of giving me the shakes." His hand trailed down, over her shoulder to her arm, and then his fingers twined with hers, bringing their joined hands to his chest. "Your muscles still feel like overdone spaghetti?"

A laugh burst from her lips. "How'd you know?"

"I've been there." He flattened her hand on his chest, right over his heart. The rhythm was strong and steady, just like Simon himself. He was her rock in a sea of uncertainty. "Just concentrate on the rhythm of my heart, Mari. Breathe deep and slow. You'll get there in time."

She followed his instructions. Breathing in and out, focusing on his heartbeat, his comforting presence. After a few minutes, it started to work. She began to feel her heartbeat matching pace with his. Her breathing slowed and steadied as her body tuned itself to his.

"God, Simon, I feel like such a fool." Her voice still shook, but her breathing was leveling out, steadier now.

"Never that, sweetheart," he whispered, stroking her back. "You're the bravest, smartest, most beautiful woman I've ever known."

When he said it like that, she almost believed him. Simon had always had the ability to make her feel really good—emotionally and physically—with both his confidence in her, and his skills as a lover. Maybe a little of the latter was what she really needed to get her mind off the nightmare.

She rose above him on one elbow. "And you're the sexiest man I've ever had the good fortune to have in my bed." She gave him a temptress's smile. At least she hoped that's how he would interpret it. Beneath it all, she still felt a little desperate to forget all the scary things that had happened in the past few days.

"You think I'm sexy, eh?" His teasing grin told her he was willing to humor her whims. He knew her too well not to realize what she was doing, and he played along, the rogue.

"Oh, I know you're sexy. Sexy Simon. That's what my friend Claire used to call you behind your back. Do you remember her?" She trailed her fingers over his chest.

"Dark hair, kept in a bun all the time? Glasses? She was studying neurology, wasn't she?" She nodded, surprised he remembered such small details. That was a fair physical description of Claire, though she had a scintillating sense of humor under that sometimes severe exterior. They'd gone to happy hour a few times after work and on one or two memorable occasions, Simon and some of his friends had joined them at the local watering hole. "I didn't think she had it in her. Looked like an uptight librarian to me."

Mariana burst out laughing. "Yeah, I guess she does, but you know, librarians get a really bad rap. They're not all disapproving matron types. You'd like my sister, Ella. She's a librarian and she's nothing like the stereotype. She's boisterous and fun loving. She always has a smile and laughs easily. She was a real clown growing up."

"Sister, eh? Well, if she's your sister, I like her already."

She liked the way he teased her but she knew there was some kernel of truth in his words. He had always made an effort to be nice to her friends from work on the rare occasions they'd mingled. Like those happy hour gatherings. He had been polite and encouraging to Claire, who was surprisingly shy around Simon and his military buddies.

"I think she'll like you, too."

"You thinking about introducing me to your family? This sounds serious." His blue gaze glittered with an intense light and she was afraid maybe she'd assumed too much, too soon.

She forced herself to shrug noncommittally. "You'll meet them eventually, I'm sure. No doubt you'll be dragged to one of the family gatherings at some point. There are a few each year where we all get together on the farm, and pick on one another for old time's sake."

He took a minute before answering, which didn't do much to reassure her. "Sounds like fun."

It was time to change the subject. Lifting one knee, she straddled him, leaning forward over his muscular torso.

"So now that we're both awake, what do you think we should do to keep ourselves occupied?" She sent him a daring smile, hoping he'd take her up on her blatant offer. She had confidence he would, judging by his state of arousal. She could feel him stir against her bottom. Oh yeah, he'd play along.

"How about a little game?" The teasing tone of his voice warmed her once more.

"What kind of game?" She was willing to try just about anything with him and she had no doubt he knew it.

"What else? My favorite game. Simon Says."

"Oh, I like the way your mind works, sexy Simon."

One of his hands moved to her breast, cupping her with warmth and exploring fingers. "Sexy Simon then," he agreed. "Sexy Simon says to lean closer so I can kiss these nipples that both seem to want my attention." Their eyes met and fire leaped between them. "Do they, Mari? Do they want my attention?"

"Yes, Simon." Her voice was shaky already and he hadn't done much more than touch her.

"Well come on down here then, woman. Simon says."

She felt wanton as she leaned over him, following his orders. She had always enjoyed making love with him when he exercised his dominant streak, but this new, teasing, *sexy* Simon was something very exciting indeed.

He latched on to her nipple with his tongue, swirling it

around the eager peak with just the right pressure. He used his teeth gently, never hurting, always enticing, and the suction of his mouth felt oh so good. Then he switched to the other side, letting his fingers take up where his mouth had left off, sliding in the wetness left by his lips to pinch and tease.

She moaned with pleasure and he drew back, releasing her nipple with a little pop.

"You like that?"

"You know I do." There was a breathless quality to her voice she couldn't control.

He grinned at her with pure male satisfaction. "Are you ready for more?"

She liked the new playfulness between them. "Bring it on, big boy."

His grin only widened. "Simon says bring that pussy up here."

She gave him a questioning look. "You want me to—"

He cut her off by the simple expedient of grabbing her hips and lifting her over his chest. Damn, that man was strong.

"Lean up on your knees, baby. Give me your pussy. Right over my mouth."

"You're serious?" They'd never done this before. In fact, she'd never done it in this position with anyone, ever.

"Oh yeah." He gave her a mischievous wink. "I want a taste of you, baby. I want to fuck you with my tongue and have your cream dribble down my chin."

Her abdomen clenched at his earthy words and she responded to the urging of his hands, rising above him into the position he desired. She wasn't sure about this, but the hidden temptress within wanted—no, needed—to do anything he asked. His dirty talk affected her more than she would have believed possible. If any other man had used such language with her, she wasn't sure she could have responded. Coming from Simon's lips? Those words were thrilling in a forbidden, very naughty way. He made her feel sexy, desired, and almost . . . wanton. Only for him.

A moment later, his mouth rose to her core, his tongue exploring, licking through her folds and right up into her. He set a rhythm that made her groan, stabbing into her over and over again with his tongue in an imitation of what he would do later with his cock, if she had her way.

She couldn't hold it. Not one second longer. She shattered with a shaking moan as she came against his tongue. He made a sound that vibrated against her most sensitive parts, drawing out her hasty orgasm. After a minute or two, it plateaued, but didn't fully dissipate. If their past history was anything to go by, she was in for one hell of a ride. He'd done this to her a few times before—brought her multiple orgasms, each one building on the last until she flew right up to the stars.

Simon was, by far, the most talented lover she had ever had the good fortune to be with. This was especially true when he took his time . . . and they had the day all to themselves. She shuddered just thinking of what he could do in that time.

When he came up for air, she was finally able to move away. He wouldn't let her go far. He parked her over his chest, sitting lightly on her haunches, her legs spread for him, her core displayed for him to look at. And play with.

His hands stroked from her hips to her pussy with tantalizing slowness. He watched her face, searching her reaction, then slid his gaze to her spread folds with heated intensity. That look alone was enough to make her cream.

"Spread your legs a little farther for me, baby, and lean back. I want to see all of you."

She felt very vulnerable, spread out and open to him. She wouldn't have done this for just anyone. This was Simon. He could have anything he asked of her. He was her savior, her protector, the only man she had ever loved. If she could bear to make herself vulnerable to any man, it was him. She complied, the straining muscles of her thighs shaking as she moved into the position he wanted.

One of his big hands spread her open even farther. Then a broad, male finger slid into her channel, making her gasp. He set up a rhythm that picked up on her earlier climax and drove her passion higher. He didn't let the pleasure dissipate. No, he kept her primed while he inspected her pussy, adding a second finger after a while that made her squirm in earnest. Then his thumb started to tease her clit and all hell broke loose. Again.

"Simon!" She cried out as she peaked again and heard him chuckle. That masculine sound drove her higher. It told her he was enjoying making her squeal with pleasure and come for him.

She came on his hand, moaning as she shook with satisfaction. It rose in a tide and never receded. He was definitely working her toward something bigger and better. She only hoped she would still be able to breathe when he finally got her to the destination he had in mind.

Mariana gave over all control to him willingly and followed where he led. She knew enough about him to know he would make it worth her while. If there was one thing she knew Simon wanted, it was her trust. She had trusted him with her life already. Now she would trust him again, this time with her body and her pleasure. She knew she couldn't be in better hands.

When the shudders began to subside, he removed his fingers. His hands stroked over her skin, cupping her breasts and teasing the sensitive nipples, then lingering over her ticklish abdomen and down into her wet, eager, wide open pussy. He didn't give her time to come down off the climax; instead, he built her toward another.

"Are you up for more, baby?"

She nodded, entranced by the glittering need in his sexy blue eyes.

"What would you say if Simon said to suck my cock?" His words dared her to be wanton and she responded in kind.

"I'd say, what took you so long?" The smile she gave him was full of feminine mischief and sloe-eyed audaciousness. Her inner siren had come out to play.

Her body craved the small respite and her mind wanted to even the score with her sexy tormentor. She wanted to bring him along with her on their path to ecstasy. She didn't like for it all to be one sided, with him giving her everything and her selfishly taking it all. She wanted to give to him, too.

"Then Simon says, give it your all, baby. Suck it down but don't make me come. I want to come inside you."

"I live to follow your orders," she teased with a roll of her eyes as she levered herself off his muscular body. For this, she wanted to be at his side, able to devote her entire attention to doing him right. He deserved no less after the two brilliant peaks he'd already given her.

She licked the head, teasing at first, watching his reactions to check his responses. Hooded eyes followed her every move. She liked the power he gave her over his pleasure. It made her feel more in control and supremely feminine. Just what she needed after her feeling of helplessness leftover from the dream— a little give and take. He owned her pleasure but he'd given her some control over his.

Wanting more, she opened her mouth wide and took him in. She loved the sexy groan that issued from his lips when she hollowed her cheeks and applied suction.

"Oh, baby, just like that," he praised, clenching his hands into fists at his sides, rumpling the sheets in his hands. The way the sleek muscles of his washboard abdomen rippled sent shivers down her spine. He really was the sexiest man alive. And he was all hers. A girl couldn't get any luckier than this.

She grabbed the root of him with one hand and squeezed, fondling his sac gently with the other. His grunts and groans were music to her ears as she applied herself to making him come. He'd told her not to push him that far, but she remembered his powers of recovery and amazing stamina. She knew it wouldn't take him long to make a comeback even after she had drained him dry. He wouldn't leave her hanging, and if she let him, he would give and give and never take even this small thing for himself.

She loved him for it, but he had to learn that sometimes she wanted to be the one giving in their relationship, not just the recipient of his amazing talents. She sucked him long and strong, gauging his reactions with increasing pleasure. He tried to pull away once. She held firm and wouldn't let him leave. Truth be told, he didn't put up that much of a struggle and she figured she'd won this round. Feminine satisfaction filled her with a giddy sort of triumph and she redoubled her efforts.

Mariana knew darn well how much he liked what she was doing to him. Inwardly she purred, knowing the sound would travel as vibrations down his sensitive length. He groaned her name as he came. He tried to pull away again, but she wouldn't let him escape. She wanted everything he had to give.

It had been so long. She remembered his taste, the unique saltiness of him. Of the few men she'd done this to in her life, Simon was the only man who made her truly yearn for the taste of him. He was her perfect match in every way.

His breath came in great gasps and his eyes were squeezed tightly shut as she watched him come down from his explosive orgasm.

"You're a witch, Mari. A siren sent to seduce me. And you're a little cheater. I told you not to do that." His eyes popped open to find her, still sitting at his side, trailing lazy fingers over his rippled abdomen.

"Come on, Simon. You know you liked it." She smiled slyly at him, encouraging him to admit his delight.

"Oh, I liked it all right." He lifted up on one elbow to meet her gaze. "But it's not what I told you to do. You disobeyed a direct order, woman." The teasing tone of his voice reassured her that he wasn't really mad at her. He was, however, in a playful mood, which could mean a lot of different things. Simon had always been an inventive lover. She couldn't wait to see what he would pull out of his bag of tricks now.

"It was in a good cause, sir." She gave a sloppy salute as a grin split her lips.

"I won't argue that, Doctor. However, when Simon says to do something, in future you need to learn that he means it."

"Really?" One of her eyebrows rose in challenge.

"Really." She knew from the way he answered that he was amused by their banter. "I ought to swat your ass for disobeying me."

"Would you, really?" Damn, was that breathy, porn star voice really hers?

Okay, so maybe the idea of a sexy spanking had run through her mind a few times, but she had never let anyone actually do it to her. She had never given up that kind of control to anyone. Of course, she'd never done a lot of the things Simon had introduced her to and she had loved every one of them. If there was anyone on Earth she could trust, Simon was the guy she could trust to explore all her forbidden fantasies. She was safe with him. He would never hurt her and he would listen and obey if she said she wanted to stop.

"Is that anticipation I hear?" She saw his cock stir as one of his hands trailed down from her waist to her backside, cupping one rounded cheek. As she'd thought, it didn't take long for him to rise to the occasion once more. The man was fit and had stamina to spare. That was a good thing in a warrior—and especially in a lover.

His fingers tightened on her ass, then let go, only to come back in a stinging smack that made her jump. A high pitched squeal came from her lips that she hadn't expected. Neither had she expected the slight burn of her flesh that made her want more.

Oh, yeah. Simon knew her all too well if that one swat was any indication. She wanted more.

"Well?" Blue eyes dared her as he sat up fully, facing her.

She blinked up at him and purred playfully. "Please sir, may I have another?"

Simon laughed outright and she loved the sound. He did it so rarely outside of their time together, it was a gift.

"Just for that, wench . . ." He lifted her as if she weighed nothing at all and scooted to the edge of the bed. In an eye blink, she was draped over his knees, ass in the air. "You're gonna get it."

"Oh, I hope so." She squealed again when his hand came down in a playful swat.

He didn't really hurt her, just smacked her hard enough for a delicious burn to spread over her skin. And the way her rubbed her cheeks with that big, open palm before and after the light taps was even more rewarding than the naughty feeling being spanked gave her.

It wasn't something she would like to do every night, but as a change of pace, it certainly had its rewards. She had never been all that daring sexually. Not until Simon. He'd given her everything she had ever fantasized about and more. He seemed to know what she wanted even before she did and he always put her pleasure first. Nothing, it seemed, was too much to ask.

Which was why she let him lead in the bedroom. This was a man who didn't need an instruction manual to find his way around a woman's body. No, Simon had probably *written* the damned manual.

In all, he spent more time stroking her skin than actually spanking her. He took his time, letting his fingers stray downward, between her legs, to linger and tease. When she squirmed, so near the edge, he startled her back away from it with another little tap. He repeated this process a few times until she couldn't control the moans that issued from her lips or the shivery sensations coursing through her body. She needed to come. Bad. And he had to know it.

"So responsive, my dear," he mused as he cupped her stinging cheek with one big hand. "We'll have to remember this for the future. Maybe someday you can play naughty schoolgirl for me."

Just thinking about the scene his words implied made her thighs clench. She was so close!

"Ah, I see you like the idea. I didn't know you were quite so kinky, Mari, but it's a pleasure to find out. I'll play any game you like. Anytime." He leaned over to growl the last bit in her ear and she couldn't help the shivers that went down her spine, straight to her pussy.

"Simon! Please," she gasped, wanting him. Waiting for him to push her over the edge again.

His hand came down in one final swat and she cried out, coming hard. She wouldn't have thought she could gain such satisfaction from being spanked, but Simon had always been able to pull things out of her response she never would have expected.

"Now, are you going to disobey me ever again?" She heard the laughter in his voice as he leaned over her.

"Every chance I get," she whispered, still coming down from a blissful place.

"Hmm. Maybe I ought to rethink my strategy." He rubbed her ass one final time and lifted her to lie on her back in the center of the bed as she laughed with him.

It was good to feel so carefree after the tense days they'd just spent. Especially after the years spent apart, years she had spent missing him.

"Come to me, Simon." She cupped his cheek as he laid her down, her gaze holding his. "Make love to me."

He stilled over her. "Who's giving the orders here?" The words were playful, but his tone wasn't. No, he'd gone serious on her, mirroring her mood and turning the needful moment into something much more serious.

"I need you, Simon. I've always needed you."

Silence stretched. She had to dare. She had to give him what she thought he finally might truly want.

"I love you, Simon. I never stopped loving you."

His reaction didn't show on his face, but she saw satisfaction and relief in his expression as he moved over her. Without a word, he joined with her, sliding into her body and claiming her for his own. At least, that's what it felt like. He began to move in a slow, steady rhythm that she matched eagerly.

Something big was happening here. It was different than it ever had been before. The urgency was there, but ratcheted back to let the emotion pour over and through. She felt all the things she always felt when Simon was inside her—protected, cherished, cared for in a deep, lingering way. She felt something else as well, moving deeply between them, in the space of their souls.

Her words of love had affected him. She felt it in every deep stroke, every moment he held her gaze. Nothing stood between them now. Raw emotion touched his face and she knew he saw the same from her.

"I have only one more thing I want you to do, baby." He kept his steady pace, drawing out the moment.

"What's that?" Her voice was breathless.

"Simon says, marry me?"

A laugh started from her lips as she reached up to encircle his neck.

"Yes, Simon. Oh, yes!"

He kissed her then, joining their bodies in every possible way as his strokes increased. He was wild at the last, holding her by the shoulders so his hard thrusts didn't push her up against the headboard. She was cocooned by him, surrounded and engulfed by him, and it felt wonderful.

They came together in a shower of passionate sparks that set them both aflame with rapture, flying higher than ever before. Together. Forever.

If fate allowed.

What felt like hours later, Mariana woke. Simon lay beside her, propped up on one elbow watching her.

"Did I fall asleep?"

"I think you passed out." He grinned. "I'm sorry, honey. I didn't mean to push you so hard. Are you okay?"

She stretched sore limbs, taking stock. "I'm glorious."

"That you are, my love." One big hand stroked her rib cage, tracing delicate patterns on her skin.

"Did you mean it, Simon? Do you really want to get married?"

"Yes, Mari. I know it's selfish, but I need you. I can't live without you. I . . . love you." His expression looked pained for a split second. "I've never said that to a woman before. I've never felt it before, but I feel it with you, Mari. I've loved you for a long time. In fact . . ." He reached over the side of the bed and fished something out of the pocket of his pants, then threw them aside once more. "I bought this three years ago, with the intention of giving it to you when I came back from that last mission. Then things happened, and well, now you know the rest. The thing is, I never could put this away. I've carried it all this time and now I know why."

He held out his hand and opened his fist, palm up. On it sparkled a diamond ring that took her breath away.

"This is yours, Mari. I bought it for you. Will you accept it? Will you accept me, knowing what happened to me? Knowing there's a heap of uncertainty in my life and about my future? Knowing that I love you and want to spend whatever time I have left with you? Knowing that I've loved you since we first met and it's taken me all this time to find the courage to tell you?"

"Oh, Simon." She sat up, tears in her eyes as she reached for his hand. He captured hers and placed the ring on her finger himself. The moment seemed sacred, somehow.

"I love you, Mariana, and I always will."

"I love you, Simon. No matter what comes, we'll be together." Tears rolled down her face as he kissed her, cementing their love.

They'd have a ceremony later and a big party with their friends and family, but all that really mattered was their love. Undying, unable to be destroyed by time, distance, or horror. They had each other now, and that was all that mattered.

Or so Simon said.

If you liked this book, you've got to try ETERNAL HUNTER, the latest from Cynthia Eden, in stores now from Brava . . .

She reached into her bag and pulled out a check. Not the usual way things were handled in the DA's office, but . . . "I've been authorized to acquire your services." He didn't glance at the check, just kept those blue eyes trained on hers. Her fingers were steady as she held the check in the air between them. "This check is for ten thousand dollars."

No change of expression. From the looks of his cabin, the guy shouldn't have been hesitating to snatch up the money.

"Give the check to Night Watch."

At that, her lips firmed. "I already gave them one." A hefty one, at that. "This one's for you. A bonus from the mayor. He wants this guy caught, fast." Before word about the true nature of the crime leaked too far.

"So old Gus doesn't think his cops can handle this guy?"

Gus LaCroix. Hard-talking, ex-hard-drinking mayor. No nonsense, deceptively smart, and demanding. "He's got the cops on this, but he said he knew you, and that you'd be the best one to handle this job."

Erin strongly suspected that Gus belonged in the *Other* world. She hadn't caught any unusual scent drifting from him, but his agreement to bring in Night Watch and his almost desperate demands to the DA had sure indicated the guy knew more than he was letting on about the situation.

Could be he was a demon. Low-level. Many politicians were.

Jude took the check. Finally. She dropped her fingers, not wanting the flesh on flesh contact with him. Not then.

He folded the check and tucked it into the back pocket of his jeans. "Guess you just got yourself a bounty hunter."

"And I guess you've got yourself one sick shifter to catch."

He closed the distance between them, moving fast and catching her arms in a strong grip.

Aw, hell. It was just like before. The heat of his touch swept through her, waking hungers she'd deliberately denied for so long.

Jude was sexual. From his knowing eyes, his curving, kiss-me lips, to the hard lines and muscles of his body.

Deep inside, in the dark, secret places of her soul that she fought to keep hidden, there was a part of her just like that.

Wild. Hot.

Sexual.

"Why are you afraid of me?"

Not the question she'd expected, but one she could answer. "I know what you are. What sane woman wouldn't be afraid of a man who becomes an animal?"

"Some women like a little bit of the animal in their men."

"Not me." *Liar.*

His eyes said the same thing.

"Do your job, Donovan. Catch the freak who cut up my prisoner—"

"Like Bobby had been slashing his victims?"

Hit. Yeah, there'd been no way to miss that significance.

"When word gets out about what really happened, some folks will say Bobby deserved what he got." His fingers pressed into her arms. Erin wore a light, silk shirt—and even that seemed too hot for the humid Louisiana spring night. His touch burned through the blouse and seemed to singe her flesh.

"Some will say that," she allowed. Okay, a hell of a lot would say that. "But his killer still has to be caught." Stopped, because she had the feeling this could be just the beginning.

Her feelings about death weren't often wrong.

She was a lot like her dad that way.

And, unfortunately, like her mother, too.

"What do you think? Did he deserve to be clawed to death?"

An image of Bobby's ex-wife, Pat, flashed before her eyes. The doctors had put over one hundred and fifty stitches into her face. She'd been his most brutal attack.

Erin swallowed. "His punishment was for the court to decide." She stepped back, but he didn't let her go. "Uh, do you mind?"

"Yeah, I do." His eyes glittered down at her. "If we're gonna be working together, we need honesty between us."

"We need *you* to find the killer."

"Oh, I will. Don't worry about that. I always catch my prey."

So the rumors claimed. The hunters from Night Watch were known throughout the U.S.

"You're shivering, Erin."

"No, no, I'm not." She was.

"I make you nervous. I scare you." A pause. His gaze dropped to her lips, lingered, then slowly rose back to meet her stare. "Is it because I know what you are?"

She wanted his mouth on hers. A foolish desire. Ridiculous. Not something the controlled woman wanted, but what the wild thing inside craved. "You don't know anything about me."

"Don't I?"

Erin jerked free of his hold and glared at him. "Few things in this world scare me. You should know that." There was one thing, one person, who terrified her but now wasn't the time for that disclosure. No, she didn't tell anyone about *him*.

If she could just get around Jude and march out of that door—

"Maybe you're not scared of me, then. Maybe you're scared of yourself."

She froze.

"Not human," he murmured, shaking his head. "Not vamp."

Vamp? Thankfully, no.

"Djinn? Nah, you don't have that look." His right hand lifted and he rubbed his chin. "Tell me your secrets, sweetheart, and I'll tell you mine."

"Sorry, not the sharing type." She'd wasted enough time here. Erin pushed past him, ignoring the press of his arm against her side. Her body ached and the whispers of hunger within her grew more demanding every moment she stayed with him.

Weak.

She hated her weakness.

Just like her mother's.

"You're a shifter." His words stopped her near the door. She stared blankly at the faded wood. Heard the dull thud of her heart echoing in her ears.

Then the soft squeak of the old floorboards as he closed the distance between them.

Erin turned to him, tilted her head back—

He kissed her.

She heard a growl. Not from him—no, from her own throat.

The hunger.

Sure, he made the first move, he brought his lips crashing down on hers, but . . . she kissed him right back.

And don't miss THE STRANGER'S SECRETS by
Beth Williamson, available now from Brava . . .

The dining room was nearly bursting at the seams. There was only one unoccupied table by the time Sarah and Whitman arrived to eat. Unfortunately, it was in a corner and made for two.

"Told you to hurry," Whitman grumbled under his breath.

Sarah couldn't stop a very unladylike snort, again. "Next time I'll run up the stairs and you stand at the bottom then."

He didn't respond, but she saw the corner of his mouth twitch, as if he was holding in a laugh. Perhaps the serious Yankee did have a sense of humor after all.

When they sat down, Sarah realized it was the first time they were face-to-face. On the train and even walking to the hotel, they'd been beside each other. Facing Whitman was an entirely different experience.

He wasn't classically handsome, but damn, he was exactly the kind of man Sarah was attracted to. His face was angular, the late-day whiskers only added to his appeal, his nose was slightly crooked, and a few scars were scattered here and there as if he'd been wounded by small pieces of something.

But it was his eyes that captured her attention. Deep, green, and framed by those long eyelashes, Whitman had the sexiest gaze she'd ever seen. Fortunately or unfortunately, she felt a tug of sensual awareness just looking at the tousled chocolate locks above those eyes.

Hell and crackers.

He frowned. "Why are you scowling at me?"

"I'm not scowling." She fiddled with the fork and knife on the table while hoping the missing waitress would appear to save her from the awkward situation.

Damn Mavis Ledbetter. The woman was over by the window with that same gentleman, completely ignoring the fact she'd been paid to take care of Sarah. Whit had been right—she was going to fire Mavis and leave her in whatever town this was.

"She looks to be a spinster." Whit followed Sarah's gaze. "Looks as if she hasn't given up the quest for a husband, though."

"She spent so much time declaring she was a spinster, she kept most men away from her." Sarah frowned at Mavis. "Nobody in town wanted anything to do with her because of her reputation."

"You're from the same town then?"

His question was one anyone in polite company would ask, but Sarah found herself unwilling to answer any personal questions. So she decided to insult him to keep him disliking her. "You're nosy."

"You're rude."

"You're pushy."

He barked a laugh. "And you're refreshingly honest."

Sarah found herself holding back a chuckle. What was it about this annoying Yankee that set her on her head? Aside from being handsome, there wasn't anything else remarkable about him. She needed to figure out his appeal so she could combat it and keep her distance, at least as much as she could, considering they were going to be stuck in a train compartment together for fifteen hundred miles.

"Then you won't mind if I continue being honest."

He nodded. "I wouldn't expect any less."

Why in the hell did that make Sarah's heart thump like a bass drum? Back home, when she ate a meal, it was with her friends, a group where everyone chatted and relaxed. Sitting with Whit made her feel jumpy and awkward—a condition Sarah was definitely not used to.

"You make me uncomfortable," she blurted.

His eyebrows went up. "I do?"

Now that she'd gone down that path, she had to finish her thought. "I'm sure you've heard the song before, Mr. Kendrick, but Yankees aren't high on my list of favorite folks, much less one I have to rely on. It's going to take some time for me to, ah, adjust, so if you can, be patient with me."

Whit nodded. "I'll do my best."

She didn't want to demand anything from the man. After all, there was no reason for him to help her. His actions told her more than anything that he was a gentleman. "When life kicks you once, you get back up and move on. When life kicks you a dozen times, you're less willing to forgive and trust." That was as far as she planned on going with that train of thought. He seemed like a sharp guy and could likely understand why she felt uncomfortable.

"Don't worry. I won't give you any cause to kick me back. I promise." The sincerity in his gaze made her want to believe him.

Ridiculous, of course. Why should she trust a stranger? She had to rely on him to be her companion, however that would turn out. Yet expecting him to carry her bags was a far cry from trusting him with her life. Sarah could take care of herself, for the most part anyway, and she regretted the fact she couldn't do it all the time.

"Good, because I bite when I kick." She fought back a grin.

"Somehow that doesn't surprise me in the least." He smiled at the waitress as she approached the table.

The young blond thing sparkled like a new penny when she caught sight of Whitman. Sarah wanted to trip her with the cane.

"Good evening, sir. Can I fetch you something to drink? Or an order of meatloaf? It's the best in the county." The young woman smiled while her face flushed.

Sarah harrumphed at the obvious tactics the girl used. "I'd like some of that meatloaf and hot coffee."

The girl looked surprised to see Sarah sitting there.

"I'm sure Mr. Kendrick here will have the same thing." Sarah shot Whitman a challenging look, daring him to contradict her.

"Meatloaf and coffee would be lovely. Thank you, miss." He graced the girl with another smile, sending her scurrying to the kitchen.

At least the food would arrive quickly considering the girl was already enamored of Whitman.

"Are you always this honest?" Whit picked up the spoon in front of him.

"Yes, I am. Does it bother you?" Sarah was ready to show him just how forceful she could be with her words.

"Not at all." He breathed on the spoon and stuck it on the end of his nose. Sarah almost choked on her spit as she watched a grown man play at a child's trick. What the hell was he doing?

When he smiled, the force of it snatched Sarah's breath. She could do nothing but look at the grin behind the spoon and wonder if she'd stepped into a dream of her own twisted mind. He was beautiful, a Yankee, and charming as all hell.

Sarah was afraid she'd lose more than her spoon to Whitman Kendrick.

Here's a sneak peek at Donna Kauffman's HERE COMES TROUBLE, out next month from Brava!

The hot, steamy shower felt like heaven on earth as it pounded his back and neck. He should have done this earlier. It was almost better than sleep. Almost. He'd realized after Kirby had left that he'd probably only grabbed a few hours after arriving, and he'd fully expected to be out the instant his head hit the pillow again. But that hadn't been the case. This time it hadn't been because he was worried about Dan, or Vanetta, or anyone else back home, or even wondering what in the hell he thought he was doing this far from the desert. In New England, for God's sake. During the winter. Although it didn't appear to be much of one out there.

No, that blame lay right on the lovely, slender shoulders of Kirby Farrell, innkeeper, and rescuer of trapped kittens. Granted, after the adrenaline rush of finding her hanging more than twenty feet off the ground by her fingertips, it shouldn't be surprising that sleep eluded him, but that wasn't entirely the cause. Maybe he'd simply spent too long around women who were generally over-processed, over-enhanced, and overly made up, so that meeting a regular, everyday ordinary woman seemed to stand out more.

It was a safe theory, anyway.

And yet, after only a few hours under her roof, he'd already become a foster dad to a wild kitten and had spent far more time thinking about said kitten's savior than he had his own host of problems.

Maybe it was simply easier to think about someone else's situation. Which would explain why he was wondering about things like whether or not Kirby would make a go of things with her new enterprise here, what with the complete lack of winter weather they were having. And what her story was before opening the inn? Was this place a lifelong dream? For all he knew, she was some New England trust fund baby just playing at running her own place. Except that didn't jibe with what he'd seen of her so far.

He'd been so lost in his thoughts while enjoying the rejuvenation of the hot shower, that he clearly hadn't heard his foster child's entrance into the bathroom. Which was why he almost had a heart attack when he turned around to find the little demon hanging from the outside of the clear shower curtain by its tiny, sharp nails, eyes wide in panic.

After his heart resumed a steady pace, he bent down to look at her, eye-to-wild-eye. "You keep climbing things you shouldn't and one day there will be no one to rescue you."

He was sure the responding hiss was meant to be ferocious and intimidating, but given the pink nosed–tiny–whiskered face it came out of, not so much. She hissed again when he just grinned, and started grappling with the curtain when he outright laughed, mangling it in the process.

He swore under his breath. "So, I'm already down one sweater, a shower curtain, and God knows what else you've dragged under the bed. I should just let you hang there all tangled up. At least I know where you are."

However, given that the tiny thing had already had one pretty big fright that day, he sighed, shut off the hot, life-giving spray, and very carefully reached out for a towel. After a quick rubdown, he wrapped the towel around his hips, eased out from the other end of the shower, and grabbed a hand towel. "We'll probably be adding this to my tab, as well." He doubted Kirby's guests would appreciate a bath towel that had doubled as a kitty straitjacket.

"Come on," he said, doing pretty much the same thing he'd done when the kitten had been attached to the front of Kirby. "I know you're not happy about it," he told the now squalling cat. "I'm not all that amped up, either." He looked at the shredded curtain once he'd de-pronged the demon from the front of it, and shuddered to think of just how much damage it had done to the front of Kirby.

"Question is . . . what do I do with you now?"

Just then a light tap came on the door. "Mr. Hennessey?"

"Brett," he called back.

"I . . . Brett. Right. I called. But there was no answer, so—"

"Oh, shower. Sorry." He walked over to the door, juggled the kitty bundle and cracked the door open.

Her gaze fixed on his chest, then scooted down to the squirming towel bundle, right back up to his chest, briefly to his face, then away all together. "I'm—sorry. I just, you said . . . and dinner is—anyway—" She frowned. "You didn't take the cat, you know, into—" She nodded toward the room behind him. "Did something happen?"

"I was in the shower. Shredder here decided to climb the curtain because apparently she's not happy unless she's trying to find new ways to terrify people."

He glanced from the kitten to Kirby's face in time to see her almost laugh, then compose herself. "I'm sorry, really. I shouldn't have let you keep her in the first place. I mean, not that you can't, but you obviously didn't come here to rescue a kitten. I should—we should—just leave you alone." She reached out to take the squirmy bundle from him.

"Does that mean I don't get dinner?"

"What?" She looked up, got caught somewhere about chest height, then finally looked at his face. "I mean, no, no, not at all. I just—I hope you didn't have your heart set on pot roast. There were a few . . . kitchen issues. Minor, really, but—"

"I'm not picky," he reassured her. What he was, he realized, was starving. And not just for dinner. If she kept looking at him like that . . . well, it was making him want to feed an entirely different kind of appetite. In fact . . . He shut that mental path down. His life, such as it was, didn't have room for further complications. And she'd be one. Hell, she already was. "I shouldn't have gotten you to cook anyway. You've had quite a day, and given what The Claw here did to your—*my*—shower curtain—I'll pay for a new one—I can only imagine that you must need more medical attention than I realized."

"Don't worry about that, I'm fine. Here," she said, reaching out again for the wriggling towel bundle. "Why don't I go ahead and take her off your hands. I can put her out on the back porch for a bit, let you get, uh, dressed."

Really, she had to stop looking at him like that. Like he was a . . . a pot roast or something. With gravy. And potatoes. Damn he was really hungry. Voraciously so. Did she have any idea how long he'd been on the road? With only himself and the sound of the wind for company? Actually, it had been far longer than that, but he really didn't need to acknowledge that right about now.

Then she was reaching for him, and he was right at that point where he was going to say the hell with it and drag her into the room and the hell with dinner, too . . . only she wasn't reaching for him. She was reaching for the damn kitten. He sort of shoved it into her hands, then shifted so a little more of the door was between them . . . and a little less of a view of the front of his towel. Which was in a rather revealing situation at the moment.

"Thanks," he said. "I appreciate it. I'll go down—*be down*—in just a few minutes." He really needed to shut this door. Before he made her nervous. Or worse. I mean, sure, she was looking at him like he was her last supper, but that didn't mean she was open to being ogled in return by a paying guest. Especially when he was the only paying guest in residence. Even if that did mean they had the house to themselves. And privacy. Lots and lots of privacy. "Five minutes," he blurted, and all but slammed the door in her face.

Crap, if Dan could see him at the moment, he'd be laughing his damn ass off. As would most of Vegas. Not only did Brett happen to play high stakes poker pretty well, but the supporters and promoters seemed to think he was also a draw because of his looks. And no, he wasn't blind, he knew he'd been relatively blessed, genetically speaking, for which he was grateful. No one would choose to be ugly. A least he wouldn't think so.

But while the looks had come naturally, that whole bad boy, cocky attitude vibe that was supposed to go with it had not. Not that he was shy. Exactly.

He was confident in his abilities, what they were, and what they weren't. But confidence was one thing. Arrogance another. And just because women threw themselves at him, didn't mean he was comfortable catching them. Mostly due to the fact that he was well aware that women weren't throwing themselves at him because of who he was. But because of what he was. Some kind of quasi-poker rock star. They were batting eyelashes, thrusting cleavage, and passing phone numbers and room keys because of his fame, his fortune, his ability to score freebies from hotels and sponsors, and, somewhere on that list, probably his looks weren't hurting him, either.

Nowhere on the list, however, did it appear that getting to know the guy behind the deck of cards and the stacks of chips was of any remote interest.

And there lay the irony.

GREAT BOOKS, GREAT SAVINGS!

When You Visit Our Website:
www.kensingtonbooks.com
You Can Save Money Off The Retail Price
Of Any Book You Purchase!

- **All Your Favorite Kensington Authors**
- **New Releases & Timeless Classics**
- **Overnight Shipping Available**
- **eBooks Available For Many Titles**
- **All Major Credit Cards Accepted**

Visit Us Today To Start Saving!
www.kensingtonbooks.com

All Orders Are Subject To Availability.
Shipping and Handling Charges Apply.
Offers and Prices Subject To Change Without Notice.